I0607726

A Shot of Trouble

A Cassidy Adventure Novel

by
Kelly Rysten

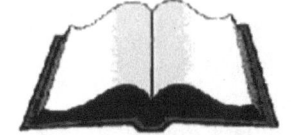

CCB Publishing
British Columbia, Canada

A Shot of Trouble: A Cassidy Adventure Novel

Copyright ©2013 by Kelly Rysten
ISBN-13 978-1-77143-107-1
First Edition

Library and Archives Canada Cataloguing in Publication
Rysten, Kelly, 1960-, author
A shot of trouble : a Cassidy adventure novel / by Kelly Rysten. -- First edition.
Issued in print and electronic formats.
ISBN 978-1-77143-107-1 (pbk.).--ISBN 978-1-77143-108-8 (pdf)
Additional cataloguing data available from Library and Archives Canada

Cover artwork by Kelly Rysten: www.kellyrysten.com

This is a work of fiction. Names, places, and characters are a product of the author's imagination or are used fictitiously and are not to be considered as real. Resemblance to any events or persons, living or dead, past or present, is purely coincidental.

Extreme care has been taken by the author to ensure that all information presented in this book is accurate and up to date at the time of publishing. Neither the author nor the publisher can be held responsible for any errors or omissions. Additionally, neither is any liability assumed for damages resulting from the use of the information contained herein.

All rights reserved. No part of this publication may be reproduced, stored in a retrieval system or transmitted in any form or by any means, electronic, mechanical, photocopying, recording or otherwise without the express written permission of the author, except in the case of brief quotations embodied in critical articles and reviews. For other permission requests, please contact the author. Printed in the United States of America, the United Kingdom and Australia.

Publisher: CCB Publishing
              British Columbia, Canada
              www.ccbpublishing.com

To my family: my kids who kept me hopping and gave me plenty of childish wisdom to draw from, and my husband who is infinitely supportive and helps me through all the stages involved in putting a book into print.

And to my elementary school, which probably prefers to remain anonymous considering they taught me, amongst other things, how to climb to the roof of a building using the meters on the side. I promise I didn't harm anything up there. I only retrieved the balls the kids lost on top of the flat roof.

Other books by Kelly Rysten

Triple Trouble

Read about Cassidy Callahan's first
tracking adventure with trouble at every turn.

Published 2009 – ISBN 978-1-926585-41-3

Car Trouble

Car trouble abounds as Cassidy sets her sights on Police Academy.
With a serial killer on the loose determined to send the police
department a message, Cassidy's attendance is in question.

Published 2010 – ISBN 978-1-926918-03-7

A Cache of Trouble

A cache of banknotes lies hidden near Cassidy's mountain
hideaway and a greedy criminal is determined to find the stash.
Cassidy and her entire search and rescue team are drawn into the hunt,
but while some seek riches, others just want Cassidy to survive.

Published 2011 – ISBN 978-1-926918-87-7

A Double Dose of Trouble

Two Cassidy adventure novels in one softbound edition including:
<u>A Pit of Trouble</u> and <u>Merry Troubled Christmas</u>.

Published 2012 – ISBN 978-1-77143-025-8

Chapter 1

I heard the shots echo down the hall. If anyone could recognize such an ominous sound it was me, but it was out of place. Nobody expected the sharp sound of a gun to shatter the quiet studies going on inside the classrooms.

I was giving a presentation to Mrs. Peabody's third grade class. I was winding up my speech about getting lost in the woods and had given examples on how to prevent it. I'd just advised the class on what to do if they ever believed they were lost, and had handed out a little plastic safety whistle to each student. Teachers hated it when I handed out whistles. The kids always brought them out on the playground and disrupted the teacher's signals for recess. Mrs. Peabody glared at me because recess was the next thing on the schedule. I asked the class for additional questions and a little girl dressed in purple raised her hand.

"Are you a policeman?"

"Sort of," I answered her. "I went to police academy. I'm qualified to act as an officer as long as a senior officer accompanies me. But my real job is in search and rescue. I am a tracker and I find lost people. That's one reason I don't want you to get lost in the woods, or anywhere for that matter. Getting lost is scary and dangerous, especially if you don't know what to do. That's why I like to talk to kids like you, so you will know what to do. But normally I don't do police work at all."

This is when the shots began to get worrisome. I felt for the 9mm at my side and glanced towards Mrs. Peabody. She appeared to be as worried as I was. I looked to the hall.

"Excuse me," I said. "Lock the classroom door behind me. I better check this out."

Stepping into the hall I was met by agitated students rushing my direction. I walked upstream looking for the source of trouble. It wasn't hard to find and what I saw stopped me cold in my tracks. A man about five-eight was stalking down the hallway. He had a paranoid look in his eye. When he saw someone he'd whip around, take aim and fire one round. He didn't wait to see if the bullet hit. He just fired and kept walking, reading classroom numbers and teachers' names on the doors. So much for not doing police work, I thought.

A door opened. "What the…" a teacher said.

"Get inside! Lock the door!" I yelled and the man turned, aimed.

Oh hell, this never works, I thought. I'm dead meat, but I have to try. I ducked into a doorway as a bullet went by, ricocheting off the metal doorjamb behind me. I drew my weapon, tentatively surveyed the scene, then stepped out, gun ready.

"Freeze! Police!" I yelled. "Drop your weapon and put your hands over your head!" It sounded like kids playing cops and robbers and it didn't help that, even in uniform, I looked like a kid myself. Please freeze, please freeze, I thought frantically. The gunman didn't freeze and I was getting cold feet. I'm not a cop, I'm not a cop, I thought. I heard a shot from another part of the school. This situation was getting worse by the second. Two shooters? There must be an agenda of some kind. I had to get over there but this guy was the immediate threat. This gunman was going to kill me. He brought his weapon around leaving me no choice. It was him or me, and if he got past me then it was also a wing full of kids. I aimed and fired in one quick stroke. If there had been any time to sit and cry, I would have. Hitting him was like killing a part of myself. I hated it. It was one of those reflex decisions, and although I was right, sometimes being right feels awfully wrong. I ran over to him with my gun still aimed. He was alive but fading fast. I jerked his gun out of his hand even though my training dictated that I wasn't supposed to touch it. It was evidence, but I also couldn't leave the weapon behind. A student could take it or the guy might not be as bad off as he appeared. I turned the man over and frisked him quickly. I jammed his gun in my pocket. The battle of the century roared to life inside my head. Leave this guy or stay? Every bit of training I had said I couldn't count on this guy to stay incapacitated. Yet there was an able bodied shooter somewhere in the building. I took off running.

The other shooter wasn't as aggressive. Or maybe the school had gotten wise and had gone into lockdown. I ran down a long hallway with adjoining wings leading off of it. The shooter was down the second wing and I skidded to a halt, hid behind the corner, then made my way from doorway to doorway down the corridor, stalking him until I could get within range. When I only had two classrooms between us, I finally stepped out.

"Freeze! Police!" I said again, this time with a little more authority. The man turned, his eyes narrowed as he spotted me with my gun leveled and ready for action. Then he fled towards the end of the hall and the glowing red exit sign. I couldn't let him get away. Who knew what was on the other side of that door? He could bust through the doorway and into a group of kids so I aimed again and fired knowing I was going to lose my nerve pretty soon. It wasn't in me to hurt people. Only my training allowed me to perform and think in such terms. Four years in the Marines, then police academy. I knew it had to be done. The man fell, then got up and pushed his way through the metal door. I chased him out the door and across a lawn, until I was forced to watch helplessly as he jumped into the passenger seat of a green SUV which roared off and laid rubber on its way out of the parking lot. The 9mm wouldn't do much at this distance. I memorized most of the license plate number and, numb with fear, made my way to the office. I could hear the sirens from the squad cars closing in on the building. Kent Jacobsen was one of the first officers on the scene.

"Action's over, but I need some help," I told him. "Green Ford SUV heading east. There's a driver and a passenger. At least one of them is armed and the passenger is wounded. I've got a suspect down." My emotions were catching up with me. "Kent, I know I'm supposed to know what to do with him, but I don't. I had to leave him to go after the other guy. But…"

He spoke to some other officers and they took off after the SUV. Then I led the way to my suspect. I didn't know if I could look at him again. I knew it was important to get there as soon as possible, but I had to force my feet to keep going.

"Can you call Rusty?" I asked him. "I don't think I can do this without Rusty."

As we walked along Kent radioed a request for Rusty Michaels, and with relief I knew my personal backup was on his way. I reported to Jacobsen what had happened. I had to pass on as much information as possible because once reality caught up with duty and smacked me one I was going to be useless. Hopefully Rusty would be faster than reality because it lurked just around the bend. We turned the corner and I looked timidly down the hallway, half afraid the suspect was gone, half fearful he was dead. I let Jacobsen check the body. He felt for the pulse and stood.

"Good shot," he said.

That wasn't what I wanted to hear.

"You took on both guys? By yourself?" he asked.

"I didn't have any choice. They didn't know I was here. And what if I wasn't? I had to do what I could. They acted like they were looking for someone, shooting people as they went. What's the score?"

"One teacher down, two kids with minor wounds."

"Is he…"

"Yep, he's…"

"Am I in trouble? I didn't have a senior officer. But I didn't have any choice either."

"You'll be happy to note you'll be taken off active duty until this gets investigated. Most cops think that's a bad thing but you're not most cops."

"What do cops do when they aren't on active duty?"

"They do desk work, go give talks at schools…"

"Oh, great."

Suddenly the school was abuzz with activity, most of it police related. Fortunately, one of the staff's goals was to return the school to normal as soon as possible, which meant I would be out of there as quickly as possible. Rusty caught up to me in the office, where we were trying to reconstruct the sequence of events to determine exactly what had happened. I showed them where the SUV had been parked and explained my brief five minutes of actual participation. I provided a description of the man who got away and the vehicle they drove. It was hard to believe that so much could happen in such a short period of time. I looked to Jacobsen, then to Schroeder who noticed Rusty standing near the doorway. He nodded in Rusty's direction, granting me permission to finally leave. We walked through the front doors of the school and found ourselves in a forest of microphones. I followed Rusty as he pushed his way through the press.

"We heard there was a shooting at the school. Can you tell us what happened?"

"No comment," Rusty said flatly.

I followed in his wake. When we got to the Explorer the crowd was still behind us. Rusty unlocked the door for me and I hopped in. Microphones were shoved up to the window.

"No comment," Rusty repeated, as he climbed in the driver's seat and closed the door. "Don't tell them anything. Let Schroeder handle it. He knows what can be said without jeopardizing the case. But I'm warning you, he'll give you the credit you deserve and they're going to come knocking."

"The credit I deserve. Rusty, I just want to find a rock and hide under it. I didn't ask to be involved in a school shooting. I just came to talk to a class of third graders. I wasn't qualified to do what I was forced into."

We drove in silence. It took me a while to get my bearings and when I realized he was taking me home my walls began crumbling. I had thought we would go to the station, but I was relieved to officially be off duty. It was a long drive home up into the hills outside of town, which gave me plenty of time to build up a good solid guilt trip for myself. Rusty pulled into the driveway and stopped. He glanced over and assessed my stress level. It was easy for him to tell. If I looked like I was ready to disappear into the seat then he knew he had a job ahead of him. This time I was still visible, my mind still actively running in circles reliving the day, trying not to dwell on the shooting but instead focusing on what *could* have happened. What if I hadn't been there? It would have been even worse. I had to force myself to realize, it could have been much worse. But then I remembered my shot. I could feel the cold metal in my hands, the tension.

"Cass, babe, we're home."

I slid out of the Explorer and followed him into our home. I wanted out of the uniform. It was restrictive, stiff and a reminder of the day's events I wanted to put behind me. After changing into shorts and a tank top I found Rusty waiting for me on the old brown couch in the den. I crawled onto his lap and held on for dear life. No matter which of us needed comforting, this couch had become our source, just sitting together wrapped in each other's arms. This time both of us seemed to need it. I needed to put the shooting behind me and he, as a detective, had to put it in perspective. He knew how things could have gone. Just like me, he was thinking it could have been so much worse, except he was thinking of me and I was thinking about the students. I was also worried about the shooters. I needed to know what would happen because of the one that got away.

After we had been sitting together long enough to settle on a question the conversation started. "How close was it?" he asked.

"I wasn't measuring. He was a lousy shot."

"Cass..."

"You would have thought it was close. It wasn't close enough to scare me. I was too busy trying to stop him. What's the first step in finding the one that got away?"

"I feel sorry for anyone driving a green SUV. They'll patrol the area looking for the vehicle. They'll run the plates and pay a call on the owner. All the local hospitals will be checked. They'll talk to school officials, and try to determine a motive. A lot goes into a case like this. And those are just the first steps. Any information they can gather will bring up more questions. You know how it goes."

"They won't give the case to you."

"No, I expect it will go to Tom. He'd be a good choice."

"The gunmen were looking for someone. When they shot at people it seemed to be to get them out of the way so they could keep up their search. They weren't planning on having much opposition."

"You seem to be taking this better."

"It's because of the kids. If it was just self-defense I'd be a basket case, but I had to do it for the kids. I still hate it. It's still going to haunt me, but we'll just deal with it. I'm more worried about the man who escaped. I've got lots of questions bouncing around in my head. Like, who was the brains behind all of this? Why did the SUV take off without the other guy? They couldn't have known he was dead. Who were they looking for? It was almost like they *wanted* the school to be in lockdown, so they wouldn't have as much to deal with. It was like they knew where they were going but then something went wrong. I don't know why I'm thinking this way. It's like the profiling I do when I track. I just kind of read it from their actions, but nothing really happened to make me come to any concrete conclusions. If I were investigating the case, I'd go to the office and see if any teachers or students had changed classrooms recently. If they had it would be unusual this late in the school year. It might point to who these guys were looking for. I'd also look at the record of school visitors. See if one person stands out as having visited an unusual number of times, or for odd reasons. I hate it when I get curious about something. I can't seem to put it down. It grates on me and, right now, a few things just aren't adding up."

"Well put this down. If you need to do something about it talk to whoever gets the case. I don't want you mixed up in this."

I tried to put it down. I really did, but as the story hit the news on TV and the newspapers, word got around and everybody speculated about it, about the identity of the gunman who had escaped. As anger flared in the community about who would do such a thing, my mind started forming a plan. Although I wasn't supposed to get involved, I decided to see Tom, the detective in charge of the investigation. We talked for an hour and he agreed my ideas were worth a try. Then he made a suggestion which took me by surprise.

"In my experience, people like being around dogs. They won't open up to an officer on the school grounds but they will talk about anything while they are petting a dog. I think you and Carla Sandoval should take a dog over to the school and just patrol. When kids ask to pet the dog, let them. And while they are at it question them. Kids know everything and they aren't afraid to talk. You can at least get a feel for how the school is coping after the shooting."

Chapter 2

"I don't think I can do this," I said nervously.

"You asked for it," Miguel Cabrera reminded me.

"I know. If I run screaming out of the kennels, can I come back?"

"You're not going to run. You're going to buckle down and stay. He's not even going after you. He's coming after me. You're just observing."

"Okay, let him go."

Carla Sandoval unclipped the leash and the big, black and tan German Shepherd bounded across the field. My flight mode kicked in, but I beat it down, willing my feet to be still. The dog leapt at Miguel. He pulled and tugged at the protective padding until he brought the officer down and then Carla called him off with a simple but firm command, "Ricco, come!" The dog returned to her and sat at her feet.

There were some advantages to knowing most of the Joshua Hills police force by name. They all knew Rusty and most of them had met me. Many of them had participated in the raid when I was rescued from Teague Stern's dog-fighting pit. I asked the K-9 Unit if I could spend some time in their kennels and observe the dogs at work. I thought being around well trained but fierce dogs would acclimate me, so here I was. Every time a dog was released I wanted to run for the hills. Every time a dog barked I jumped in fear.

Carla released Ricco again but this time Miguel pretended to be a fleeing suspect. Ricco chased him down and tackled him. I remembered what it felt like to be tackled by a large, fierce dog.

After an hour's worth of training, they took a break.

"I think you need to spend time with a big friendly dog," Miguel suggested. "Do you know where there's one you can borrow for a few days?"

I thought for a minute. Amos.

"Yeah, maybe, I'll have to ask. Do you think it will work?"

"It can't hurt."

Yeah, right.

Kelly Green laughed, "You? You want to borrow Amos? You're scared to death of him!"

"That's the point. I want to get over it. Maybe if I spend some time with him I'll convince myself it's silly to be scared of dogs. There was a time when they didn't bother me and Amos is a great dog. He listens and plays fetch. If there was a big dog that could help me get over this fear it would be him."

"Amos is a pest. Can you live with a pest?"

"Do you mind if I train him a little, if I manage to get over being scared of him?"

"You are most welcome to try. So far he sits for two seconds and he steals stuff. That's what makes him a pest. He's even named after a pest."

"Amos? How is he named after a pest?"

"His registered name is Amos Quito. We had to pick a name that wasn't taken yet. He was a pest. The name fit."

"Leave it to you to give your dog a bad pun for a name. He doesn't draw blood does he?"

"He hasn't since he was teething, so it's been a while. I don't think you have anything to worry about."

"So, what do you say?"

"Sure, you can borrow Amos. It'll give us time where we don't have to guard our possessions twenty-four/seven. I suggest hiding dinner in the microwave until you are ready to eat and locking your shoes in a closet. And guard the stovetop while you are cooking. He's set himself on fire a few times."

Oh great. Well, if I spent my time training him, I certainly wouldn't have time to be scared of him. It sounded like he just needed a firm hand.

"Will he run away if he's not on a leash? I don't have a fenced yard."

"He won't run away but he might wander off. You'll have to keep an eye on him and call him back to keep him close."

"I think I better wait for the weekend to take him. Maybe Rusty will be here for backup."

"Good idea."

"See if Rhonda wants to come for dinner on Friday."

"We're having company Friday," I announced at dinner that night.

"Oh?" Rusty answered.

"Umm, yeah, I hope you don't mind. If you don't want him to stay we can send him back."

"Him?"

"I'm taking care of Amos for a while. Kelly and Rhonda are coming for dinner and Amos is going to stay with us."

"Kelly asked *you* to keep Amos? He knows you're scared to death of that dog!"

"Rusty, don't be angry. I asked Kelly if I could borrow Amos because I thought having a dog around would help me get over being scared of him. It was my idea. Kelly will take him back any time we want him to."

I watched out the front window as the big black Labrador retriever pulled Kelly to the front door while Rhonda followed behind. I opened the door and they came in. Amos tugged on the leash, eager to investigate this new place. Kelly braced himself against the tugs. Kelly was a big, strong guy. How was I going to manage a dog this size if Amos gave Kelly a hard time?

"Food and shoes hidden?" Kelly asked.

"Yup, safely stashed away."

"Are you sure you want him loose?"

"No, but go ahead. It's got to start some time and it might as well begin while you are still here. Did you bring his food and training collar?"

"Training collar? Ha! What you see is what you get."

A red nylon collar, red nylon leash and fifty pounds of dog food. Was it a rule that black dogs had to wear red? There had to be one. I couldn't remember ever seeing a black dog wearing any other color besides red.

"How much does he eat?"

"Depends on how much he can steal. I'll leave that up to you. If you work with him the same way you work with Shadow maybe he'll be healthier when we pick him up."

"How much does he weigh?"

"A hundred twenty pounds, last time he was at the vet."

"He's bigger than me!"

"Yeah."

"I need to work on *that look* that dogs don't like."

"That look?"

"Yeah, it works on men and kids too."

"Oh, that look."

"It can stop a dog in his tracks if you do it right."

"I wish you the best of luck."

Amos sat at an empty spot at the dining room table. His nose was just table height and he watched the bowls with a hopeful expression. Kelly watched Amos carefully. Shadow lay in a corner observing the proceedings with interest, knowing his turn would come. I was glad Amos was across the table from me. He looked big staring at me over the tabletop. When Kelly reached for a second helping of potatoes, Amos jumped, placing two big black paws on the table. I reacted on instinct. It was just a training reaction. I leapt to my feet, glared at Amos with *that look* and said sharply, "Ak, no! Down! Sit!"

Amos looked at me puzzled and sat.

"Good sit, stay," I said firmly.

There was a moment of silence.

"Wow, I'm impressed," Kelly said.

"Sorry, I am just used to jumping on Shadow."

"Don't apologize to me! I'm taking notes!"

"What do *you* say when he does that?"

"It isn't very repeatable."

"Only use words he knows. He obviously knew no, down or sit. Use a firm tone and limit your words to what he knows and he will tune in better."

"I can't wait to see what kind of a dog we end up with," Rhonda said.

"Don't get your hopes up. I still have to force myself not to run away from him."

Kelly and Rhonda obviously were used to clearing the table with Amos around. They took all the food and put it on the counter. One person guarded the food while the other cleared the dirty dishes. They had the system perfected. I'd have to work out my own system. I thought it would involve a confrontation and some firm commands. At least the evening was getting my mind on training and not on irrational fear. Amos wasn't a bad dog, I told myself, he was just used to getting his way. I had to persuade him that my way was better than his.

I found a small bite of meat and called Shadow. The sheltie rushed over and sat in front of me. I placed the piece of food on the floor and he eyed it expectantly. I waited several seconds and said brightly, "Okay!" Shadow pounced on the morsel.

"I dare you to try and teach Amos that," Kelly said.

"I don't think I can yet. It's going to require a few more words and some physical contact with a dog that big."

"Give it a try."

I had Amos' attention so I placed a piece of food on the floor. He went for it and I scolded him sharply. "Ak, No! Leave it!" I grabbed his collar and hauled him back. "Sit! Amos, sit!" He looked puzzled. I glared at him. "Sit." He obviously knew what *sit* meant but he ignored my command. I picked up the piece of meat and held it up where he could see it. "You want it? Sit." I waited patiently. I added a glare to my next command. "Sit!"

Amos sat.

"Stay."

I took a step back and put the food on the floor. I didn't make him wait long. "Okay!" I said, allowing him to break his stay. He didn't know what *okay* meant so I picked up the meat and handed it to him. "Gentle, gentle." I thought I was going to faint when he lunged for it but I toughened up and pulled the bite back. "Gentle," he took the bite and half my hand. I yanked my hand back, rinsed it off in the sink and flopped down on the couch. I was nearly shaking. Being in training mode helped but the dog was frighteningly big. "We need to work on being gentle."

"I think you two are going to get along great," Kelly said.

Bedtime came and the dogs needed to go out. I clipped the leash to Amos' collar.

"You want me to do that?" Rusty offered.

"No, this is my project. I'll do it."

"You don't have to do everything."

"I took this on. I'll stick with it. I hadn't counted on having to get so close to him this soon but now that I've got him I need to take care of him. I wouldn't want to lose him outside."

By the time I returned it was obvious we needed to make a trip to town because Amos needed a training collar if the leash was going to be of any use at all. My plans had been to let Amos laze about the house and be near me but it wasn't going to work that way. Amos' lazing needed constant attention, which meant training. I had to start at the beginning. First a training collar and a very short leash. I needed to be able to correct him without fiddling with a long leash so the leash I bought was only a handle and clip. With the six-foot leash we practiced heeling. Inside he learned *sit* and *stay*. When he'd mastered those commands we learned *leave it*. That phrase would prevent a lot of stolen food.

Dogs hate to have their nose thumped so I held out a piece of food. When he tried to grab it I thumped his nose and said, "Leave it!" Pretty soon he was shying away from the food when he heard "Leave it." Next he had to learn to leave plates alone. When he approached the plate it was a correction and "Leave it!" All this training involved getting in Amos' face and standing up to him.

Saturday night Rusty was on the phone to Kelly. "I don't know how much more of this I can take." A pause while Kelly talked. "No he won't hurt her. He's stubborn, but Cassidy is just as stubborn. I see the fear but she just wrestles that big old dog anyway. It's like watching her walk into the line of fire." It felt a lot like that too. Every time I got in Amos' face I expected to lose a limb. "No, I don't think so. She's making progress on both of them. It's just hard to watch."

Next was *down*. If I could get him to obey just those commands we'd be in business. I didn't expect miracles. I knew he'd break his stay and I'd have to correct him and put him back in position. Repetition was the key. Mealtime was the hard part because to correct Amos I had to keep him close. I put him in a down stay and we began eating. When Amos got up I scolded,

"No, down, stay!" Amos looked at me like a little kid in time-out. He could only stay for a minute, but was doing well. I thought the constant corrections were going to drive Rusty batty. He thought I'd give up in fear and desperation but I knew an even, firm, constant hand was all Amos needed. By Tuesday he was laying under the table for the whole meal. His reward was just like Shadow's, a bit of food after a short stay. Amos gobbled the bite and I praised him. "Good boy! What a good stay! Good dog!"

Amos gave me a happy grin and planted his paws on my shoulders knocking me over backwards. I should have just gotten up and put him in a sit again but his action triggered something inside of me and I rolled away huddling in fear. Amos was happy. He lunged at me asking to play.

"Rusty! Help!"

Rusty ran in from the other room and pulled Amos off me. I bolted to the end of the kitchen and stood collecting my thoughts and feelings.

"Babe," he said in exasperation, "you don't have to do this. You're pushing yourself too hard."

"No, I just reacted badly. It was actually a breakthrough and he was happy because I told him he did a good job. I just need to be prepared when he does that again. Now it's time to teach him not to jump up. He should be happy when he does a good job but he has to learn to control his enthusiasm."

"You don't have to do this," he repeated. "This is for *your* good. This isn't a project to make Amos a reformed dog. When this ceases to be of benefit to you we call Kelly."

"Well, I obviously need more work," I replied.

If I knew how hard this was going to be I'd have called Kelly sooner. Every afternoon I took Amos out for a walk. We practiced heeling so he would walk on a leash under control. He was doing very well with the training collar on. I even considered leading him through some of the agility obstacles, but Amos soon put a halt to that idea. I was walking him in the hills behind the house when a rabbit darted out of the brush and bolted away. Amos took off after it, and my hundred and fifteen pounds didn't slow him down much. He had four feet to pull with. I ran after him pulling back with all my might.

"Heel! Amos, heel!" I commanded as he dragged me along. I planted my feet to give him a good solid correction with the leash, but the rabbit darted under a prickly pear cactus and Amos leapt through it. Oh hell! We hit the cactus and went through it with terrifying quickness. Amos yiped loudly and skidded to a halt. He began pacing, lifting his legs and shying away from the fiery stinging needles lodged in his legs and chest. Every time he moved the spines rubbed and stung. I felt his pain because I was full of spines too and wasn't quite sure what to do. We couldn't walk back home in this condition and Rusty wouldn't be home from work for hours. I couldn't pull out the spines with my fingers. It was going to require pliers. I pulled my way down the leash, closer to Amos.

"Amos, boy, DOWN, lay DOWN."

Although it was a painful position, at least he wouldn't be moving around as much. After pinning Amos down I began petting him, talking to him gently but firmly, trying to calm him. We needed help. Rusty was in town and Kelly was in the mountains, and both men were probably at work. This situation required a man's help though. I couldn't think of any woman I knew who would pull cactus spines out of me with a pair of pliers. I opted for Kelly. He'd have better luck controlling Amos. I was glad I had my cell phone on me and hoped Kelly had his too.

"Hey Cassidy, how's the dog sitting going?" he asked when he answered.

"Kelly, I need help. Are you busy?"

He stopped what he was doing. "What kind of help?"

"Amos and I are full of cactus spines. I need pliers quick."

"Where are you?"

"In the hills behind my house."

"How will I find you?"

"Head south west from the barn. We left a pretty good trail."

"Where's Rusty?"

"At work. He doesn't know. I thought you could handle Amos better. If you're busy then I'll just try for the house but this hurts like crazy."

"No, stay put."

"Bring two pairs," I added quickly before he hung up.

I pinned poor Amos down for nearly an hour before Kelly found us. He saw all the thorns poking out of my jeans and grimaced.

"Why didn't you just let go?"

"It happened too fast and I wasn't going to lose your dog."

"Cassidy…"

"Give me a pair."

He handed me a pair of pliers and I found a spine. I grabbed it and pulled. Amos jumped and yipped. I pinned him down, found another spine, grabbed and yanked. Amos struggled.

"I'm sorry boy! We have to do it. It's okay, hush, hush. It's okay. Down, down. Stay. Amos stay. Good boy, good stay."

Grab, yank. Grasp, pull. Kelly and I worked over the dog while he wriggled, squirmed and whined. I lay on top of him, pinning him to the ground and talking into his ear as we searched for more cactus needles, giving him only the simple commands that he understood over and over again. Down, stay, good.

"What a good boy. No, no, stay down."

It got harder and harder to find thorns until finally after rubbing our hands over him we couldn't feel any more. He whined but didn't jerk as he had before when we hit something sharp. We brushed all the spines into a pile and released the dog. He paced a bit, whining, then sat and started licking his leg.

"Okay, my turn," I said. I grabbed a spine and yanked. Oh man, this was going to hurt. I buckled down and set my determination to maximum.

"Cassidy... I can't. I can't hurt you like that."

"Okay, then take Amos back to the house. I'll do it."

"No, let me take you to a doctor."

"They'll just do the same thing I'm doing now. I can do it without having to figure out how to get to town in this condition. Just let me get it over with. Take Amos to the house."

"I can't leave you like this."

"Then sit down and make yourself comfortable. This might take a while."

I never, ever want to go through something like that ever again. I thought it would never end. Every pull brought a ripping, pulling feeling and a stab of pain. I thought Amos was lucky because he hadn't been wearing jeans. Each time I pulled a spike out of my jeans the fabric moved and made all the other spikes pull. I had to phase out the pain and just pull them as quickly as possible. After a while Kelly couldn't stand it anymore and picked up the other pair of pliers. We timed the pulls so there was only one jab of pain for our two yanks. When I couldn't see past the tears I had to pause.

"Kelly, stop. I can't do it anymore. I need a break."

I lay on the ground trying not to move. Amos came up, whined, then licked my face but this time I was too sore to be scared. I looked up into his big brown eyes and patted the ground beside me. "Down, Amos, down." He lay down beside me while Kelly watched in surprise.

"How did you get him to do that?"

"Amos knows what *down* means. He's a smart dog. He just needs a firm hand."

"That wasn't a firm hand. That was a polite request."

"Maybe he's just in a down sort of mood. I certainly know I am. How many more are there?"

Kelly looked at my jeans. "Maybe a dozen."

"Okay, I think I can handle that. Let's finish it."

When we were through I ran my hands over my legs and found a few smaller spines that had penetrated right through the denim. I had to roll up my jeans to remove them.

"You ready to go?" I asked Kelly.

"You're going to walk home like that?"

"I don't have much of a choice. Do you think I should take Amos to the vet?"

"Nah, he'd just lick off any medicine they told you to put on it."

"Are you sure he'll be okay?"

"Just don't let him bleed on the furniture."

We all stood and Kelly picked up Amos' leash. Amos walked to the end and started pulling Kelly home.

"Kelly stop. Don't let him do that. Watch."

I took the leash and Amos tried to pull me, so I jerked suddenly and firmly on the leash and he stopped. I stood beside Amos and gave him a command. "Amos, heel!" I stepped out with my left foot to give him a visual cue and he started walking calmly beside me. "No rabbits," I admonished him. "Good heel." When he pulled ahead I gave a quick correction and a firm command and he fell back. Kelly just shook his head and followed us back to the house.

"Rhonda would be appalled if she saw that collar."

"It's not as bad as it looks. Put it on your arm and pull the leash. You'll see it doesn't hurt him. If he's willing to pull a hundred pounds behind him at a run you know the collar isn't hurting him that badly. He is actually doing very well but needs to learn to ignore distractions. You let him chase rabbits, don't you?"

"Yeah, I get tired of trying to hold him back so, if we're alone, I let him go."

"Maybe I should have let him go, but I didn't know how far he'd run or if I'd be able to get him back."

"It's my turn to give you a command," Kelly said seriously. "Do *not* let him hurt you. If I hear that you let him hurt you I'll be right back down here…"

"Amos didn't hurt me. He chased a rabbit. That's all he did. I was the idiot who wouldn't let go of the leash. That's not his fault."

"I'm still telling you. Don't let him hurt you." Then his eyes softened. "I think you've come as far as he has. Do you know how close you were to his face while we were pulling out the cactus needles?"

"Yeah, but it had to be done. Necessity is the mother of bravery."

"I thought it was invention."

"Necessity is the mother of a lot of things."

We arrived at the back door of the house and Amos lunged, eager to do something new. I corrected him. "Amos, sit!" No response. "Amos, SIT."

Oh, all right, he seemed to be saying and finally sat down. I calmly removed the leash. "Wait." I opened the backdoor. "Okay!" He dashed into the house.

"How did you do that? You've only had him a week."

"Necessity is also the mother of training. He needed some manners. I needed him to have some manners so we forced some manners onto him. Do you want a sandwich before you go back? I'm going to start soaking my jeans and then I'm going to make one for myself."

"Sure, but then I need to get back."

I went to the bedroom to quickly change my jeans. I put the bloody pair into a sink to soak in cold water. I washed the puncture wounds, though they stung like crazy, put on a new pair of jeans, then went to the kitchen to make our lunch. I got one slice of bread and one slice of lunchmeat, folded it together and placed it on the edge of the counter. Then I moved to the side and made sandwiches for Kelly and myself.

"I wouldn't leave that there if I were you," Kelly warned.

"It's his. It's bait. But Amos can't have it until I'm ready to give it to him."

Amos eyed the sandwich, ignoring the much larger preparations right next to him. I saw a shift in his attitude. He checked to see if I was watching. Without turning I said sharply, "No! Leave it." He backed off, disgusted with me. "Do you want lettuce? Tomatoes? Onions?"

"Sure, you know I'll eat anything."

As I worked I kept tabs on Amos. Every time he decided I wasn't watching I'd remind him sharply, "Amos, leave it." When the sandwiches were done I put them on plates and walked over to the bait. I picked it up and Amos looked hopeful. I tore off a small piece of bread for Shadow and placed the sandwich on the floor. "Wait. Stay," I commanded. He wriggled in anticipation. I let him wait several very expectant seconds before releasing him with an "Okay!" Amos gulped the sandwich in one bite. Then I repeated the same command with Shadow and the little piece of bread.

"I still haven't figured out how much to feed him," I said over lunch. "If I fed him whenever he acted hungry then the food would be gone. I know the instructions on the bag are always high. If I fed Shadow what the bag says to feed him he wouldn't be able to walk. So I feed Amos a cup and a half twice a day and he still gets unhealthy amounts of people food, but it's controlled amounts."

"How did you get him to quit stealing food?"

"I can read canine minds and head off bad behavior before he can do it. You saw. You know your dog. You know when he's planning something. So, nip it in the bud. Don't even let him plan."

"Easier said than done."

"Half the training is for the dog. The other half is for the owner. Once you learn to watch and jump on bad habits he'll listen to you, just like he does with me. You know, I had really only planned on letting Amos live in the house with us. I wasn't planning on training him at all. I only trained him out of self-defense. It was train him or live in fear of him, so I buckled down and trained both of us. I think it's about time I went back to the K-9 kennels. Maybe I won't run when I see all the police dogs now."

"Why are you doing this? Most people would think, hey, I don't see scary dogs that often. I can live with that. But you go out of your way to confront the one thing that scares you the most."

"I guess I'm just stubborn that way."

Kelly polished off his sandwich. "Are you sure you're okay? Some of those spines were buried pretty deep."

"I know, it still stings like crazy. Thanks for coming out. I'm sorry I had to drag you away from work. I hope it wasn't something important."

"I can catch up."

"Do you want some help? You can put me to work."

"No, just take care of yourself. Tell Rusty 'hi' when he gets home."

"Will do."

Kelly headed to work and I quickly put my jeans into the wash before Rusty could see them. Then I showered, trying to erase as many of the scratches and scabs as possible. I felt every one of the little scratches and puncture wounds when the water hit them. They stung like fire. I scrubbed anyway and by the time I was through I was exhausted. I'd had enough pain for one day and flopped down on the bed to rest. Amos walked over and dropped a tennis ball on my stomach.

"You just don't know when to stop, do you?" I scolded the dog.

I had to admit, Amos didn't strike fear into me whenever he approached. He was big and powerful, but he liked me and he trusted me and I was starting to feel the same way about him. He eyed my shoes sitting on the floor by the bed.

"Leave it!" I told him and he lay down with a huff of disappointment.

I was moving mighty stiffly when I got up to make dinner. Each little puncture wound rubbed my jeans the wrong way and I debated whether to change into shorts. I decided to put off the inevitable questions from Rusty and kept my jeans on. I made a simple meal of tacos, hiding the meat in the microwave and the toppings in the refrigerator until Rusty got home. I had a long list of things I was supposed to do that day but none of it sounded like much fun after taking a run through a cactus. I took the jeans from the washer and put them in the dryer and decided to ignore the list.

Rusty came home and gave me a big hug and kiss just like usual. Then he went to his office to put some files away and then to the bedroom to hang up his coat and tie. I warmed up the taco meat again and started frying taco shells.

"How was your day?" he asked.

"You mean besides my daily disaster?"

"No, including."

"Oh, then it was lousy. But now that you're home it's improving remarkably. How was your day?"

"I got into a little bit of a sticky situation, but it all worked out."

"Sounds like my day too."

The evening was quiet and peaceful which left us wondering if perhaps too many of our evenings were becoming a bit too quiet and peaceful. Typically Rusty came home from work and we would eat dinner. Later Rusty usually went over some files from the station. I either worked with Shadow or Amos or found something else to keep me occupied. We decided, before heading for bed, that an evening in town was what we needed.

That night I kept the lights dim hoping Rusty wouldn't notice the hundred or so little puncture marks that covered my legs. I thought I'd managed to put off the inevitable until he wrapped himself around me and I gave a startled jump. Every time he touched a spot where we had pulled out a cactus needle it stung sharply.

"Mmm, this isn't the way you usually react to me," he said softly.

"Sorry, my sticky situation is telling on me. Where were we?"

"We were going to turn on the lights so I can see what you're hiding from me."

"Rusty, it's not that big a deal."

"That's the magic phrase that confirms my worries."

I'd have to remember not to say that again. He flipped on the light and I lay there in all my red, scabbed up glory.

"Cassidy! What did you do today?"

"I took Amos for a walk. We chased a rabbit."

"You look like you've got localized chicken pox."

"Okay, now that you've seen my legs and you know it's nothing, lay down with me and I'll tell you about it. By the way, Kelly says 'hi'. I had to call him because Amos and I were covered in cactus needles. I felt so sorry for Amos. He didn't understand what he'd done at all. One minute he was chasing a rabbit and the next he was full of cactus spines and he couldn't move without them hurting. I had to pin him down so he wouldn't hurt himself worse and then Kelly and I had to pull them all out."

"You felt sorry for the dog."

"Don't worry so much. It was just a cactus."

"I'm calling Kelly in the morning. I want to know how much you're not telling me."

"Please don't. You'll get mad at him, but he didn't have any choice. You know I wouldn't let him take me to a doctor. He tried, but I just started pulling them out myself, and he was forced to grab a pair of pliers and make it go faster. He didn't want to pull them out, but when he saw me doing it, and how long it would take me he started pulling them out, too. So we finished faster. He did what he could. So don't get mad at him."

"Why wouldn't you go to a doctor?"

"Because it hurt. I'd have had to walk home with those needles in me and ride to town with needles in me and then they would just do the same thing that we did out in the hills. So it seemed smarter just to get it over with. Some things you just have to toughen up and get through. It hurt, but it wasn't serious. It just had to be done, so we did it."

"Find a way to lay down where it's comfortable. Just let me hold you without hurting you. Why didn't you call?"

"I knew Kelly was closer and Amos knew him. I thought he could handle the dog better."

"Why didn't you call me afterwards?"

"Should I? I didn't want you to worry and there wasn't anything you could do."

"I could have been here. I'd have felt better just being with you."

"I can't call you for every minor disaster that happens to me. You'd never get any work done. And there *is* a plus side to all this. I'm not afraid of Amos anymore. After pinning him down and wrestling with him to get out the cactus needles I mostly just felt sorry for him. There wasn't any time to be afraid."

Chapter 3

"Where have you been?" Carla asked as I entered the K-9 kennels again.

"Acclimating, just like Miguel suggested. Ricco is your dog?"

"Yeah, he rides shotgun for me in the back seat."

"You want to go patrol that school? I have some ideas. Tom checked out some of them, and he suggested we talk to the kids, see how they are doing after the shooting, see if anybody will talk about anything fishy. Are kids allowed to pet Ricco?"

"Sure, he may look fierce but he is also well socialized. He doesn't just bring down fleeing suspects. He sniffs for drugs and he's learning how to find people in situations like avalanches and earthquakes. You two have a lot in common. You've got the eyes and he's got the nose."

"Look! A dog!"

"It's a police dog!" Carla said brightly.

"Hey can I pet him?"

"Sure, and thank you for asking. It's always smart to ask before you pet any service dog," Carla said. "He might be working and you shouldn't interrupt a service dog when he's at work."

"What's his name?"

"His name is Ricco."

"Hi, Ricco, what are you doing at school?" the boy asked.

"We're just keeping an eye on things, seeing how the school is reacting to the things that happened last week."

"What's Ricco doing?"

"He's just visiting the students. He likes kids."

"That's cool, Ricco, you get a uniform and everything. I wish my dog had a uniform. My mom puts bows on his ears. But a uniform, *that's cool!*"

More kids talked to Ricco than they did to us. Ricco basked in all the attention. I was beginning to think the day was a waste of time when we met a little girl on the playground. She was timid, afraid at first that the big dog was as mean as he looked. Boys thought Ricco was cool. Girls stayed back for some reason. This little girl was an animal lover. There were bunnies on her sweatshirt and her shoes had Dalmatian spots.

"Will he bite?" she asked.

"No, he won't bite. He only bites bad guys and only when he's told to."

"Hey doggie, you should have been here when we *did* have bad guys. It was scary. But you're lucky you weren't. He'd probably have shot you too."

"Did you see the man?" Carla asked reluctantly. Well, it seemed that way but she didn't want to appear eager to hear something that bothered the girl so much.

"No, my teacher locked the door so he couldn't get in. But she was scared. She was real scared and she kept saying, 'How did they know?' which I didn't understand at all. If Mrs. T was scared, I was scared, too, because Mrs. T is a smart lady. She is the nicest teacher. I used to hate school until I got in her class. She tells us interesting stories and she grew up on an island far away."

"I bet all the teachers were frightened. It's scary to have people shooting nearby."

"Yeah, I think most of them were, but not the same as Mrs. T. She called in sick two days in a row and we had to have a sub. The sub was no fun. It was just work, work, work. Does the dog shake hands?"

"Yeah, just say, 'Ricco, shake.'"

The little girl shook Ricco's hand then ran off to play.

Carla and I looked at each other. We patrolled the grounds for the rest of the school day and when the kids lined up we asked where we could find Mrs. T's class. We watched Mrs. T as one by one her students were released to their parents or sent to the bus. She was a middle-aged Filipino woman, dressed conservatively in navy blue slacks and a colorful tropical-patterned blouse. Her long black hair was pulled up into an immense ponytail and she smiled broadly when she spoke of the students. She greeted each parent warmly and ruffled the hair of the kids as she spoke. When she wasn't busy, though, she seemed nervous, glancing around her as though she was expecting an ambush.

"What do you think?" Carla asked me.

"Technically, this is Tom's case. I don't think we should interfere."

"Right, I just wish we had a name."

We went to the front desk and after asking for Mrs. T we were told that Miss Tumibay had left for the day. Apparently Mrs. T was single and in a big hurry or possibly she was refusing visits from outsiders. We left the office satisfied that we at least had a name. Then Carla and I walked the halls until we found the classroom of Miss Kima Tumibay.

"I say Tom takes it from here," Carla suggested.

Riding back to the station, Carla radioed for Tom's twenty and found out he was not at the station. She left a message for him to call one of us when he returned to his office.

When we arrived at the station I headed for Rusty's office. I knocked quietly and peeked in the window. He recognized the knock and came to the door. His smile lit up the room. He glanced at my uniform and sidearm. I'd had to be in cop mode for the day even if I was just talking to kids.

"I didn't expect you in town today. What have you been up to?"

"Information gathering. Carla and I patrolled the school to see how the kids were coping. Since we decided we spend too many quiet evenings at home, I thought you might like to stay in town for a while."

"It's still early. I just stopped by the office for a file. I have an appointment in fifteen minutes. Can I catch you back here in an hour or two?"

"Sure, but it's going to cost you," I answered.

He raised an eyebrow.

"I'm going to see if I can find an outfit I can enjoy the evening in."

I was tired of this always happening. I was beginning to think I needed a closet in my Jeep. If I wore my uniform I ended up needing civvies. A couple of times I had stopped at the station to take out my frustration on the punching bag only to find myself dressed all wrong. I needed a dress, a jeans outfit, my uniform and exercise clothes at the station. What I really needed was a locker but maybe a gym bag in the back of my Jeep would do for now.

I am not Ms. Shopper by a long shot. I don't enjoy shopping unless I am with my mom or sister and they help get me in the proper shopping mood. When I'm shopping alone I'll decide on precisely what I need and only look for that one item. This time I decided that whatever I wore would tell Rusty what kind of an evening he was in for. But I also decided that I wanted something wrinkle resistant that would pack easily so that if I kept it folded and stored in a gym bag maybe it would remain wearable for when it was needed. Finding outfits that fit had never been a problem. Anything in a 5 or 7 usually worked well. The problem was finding something that looked like my style. Looking like Skipper had some disadvantages. If I bought anything typical then I looked like a kid playing dress up with my mom's clothes. If I bought juniors clothes I looked fifteen. I had to think cute and perky, but older cute and perky, and not grandmotherly cute and perky. I was only twenty-six. You'd think it wouldn't be that hard. I suddenly realized that Lavene would know what to do, so I jumped into the Jeep and headed for the mall.

"Girl, would you look atchoo! I thought you said you wasn't becoming a cop. You said you were tracking."

"I am, but occasionally I find myself in a uniform. Only problem is I have a date tonight and I don't want to go dressed like this."

"All right! Date clothes! That's the kind I like! And you got a ring on your finger! How's married life treating you?"

"Wonderfully, it's been quiet though. That's why we're going out tonight."

"I got just the thing to add spice to your life. Lookie here."

The dress she held up was like Swiss cheese. I couldn't even figure out where the head and arm holes were when it was on a hanger.

"Lavene, I couldn't wear something like that."

"Aw, come on. You're smart. I'm looking for a customer who can figure out which way it goes."

"It's not that kind of a date."

"Aw, I bet it comes off easier than it goes on."

"Think Skipper. That usually works."

I took an armload of outfits into a dressing room. Too stiff, too flouncy, too old, too young, it seemed everything was too *something*. I worked my way through the pile and found the Swiss cheese dress on the bottom.

"Lavene! I am not trying on this dress."

"Aw, come on. Be a sport. You and I are the only ones who are gonna see it."

"Oh, all right, but I am not going to buy it."

I turned the dress this way and that. It was made of spandex. Why Lavene would take me for a spandex girl, I didn't know. I finally figured out that all the holes ran down the sleeves and around the front of the dress so the one large hole for the head was plainer. I slipped it on and pulled it around until all the holes were in the right places.

"Lavene," I called out, "if Cat Woman ever became a hooker, she'd wear this dress."

"Lemme see." Then, "Hmm, it does fit you though. And it makes you look, umm, curvy. You're sure you won't buy that dress?"

"Rusty would think I'd found a different profession."

"You're not going to a disco?"

"I don't even know how to dance. This is more like a quiet dinner, maybe a drink."

"Maybe some hanky panky? If so that's the dress."

"No, I couldn't."

"Couldn't buy the dress or couldn't hanky panky? Ready for round two?"

I sighed, "Okay."

I worked my way through the second armload of dresses and came to a quick halt.

"Lavene, I think we can stop now."

The dress was white and silky, almost gauzy. The top was fitted, almost like a swimsuit and the skirt floated and swished in interesting ways.

"What do you think?"

"Cat Woman it ain't, but neither are you."

"Do you think he'll like it?"

"Girl, they like anything with a skirt."

"Okay, hold this for me while I run over and look at shoes. I doubt my uniform shoes go with a white dress."

By the time I got checked out it was time for me to head back to the station. I peeked in Rusty's window and opened the door a crack.

"Give me fifteen minutes," I said and then went off to the locker room to change. I slipped on the white dress, slip and shoes. I definitely had to stop going shopping whenever I got stuck in town. I looked up and down at all the lockers. Fifty women's lockers and maybe ten women were working at the station. I needed to find out who was in charge. I brushed my hair. I didn't have a curling iron or make-up so there wasn't much more I could do. When I found Rusty again he was talking to Tom in the lobby.

"I'll have to send you out shopping more often," he said smiling. The woman manning the front counter sighed.

"You wanted a date, Lavene helped me find a date dress. Hi Tom, I guess Carla filled you in on our trip to the school."

"Oh yeah, definitely. She had to go bail out her husband, who broke down on the freeway, and she left me a message. 'Check out Kima Tumibay' was all it said. A little more information would have been helpful."

"Kima Tumibay is a teacher at Del Sol Elementary School, room 16. What we got out of one of her students was that Mrs. T was unusually agitated, so much so that she took two days off afterwards to regroup. Ordinarily, I wouldn't see that as being unusual. I'd expect the people most affected by this to need some peace and quiet after a school shooting. But the little girl said that while the shooting was going on her teacher kept saying, 'How did they know?'"

"How did they know what?"

"I don't know but it sounded like Mrs. T thought the shooters were looking for her. Her room is down the wing where the shooter got away. Carla and I watched her for a little while. She's a very pleasant Filipino woman. The kids love her. I can't imagine her having any enemies."

"We'll have to see about that. Thanks for the information. Was there anything else?"

"Yeah, Ricco is a cool dog and he's lucky because he gets to wear a uniform. Three boys want to be policemen when they grow up and two kids wanted us to arrest the school bully."

"Are you ready?" Rusty asked.

"Yeah, I chose an outfit, you choose dinner."

"What kind of place is this? The sign is in four languages, but none of them are English. None of them are our alphabet. I've ruled out Mexican, German, French, Greek, Italian…"

"It's Asian."

"Well, I'd kind of narrowed it down that far."

"That's right. It's Asian. It's a good place to try new things because they have lots of different kinds of food. By the way if they say a fish is fried it could be that the *whole* fish is fried. I know you don't like your food to watch you when you eat it."

"Thanks for the warning."

A maitre d' seated us in a booth next to an indoor water fountain. All the tables had starched white tablecloths and matching napkins. The servers were dressed in black and white with complimentary starched, white aprons. Flowers adorned the tables.

I was glad I was feeling brave because none of the dishes had names that told me anything about them. Should I try Delightful Threesome? Raging Volcano? Enchanting Sunset? I noticed Raging Volcano had a little pepper symbol by it.

Rusty saw my confusion. "Avoid this part of the menu. You're likely to get whole tiny octopus," he said. He pointed to another section. "These are more normal dishes like you are used to."

"What's a little risky but somewhat normal?"

He smiled at me. "How about Risky Business? It sounds like you. It's a businessman's lunch, slightly spicy but pretty much a normal stir-fry dish. Plus I don't see Trouble Magnet on the menu. Should we suggest it as a title?"

"I wonder what kind of a dish it would be. What are you going to order?"

"How about Twilight Romance? Or Bold Adventure? That one's spicy."

"Are you telling me you order by the title, not by what it is?"

"Only when the title might tell something about my intentions."

"So, what do we get if we mix Risky Business with Bold Adventure?"

"I don't know, let's find out. By the way, Sex on the Beach is not a drink here. It's bunch of naked seafood basking in a brown sauce with steamed vegetables and rice on the side."

"You didn't order Sex on the Beach when you were with me."

"I didn't order it at all. I saw it go by and knew I didn't want it so I asked what it was called. It was a little disappointing to know I didn't want Sex on the Beach."

"Maybe one of these days we can go looking for a deserted beach."

A waiter came over to our table to take our order so Rusty ordered Risky Business and Bold Adventure served family style. As the waiter turned to leave I noticed two women being seated a couple of tables away. It took me a moment to realize one of the women was Kima Tumibay. I watched discreetly.

"This is really not necessary…" I heard Mrs. T say. Her friend, also an Asian woman, seemed apologetic. They glanced around themselves frequently but they seemed calm. I noticed her friend spoke very little English and frequently reverted to some foreign language that I didn't recognize.

"He may be an activist but he's never been dangerous."

Her friend spoke and she thought for a minute and then seemed to repeat the statement in the foreign language.

"Cassidy, are you home?" Rusty asked.

"Oh yeah, sorry."

"What is it?"

"Remember the teacher I told Tom about at the station? That's her in the navy slacks and Hawaiian shirt."

Rusty watched. I knew I shouldn't eavesdrop, but I knew I could get valuable information for Tom. I wished I could have switched tables.

"I'm sorry," she said. "English first, Chinese second. It's a rule…."

More Chinese.

"Mai, try short sentences in English, first. Tell me about your life before you came here. Short sentences."

They began a choppy conversation with Mai struggling and Mrs. T correcting her gently. I turned to Rusty.

"So, how much can we use and how much must we ignore?"

"Let's just open our own restaurant and then you can run it and all the people we are looking for can just come eat there, blow their cover, tell us their secrets. I can go undercover as a waiter and arrest them as I take their order. I was going to suggest we go to Trujillo's for a drink but maybe we better not."

"Rusty, you're getting superstitious. Admit it."

"At least she isn't dangerous."

"I don't think you'd be able to pass as a waiter. No one would believe for a second that you were really a waiter."

"Why not? I already carry a pad of paper and a pen. I could trade my gun in for a cheese grater or a pepper grinder."

"The tips would be great. I'm for finding a deserted beach."

Our food arrived and I looked at it suspiciously. It didn't look too risky. I looked at the Bold Adventure and I could see little heat waves floating over the top of the dish. Or maybe it was just the spicy aroma which seemed hot. Rusty took some rice then spooned Bold Adventure over the top. He took a bite then reached for his glass of tea. Boldly going where many men had gone before, straight to the tea.

I scooped out some sticky rice and topped it with some Risky Business. I smelled it but I couldn't detect much of anything over the Bold Adventure. I took a bite. It was a little spicy, but I dug in while Rusty carefully searched his plate pulling out little peppers.

"Don't eat these," he warned me. "They'll set you right on fire."

"This is good. Do you want some?"

"Maybe after this."

The meal was interesting. Eventually I did try a little Bold Adventure. I didn't find it as spicy as Rusty did. Maybe bold adventure was becoming more normal for me. I tried to keep track of the conversation at both tables at once but I wasn't very successful. Whenever I caught a few words from the other table it was Mai talking about her family in very broken English. I knew Rusty didn't appreciate work infringing on his date. I tried to remember this was Tom's case; he'd talk to Kima Tumibay. It was none of my business.

Rusty attempted to use the chopsticks. He did okay while he was just grasping bite-sized pieces but gave up when he was left with only rice. I wasn't going to try chopsticks in a white dress. That seemed like an invitation for a fashion disaster. Bold adventure had a habit of leaving stains behind.

When we left the restaurant I caught Rusty following and watching me from behind. I sashayed a little and he smiled and winked at me. It was odd; in the beginning I'd never really done anything to attract Rusty. I didn't encourage him in any way but now that we were married I enjoyed flirting with him. In a way that was good. It opened up new and interesting twists and turns to our relationship. It was fun. And I thought he rather enjoyed seeing this new side of me.

Trujillo's was busy but, since I was with Rusty, no felons tried to strike up a conversation with me. Rusty scared them all off. Benny and Marco, the Trujillo brothers were there working the crowd.

"Ey, Rusty, long time no see! Are you working tonight?"

"Trying not to. How's business?"

"Is good, I've been trying to think up some gimmick to bring people in, like Mexican karaoke. You think Mexican karaoke would work?"

"Um, no."

"Aw, why not?"

"Your clientele is too mixed. Not enough customers who know Mexican songs."

"So," he asked, "what brings you here?"

"An evening when Cassidy and I are in town together."
"Oh, can't make a gimmick out of that."

Chapter 4

The call came midmorning the next day.

"Cassidy? I've got a job for you. Can you be at Elk Meadows in a few hours?"

"Yeah, I've got a pack ready to go. I just need to call Rusty. Any details?"

"Man and wife camping at Elk Meadows. They went out for a hike and the wife wanted to turn back early. The husband kept going and when he got back to camp his wife was nowhere to be seen. He went out looking for her yesterday evening and called early this morning, concerned because she was still out there."

"Were they following the trail?"

"No, they crossed the meadows and headed up into the hills nearby."

At least I knew the area a little bit. I'd hiked behind the meadows once before. The trail was fairly fresh. I was hopeful that this would be a successful search.

"How old is she? Does she have experience in the outdoors?"

"Not much but she doesn't sound like a wimp either. They take their grandkids camping and she'd always told them that if they got lost they should find a place that was safe and wait to be found. Hopefully she listened to her own advice."

"Grandkids? How old is she?"

"Fifty eight."

Rusty answered on the second ring.

"Hey there."

"Hi, I've got a call. It doesn't sound like a long one but I thought I ought to let you know. Base camp is Elk Meadows. I'll be heading into the hills behind the meadows. You know the area. Tracking should be about average for the mountains. She's been gone overnight but she sounds very level headed so hopefully she found a rock somewhere and she's just out there waiting for me."

"You take care of my girl out there."

"I will, I miss you already, but I shouldn't be gone long."

I met Landon at the compound. He smiled broadly as I stepped out of my Jeep, shouldered my pack and made my way over to the car he had packed and ready to go.

"I doubt you need me on this one," he said. "But at least I get to go on a hike in the mountains with a beautiful girl. I can't knock that."

If there was anybody I'd rather go tracking with besides Rusty it was Landon. He was an EMT and very capable, but more than that, he was good company, he looked out for me. In fact, he was loyal to a fault. When I got so involved in the trail that I forgot the time he reminded me to eat. When I pushed too hard he slowed me down. When things turned out badly he was there, first to take over medically, then as emotional backup. That wasn't part of his job but he was always there for me. When a search ended badly I tended to withdrawal and blame myself. He never let me get away with any negative thinking and he knew the routine. Landon drew me out, encouraged me, and beat down my guilt trip before calling in the troops, which meant Rusty, and then... then he sat back and wished it could just be him.

Victor was the other EMT I got paired up with a lot. But oddly enough, it was because Victor didn't do all those things that made me like working with him. Victor was Steady Eddie. He followed me and stepped in when I got to the end of the trail. And he let me be. He was good company and he always needed a tale of my latest catastrophe, even if he'd heard it before, but we worked more independently, and I appreciated the space. Victor wouldn't be on this search. He was a family man, with an outside job and wouldn't be needed. We didn't need Landon either, except that Strict wouldn't send me out alone and Landon was a willing participant. Rosco and Thez would be willing to go out, too, but Strict chose wisely when he paired me up with Landon or Victor. Tracking with Rosco was like pulling a trailer behind me. And Thez was entertaining but always brought along too many surprises.

"I got a new toy," I announced as I loaded my gear. "I hope it doesn't scare our ten sixty-five, but I wanted to take it for a trial run."

I handed him the rifle Rusty had given me for Christmas. Landon took it from me and looked it over, hefted it. It definitely wasn't the gun for him, but he admired the work that went into choosing a gun that was right for me. The public expects the officers to carry weapons. They see the uniform, the attitude and the rifle fits in. Not so with me. They wonder if I know which end is which. And this rifle didn't help in that department. It was more of a commando style. But the fact that it wasn't made out of heavy wood and metal made it extremely light and the molded stock and butt were tailored to a smaller person, so it made the rifle a perfect fit for me.

"I've been going to the range about once a week. I still aim a little high on the first shot. So I skip the first shot and go for the second one instead."

"That works. You're probably just rushing your first shot."

Elk Meadows was green with melting spring snow. The grass of the meadows, usually a dull yellow, looked alive with new growth. I almost expected to see elk grazing but knew they rarely came this close to the campground.

Strict hugged me in greeting.

"You're looking good," he said. "You ready?"

"Yeah, it's been a while. You didn't call me to tromp through the snow like you did last year."

"That's because we could see the tracks though the snow. When we need a real tracker we call you."

"So you need a real tracker?"

"It would help."

"Where's the campsite?"

Strict took me over to a camping spot with a large cabin tent. The picnic table had a red and white checkered tablecloth clipped down to it. A lantern stood at one end and an ice chest sat comfortably on the picnic table bench. A white Suburban was parked next to the campsite. A large golden retriever mix strained at the end of a chain wrapped around a tree. He barked, half warning and half greeting. This couple was settled in their outdoors ways. A man sat at the picnic table, head in hands. He stood as we approached.

"Peter? This is Cassidy Michaels and Landon Wilson. I'm sending them out to find Alisondra."

Peter looked at us dubiously.

"Don't worry," I said, "I'm more capable than I look."

"Cassidy is our tracker," Strict said. "She's why we don't have twenty people up here ready to canvas the hills. She'll stay on Alisondra's trail until she's found. Landon is here for medical support. If Alisondra did as you expect and found a place to wait for searchers we should have her back safe and sound soon. If she tried to find her way back it might take some tracking. We'll maintain radio contact so we can check the progress whenever we want. Cassidy needs a few things before she heads out. If you have a pair of Alisondra's shoes, a picture of her, and a sample of her tracks it would help."

I began walking around the campsite. I'd already noted the kind of shoes Peter wore so I could distinguish Alisondra's tracks from his. Peter ducked into the tent and came out with a pair of canvas tennis shoes.

"She wears these around camp. She wears sturdier shoes for hiking."

I took the shoes from him and noted the wear patterns. She must wear these shoes around the house too. The insides of both soles were worn smooth. The inside of the right shoe had a hole worn through it. The laces were ready to break. This lady wasn't into the latest styles either. She was all business, but a pleasant, comfortable business. I thought she must have a lot of fun with her grandkids. I put the shoes down and walked around camp trying to pick up the tracks of Alisondra's sturdier hiking shoes. I located a good track and squatted down to study the tread pattern. The wear marks that I had seen on her canvas shoes didn't show up on the hiking shoes. Perhaps the hiking shoes were newer. It helped that the tread was crisp and recognizable. The tracks would show up easier in the rougher terrain of the mountains.

"Are you ready?" I asked Landon.

He walked to the car and shrugged into his pack in response. I took out my own pack and shouldered the rifle. Peter looked alarmed. I looked to Strict and he was just as curious. I'd never taken a rifle with me before.

"Rusty got it for me for Christmas. I'm just seeing if it packs well on the trail. You wanted me to have one for scouting. Well, now I've got one."

"I'd like to take a look at it when you get back."

"Okay, show me what we're up against. Peter, you and Alisondra hiked out of here and she headed back early. You can save me some tracking time if you can show me on the map where it was that Alisondra turned back. Do you know where it was?"

He bent over the map and pointed to the meadows. "The campground is here," he said, pointing. "We crossed the meadows in this direction and followed the side of the hill around until the little valley split. Then we continued down the left fork. When the valley ended we began following the terrain up into a saddle and came down the other side. That's when Ally wanted to head back. I was sure she could find the way since all she had to do was go over the saddle and follow the valleys back to the meadow. It seemed very straightforward to me. But when I got here there was no sign of her."

"So the last time you saw her was just south of the saddle? Can you give me a landmark where I can pick up the trail? The more specific the better."

"Yeah, Ally took my picture standing next to a tree that was growing in a corkscrew. If you can find it, it'll make a good starting point. There should be plenty of tracks in the vicinity too."

I asked Landon, "Got your hikin' boots on? We're taking a fast hike to the saddle with minor information gathering on the way."

I circled the campsite finding the trail leading out and through the meadow. I walked quickly, keeping an eye on Peter and Ally's tracks. I noticed they stayed close. Occasionally Ally's footprints would stray to the side and Peter's would stop as Ally stopped to investigate something. She would kneel in the grass and look closely at small things, sometimes getting down on hands and knees. I thought I might like this lady when I finally caught up to her. I imagined a woman with dirt smudged jeans and a curiosity about the world that matched her grandkids'.

Landon followed me quickly across the meadow. My pack was heavy. It always took me a half mile or so to get used to the weight. After that, the pack seemed to settle and I could move as if it were a part of me.

"Since we're just hiking and we know where we're going, tell me about your latest adventures," Landon said.

My heart sunk. I should have seen it coming but it hit me like a ton of bricks.

"Landon, you've heard all about it. It's been in the news and I'm sure Jacobsen has made sure the station has heard his version. Isn't that enough?"

"Jacobsen?"

"Yeah, he...you're sure you haven't heard about this?"

"Considering you haven't told me anything yet, yeah."

"I don't know if I can talk about it. I thought you'd heard. You watch the news, don't you?"

"If I'm not on duty, or out."

"Shoot. I don't think I can do it yet. Get it from Jacobsen."

I could feel the look he gave me burrowing through my back. It was a mixture of irritation and concern. He knew the things that set me off.

"If Jacobsen was involved it means he was senior officer."

"Not necessarily."

I doubled my pace trying to out hike my brain. Maybe if I hiked fast enough we'd leave the topic far behind. When Landon got tired of trying to keep up he huffed impatiently, "Cassidy, you can run but you cannot hide. I won't push you to talk about it but eventually you've got to come to grips with it or it's going to eat you up."

"Not if Tom can put the guy away. If we can just get him before he hurts someone I'll be okay. I keep running the pieces of what I know through my mind and it's taking shape but it still doesn't make sense. Like, why is Kima Tumibay worried about gunmen? She's just a teacher. What could a teacher possibly have done to cause two armed men to go looking for her? I saw her at the school. She loves the kids in her class. The kids all think she's great. She's personable and friendly and kind. It doesn't make sense."

"For not wanting to talk about it you're doing a pretty good job, although I don't have answers to any of your questions."

"Rusty and I saw her at a restaurant last night. She didn't know who I was. It was odd seeing her there too. Again, she was personable and friendly. She was with a foreign woman who spoke very little English and she was helping her learn English, not unusual for a teacher, but something seemed odd about it anyway. Her friend appeared to be worried about something and one sentence that I overheard was out of place and it kind of tied in with why the woman might be worried or why the gunmen were at the school. She said a certain man was 'an activist but usually not dangerous.' And yet these two gunmen turn up at the school. I think it must tie in somewhere. And I worry about exactly where. I've had enough gunmen after me to learn it doesn't take much to set some people off. I've had guys try and kill me for the oddest reasons."

"It's because you're a trouble magnet. You attract people like that."

"Gee, thanks. Even if that's the reason why I get into trouble it doesn't explain why it would happen to her. I wish I could talk to her but she doesn't even know who I am or how I know about her link to all this. And I'm not sure she should know."

"Cassidy, you're not making any sense unless I have some background to go by."

"It doesn't help."

"Why can't you just start at the beginning?"

"I can't. Landon, just ask Jacobsen or Rusty or Strict or almost anybody else at the station. Where have you been that you haven't heard about it? It was on TV, probably nationwide. You couldn't have missed it. Schroeder was on the news. I couldn't watch it because it brought too many flashbacks. Schroeder told them in no uncertain terms that they would not get an interview with me no matter what. I think it's because Schroeder is worried about how much I might say but he also knows my aversion to television reporters."

"You know you're just digging yourself in deeper and deeper."

We were headed up the first little valley, still following Peter and Ally's tracks but only enough to verify their passage. I was more interested in what had happened to Alisondra after she left Peter and headed back. I was hiking at a good steady pace because I knew time was ticking away. The trail wasn't exactly a valley, but more of an area where two hills met and resulted in a little wash. When it rained the wash would turn into a small creek but now, even with the snow on the mountains quickly melting, the wash was dry.

"If you really want to find out, drop back a bit and talk to Strict."

"I couldn't do that. Everybody within range would listen in."

"You can go to another frequency, but really, I'm telling you you're probably the only one who doesn't know. Maybe Peter will feel better about me carrying this rifle. Or maybe he'll worry more. Oh hell." I stopped, turned around and confronted Landon with the truth. "Okay, here's how it was, I went to Del Sol Elementary School to talk to a third grade class about my job, how to prevent getting lost, you know the drill. I hear shots. There's a gunman walking through the school taking pot shots at people. I was the only one armed. I had to shoot him...Landon I had to. Everybody else was locked in classrooms or running down the hall in fear. There were two gunmen and I killed one and wounded the other. He's the one we've got to catch. But I can't fit all the pieces together. And I can't put it down. I just relive it and think about it and try and piece it together but I can't make sense of it. I try but I don't have enough pieces yet. Now let me hike before I get all tied up in knots and become useless." I kicked a rock, turned around and trudged off down the trail. Landon stood still letting this new information sink in. He knew to give me some distance. He followed silently but I knew what was coming and I didn't want to hear it. I stopped to clear the tears from my eyes. No use trudging off if I couldn't see, I'd only lose the trail. Even if I was just verifying their tracks I still needed to see them.

"And this teacher thinks the gunmen were after her? An 'activist'? That's an odd word."

"She was trying to think of a word her foreign friend would understand. That's just what she came up with."

"Activists have an agenda. An issue they address. What's this guy against?"

"That's just it, Landon, I don't know." But I was thankful he wasn't trying to justify my actions like I had been expecting him to. "I keep thinking, though, that if she knows he's an activist, maybe she knows who he is. And if she does, why would she protect him? It seems like she'd be running to the police and reporting him but that hasn't happened."

"You said there were two gunmen. Maybe she's afraid of a radical militant organization."

"This is Joshua Hills. What kind of organizations do we have here?"

I climbed up a few rocks and located Ally's footprints on the other side. I was glad hikers preferred following sandy washes. It made my job a lot easier. I expected it to get tougher at the saddle.

"Cassidy, you know it had to be done, right?" Oh boy, here it comes. Instantly my walls went up.

"My head knows. It's the rest of me I'm having trouble with. Just because something has to be done doesn't make it right."

"Look at the alternatives. I know it goes against your principles to shoot someone. If you hadn't shot him then what would have happened? You couldn't fight the guy, you'd have been beaten until he shot you or you shot him. You couldn't wait for help. Help could have been too long coming." My pace picked up as the thoughts flailed around in my head.

"I don't want to hear it. I've heard it several times a day since this happened. I go over and over it but I still can't justify it to my heart. I just need to forgive myself and maybe that will be come sooner if we can just get this guy who got away and I can make sense of the whole situation. Now find a different subject to talk about."

"Cookies. Did you bring any cookies?" he asked.

"Depends, did you bring anything to trade?"

"You're kidding."

"Victor brings cinnamon rolls."

Of course Victor had never actually *offered* me a cinnamon roll. He just unknowingly taunted me with them. Landon's face fell.

"Oh, all right, I only brought a few, because I expected this to be a short search, but I'll split them with you."

"Chocolate chip? With nuts?"

"Chocolate chip, no nuts."

"This is Mickey Mouse tracking," he said looking at the ground. "Even I could do this."

"We'll have our work cut out for us after we reach the saddle. It'll be more woodland tracking and it'll only be one person. I'm not even really tracking at this point. Just trying to get to the saddle in time to leave us some real tracking time. She shouldn't be far from the saddle though. We can't be two miles from the campground. She should have been able to find her way back from the saddle. It seems impossible to get lost on a hike like this. Judging from the hints in the meadow she probably got distracted and followed her curiosity away from the campground instead of returning."

The day was warm and pleasant. We watched ahead for trees and shady spots then eyed the saddle ahead and kept walking. As we neared the saddle I paid closer attention to the tracks. A mountain pass could be a broad area and one tree could be hard to spot so I followed the tracks. When we stood before the corkscrewed tree Landon and I glanced at each other. My look said, okay, now the real work begins. His look said, didn't you say you had cookies? I rolled my eyes then took off my pack and fished around inside until I found a Ziploc bag of cookies. I handed him four. Then I took out trail mix to snack on while tracking. I put on my pack, shifted it around, fastened the hip belt, and shouldered the rifle. The rifle was packing surprisingly well. As I put it back on I realized I hadn't noticed taking it off. It fit me and moved with me as though I had always owned it.

Now it was time for some real tracking. We had to find Alisondra today. I was determined. Examining the tracks around the corkscrewed tree, I located Peter's tracks standing next to it, then discovered Alisondra's tracks several yards away where she had stood to take the picture. I followed her footsteps carefully as she hiked with Peter over the saddle. They stopped and talked once about halfway down the hill, their footprints milling about casually. She followed him to the bottom of the hill before turning back. However, when she returned to camp she did not want to climb to the top of the saddle again so she circled the hill hoping to see some new sights and find her way back to Elk Meadows from the other side. If she thought the hill would lead back around to the first little valley she was mistaken. It didn't lead her that way at all. At first she just hiked along with a spring in her step, seemingly enjoying the day. When the hill began curving in an obviously different direction from Elk Meadows she turned around. She followed the hill around but didn't recognize the saddle when she got back to it. She kept on. The further south she hiked the rougher the terrain became. She was approaching the big shale mountain, its flimsy rock chips visible even from this far away. Ally stopped frequently. I imagined her thinking about the path she had been hiking and trying to figure out a way back, or picking up the odd-shaped pieces of shale, like I tended to, thinking they begged to be painted on. I never was much of an artist though so I always left the shale where it had fallen. It became more difficult to track Ally near the shale mountain because the ground was coarse bits of shale. I had to study carefully trying to piece together what little information the ground would yield. I was glad I hurried to the saddle because this was the kind of tracking that couldn't be rushed. Landon walked to the bottom of a jagged looking ledge jutting up to the east.

"Don't climb it," I said. "It flakes away. If we were on the other side of the mountain you could see Elk Meadows from up there. The mountain overlooks a couple of miles of meadows and the campground is at the end of it."

"Maybe I can see something from up there anyway," he said and began climbing.

"The shale isn't trustworthy. Test the rock before you put your weight on it."

"You climbed up there and now you're warning me about it?"

"The way I climbed up doesn't require handholds and footholds. Go ahead, you have a little while. I won't go far while you climb up and back. This ground is useless."

I turned my attention to Ally's partial track. I followed the direction it was pointing and looked for the next one. Maybe. Maybe this rock had been stepped on. It looked like it had been pressed into the soil fairly recently. I removed the rock and examined the indentation, imagined what kind of a step would make it press into the ground at that particular angle, then looked to the place where I imagined the other step would have fallen. I kept the last sure track in my mind so I could go back to it if necessary. Step by step I figured out Ally's route. It felt like it took ages but finally she headed away from the shale and the ground became readable again. I didn't want to leave Landon behind so I found a stick and drew a circle around the track. Then I dragged the stick behind me marking my trail back to the ledge.

"Landon!" I called. "Time to get a move on!"

I heard a motion from above and saw Landon descending the mountain, carefully feeling for footholds.

"I didn't see anything but empty forest from up there," he said.

"I got past the tough part."

"Okay, give me a minute, I'll catch up."

"Follow the stick mark in the dirt."

"Okay." I knew he'd catch up to me quickly, so I set off again to find Ally's last track.

Fifteen minutes later Landon still hadn't appeared. He's a big boy, Cass, he can take care of himself, I told myself. He's been doing this a lot longer than you have. But then I thought that even if Landon was a big boy, he'd never considered me to be a big girl and wouldn't have let me go this far alone. So, again, I went back expecting to meet him hiking down my clearly marked trail. Instead I found him at the bottom of the ledge surrounded by a small pile of handholds and footholds that had been truly untrustworthy.

"It's about time," he said.

"I won't say it."

"Say what?"

"I told you so."

"Thanks, now help me. I did something to my leg. Is it broken?"

"You, the EMT, are asking me, the tracker, if your leg is broken? If I saw your tracks and you fell I'd say, 'Ouch, bet that hurt! I bet that guy's leg is broken.' But show me a leg and I have no idea."

I gave him a hand up. He stood without putting any weight on his leg. He put an arm over my shoulder and I helped him to his pack, then lowered him back down. His blonde hair was a mess and his blue eyes reflected the pain.

"Did you call Strict?"

"No, I was waiting to make a decision."

"Well, you aren't hiking anywhere in this condition."

"Open my pack. I've got splints in there. It's a little plastic bag." He began poking at his leg, not the gentle feeling motions he used on other people. He'd checked me over for broken bones before and had been very gentle. When he found the most painful spot he began running his fingers over the area but didn't come to any firm conclusions.

"If you're in too much pain to put weight on it you can't hike. I may have miles to go. We can't tell from here. If you call Strict and he sends a copter in for you maybe Alisondra will hear it and head this way."

"You're not going by yourself," he said determinedly.

I shot him with *that look* and said with the same determination, "I'm not quitting. Maybe Strict can get someone else to come in on the helicopter. Is this it?" I asked, holding up a little packet of clear plastic.

"Read the label. I've got different kinds in there."

I read a few little plastic packets before I found it.

"Okay, lower leg, got it. This is a splint?"

"Yeah."

"It's not the kind of splint I learned to use in school."

"That's because in school you didn't have to pack several of them in a backpack."

"True."

"Find the scissors."

I followed his instructions and located the scissors. I cut away his pants leg just above the knee because the leg could be x-rayed though the splint if the material wasn't in the way. While I worked he radioed Strict. Strict wasn't very happy. There was a long discussion where Landon told him I wasn't coming out and that Strict should call Victor. Strict informed us that Victor wasn't available. How about Rosco? Thez? I untied Landon's shoe and loosened the laces. I pulled his shoe off as gently as I could and he stiffened with the pain.

"We still have the sock to go. Ready?" I gently pulled off his sock making sure it didn't catch on his heel.

The splint was like a giant inflatable sock. I opened it and got all the creases out then made sure it could be pulled onto his leg without putting undo pressure anywhere. I slipped it on. Now what?

"Just blow it up," he instructed. "See the valve?"

"Yeah, I'm just imagining how this is going to get back to Rusty. If I know you…"

He gave me a mischievous smile. "Guess you'll have to tell him first. Wouldn't want him getting any wrong ideas. Pinch it a little, then use long, slow breaths. Release the valve to keep the air in between breathes."

I blew up the splint until it fit snuggly and I couldn't get more air inside.

"Did you give Strict our coordinates?"

"Yeah."

"Think I should spread out your tent so they can find us easily?"

"Wouldn't hurt."

I pulled Landon's tent from its bag and went looking for an open area. After spreading it out I put a couple of stakes down to hold it in place. When I got back to Landon he was removing the radio and burrowing in his pack. He handed me several packets.

"I'll trade you, the basic first aid kit for the rest of the cookies."

If I was going to have to pack his medical supplies and the radio I wanted to get rid of some weight from my pack anyway, so we struck a deal.

I ate one cookie and gave him the rest. When he saw there were more than four he looked at me like I had been holding out on him earlier. I just couldn't imagine anybody eating more than four cookies at a time. Two was my limit. I unpacked both packs, except for his personal things in the bottom pocket, then we picked and chose what he thought I might need or was authorized to use. I packed them hoping all the identical little packets wouldn't be needed. I sent some of my backpacker food with him since I didn't expect to be out for more than another day. He took my water purifier since I didn't expect to see any water to purify. This little detour was seriously cutting into my tracking time.

As we heard the helicopter closing in I got up and walked to the clearing to flag it down. I didn't think there was enough space to land but at least they could spot us easily. When they spotted us I helped Landon hobble over to the clearing, then rolled up his tent and hastily stuffed it back in its sack. A basket was lowered along with a volunteer and together we helped Landon onto the stretcher.

"I'll call when I get out of here," I yelled over the noise.

"I'll be sure and need some help."

I gave him a friendly punch to the shoulder and he was pulled up into the bay. The helicopter flew a wide circle searching for our missing person, then headed back to town. I noted grimly that they didn't leave me an EMT. I was on my own but I didn't mind so much. I could track, camp and find my ten sixty-five alone. I just hoped Ally wouldn't need medical attention. It was possible that the helicopter hadn't taken Landon to town, but only to base camp where an ambulance took him the rest of the way. If that were true then maybe Strict still had someone who would be joining me later. I watched the helicopter, then turned and jogged to the last track I'd found. I was glad I had passed the hardest part of the search and Ally was pointed in a good direction for tracking. The tracks led on and I followed them as quickly as I dared. When I had started out I'd hoped to find Ally that day. Now it was doubtful.

Chapter 5

Strict checked in with me frequently. It was always just a quick, friendly check up and he never kept me on the radio long.

Ally's tracks reflected a change in her mood. She had started out with a spring in her step which gradually faded to a cautious but steady hike. She had a nice, ground eating stride, unless she became distracted, which happened occasionally. I followed her as she investigated an animal den and I was surprised to learn that it was empty at this time of year. Later she climbed a tree looking for the right direction but the tree she chose was over the mountain from the meadows so she wasn't able to see it. She stopped frequently but the reason for her stops weren't always apparent. It was always in a place where there was no shade or other tracks, and she didn't sit to rest. Perhaps she saw a bird or heard a noise. It wasn't clear, but I was glad she was taking her time.

I tracked until it grew dark and I could no longer see footprints on the ground. I stopped reluctantly because I still hadn't found the place Alisondra had spent the night. Usually I stopped earlier than nightfall, so I could cook, clean up and set up camp before it got dark. Since I was alone I could rough it a little more. When I was with the guys I made a point to set up a tent and roll out a sleeping bag. If I didn't have everything they felt I needed they felt guilty and began providing for my comfort. It was a relief to be able to camp however I wanted so I didn't set up my tent. I just rolled it up loosely and used it like a bivouac sack. After pumping up my little one burner gas stove, I heated up water and added it to the pouch of a backpacker meal. Then I used the rest of the water for hot chocolate. Backpacker food, oatmeal, trail mix and hot chocolate were my camping staples. I always came home craving fruits, vegetables and sweets. Preferably cheesecake.

When my meal was finished I folded up the pouch, tucked it into a trash bag, then rinsed the cup and fork. As I lay in my makeshift tent, the smooth nylon brushing my face when the wind blew, I pictured Rusty, just like I always did before falling asleep. I'd told him this would be a quick trip but I hadn't planned on spending hours helping Landon. I hoped Rusty wouldn't be angry if he found out I'd continued alone. I knew he wouldn't be mad at me. He would expect it of me, but he might be mad at Strict, telling him he should have called and Rusty would have jumped on the helicopter himself. I fell asleep with thoughts of Rusty and awoke in the morning determined to find Alisondra and get back home. I enjoyed the solitude and my time in the woods but each night I was away I felt more and more guilty and homesick.

Mornings in the mountains were my favorite time of day. Everything felt crisp and new. The sun didn't pound down, it filtered in sideways through the trees. Everything was still and peaceful. I went through my morning routine on automatic, only because I knew I'd last longer in my tracking if I ate properly. I took note of how much water I had left. I was tempted to pour some out to cut down on weight but knew I might need to share when I found my ten sixty-five. I found the end of the trail and started out, reading carefully and as quickly as I dared. I'd been on the trail for an hour when Strict checked in.

"How are you?" he asked. "Holding up okay?"

"Yeah, I'm fine."

"Got a call from Rusty last night."

"You knew to expect that."

"Yeah, I should have. Should have kept my mouth shut too. He wasn't as upset as Peter was though. I had to outline your many successful tracking expeditions before Peter was convinced you'd be okay out there."

I gave him the coordinates off the GPS and he plotted my location on a map then let me get back to my tracking, not that I'd quit. It was just easier to track without dealing with the radio.

If there was ever a search for me to do alone, I thought as I tracked, this is it. I had learned a lot about Alisondra as I followed her footsteps. She was a sturdy and practical woman who was also whimsical and fun. She became distracted by the simplest of things yet she kept her head and didn't panic even though her path never made any sense. I found myself thinking, if I needed to get back to Elk Meadows from here I'd just go over this hill, turn west at the big shale mountain and I'd be there. But Ally didn't seem to own a sense of direction.

I was tracking along, still worried that I hadn't found the place where Ally had spent the night, when I heard a movement ahead in some rocks.

"Are you looking for me?" a voice called out from above.

"Are you Alisondra?" I asked.

"Oh, don't call me that. It makes me feel so old. When I was five, people told me it was a pretty name because I was pretty. When I was in high school guys told me it was a sexy name because they wanted me to feel sexy. By the way, how old are you? Maybe I shouldn't be telling you these things."

"Don't worry, I'm old enough."

"When I was thirty it was a stately name and when I was fifty it was regal. Now that I am nearing sixty I'm afraid to hear what it's considered next. So I go by Ally and now I can be whatever age I want."

"So what age do you want to be?" I asked.

"I liked thirty-five the best. That was a good year. I was old enough to know I didn't know everything but young enough to enjoy it. And I was old enough to know there was a lot of learning still ahead of me." She climbed down lithely from the rocks and joined me on the ground. "I was hoping for a nice young man, maybe thirtyish."

"He was twenty-nine and he broke his leg. Don't worry, there will be more of them when we get back to base camp. Have you had water?"

"I knew to conserve that. I've got a tiny bit left."

"You can finish it. I've got more. How long has it been since you've eaten?"

"About a day and a half. I look on it like a forced diet. Maybe I lost a little weight," she said hopefully. She wasn't fat but she wasn't thin either. She was huggable to her grandkids but attractive to men her age. Her gray hair was in an easy care cut and her eyes smiled behind stylish glasses.

I found a comfortable spot to sit for a while, removed my pack and rifle, then opened the pack and began digging around inside looking for something to eat. I brought out my camp stove and a packet of backpacker food. I handed Ally the remains of my trail mix and a bottle of water. A few quick pumps and a flick of a Bic and I had the stove working, then water heating. Even after going a day without food she picked out her favorite parts of the trail mix.

"The one thing I missed out here was a bath. That water makes me want to go home and take a long, hot bath. When night came yesterday I knew it was time to stop running around in circles. I've always liked rocks. Rocks and trees are friendly. The trees close me in and the rocks are fun to climb around on. So I decided to stay here and wait."

"Smart move. I wish more of the people I find would do that."

While the water was heating I located our position on the map and figured out how to get back to Elk Meadows. I was relieved to see it wasn't far. I poured the hot water into the pouch, folded the top over and shook it a little.

I called Strict on the radio. I always felt self-conscious when I spoke on the radio. I let the guys carry the radio most of the time. It was a gadget and guys like gadgets.

"Strict?"

"Go ahead, Cassidy."

"Ten Sixty-five found."

"Ten forty-five?"

"Ten forty-five A. We're fine."

"Need a lift?"

"Negative. I found us on the map. We can make it out today."

"Give me your coordinates."

I read them off the GPS, he located our position on the map and agreed to let us hike out.

"We're just eating some lunch and then we'll head back."

"Ten four."

"Your name is Cassidy?" Ally asked.

"Yeah, my dad is an old west buff."

As Ally ate her reconstituted noodle lunch she said, "I have a better recipe for this if you're interested."

"I bet you do. What is it?"

"I think it's trying to be lasagna but it has a bit of a stroganoff flavor to it, too, like beefy sour cream. What would that make it strogagna? Lasanoff?"

"I think the label says lasagna on it."

"So," she said changing the subject, "what do your parents think of you traipsing around in the mountains by yourself?"

"They are glad I'm doing this because it's a lot safer than what I do when I'm not traipsing around in the mountains."

"What do you normally do then?"

I laughed, "I'm a housewife and trouble magnet."

"You, a housewife? You look like…"

"I'm still in high school, I know."

"You remind me of those pictures they used to show of kids in the Mid-East carrying machine guns."

"Gee thanks."

"I didn't mean…"

"It's okay, actually, I *have* been one of those kids in the Mid-East carrying a machine gun. I didn't use it though. I spent six months in Afghanistan. Your husband looked worried when he saw me packing the rifle, but I'm used to that."

She laughed, "I bet he did. He thinks women should fit into his little mold like his mother did. I'm afraid I haven't stayed within that mold myself. There are too many interesting things outside the mold so I end up hopping out and getting lost in the mountains. By the way, how did you know where to find me? I expected a dozen men to be searching the hills calling out my name, not some teenager walking quietly up to me and introducing herself."

"I followed your tracks. If I'm not around I guess they do send out a dozen guys to search the hills and call out people's names, but since I am here they only sent out two."

"And the other guy broke his leg?"

"Yeah, he was flown out by helicopter. I was hoping the helicopter would catch your attention. Did you see it?"

"No, I heard something in the distance but I was up in the rocks wondering how trees manage to grow there. If I were a tree I sure wouldn't pick solid rock to try and grow in. Seems like it would be hard to get water out of solid rock and even harder to grow roots."

"Thinking like that is exactly how I got to be a tracker. I was curious about tracks, how they were made, what kind of animals made them, where the animals went. What did they do? The more tracks I followed the more I learned until it was the most natural thing in the world to just follow tracks to see where they led, and what kind of people made them. I like your tracks. I could tell from your footprints that you were an interesting person and someone I would like to meet."

"And I think you are an interesting person who my class should meet."

"Your class?"

"Yes, I teach kids how to be interested in the world around them. Well, technically I'm a kindergarten teacher but at that age curiosity gets them further than book learning."

"I speak to classes every once in a while, usually about safety in the woods. Last time I spoke my presentation was cut short by that shooting. I suppose you heard about it in the news."

"Heard about it? I was there. I was grateful that the kindergarten classes are separated from the rest of the school. My kids did great though. I was so proud of them. When they heard the alarm they all got under their desks like for an earthquake drill. I wasn't going to tell them to do otherwise. I locked all the doors and turned my desk so I could see the kids while I sat under my desk too. I kept telling them what a good job they were doing and we read stories. We were lucky an officer was on hand at the time. It could have been so much worse."

"Well, that wasn't exactly an officer. It was me."

"You? You mean you had to... How did you do it? I mean you had to, I know that, but I don't think I could even if I had to. I could see some cops springing to action, taking aim, firing, no problem. I just have trouble picturing you doing something like that."

"I know, me, too. And it was very hard. It's always hard to make a choice like that. If it weren't for the kids, I'd be haunted by something like that. And it still bothers me. It bothers me a lot. If I talk to your class, I'd rather they not connect me with the shooting. I'd like to make it fun for them. You know what would be fun? A tracking demonstration. I can tell from the kids' tracks what they have done. It's always fun to let a few kids lay a trail for me and then let me tell them exactly what they did. I get kids who do handstands and back-flips trying to trip me up and I always figure it out."

We kept talking as we cleaned up the cooking gear and packed it away, then headed back to Elk Meadows. Ally was a fun person to talk to. She was bright and attentive and knowledgeable and yet she was curious about everything. Maybe she became knowledgeable by being curious about the world around her. However it happened, Ally made the trip back enjoyable for me.

"How do you know where we are?" Ally asked.

"I found us on the map while the water was heating for lunch. And I can see on the topo map where the hills, mountains and valleys are. I have a GPS device that tells where we are."

"So show me. Where are we?"

"I thought you wanted to get back soon. I know Peter sure wants you back today."

"Oh, it won't take that long, show me!"

"Okay, here's the map. I'll read off the coordinates to you and you find them on the map."

I gave her the longitudinal coordinates and showed her how to find that on the map. Then I gave her the coordinates for our latitude and let her find it herself. After putting the two together we located our position on the map.

"You mean, that's us, standing on that elevation line, right there?"

"Yup."

"I don't see any line."

I hoped she was kidding. "Now, you see how the lines are spaced to our right, it shows this hill to our right and we are following this line here because it is a natural pass through the hills. See where the lines are far apart? Those are the meadows. That's where we are trying to go."

"Oh! And it doesn't look far!"

"Well, it's two miles but it won't take long if we keep going."

It felt strange for me to be teaching a fifty-plus-year-old woman how to read a map. But she learned eagerly and it reminded me of my nephew, Patrick, who was only six.

I was surprised just how quickly the miles passed while we talked and walked. When the meadows appeared before us Ally got excited.

"I know where we are now! Oh look! Look at all the cars!"

But it didn't keep her from being curious about other things either.

"Look," she said pointing, "the grasses make like a tent for little animals to run through. I could sit for hours waiting to see what little animals come running through that tunnel but they never appear."

"That's because they think you're big and scary." I examined the small game trail and found evidence of several animals. "Well, it's at least mice and rabbits, perhaps voles. Have you ever seen a vole?"

"No, never, but maybe if I am careful I can someday."

"That would be highly unlikely because they are extremely timid. I've only seen a vole once." I didn't tell her that I ate it on a survival trip. "Come on, the guys are waiting for us."

"Is Peter there? Maybe he'll come back and watch for voles with me."

"Yes, Peter was there when I left. I'm sure he's still at the campsite. I bet your dog missed you too."

"Oh, Livingston, I'm surprised he didn't run off somewhere just like me. He's an explorer, that dog is. I have to watch him every minute."

As we got closer I noticed Rusty's dark blue Explorer in amongst the county cars.

"Oh yay! Rusty's here!"

"Rusty?"

"My husband."

"I still find it hard to believe you're not in high school. Now watch him be this big tough guy. You need a big tough guy to watch out for you, especially if you're a trouble magnet."

"He's tough enough. But he's also the most patient, gentle person I've ever met. You'll like him. He's one of those thirtyish guys you were hoping would find you."

"Well, well, then, let's get a move on."

She tromped through the knee-high grass and a group of guys gathered watching us approach the campsite. Rusty stood, hands on hips, big smile plastered on his face. Oh man, if he just knew how good he looked... He spoke with Strict and then they both smiled. Peter stood there with a look of fondness in his eyes. Ally might not fit into his cookie cutter world but he loved her just the same, perhaps more, because of it. I shed my pack at the nearest picnic table and ran over to Rusty for my welcome home hug. It felt so good wrapped in Rusty's arms. I could live there. Ally watched and just shook her head wondering what that little kid was doing with a big hunk like him. Strict came over and gave me a polite shoulder hug, his way of saying job well done. EMTs closed in on Ally but she eventually fought them off.

"Ally, you met Rosco. This is our search commander Lou Strickland, my husband Rusty Michaels. Guys, this is Alisondra but you can call her Ally. How's Landon doing?"

"He's sitting at home with a stack of pizza boxes," Strict replied.

"I need to go over and cook up some backpacker spaghetti, backpacker stroganoff, and backpacker macaroni and cheese. I bet he missed all that."

Rusty warned me, "Actually he has a wish list. Chocolate chip cookies with nuts is on top, followed by mayojar steak with fried rice and steamed vegetables."

"He ate all my chocolate chip cookies and now he's asking for more? After I spent two days out in the hills?" I said, then added with resignation, "I bet he gets them, too."

"You might look tough but you're a big old softie," one of the guys quipped and Ally looked totally bewildered by that.

"Yeah, I guess I am," I replied.

"Will you come talk to my class?" Ally asked hopefully.

"Sure, just give me some time to get things back to normal. I need to make cookies and go grocery shopping, but later in the week I can do it. Just tell me what time, what room and I'd be glad to."

"Oh goodie!" she exclaimed like a little kid. "Room Two A in the portables by the little playground."

Home felt unusually quiet. Shadow had given me his customary wild welcome then settled back into his usual routine. Rusty and I snuggled on the couch catching up on minutes.

"I missed you last night," I confessed.

"Mmm," he said snuggling closer.

"I probably could have found Ally yesterday if Landon hadn't broken his leg. But I doubt we could have hiked out yesterday, anyway."

"I suppose you're going to spend hours making cookies."

"I can do it tomorrow while you're at work but I did tell Landon I'd call him when I got back. He'll probably just try and make me feel sorry for him. If he cons me into making dinner would you mind having mayojar steak at his place tomorrow night?"

"That would be up to him."

"He's not getting me over there without you. If he wants cookies and dinner he's got to invite you too."

"Next time your partner breaks a leg and needs to be airlifted out let me know. I'll track with you. I don't like you being out there all alone."

"All alone? Just me, the radio, the GPS, the maps, and my rifle. You know I'll be fine. The only thing I was worried about was that Ally might need more medical attention than I could provide, but that wasn't the case. She was just lost. She didn't even really think of it as a bad thing to be lost. It was more like an adventure to her. But if you'd have been on that helicopter to take Landon's place I sure would have been glad. Ally would have too. She was a little disappointed to be found by a woman. She was hoping for a bunch of handsome guys, not one woman tracker all by herself." I laughed, "She asked if my parents approved of me being up in the mountains all by myself."

He laughed with me, "What did you tell her?"

"I just answered her question. It was still an appropriate question to ask. You know," I said lazily snuggling even closer, "you'll be lucky if you get a homemade dinner tonight. I may just stay right here all night long. You're going to have to kick me off if you get hungry and even then I need to shower before I cook."

"How about I help you with the shower, then we figure out dinner?"

"Seems like I need help with everything today."

Chapter 6

Rusty and I had the sexiest shower this side of the Mississippi. It was large, with glass walls and had a bench positioned right in the middle. There were two shower heads: one normal one and one on a long hose that could be used almost anywhere in the shower. It had been made for a disabled man and we put it to good use. The widow who had sold us the house was moving to senior living apartments and wanted her home to go to someone who would liven the place up again. Rusty and I definitely livened up the shower. Any time the bathroom door was left open it was an invitation for shower play. Sometimes it was play. Other times it got hot, steamy and sweaty and we ended up in the bedroom in a tangle of bed sheets and limbs.

I awoke with my hair sticking out in all directions. So much for my shower. Now I needed another one. Instead I rolled over and snuggled closer to Rusty's side.

"Look what you did to me. I'll never get my hair to stay down. I'll have to shower again. We're in a never ending cycle. We're going to make love and shower for the rest of our lives and it's all your fault."

He lazily turned over and wrapped his arms around me. My hair tickled his nose.

"Sounds good to me. But it's not all my fault. You lured me into the shower."

"I lured you? You were the one who said I needed help showering."

"You lured me all the way from the den to the shower to the bed."

"I led you into a trap."

"The most wonderful trap. How did I live without you for so long?"

"Patiently."

Landon had only spent one day at home in his cast and he already had cabin fever. Rusty and I stopped by for a visit on our way to dinner and ended up taking him along. He already had a stack of pizza boxes by his chair in the living room although it didn't make any sense how he could eat more than one pizza in a day. Rusty offered to take him to Zeke's but he quickly turned down more pizza. We settled on Trujillo's, an old standby frequented by most of the members of the police force.

"Hey Landon!" Benny Trujillo called in greeting. "What did you do to your leg?"

"I fell on it rock climbing," Landon answered.

"Can I sign your cast?" Benny asked.

"Sure, why not?" Landon said.

Benny disappeared then returned, not with a marker, but instead carrying a business card covered in clear package tape which he stuck to the back of Landon's cast.

"There. It's like a bumper sticker."

I read the card aloud, "Trujillo's Bar and Grill serving lunch and dinner daily 11AM-11PM."

"Great, I get to be a walking advertisement," Landon said.

"You're not even walking. You're a crutching advertisement."

"Yeah," Benny said, "but Landon knows lots of people. I can count on him getting around, you see, so everybody will wonder, what's that thing on the back of your cast? And so they'll read it."

"Yeah," I said, "he knows the whole police force, the ambulance company and ER at the hospital, but they are already your most faithful customers."

"You'll see, he'll reach more than you think. You just watch, he'll run out of clean clothes and he'll go out and buy shorts that fit over his cast. He'll get around."

"Oh shoot," Landon said, "that reminds me, I have uniforms at the cleaners."

"You see?"

"How bad do you want to get out of the house?" I asked Landon.

"I'd hitchhike."

"Do you want to get out bad enough to go talk to a class of kindergarteners?"

"After what happened last time I'm surprised you're ready to go back."

"Yeah, but this is Alisondra's class. She was rather disappointed to be rescued by me. I thought she might like to meet the other half of the team. I think this talk is going to be a little different than usual. I expect it to be more storytelling and tracking demonstration than the usual safety lecture."

The next day I dropped off the groceries at Landon's apartment and we drove to the school. Ally's class was still out for recess so we were able to find her on the playground easily.

"Oh! I'm so glad you came!" she said enthusiastically. "And this must be the other half of my search party."

"Ally, this is Landon Wilson."

"It's too bad about your leg," she sympathized.

When recess was over she gave two sharp blasts with her whistle and the kids all lined up.

"Boys and girls we aren't going back inside to do math today. Instead my friend is here to tell you about her job so we'll stay outside a little while longer. Follow me. We are going to find a place where she can show you what she does."

Ally led the way to a large sandy area of the playground and had the kids all sit cross-legged on the ground. She sat down too and began addressing her class, "Last weekend my husband Peter and I went up to the mountains. You know how I get curious about things. Well, I found out my last name means *deer meadow* and I was so excited to know my last name had a meaning that I wanted to actually find a deer meadow. I was looking on a map and I saw that up in the nearby mountains there was a campground called Elk Meadows! Peter and I decided to go camping there so we could see if there really were elk in the meadow. We didn't see any but we did some hiking around and guess what I did." She waited a short time for a response. Several hands shot into the air. "Devon?"

"What did you see instead?"

"I saw lots and lots of countryside because...I got lost! I know I've told you before, how to be careful and never get lost, but I did it anyway. I just kept seeing interesting things until I didn't know where I was anymore! Then I tried finding my way back. I did that until night came and I had to stop."

"What did you do, Mrs. Rawleigh?"

"I found a place to sleep and the next day I did what I always tell you to do. I waited for help. And do you know who my help turned out to be?"

"Him and her!" the kids said, making the connection.

"Yes, Cassidy found me. She followed my tracks all the way from Elk Meadows through the mountains. She knew exactly where to look for me because she followed my tracks on the ground. As we were walking back to Elk Meadows we got to talking and I found out she is a very interesting person so I thought you might like to meet her!"

"Good afternoon boys and girls, I'm Cassidy and this is my tracking partner, Landon Wilson. Landon is an EMT. Does anybody know what an EMT is?"

"He's like a fireman except he doesn't put out fires."

Landon smiled at that. "It stands for Emergency Medical Technician. I go with Cassidy on search and rescue calls in case somebody gets hurt. I patch them up and get them the help they need. If they need to go to the hospital I call an ambulance or a helicopter and I go with them to the hospital."

A hand shot up. "Yes?" I asked.

"What if *you* get hurt? Then what do you do?" a little girl asked, eyeing Landon's cast.

"Then Cassidy patches me up and sends me to the hospital."

"Did you get to ride in an ambulance?"

"No, but I got to ride in a helicopter. I ride in an ambulance every day for my normal job and I ride in helicopters a lot for our search and rescue job."

"Lucky!" exclaimed several boys at once.

"Cassidy, tell us how you became a tracker," Ally said.

"Well, when I was five or six years old, about the same age that all you kids are, I was very curious about everything and one of the things that fascinated me was tracks. I would study them and try and figure out what made them and I would follow them to see where they went. I grew up on a quarter horse ranch and there were lots of people on the ranch. I got so used to following tracks that pretty soon I could tell you who on the ranch had made each track. I knew which dog had walked where and I recognized each workhorse's track by the angle of their horseshoes. When I got a little older my parents let me explore the hills near the ranch too. There I got to track deer, coyotes, foxes and rabbits. When I went to school I tracked the kids on the playground and even animals that had crossed the playground. A time or two I got into *big* trouble because I was so interested in the tracks that I followed an animal right off school grounds and to its house! I should never have left the grounds during school hours. I was sent to the principal's office. Over the years my tracking got better and better until I could follow most people anywhere they went as long as it wasn't on cement or rocks. As long as there is dirt I can pretty much stay on a trail until I find the person. One day a detective found out I could track and he sent me on a long search for his friend who had been missing for a week up in the mountains. I had to follow his tracks for four days before I found him and even met a bear on that trip that chased me up a tree. At that point I didn't know about getting involved in search and rescue so I just went out looking for this guy alone, just like I had always tracked. But when I found the man he needed a doctor. He had been shot and tossed over a cliff, and all I could do was give him food and water and call on the radio for help. I am glad to say that man lived and he is now a very good friend. That trip taught me the value of teamwork."

"Who shot him?" a boy asked.

"There was a farm up in the mountains that grew marijuana and made drugs, something you should never get involved in. It is bad news. The people at the farm were scared of being discovered doing illegal things up there and they thought the man would send in the police so they tried to kill him."

"Just like on TV?"

"Can you tell us what you had to do to be on a search and rescue team?" Ally asked, dodging the TV issue.

"I had to go to school and study really hard. Landon went to the same school. It's called Police Reserve Academy. It is almost like being in the Army or the Marines. I know because I have been in the Marines. We had to do exercises and run obstacle courses. We had to learn to shoot accurately. We had to learn a lot about the laws and how they work. We had drills where we practiced all kinds of police activities: knocking doors in, subduing suspects, arresting people. The people in the drills were just other officers but they acted like real criminals and sometimes they resisted arrest and we had to figure out how to handle the situation. It was a tough school."

"What was the hardest part of academy?" Ally asked.

"For me it was studying the laws and procedures and participating in the drills. I knew I was never going to be a real policewoman so I never cared for the drills. I just had to get through it so I could track for the police."

"Landon, what about you?" Ally asked.

"It was the physical conditioning. I hated the running and we ran for miles. As a guy I really got into the drills and could handle the academics but I hated the constant exercise and running. You didn't mind the running?" he asked me.

"I knew there would be exercises and running so I trained for that. I made sure I could run the five miles even before I started academy."

"Can you tell the kids what *procedures* are?" Ally asked, zeroing in on a new concept.

"Procedures are like a recipe. It is a given set of instructions designed to bring about a positive goal. All the police have procedures that they have worked out for different situations. It's a set of actions. It helps the police in two ways. One, it has been proven successful and two, if they are working in a group everybody knows what everybody else's job is, so there are no surprises. You have procedures at school. If everybody just did whatever they wanted it would be confusing. So your procedure for talking is to raise your hand first and wait to be called on. Your procedure for recess is to line up calmly and walk in a line. It works and if you didn't have those procedures then everybody would be talking at once and kids would come and go as they pleased and Mrs. Rawleigh couldn't keep track of you."

Ally stood and then announced, "Cassidy promised to do a tracking demonstration so we need two volunteers."

Hands shot up.

I'd been watching the kids as they lined up and observed them as they walked and I talked. I chose a little girl who was a natural born dancer and a boy in a black jersey.

I explained how the demonstration worked. "I'm going to hide my eyes and I want you both to lay a trail for me. You can do anything you want, walk, run, skip, do handstands, or crawl. It doesn't matter. Then when both of you are finished I will follow your trail and tell the class what you did."

"That's no fair! He can tell you what we did," they said pointing to Landon.

"I wouldn't do that," he said. "I want to see if she can do it too. I've seen her follow tracks but she's never told me what they mean before."

I hid my eyes and let the kids go to work. There was some giggling and snickers before I was allowed to turn around.

I glanced at the area. I knew to the class it just looked like dirt, especially since there were a hundred footprints on the ground before the two kids had even laid their trails. I decided to do the boy's trail first. I pointed to the boy and asked, "What is your name?"

"Michael," he said simply.

I studied his tracks picking up mannerisms and forming patterns in my mind, then I profiled as I went.

"Michael did a good job," I told them. "He tried to trick me a time or two but I bet I can figure it out. First Michael ran from this spot to right about here. Michael, do you like hockey?"

"Yeah, but I'm not old enough to play," he said.

"But you practice on the street, right?"

"Yeah, with the neighbor kids. How did you know?"

"Your footprints told me. You run almost like you are rollerblading. You push out and back when you run. I bet when you get on a team you'll skate really fast!"

Michael looked smugly at the other boys.

"After Michael stopped running he turned, well, not really turned, he twisted, like this," I said turning on one foot and leaving a well defined matching twist in the dirt. "Then he hopped on one foot for one, two, three hops. That's when he lost his balance and fell a little bit. He put his hand out to catch himself and then scrambled to a standing position right here. He stood and thought about what he was going to do next. Then he took really long steps, across the field in this direction, all the way over to here." I looked at the trail leading back to the group. "He took a run and then leapt as far as he could, which was pretty far, and he landed in a cloud of dust, then he walked backwards trying to make me skip over the jump. He wanted me to think he ran and then walked but he ran and jumped, then backed over his jump. Then he stepped to the side and very carefully tried to trick me again. He tiptoed around this way and hit the end of his trail and then went and sat down in the same spot where he had started. Then he ran around to another spot to see if that would trick me too."

"Wow! How did you do that?" a boy asked.

"Your footprints are like stories in the dirt. All I have to do is read them."

"Now do Rachel's!" a little girl in pink cried out.

I walked the area, careful to not disturb any footprints.

"Rachel has little feet and she is very quick and graceful since she has had gymnastics and dancing lessons. I can tell because when she stands her feet are in ballet positions. And she walks with her toes pointing in the same direction she wants to walk. Her toes lead the way. She almost comes down toe first when she walks. Rachel started out right here, the same place where she finished. She didn't try and do sneaky tricks like Michael did but she tried some gymnastics stunts so let's see if I can figure it out." It was really just a matter of puzzling everything out. The kids always thought that doing tricks would confuse me but the movements to do them were very distinctive and upset the normal pattern. So any tricks the kids played actually made my job easier. "This is almost like a floor routine in the Olympics," I told the class, making Rachel feel very proud of herself. "She went step, step, step, turn, step, step, step, leap! She came down on one foot and skipped across the playground until she got up enough speed and then she did a cartwheel, not quite landing right, but a good cartwheel nonetheless. Then it looks like she twirled around and around maybe six times. When she stopped to think of what to do next she stood heals together, toes apart. She ran this way, then dove into a somersault so she'd have enough momentum for a good leap at the end. Then she walked in and out of Michael's trail on the way back to her spot."

"That is so cool, how did you know Rachel walked on Michael's trail? Maybe Michael walked on Rachel's trail."

"Good thinking. That shows you were paying attention. If Michael had gone over Rachel's trail his footprints would have been on top, but they weren't. Rachel's footprints overlapped Michael's so I knew Rachel was the last person over that spot."

"What about him?" a girl asked, pointing to Landon. "Can you track people on crutches?"

"That's even easier. The points of the crutches are small so all his weight is on a small area. That pushes the ends down harder than just a simple footprint. With a footprint the weight is divided over a larger area. So the prints of the crutches show up easier. Also, you can tell what direction a person on crutches is going because their body is always between the two points."

"Okay, boys and girls, everyone sit back down cross-legged in a group," Ally said. "Does anybody have a question for Cassidy or Landon?"

"How long does it take to find a lost person?"

"That depends on how long they have been missing and how far they traveled. I have been on four day searches and searches that only took three or four hours. When Mrs. Rawleigh got lost it took me a day of actual tracking and then I had to camp out because it got dark. So I was on the trail a day and a half."

"Do the men give you a hard time, since police and searches are mostly done by guys?"

"Not since I proved to them that I know what I am doing and that I stick to only things that I know how to do. I don't try to be a policewoman. I am a tracker and occasionally a scout."

"What does a scout do?"

"A scout checks things out, like a spy, except from a distance."

Landon added, "In the woods Cassidy can almost disappear. She knows how to hide so that people can't see her and so when she scouts she stays out of sight of the thing or person she is scouting, then she comes back to the officers and tells us what's going on."

"When you were a kid on a ranch did you get to ride horses?"

"Yes, I rode horses a lot. I still have a horse at my parent's ranch. He is gray and his name is Shasta."

"That is so cool! I ask my parents every day for a horse but they won't get one."

"Horses take a lot of upkeep. The ranch is set up specifically for raising horses so it's easier for my parents."

"How many horses do they have?"

"Oh, golly, I've never counted. They have twelve in the barn and several more out in the paddocks."

"What do you do when you're a policeman?"

"I have been through police school, but I leave the police work to the real officers. I don't have the right mind-set for police work. I am too tenderhearted. When I have to be tough I just can't do it. And if I ever have to hurt someone it hurts me worse and I feel sad for a long time."

"Are you sad now?"

"Lexie! What a thing to ask!" Ally scolded.

"What? She was the one who was at my sister's class when we had lockdown. Ashley said the lady that was there had to shoot the bad guys."

Ally looked at me apologetically.

"Yes, Lexie," I choked out, "that day still makes me very sad. I was happy while we were having fun with tracking but that day did make me very upset. Every time I remember it I get sad. It was a choice I had to make and I hope you never have to make a decision like that as long as you live."

Ally decided it was time to change the subject and said, "When I got lost and Cassidy found me she had a little stove and packets of food to cook. All she did was add boiling water and it made lasagna in a pouch. We didn't even have dirty dishes to wash. She brought me water. She taught me how to find my location on a map. Not only did she find me when I was lost but she stopped those bad men from hurting more people at the school and I will always be thankful to her for that. Does anybody have any tracking related questions?"

"If we wanted to be a tracker how would we learn how to do it?" a little boy in a red shirt asked.

"Well, start out by noticing anything that makes tracks. If you are watching the person or animal actually making the tracks, go look at the results. Match the tracks you see with the motion you remember. Later when you see a track try to decide what made it. Is it an adult or a kid? A man or a woman? If you stay interested in tracking one question will lead to another and then just try answering as many as you can. In time your brain will start sorting the information when you see a track. You'll look at a track and narrow down your choices really quickly. It's like identifying birds. If you see a bird there are certain characteristics that bird watchers notice automatically: size, mannerisms, markings, color, what kind of things it eats. All these little facts get categorized and then all of a sudden *ding!* Your brain comes up with the name of a bird. Well, the same thing happens with tracks. Who has a dog?"

Half the kids raised their hand.

"You," I said pointing, "what kind of a dog do you have?"

"A beagle."

"And how do you know it's a beagle?"

"It looks like a beagle and it sounds like a beagle and it acts like a beagle."

"So, tell me, what does a beagle look like?"

"They have long ears and big brown eyes."

"And?"

"And it's not big and it's not small."

"So far you've only narrowed it down to half the dogs in existence. What makes a beagle a beagle?"

"Its nose. Beagles have a nose for sniffing and they follow their nose all the time."

"What color is a beagle?"

"He is white and black and tan."

"Short-haired or long?"

"Short."

"So a beagle is a medium-sized, short-haired, white, black and tan dog with long ears and big brown eyes and he follows his nose everywhere. And he sounds like…what?"

"He howls at fire trucks and he has a long, sad bark."

"Wow, that's a lot to remember just to identify a beagle, but you kids do that all the time and the same kind of thing happens in tracking only it is more subtle. Tracks are big or small, wide or narrow, slow or fast, sad or happy, fresh or worn. They have patterns and different kinds of animals make different shaped tracks. All these things need to be taken into consideration when you track and it takes time to learn to identify them."

"Well, boys and girls we covered a lot of territory today. We talked about getting lost, tracking, the school shooting, beagles, and birds. I think it's time for us to get back to our lessons and let Cassidy and Landon go back to work."

Ally ducked into her classroom for a minute, then a young woman followed her back to the playground and instructed the class to line up. They followed the aid into the school, waving to us as they left. Ally then led us to the office where we checked out.

"I'm sorry about the shooting coming up. I know that was awkward for you."

"It's okay. It is hard on me to remember it, but each time I do I deal with it a little more. The loss of life is what hurts, but the guy that got away is what worries me. I got the impression they were looking for someone here. And I worry for that person."

A hand appeared gently on my shoulder. "No need to worry," a voice said next to me. I turned and there stood Kima Tumibay. If anybody should worry it would be her.

"I've been helping the detective assigned to this case," I said. "Since I let the man get away I feel it is my duty to do what I can to bring him in. I may not have much jurisdiction but I've got a sharp eye and discerning mind."

"The detective will get nothing from me," Mrs. T said.

"Why? You don't want to help the police?"

"No," she said simply, "I don't agree with his tactics but McPherson is only following his heart like I must follow mine. The fact that we disagree means little."

"Even when he harms others to 'follow his heart'? What kind of a heart does this guy have that he's willing to shoot up an elementary school?"

"He thinks of himself as a patriot. Is there anything wrong in that?"

"There was as soon as he fired a shot in this school," I said resolutely.

"I have seen worse," she replied. "It is why I do what I do. So others may escape what I have seen."

"What is it that you do?" I asked. I was curious what she could possibly do to set off this McPherson guy, but I was also curious about Mrs. T as a person.

"I help people," she said simply, "and he helps people in his own way, yet we disagree." Then she gathered up some mail and papers and quietly left. I wanted to chase her down to ask more questions, but I knew she had to return to class, so I stood there watching my only chance at new information walk down the hall and disappear around the corner.

"Cassidy, thank you for coming. The kids enjoyed it or they wouldn't have asked so many questions. Many times I end up asking all the questions that I think they would like to ask. How did you know Michael was a skater and Rachel was a dancer?"

"That's what I thought even before I studied their tracks and then their tracks confirmed it. With Michael it was either hockey or football and his tracks leaned towards skating so I went with that."

"But how did you know?"

"Like I said, I have a discerning eye. Things like that just stand out to me. There was a little black girl in pigtails. She is an artist. And there's about four of the girls who are horse crazy. There's a boy who is into dirt biking. School's almost over. You better get back to class."

We departed amongst more thanks from Ally, then Landon followed me on his crutches to the Jeep. I got in and started the engine as he finished loading his crutches.

"We're not going home, are we?"

"I'll drop you off there if that's where you want to go."

"We're going to the station, aren't we?"

"I've got a name for Tom."

"You could just call him."

"I thought you wanted to get out."

"You've got an appointment with the punching bag, don't you, only now its name is McPherson. I could see the punching bag coming as soon as that little girl asked if you were sad."

"It's just a form of exercise. I could do the same thing running. The punching bag just happens to be handier. If I run I find myself three miles from home. If I use the punching bag I'm still near the Jeep."

"Makes sense."

"I don't want to fight McPherson. I just want to find out what this is all about and send him to jail."

The station was a beehive of activity and I snuck through the crowded lobby leaving Landon behind. He had many friends at the station and would make the rounds of those who weren't neck deep in work. Later he'd find me in either Tom or Rusty's office or in the gym. I peeked in Rusty's window to see if he was busy but he was meeting with someone so I went on to Tom's office. Rusty was quick, though. Before I could get to Tom's office he was standing in the hall.

"You're busy, I'll let you work," I said.

"It's okay, what's going on?" he asked, knowing I didn't make a trip to the station for just anything.

"Nothing, I finished at the school and managed to get another little tidbit of information for Tom so I came to deliver it. When can you make it for dinner?"

"It'll be a few hours."

"That's fine. I don't know how long I'll be here and then after that I'll still need to cook it."

"I'll see you then."

"Okay."

I continued on to Tom's office. Tom was busy, too, but he nodded so I opened the door and stuck my head in.

"I'll be around for a little while. I have a name for you."

He bolted out of his chair, "What?!"

"I don't know if it's an important name or not. It's just a name."

"What is it?"

I stepped out of his office and he followed.

"I spoke at the school again. The subject of the shooting came up and the teacher followed us to the office and was apologizing that the kids connected me with the shooting. I told Mrs. Rawleigh I was more worried about the guy that got away and Mrs. Tumibay told me not to worry about it. We got into a little bit of a discussion that didn't yield much information but she did say that McPherson thought of himself as a patriot and that there was nothing wrong with being a patriot. When I steered the conversation around to ask why McPherson was after her she said simply, because she helps people. She said that McPherson thinks he helps people in his own way. She doesn't agree with his tactics but she isn't going to help the police because McPherson is just 'following his heart' just like she does herself. So you see, I didn't get any really useful information but I thought you might want to look McPherson up in the computer and see if there is anything linked to him. If something turns up give me a call and I'll try and identify him for you."

Tom scratched his head thinking over what I'd told him and maybe fitting it with things he already knew. "Us? You said the teacher followed us to the office. Who else was there?"

"It was Mrs. Rawleigh, Mrs. Tumibay, Landon Wilson and I. Strict had a call to find a missing person over the weekend, so I was sent out. Landon was my partner. Turned out to be a kindergarten teacher at the school. Landon fell off a rock, broke his leg and had to be airlifted out so when I found my ten sixty-five I was alone. Ally was disappointed to be rescued by a woman so I brought Landon along for the talk so he could get out of the house and she could meet the guy who was supposed to have rescued her."

"How'd the talk go?"

"Fine, except the kids linked me to the shooting. I gave a tracking demonstration and talked about how I got into tracking. There were lots of questions."

"So word has gotten around through the kids?"

"I don't know how much. Mostly it was kids who had siblings in the higher grades in the classrooms near the shooting. Or older siblings in Mrs. Peabody's class."

"Mrs. Peabody?"

"That's the class I was speaking in when the shooting started. I didn't mean to take you from your work. I'll let you go. If you have more questions give me a call."

Chapter 7

For some reason the punching bag had suddenly lost its appeal to me. My sharp sadness had mellowed to a general bummed out feeling that I thought would go away on its own. I went to the Jeep and pulled out my rifle with plans of heading to the range to practice, but first I stuck my head into the gym.

"If Landon Wilson comes looking for me send him to the practice range."

"Okay," several of the guys answered.

At the practice range I took aim with the rifle, waited for my first reaction to pass, saw that, sure enough, it would have been too high, then squeezed off the shot. I had to get past that first reaction, so I practiced my first shot over and over again. Landon made his way in on crutches and waited to be acknowledged.

"Do you want to try it?" I asked. "Most of the guys agree they like the service rifle better."

"That's because this rifle was made for you. They are used to their trusty service rifles."

"Me too, but I am trying to get better with this one since it packs so easily. See what happens when you try it."

"You're trying to get better? Look at your target. I'd be glad if I could shoot like that."

"That's because I skipped my first shot. When I bring the rifle up and take my first shot it always comes out high."

"One of those has to be your first shot," he argued.

"I only did second shots."

"You can't just do second shots. One of them has to be a first shot."

"Not if I skip it."

"Cassidy, sometimes your logic eludes me."

"When the second shot and the first shot happen at the same time I'll be in business."

"How will you know when that happens if you always skip your first shot?"

"Oh, all right, I'll show you." I found a fresh target, took my stance, rifle at my side. I brought it up aimed and squeezed off the shot and it hit high. I squeezed off the second shot and it hit right on.

"Two inches. You're worried about two inches?"

"Two inches is a long ways when you are talking human anatomy. If anybody should know that it would be you."

"I still wish I could shoot like that, even with the high shot. You ever try those target shooting booths at the fair?"

"I did when I was a kid. I feel kind of bad about it now."

"Why?"

"Well, you know how I look now."

"Yeah…"

"Well imagine when I was fifteen and I looked twelve. Now imagine some poor hawker trying to talk this girl into trying a gun for the first time. 'All you have to do is hit it once and you win this stuffed animal.' My sister Jesse and I would exchange glances and we'd walk away. Then Jesse would say, 'Aw, come on Cass, you only have to hit it once!' and the guy would up the ante and upgrade us to a bigger animal. I'd finally give in and pretend to figure out how the gun worked. I'd take a long time aiming and accidentally hit the star. Then he'd want me to try again because the first shot was beginner's luck. I kept accidentally hitting the target until I'd won whatever Jesse wanted. The trick was to look innocent and take my time aiming. They'd hand over just about anything thinking there was no way I could do it again. I won her a bicycle and just about every stuffed animal she liked."

"For your sister?"

"Yeah."

"What about you?"

"I didn't have any use for all that stuff. I just enjoyed the hunt. The deal was I'd win it, but she had to carry it. So she'd walk around with this huge toy looking all smug with herself and I'd walk with her secretly knowing I'd won it all along. I haven't been to the fair in years. I bet I could still do it, but I still don't know what I'd do with a stuffed animal or a bicycle."

"You could donate it at Christmas to the toy drive."

"Hey that's an idea. Five bucks for a bike isn't too shabby."

"Can I go watch? I want to see the guy's face."

"Rusty would think it was dishonest."

"Why? Just because they misjudge you? That's not your fault."

"Isn't it a little dishonest to take advantage of it?"

"What, you think these guys don't go pick up toys for their kids at the fair?" he said, indicating the other officers. "It's not dishonest to go for the games you are good at. It's only common sense. If you're good at throwing rings you throw rings. If you're good at picking a lucky duck, then you pick up ducks. So, you're good at shooting."

"The fair isn't until August so you've got a wait ahead of you."

"There's a little traveling carnival at the corner of Foster and Grant. I want to see you try it."

"You're kidding."

"No, it'll be fun."

"Oh, all right, but after that we need to think about dinner."

The carnival was dead. As soon as the schools got out it would fill up but there were only two families there letting their kids ride the train and jump in the bouncer. Landon and I wandered in and out of the arcade turning down multiple hawkers. When we passed the shooting booth again we paused.

"Come on, try it," said Landon.

"I don't want to."

"Why?"

"It feels wrong."

The hawker joined in, "There's nothing wrong with these guns. They can't hurt anybody. Here, I'll show you." *Bam!* He hit a target. "All you have to do is hit the star and you can win this toy right here."

"How much is it?"

"A dollar a shot or six for five dollars."

"And what do I win if I get all six shots?"

He tried not to laugh, but barely succeeded. I had him.

"One shot gets you this animal, two this one..." he kept increasing the shots and pointing to bigger animals. "If you hit the star six times I'll throw in two free shots for the biggest one."

"And when I miss?"

"If you miss, that shot isn't counted."

"And I have to get the shots all in a row or do you add them up at the end."

"You can add them up at the end."

I looked to Landon. He wasn't playing his part very well. He was trying not to laugh.

The hawker looked to Landon. "Aw come on big brother, chip in a dollar for her first shot?"

Now I was laughing, too. Big brother! Landon glared at me and slapped a five on the deck. The hawker smiled greedily.

"There ya go, that's what big brothers are for, right? Now, let me show you how it works."

He showed me the gun and walked me through how to aim and fire. He even warned me about the gun kicking. Compared to what I was used to, it didn't kick at all but I let him explain it all anyway.

I looked to Landon. "You really want me to do this?"

Landon explained to the hawker, "I keep telling her she's got a good eye for this but she won't believe me."

I slowly took aim, felt around for the trigger, took aim again, pretended to be off and corrected it. I fired hitting slightly off center. The guy looked surprised.

"Well, well, maybe you do have a good eye for this. You have four more shots."

"Five, you said it was six for five dollars."

"So I did. Go ahead try again."

I looked the gun over like I needed to familiarize myself with the workings again, then slowly took aim and took my second shot, which hit at the base of the top point of the star.

"You're shittin' me!" the hawker exclaimed in astonishment.

Now the other hawkers were starting to get interested. They were watching from their respective booths. A few of them, who saw how dead the carnival was, wandered over to get a better look.

"I think I'm getting the hang of it now," I told Landon.

When I made the third shot Landon and I exchanged high fives, just like a good sister and brother should. The crowd was growing. A dad decided he needed to win a toy for his little daughter, but waited to watch my last shots.

"I get three more, right?"

"Right, but you can quit whenever you earn an animal you like."

"Okay."

I aimed, slowly squeezed off the fourth shot, and feigned disappointment when it hit in the lower point of the star.

"It's okay," Landon consoled me, "it's still in the star so it still counts."

On the fifth shot I "accidentally" pulled the trigger twice and the shots hit about an inch apart, still within the star.

"Oops, I think I did two at once. Does that count?"

"Yeah," the hawker admitted grudgingly.

"Do I still get my two free shots?" I asked hopefully. I had my eye on a huge, ugly, pink bear that I couldn't wait to leave on Landon's couch as a permanent reminder not to put me in situations like this again. He'd have to live with it forever or figure out how to get rid of it. It was worth the trouble and I was determined to get it.

"Okay," I told myself, "two more, you can do it!"

The seventh shot came after tense aiming. All the hawkers were sitting on the edge of their booths. All the kids were looking hopefully at their daddies. Well, at least this guy is going to recoup some of his money, I thought. When the seventh shot hit home I reacted excitedly. The hawker looked at me.

"What *are* you?" he asked suspiciously.

"Just a second," I said, and took my last shot as almost an afterthought.

"Me? I'm just a housewife, tracker, reserve deputy and former Marine here with my big brother to win a bet, and I'll take that big, ugly, pink bear."

"Are you sure? It's not the biggest one."

"No, but it's an appropriate prize for my big brother."

He gave me the bear and I handed it over to Landon.

"Here you go big brother!" I said with a big grin.

Landon couldn't carry the bear and manage his crutches so I carried it to the Jeep. The bear filled the back seat and rocked and moved with the Jeep's movements, looking like some cuddly alien passenger. We drove silently to Landon's apartment where I carried it in and set it down with a flourish in the middle of his couch.

"You are a mean, cruel person, you know that?"

"You put me up to it. You deserve a big, ugly, pink bear."

I looked at the grocery sacks still on the kitchen table.

"You were supposed to put the meat in the fridge."

"Oh, is it bad?"

"No, well, I'm sure every doctor and dietician in the country would say it's unsafe but I've backpacked all day and then cooked it and it has been fine. Maybe we fooled it into thinking it was up in the mountains all day. This stuff is really better up in the mountains."

"Why do you pack it all in a mayonnaise jar?"

"Tradition. It's mayojar steak. How can it be mayojar steak without the jar?"

"Okay, you got me on that one."

"You sure aren't acting very helpless today. I think the broken leg is just an excuse."

He sat on the couch with his foot up on the coffee table, eyeing the pink bear with disdain.

"You didn't give me much choice."

"Was the school boring?"

"No, it was definitely different from my other trips to school classrooms."

"Yeah, me too."

"This shooting really has you riled, doesn't it?"

"At times."

We talked as I cut up stir-fry vegetables and made fried rice.

Rusty arrived halfway through my preparations. He eyed the pink bear curiously.

"What's with the bear?" he asked.

"Landon won it in a bet," I answered.

"On purpose?" Rusty inquired.

Defending himself in the face of total embarrassment Landon said, "Your wife has a cruel streak. I bet her she could win the shooting game at the carnival and when she did, she picked out this big, ugly bear. Now what am I going to do with it?"

"You could donate it to the toy drive," Rusty said, helping my cause without realizing it.

"And until then I have to explain it to everybody who comes over."

"Don't make bets unless you can deal with the consequences," I admonished him. "I'll pay you back for the shots, though."

I dug out a five dollar bill and gave it to Landon. "Here you go, big brother."

"Would you, please, stop it already?"

"How many shots did you make to earn an animal that big?" Rusty asked me.

"Eight and I could have chosen a bigger one but this bear looked like an appropriate way to get my revenge."

I stirred and cooked the rice, then put the steak under the broiler as the vegetables steamed.

"You sure threw Tom for a loop today. He jumped on that name and looked up everything he could find. He came up with a few McPhersons but none of them seemed likely to be candidates. It would help if we knew what to connect him to."

"Kima Tumibay knows but she's not talking."

"Does she know not talking could land her in jail?"

"It's Tom's job to tell her that but I'm afraid it will just push her further away. Did you ID the dead guy? Maybe he's linked to a McPherson somehow."

The steak turned out better than I had expected. It was always good up in the mountains but everybody seemed to enjoy it no matter where I made it. We ate and told Rusty about the events of the day.

"I wish I could have been there at the carnival."

"I could try again."

"I doubt they'll let you try again," Landon said.

"I bet they would."

"Don't make a bet unless you can deal with the consequences," Landon reminded me.

"If they let me shoot again you keep the bear. If they turn me down I keep it."

"It's a deal."

"You know, if I win another bear you'll have two of them, but this time I'll get you a blue one to go with the pink one. How late do they stay open?"

When I appeared at the booth again the hawker rolled his eyes. "Oh, no, not you again!"

"Can I try again?" I asked innocently and Rusty grinned, knowing how hard it was for a man to turn me down. "My big brother made me a new bet."

"Why don't you go to a practice range and use real guns?"

"That wasn't part of the bet. Plus the big, ugly, pink bear's home is on the line. I'll make you a deal."

"Yeah? What kind of a deal?"

"Let me see a target."

I took a pen and drew a dot in each of the five points of the star.

"If I can take out just the dots with five shots, I win."

"Just the dots? So if you miss once then you lose?"

"Yeah."

The hawker sat back on the board framework of his booth recalling how my earlier shots had been all over the star.

Landon gave me a "that's no fair" look. Rusty just leaned back on his heels and enjoyed watching me work.

"You're a cop?"

"Not exactly, I'm a reserve deputy but my work mostly involves tracking."

He looked at the guys, they agreed, that's what I did.

"And you were in the Marines."

"Yeah, a few years ago."

"A few years ago? You're not old enough to…"

"Yes I am. The guy you thought was my big brother is my search partner. And this is my husband." The guy's mouth fell open. "Now, what do you say? Do we have a deal?"

"You're going to take out the dots in the points of the stars. Five dots with five shots?"

"If you let me."

"Five shots for five dollars."

"Okay." I put down my five dollars.

He hung up my target and I picked up a rifle.

"You want me to show you how it works?"

"No, I think I remember."

"I bet you do." Then he raised his voice to address the crowd. "Okay! Ladies and gentlemen! I have a *challenger*! *This* little lady right here is going to try the *ultimate* shooting challenge! And *you* can too! Step *right* this way!

This little lady is going to try to shoot *all five points* of this star with only *five* shots of the gun! Step up! Step up and *see* if she can do it!"

A group of people gathered to watch, mainly skeptical guys and kids who wished they were allowed to shoot. I wondered if the hawker thought it would make me nervous to have a crowd watching, but after shooting in front of soldiers, ranch hands, cops and friends a group of people didn't bother me much.

I raised the gun and took aim. The first shot was always the riskiest. The first shot always taught me how to correct for the others. So I aimed carefully and squeezed the trigger smoothly, without jerking or jarring. I felt the shot come off clean. I knew I'd done well when the crowd fell silent.

I'd already won the bet with Landon. His bet had only been whether or not they would let me shoot. Now I had nothing to lose but a big, ugly, blue bear which didn't concern me. This was really all about the challenge.

I took aim again and carefully shot out the second dot amid oohs and aahs. I kept the gun up and moved to the next dot, aimed and fired, aimed and fired, aimed and finally fired the last shot. The crowd applauded and the guy took down my target. There was a little speculation on one of the shots. The hole touched the dot but didn't wipe it out.

"What do you think?" the hawker asked addressing the crowd. He held up the target and they all applauded loudly.

"Thanks for the publicity," the hawker muttered, "choose a toy." Then loudly. "Okay! *Who* will be next to shoot the star! Just think, if this little lady can do it, *you can too*! Step up! You sir! Give it a try!"

I looked around me. Landon gave me a "don't you dare" look so I turned to Rusty.

"Your turn," I told him, "which animal do you want?"

He chose a normal sized teddy bear and then found a family with a little girl.

"Here," he said, handing the bear to the dad, "we just came to win a bet."

The dad handed the toy to his daughter and thanked us by saying, "I never could have won it. That was some nice shooting."

"Thanks," I said. Then to Landon, "So, are you satisfied now?"

"That's no fair," he replied accusingly.

"You didn't make any rule about changing the odds or bargaining with the guy. You just bet they wouldn't let me shoot. Besides, I bet if you had brought the big, pink bear back he would have let you return it. Now you are doubly stuck with it. You were lucky Rusty was nicer than me."

We took Landon home where I washed up the dinner dishes and packed up my containers. I put the leftovers, neatly sealed in plastic storage bowls, in his refrigerator and gave him a bag of cookies.

Chapter 8

A few days later I had cabin fever and my Jeep seemed bored too. I'd made a point, when buying it, to ensure it came equipped with a winch but then I never had a chance to use it. Not that I was intending to get stuck this morning and need my winch, but I was determined to see something new, maybe find some tracks to follow, get out into the hills and get rid of that boxed in feeling. I really should have known better. I left a note for Rusty on the white board on the fridge, as I always did. It wasn't very specific because I didn't know where I'd be going. Even when Shadow and I jumped into the Jeep and took off I didn't know where I was going. The note just said: Went exploring @ 9 AM, destination unknown. ETA before dinner.

I made sure my pack had the bare essentials: trail mix, water, knife, magnesium stick and a change of clothes. I switched the clothing in the pack to shorts and a tank top in case the day heated up and I became uncomfortably warm.

Shadow was happy to be going somewhere for a change. We had been working the agility course in the backyard and he did well on most of the obstacles I had built. I was pushing him a little because I'd been thinking of entering him in a competition. We weren't ready yet but we were getting closer, slowly but surely. However, even agility work didn't relieve the cooped up feeling of being home too long.

As one road led to another I noticed we were driving along the foothills until finally a tendril split off and entered the mountains. I wound my way up into the pines and absentmindedly took the most interesting looking turns. As the road became more and more degraded I eventually needed the four wheel drive. The Jeep bounced and lurched over the washed out road until around noon when I ended up way back in a tiny campground that hadn't seen a camper in at least ten years. I wondered which campground I'd discovered as there were no trashcans or water. An absence of facilities meant there were also no camping fees. The parking places were overrun with weeds and the fire pits had been swept clean of ash by the wind. The campground felt lonely and ignored so I stopped. Any campground this forgotten probably had wildlife that had grown used to the absence of people. I got out of the Jeep and Shadow bounded out, following his nose to the nearest interesting smell. I followed him, since the nearest interesting smell probably belonged to a recent visitor. I watched the ground as I walked.

Deer passed through the campground often. There were tracks on top of tracks in the dense undergrowth and the plants looked trampled and grazed on. There were many different wildflowers in the campground because the cleared trees let in plenty of sunlight. There were too many tracks to follow any one deer so I headed for the outskirts of the campground looking for some less common tracks. I started a wide circuit of the area and discovered the campground was bigger than it looked. There were actually two sections to it with a rough road connecting them. I counted maybe fifty campsites. Glancing at the mountains surrounding the campground I thought of how easy it would be for tourists to get lost. Maybe it was a good thing the tourists didn't know this campground existed. Shadow followed as I searched the ground watching for something of interest to track. It took me a couple of hours to decide deer and field mice were about the only animals that frequented the site. Still, I wondered what had made the area interesting enough to have built a campground here. The site would have been pleasant enough when it was maintained but I thought maybe there was a trail or a spring or a creek nearby. After searching the surrounding land for any signs of water or trail I finally found a tiny track leading away from the far end of the campground, so I followed it. It led deeper and deeper into the woods. The track passed along sunny ridges and ducked into shady pine filled canyons but there was no sign of water. When I got hungry I dug out the trail mix and the little Ziploc bag of dog food. I sat down to eat while Shadow ate the dog food, then I gave him a drink of water by pouring it into the Ziploc bag and holding it out for him.

It was hard to believe I was this far away from people and I couldn't find an animal track. The forest was quiet, the ground was silent, even the wind was still. I followed the trail until I noticed the sun had dipped behind the mountains then I turned around and headed back to the Jeep. I watched the brush for signs of life but the forest was eerily silent. Not a birdcall, not a snapping twig. No clouds in the sky, no sun bearing down. The sun sank as I walked and the sky was just becoming dim when I reached my Jeep. I opened the door and let Shadow jump in and then climbed in and buckled up. I put the key in the ignition and turned and…nothing happened. The Jeep's engine was as silent as the forest. Now that was odd as this was practically a new vehicle. What could have gone wrong with it so fast? I got out and popped the hood open to check the engine. I jiggled the battery cables. They seemed tight, no corrosion. I poked around in the engine knowing it had to be something electrical since that's what started the Jeep. I looked and looked. I pulled wires out to look at them and when I did little sharp pieces of casings scratched my hands. Oh great. Mice had gotten into my Jeep and had eaten the wiring! Now what was I going to do? After three hours of driving down road after road I'd paid little attention to my location. For all I knew I could be twenty miles from a paved road and due to my training I knew to never cut cross-country. I'd tracked down too many missing people to follow their example. In the fading light I searched the Jeep for anything useful and found one more water bottle and a two-foot long mag light. I checked the bars on my cell phone but had zero reception due to the surrounding mountains. It was going to be a long night.

I took note of the position of the sun as I set out hiking toward the highway. I didn't have much light left. While walking I wondered how the Jeep's engine had functioned at all if the mice had chewed the wires. Did all my bouncing and jostling of the Jeep cross some live wires that shouldn't have been crossed? I knew a thing or two about cars. I could check my oil, change out the battery, brake shoes, filters and change and rotate the tires. But I couldn't rewire a car in the middle of nowhere. In fact, I wondered how I was going to get the Jeep home again when it had taken a four wheel drive to reach the campground in the first place. It was going to be one very expensive tow job, if I could find someone willing to haul it all the way back.

The light faded. I kept walking. When I hit the washed out patches of road I turned on the flashlight and picked my way over them, then took note of the right direction and walked in the dark, feeling my way along. It was slow going. Whenever I wandered to the side of the road I'd turn on the flashlight, center myself and try again. I didn't want to run out of batteries so I only used the flashlight when necessary. I only used my cell phone to check the time twice. When eleven o'clock neared I thought it was time to stop and find a place to sleep. I wanted to be close to the road so I could hear a car, but I didn't want to be on the road and risk getting run over. I found a hillside that faced the road and dug a small ledge in the loose dirt. If cars came down the road the lights would wake me. I curled up on the ledge and put Shadow in a down stay behind me. Then I went to sleep willing myself not to move. It used to be hard to sleep in one position but in the Marines there were times when space was cramped or conditions were hazardous and I learned to sleep in almost any circumstances. Unfortunately, I was four layers deep in little four wheel drive tracks and I wasn't expecting any cars. I slept through the night and woke hungry at first light. I checked my meager store of trail mix. There was plenty. I wasn't going to starve, but wouldn't be full either. I poured out a handful and ate it. I never did care for the taste of it all mixed up. Once my hunger was satisfied I just picked out the nuts, pieces of dried fruit, or M&Ms as they appealed to me.

I wondered what Rusty was doing. I hated when these things happened to me, not because of what might happen to me but because of the worry it caused him. To me this was just an inconvenience. To him it was more. To him I was a missing person. He would know that I went exploring and he could guess that I got distracted or had mishaps come up. What he didn't know was, I was in the middle of nowhere, perfectly fine, just a long ways from where I should be. I wished I had a way to tell him.

I reached the first intersection by midmorning but unfortunately it was just the beginning. I found a branch and marked the turn so I'd be able to find my way back to the Jeep. I examined the intersection to see if another car had passed through after my Jeep. It looked like mine was the last vehicle over the road. I'd come through here before noon yesterday, so that meant I couldn't expect much traffic today either.

The sun rose in the sky and miles fell beneath my feet. I marked the second intersection, then sat down to rest. When I got up I examined the road and followed the tracks of my Jeep to the next leg of my journey.

I spotted some coyote tracks crossing the road. At last! An animal to track. Too bad I couldn't take time to follow it. The tracks were fairly fresh and crossed over my tire tracks. Half an hour or so after I saw the coyote tracks a motorcycle suddenly came down the road and drew to a stop before me.

"Are you okay?" a stout man dressed in black leather yelled over the rumble of his bike.

"Yes, I'm fine. Can you tell me how far it is to the highway?"

"You're kidding."

"No, I came in yesterday and didn't keep track of the miles. I'll be fine. I'd just like to know how far I have to go."

"I'll give you a ride."

"No, thanks, I have my dog along. I'm afraid he doesn't do motorcycles."

"Can I call someone for you?"

"Yeah!" I opened my pack and pulled out my wallet and then leafed through my cards. I found Rusty's business card and handed it to him. "Tell my husband that I'm fine and point him in the right direction. He's used to this happening and he'll find me."

The guy sped off and I glanced down at Shadow hopefully.

"It shouldn't be long now and Rusty won't be as worried so we can ease up."

Shadow just sat there with his tongue hanging down to his knees. I poured some water into the plastic bag and he lapped it up. We set off down the road feeling a little better.

A mile or so later I heard a rumble coming up behind me. I pulled off the road and crouched in the brush as a motorcycle gang cruised by looking around. Somehow I didn't think they were looking to help me out. If they were worried about my well being they would not have ridden their motorcycles. They knew I had a dog with me and wasn't going to abandon him in the woods. I let them pass and put a few turns between us before I climbed up onto the road again. A half mile later and they were cruising back. What were they up to? I'd met friendly bikers and violent bikers. If they really meant to help they would have called the ranger station, Rusty, or at least brought a car. I briefly considered whether or not my Jeep wouldn't start because they had tampered with it, but quickly ruled that out. I had been within sight of the Jeep most of the time and I didn't think they would ride their shiny motorcycles over a four wheel drive Jeep trail. I had seen the wires. The Jeep had only been tampered with by my desert pests.

Each time I heard the rumble of motorcycles I commanded Shadow to heel and put him in a down stay well off the road. Shadow growled at them as they went by. Fortunately, they couldn't hear a thing over their motorcycles. After three passes Shadow finally lost his patience. Barking loudly, he darted up onto the road and chased the group of motorcycles. One of the men turned and spoke into the radio inside his helmet. Then they all stopped and turned around. I shrank back into the woods. Now I was in a tight spot. Shadow could find me easily enough but if he did he would also lead the men in my direction and I didn't trust them. Further and further I slipped into the woods until the men didn't want to leave their bikes behind to pursue me. Shadow followed so they knew approximately where I was but they didn't want to go that far from the road. I continued on my way, paralleling the road but it was much slower going and I couldn't watch for Rusty or any real help. Nighttime found me low on energy, trail mix, water, and trust, off beside the road a fraction of the distance I could have gone without the "help" I'd encountered.

I didn't really expect the motorcycle gang to continue their little game into the next day, but I felt better concealed in the woods, so I slept out of sight of the road. I kept my ears tuned for cars or radios. When the rangers were out and about I frequently heard their radios long before I could see them.

On day three I was determined to hit pavement. It seemed impossible to have been three days away from pavement in these mountains. When I stood on a mountaintop I could see Joshua Hills to the north and LA to the south. How could I be three days from pavement? I picked all the fruit and chocolate from the trail mix and gave the nuts to Shadow. We were going to hit pavement today. We had to. I set my feet to marching tempo and pointed myself down the road and kept it up. There was only one reason to stop, and since I hadn't eaten or drank very much I wouldn't be taking pit stops very often. I could eat trail mix and drink my meager supply of water while walking, for a third of a bottle, anyway. Come on, Cass, just keep on keeping on.

I was marching down the road, carrying the last third of my bottle of water, when I heard a vehicle approach from behind. I heard the brakes hit, the truck slide to a halt. I turned around and there was Kelly Green, shocked as shocked could be. He jumped out of the truck and bowled me over in the biggest hug I'd ever received. Luckily Rhonda wasn't with him.

"You good for nuthin' little troublemaker, you!" he exclaimed affectionately. "Rusty's never going to let you out of his sight. Where have you been?"

"Walking," I said tiredly. "Just walking. It's been a hell of a long walk."

"Come on," he said, "let's tell everyone they can go home."

"Aw, Rusty didn't call everyone out, did he?"

"Not everybody. We didn't know where to start."

"Me, too. I have no idea where I ended up, but I need to figure out how to get the Jeep back. Mice ate the wiring and it won't start."

He bundled me into the ranger truck and got on the radio. "Ten sixty-five found and we're A-okay." He then turned to me and said, "We figured it was somewhere in the mountains because you didn't have cell phone reception but we've got guys driving the back roads out in the desert too."

Rusty came on over the radio and said, "Cassidy?"

I took the microphone from Kelly. "Hey!" I tried to respond brightly but I just didn't have enough energy. Rusty didn't know what to say over the radio. I could think of a dozen things he'd want to say when we were alone but all I got was a relieved silence. "It's okay, I'll see you soon."

The truck bumped and lurched down the old dirt road and I realized I would have had a long walk ahead of me if Kelly hadn't found me. I curled up on the seat and tried to ignore Shadow who was trying to look out the window to my right. I moved over to give Shadow some space but the seat wasn't as stable and I often bumped shoulders with Kelly as he eased over the rough spots in the road.

"You think this is rough. You ought to see where my Jeep is."

Kelly pulled into the ranger station and I opened the door. Shadow bounded out and I tried to stop him but I didn't have the energy, and when I stepped out of the truck it was all I could do to stay standing. I dragged my pack over and looked for anything edible but it was all gone. I zipped it up, walked to the steps of the ranger station and sat heavily.

"Cassidy, what's wrong?" Kelly asked.

"I just haven't had enough to eat. If Rusty hugs me like you did, he's going to knock me over and I won't be able to get up. Do you still have that map laminated to the counter?"

"Yeah."

"Let me show you where my Jeep is."

I got up awkwardly and found my way into the ranger station.

"Show me where you found me."

He pointed to a road. I followed the roads picturing the directions I'd marked while hiking out. I traced the route with my finger until I came to the end of the road. There was no campground symbol. Nothing. Just a dead end road.

"There's an old, abandoned campground at the end of this road. My Jeep is there. I was just going to spend a few hours exploring in the hills but when I got back to it, my Jeep wouldn't start. So I started walking."

"You walked all that way?"

"Yeah, it was a long walk."

"I'll say. Look at me."

I looked up into the eyes of my long-time friend and his brow furrowed.

"We really need to get you something to eat. You're ready to drop."

"I was doing fine until I slowed down. Now everything is catching up with me."

"When was your last meal?"

"Breakfast two days ago."

I heard the vehicles arrive one by one and then joyful volunteers filed in and slapped me on the back nearly knocking me off the stool that stood in front of the map counter. Victor and Paul. Rosco and Strict. Jacobsen, and finally Rusty. He rushed to the entrance and the door banged open in his haste. Rusty stopped, almost too fearful to look. I slid off the stool afraid if I didn't he'd knock me off. I took a few shaky steps and he barged through the room and clasped me tightly. Everyone looked a little uncomfortable and then they all filed out onto the porch again.

Rusty held on for a long time, rocking back and forth, his head buried in my filthy hair. It almost felt like a slow, intimate dance, filled with emotion. His worry soaked into me and his relief enveloped me.

"Oh, babe, don't ever do that to me again. I don't think I could stand it."

"I didn't do anything, my Jeep broke down. I would have been back by dinnertime if I could. Nothing bad happened. I've just been walking, trying to find the highway. I might have found it today if Kelly hadn't picked me up.... Rusty, stop... stop for a second. I need to sit down. I've been running on empty too long."

He held me out at arms length to look me over and then led me into the radio room of the ranger station. Two utilitarian, plastic and metal chairs sat in front of the radio and across the room they had placed a big, plaid, country style couch. A six-foot long table full of papers separated the two. He led me to the couch and I sat with a sigh of relief.

"You just went out exploring. That's all," he said.

"Yeah, that's all. No trying to track down McPherson. No chasing after mountain lions, no getting kidnapped by men in yellow vans. I just got stuck in a very hard place to walk out of. I don't think the Explorer will make it back there. I had to use four wheel drive."

"Let's trade that Jeep in for something safer. How about a sexy sports car?"

"I'd rather get stuck in remote places than pick up your felons at red lights. You have to learn that just because I disappear doesn't mean I'm in danger."

"Cass, you had three ounces of water left. You're fixing to collapse. Do you really think you'd have made it out of there today?"

"Yeah, I know I would. As long as I was in work mode I was fine. And I could have found food along the way but I was more worried about you."

"You were worried about me?"

"I wanted to get out of there as soon as I could so you wouldn't worry and call out the troops. Guess I was too late for that."

"That reminds me," he said, and picked up his phone. He called the station and told them I'd been found. They called off the search for the sand colored Jeep. After he hung up he said, "And you get to do this one." He punched in the number and handed me the phone.

"Yeah?" the voice said.

"Hello?" I answered.

"Cassidy…it's been two days!"

"Chase?"

"If you want to be found you have to give us a starting point."

"I'll keep that in mind next time the mice eat my wiring. Only break down where I'm findable. Got it."

"Where are you?"

"Kelly's ranger station."

"I'm glad you're okay."

"Thanks."

That was enough of a conversation for Chase. He hung up. I closed the phone and handed it back to Rusty.

"Are you okay now?" I asked him.

He sighed, a calmer more thoughtful sigh. "Yeah, let's go meet the troops."

"I still need something to eat, troops or no troops. I've survived on half a sandwich bag of trail mix for two days."

"Don't tell me you're going to eat cheesecake for lunch."

"No, I don't think my stomach could handle it yet."

We got up and made our way out to the porch. The crowd had doubled. I was guessing the people searching the desert roads had caught up with us. Landon made his way up on crutches. He grinned at me looking as though he was counting down my remaining nine lives. "Do we get the full story or are you going to leave us hanging?"

"You get the full story but there isn't much to it."

"Oh yeah?"

"Yeah." So I told them about it and when I was finished they all looked at me like, "And then what?"

"I told you, you guys worry too much. A girl can't even go exploring and break down without the National Guard going on alert. I'd have called as soon as I reached a phone. I just hadn't gotten there yet." Then I realized who I was speaking to and backed up a bit. "I'm sorry, guys. I know you meant well and you were only out there because you care. I'm lucky to have you."

I was starving but wasn't sure how to make a graceful exit to find something to eat. I couldn't just walk out on these guys, but if I didn't eat soon they might end up carrying me out. Kelly came to the rescue again.

"Gilson's Grill has prime rib for eight ninety-nine. I say if we want to continue our celebration we can take it over there."

Those who really ought to have been doing other things rather than looking for me now had a good excuse to leave, while the others who felt compelled to stay were free to stick around. More importantly, I could finally eat a real meal.

Gilson's was a dimly lit bar and grill that bikers frequented on their many rides up into the mountains. They stopped there regularly because the food was good and there was plenty of it. I glanced around trying to find some real lights in the place but the closest I found was neon signs for every beer company imaginable. One thing Gilson's wasn't good at was providing lighter fare. I could get an inch thick steak smothered with anything imaginable but I couldn't get a small bowl of fruit. I settled on grilled chicken and wasn't surprised when it arrived with a heap of mashed potatoes smothered in gravy. I poked around in the gravy hoping for a vegetable of some kind but couldn't find one.

After a few bites my stomach realized that I hadn't completely forgotten about it. Then I settled into the flow of things and started listening to the conversations around me.

"Landon," Rusty said, "how are you getting along with your new roommate?"

All eyes swiveled to Landon.

"Very funny," Landon replied. "First you curse me with the thing, now you want me to talk about it in front of everybody."

"No, I thought maybe if everyone knew you were looking for a new home for it someone might offer to take it off your hands," Rusty said.

More eyes swiveled his way.

"Okay Wilson, so what is this 'roommate' you've been cursed with?"

"It's a huge, pink bear. Anyone need a huge, pink bear?"

The whole room busted out laughing including a table of bikers in the corner. Landon shrank in his chair. I felt kind of sorry for him. Then I noticed a single biker buried up to his elbows in barbecue sauce. There was a pile of baby back ribs stacked on a plate to his right. He tossed one more bone unto the pile, got up ponderously, and walked over wiping the sauce off his face with a big napkin.

"Don't go away," he told Landon. He disappeared into the men's room and we soon heard the sound of running water as the man washed away the sticky sauce. Ten minutes later the biker reappeared sauce free. A tiny woman dressed in black leather pants and a red, white and blue striped shirt came out of the ladies room and joined him. He was at least twice her size and wore a bandana around his head sporting the same patriotic colors. His face was tanned with a raccoon pattern from spending time outside and wearing sunglasses. "I'm Clarence," he said politely. "I may be able to help you with the curse of the big, pink bear. Me and the missus are going to take a bike trip across the country and we need a mascot to ride along. We have matching purple Harleys with purple trailers. The pink bear would look just goofy enough strapped to the top of a trailer to make a fitting mascot. Do you know where we can get another one?"

Our table fell silent.

"Umm, how well can you shoot?" Landon stammered. "Cassidy won it in a shooting booth at the carnival."

"Cassidy?"

"Yeah," it was my turn to stammer. "I think you have to hit the star six times in a row."

"You? You're Cassidy? You won the big, pink, bear?"

"Yeah."

"Think you could do it again? I can't shoot worth beans unless someone bashes my Harley."

"I don't think they'll let me shoot again. I already took them to the cleaners twice."

"I'll pay you fifty bucks to try."

Rusty and I looked at each other.

"Meet us at the corner of Foster and Grant in Joshua Hills at three-thirty tomorrow," Rusty finally said.

"Why three-thirty?" I asked.

"That's when all the kids show up. People see you shoot and then all the dads think they can do it too. So the guy is more likely to let you shoot and win if he has an audience to work afterwards," Rusty explained.

"You got a deal, don't forget the big, pink bear," Clarence told Rusty. Landon grinned, relieved to see a happy ending for the big, pink bear that didn't include him babysitting it until Christmas.

"If I have a choice between a pink bear and a blue bear, which one should I choose?"

"What do you think, honey? Do we want matching pink or pink and blue?"

"We could put the blue one on your trailer and the pink one on mine. Or we could match; it doesn't matter either way to me. Blue goes with purple, too," she answered.

"I don't know, I like the idea of matching bears," Clarence said.

"Okay, then go for pink. Why do you ask me if you're just going to do what you want anyway?"

Clarence looked at us sternly, "Three-thirty tomorrow?"

"We'll be there."

"It's a deal."

"Thanks!" Landon added.

Clarence and his wife left and everybody looked to Landon.

"Okay, what's the story of the big, pink, bear?"

The carnival was bustling with activity when Rusty and I pulled up and met Clarence and his wife at the gate.

"This is Twila," he said apologetically, having failed to introduce her at the restaurant.

"It's good to meet you, Twila. I'm Cassidy and this is my husband, Rusty."

We all shook hands and they followed us into the carnival. We walked up to the shooting booth and the hawker just stood there, his arms folded.

"Well, well, if it isn't miss publicity!" he said.

That was encouraging.

"I need another bear. Tell me how I can get one."

"Shoot the star six times. If you get six in a row I'll give you two free."

"That's it? Just six in a row?"

"Yeah, you're great for business. I like you. All the guys think if you can do it they can too so they line up by the dozens. Mind if I drum up a little business?"

"No, I kind of expected it. You mean I really can shoot again?"

"Yeah, besides, I don't meet many people like you."

"Six shots for five dollars?"

"Yep and two free if you make those."

I put down my five and he handed me a gun.

"Just a sec. Ladies and *gentlemen*, I have a *challenger*, a little lady here who thinks she can hit the star *six times in a row*! *Can* she do it? Most people would say *no*! There's no way she could do it but she's here to show you it's *easier than it looks*. Come watch as she gives it a try. *You* sir! Do you think you could hit the star? If this little lady can do it so can *you*!"

I waited until a good size crowd had gathered and then I took careful aim. Clarence stood behind me, arms crossed over his massive chest. Twila stood quietly beside him. Rusty grinned and Landon crossed his fingers. If I lost there was a chance that Clarence wouldn't want Landon's single big, pink bear.

I took my time on the first shot, then without lowering the rifle I remained steady and squeezed off five more. The crowd broke into applause and it was Clarence's turn to stand there open-mouthed. Rusty pulled me into a joyful hug. I chose another big, pink bear and told the guys standing around, "It's not that hard. I'm sure if I can do it, you can, too."

We walked to the parking lot and handed over both big, pink bears to Clarence and he happily strapped them down to the tops of their purple Harley trailers. Clarence pulled out a fifty-dollar bill.

"Thanks," he said. "The trip will be a lot more interesting with people razzing us about the bears all the way. Now I have a good story to go with it. Helps break the ice when I meet up with people at pit stops." They pulled on their matching purple helmets, got on their matching purple Harleys and rumbled out of the parking lot.

Thus ends the saga of the big, pink bear. He started out his trip on the beach at Santa Monica and I never heard if he made it all the way to the east coast or not, but he certainly had a different life than most stuffed toys. I also wondered over the next few months if the big, pink bear got to visit any more carnivals in his travels. I hope so.

Chapter 9

After the carnival Rusty and I went home and spent a long quiet afternoon together. From time to time I caught Rusty just watching me do everyday things, so finally I sat with him on the couch.

"What's wrong?" I asked.

"Nothing's wrong," he answered, not very convincingly.

"Something is on your mind or you wouldn't be watching me so closely. I see the wheels turning."

"I keep thinking…babe, you just scare me, that's all. I keep thinking one of these trouble attacks is going to get the best of you."

"I wasn't trying to get into trouble and it wasn't my fault that the Jeep broke down thirty miles from civilization. I did what I could and I would have been fine. I'm sorry it worried you. I knew it would but there was nothing I could do once it happened. All I could do was walk out."

"I know. I can't help it. You'll just have to live with me watching over you. And I'll try not to worry when trouble attacks but I can't help it. Are you feeling better today?"

"Yeah, I'm fine. If I can just get three meals a day for a while I'll catch up. Strict knows I'll take calls. I hope he waits a few days but if he called tomorrow I'd be ready to go out. We still need to figure out how to get the Jeep back. I called a few towing companies. They don't want to go that deep into the mountains. They keep giving me wild quotes. I'm thinking of trying horses. We could tow the horses in until the road gets too rough and then ride in and pull the Jeep back out."

"How far is it from the washout to the Jeep?"

"That's just it, I'm guessing about ten miles."

"So we'd have to ride horseback for ten miles?"

"One way, if my guess is right. Don't worry, you won't have to ride in. I know ten miles on horseback is not your idea of fun."

I reluctantly punched in the telephone number for the ranch. It wasn't like me to ask for help and to do so would cause a lot of concern.

"Hello?" It was Martha, the ranch cook and housekeeper.

"Hello, Martha, it's Cass."

"Cassidy! It's so good to hear from you! How are you, dear? I'll go find your mom!"

"I'm fine, but I'm not sure Mom is the right person to talk this time. I'd better start off with Dad."

"Your father? What have you done this time?"

"Is that Cassidy?" I heard in the background. A question like, *what have you done this time?* always made my family think of me.

"Yes, but she wants to talk to her dad."

"Oh dear."

"She sounds okay."

"Okay."

"Martha," I interrupted, "you can put Mom on. She can turn me over to Dad."

"Cassidy?"

"Yeah, Mom."

"What have you done this time?"

"Nothing much, I just need a hand retrieving my Jeep. It's stuck down a road that needs four wheel drive and I think I will have to ride in and pull it out with horses."

"Oh, okay," she said, sounding as though like this was an every day request. "Wayne, pick up the phone. It's Cassidy."

Dad picked up and I felt like I went back ten years.

"Daddy?"

"Yes, Cass, what can I do for you?"

Maybe I should be calling them more often if he assumed I just wanted something. It kind of set me back realizing he was right. Okay, no beating around the bush.

"I was wondering if I could borrow two horses and a ranch hand for a few days." I explained the situation.

"I think you should be able to figure this out on your own," he told me. "You're a big girl now."

Well, at least someone thinks I am! I thought.

"Dad, I did figure it out. I called tow truck companies. The road is too rough. It's going to take driving in until the trailer can't go further, then riding in, camping overnight, hooking up the horses and pulling the Jeep out. Depending on how the horses do, it might take another night out on the road. I don't know where I can get horses around here. I guess I could try, but I *know* your horses. They are all good work horses. I'd have to be working with strange horses down here."

"I can't spare Steve right now. Frank's not doing well. Steve has pretty much taken over managing the place."

That news took me by surprise. I knew Old Frank was getting on in years but he'd been old ever since I was a kid. Now to hear that he was not doing well sounded ominous to me. Old Frank would die managing that ranch, or at least die thinking he was.

The next evening a big pickup with a large horse trailer pulled up to the house. Randy, one of my dad's ranch hands, bounded out. I was in for a couple of days of non-stop chatter.

"Cassidy! You're a sight for sore eyes." He pulled me into a hug and then stood back. I was in for a scolding. "You're skin and bones! Are you okay? Rusty better be treating you right."

"I'm fine, Randy. I just lost some weight on this last little adventure of mine. You'll understand once you see where the Jeep is stuck. Let's put the horses in the corral. I bet they're tired of that trailer. I wasn't sure you still trained horses to pull the buckboard."

"Sure, we do, I keep a couple of horses ready for just about anything." He opened the back of the trailer.

"Shasta! You brought Shasta!"

"And Mack. I thought I remembered Rusty got along okay with Mack."

I clipped a lead onto Shasta's halter and backed him out of the trailer.

"Look boy, you get to visit my house!" I gave the big gray quarter horse a hug and then led him around the house to the corral. Randy followed with Mack. He took out a flake of hay and tossed it into the corral. We left the horses to get settled. Shadow walked around the corral excitedly and I had to call him into the house to get him to leave the horses alone. He ran to the front door and barked.

"No, you aren't going out there," I scolded. "Randy, can I get you anything?"

"Sure, I'll take anything you have to drink. When's dinner?"

"I aim for seven. I know that's later than you're used to. Rusty should be home a little before then."

Randy and I had known each other since we were teenagers. We had grown up with similar interests and had done the same things around the ranch. He had joined the staff at the ranch when he was fourteen, going to school with me and working on the ranch for his room and board in the bunkhouse. We had both gone on hunting trips with the ranch hands and had both learned to shoot well. So I thought he'd get a laugh out of the story of the big pink bear. Midway through the story Shadow was still barking at the front door and then he suddenly stopped and ran to the back door. What was going on with that dog? I opened the front door and didn't see anything out of the ordinary, so I returned to the den to continue my story. Suddenly I saw two little eyes peeking in through the back door through cupped hands. Oh no!

"Randy, you had a stowaway. Did you know that?"

He turned to look at the back door and his shocked face almost went white. Patrick! Randy jerked the back door open and stood there glaring down into the contrite face of my nephew. Images of my frantic sister filled my mind.

"You little troublemaker, get in here!" Randy barked. "Do you know what your mom is going to do after she gets over the panic of not being able to find you?"

"She thinks I'm at school," Patrick answered, thinking he had this all figured out.

"School has been out for two hours," Randy informed him. He pressed and held the speed dial and then handed the phone to Patrick.

From the expression in my nephew's eyes I immediately knew he'd connected with his mother. "Mom?" A very long pause. "I'm fine, Mom. I'm with Randy." More talk from Jesse. "No, Mom! He didn't know I was there or he wouldn't have taken me. I hid in the back of the truck." I could almost hear my sister's voice from several feet away. "I know, but I missed Aunt Cassidy and Uncle Rusty and the deer."

Randy sat down on the couch, looking completely stressed out. Then he took the phone back from Patrick. "Hi, Jess." More loud talk from my sister. "I'll bring him home. You know that." Would Jesse ever calm down? "We'll take care of everything." Another pause. "I don't know what I can do but we'll see. Okay, here she is."

Oh boy, here we go. At least she couldn't blame me. Patrick continued to stand there looking like he was ready for whatever came at him.

"Hello, Jesse?"

"Cassidy, I don't know what to say! I had no idea Patrick would pull something like this! He knows better than to skip school to go to your house!"

"It's okay, Jesse, as long as he's okay. One skipped day is not going to ruin the kid, but this isn't a social call Randy is making down here. We have a job to do and Patrick either has to help or stay out of the way while we do it."

"How long do you think it will take?"

"We'll go in tomorrow morning, camp overnight at the campground and then try to pull the Jeep out the next day. The amount of time depends on how far we can go with the trailer. The further we can drive in the less time we'll have to ride. I expect Patrick to be home in three days."

"I hope he won't be too much trouble. He's going to be grounded for life when he gets home."

"He won't be too much trouble, but it may not be fun for him either. He'll have to ride and camp and ride some more and I can't guarantee any deer for him on this trip because we will be gone so much."

"That's what he gets for not thinking things through before he takes off. I guess there's not much I can do at this point except wait until he gets back."

"He'll be fine. Randy will bring him home when we're finished."

"I better call the ranch and let them know they can stop looking. I'll talk to you later."

We hung up and I turned to Patrick. Although I had mixed emotions about him being here I'd actually been missing him like crazy.

"Come here, you little troublemaker, I missed you," I said giving him a big hug. "Randy has dibs on the guestroom so you'll have to sleep in the den. Did you bring any extra clothes? Toothbrush? Anything?"

"You mean I get to stay?" he asked.

"What else are we going to do with you? We can't send you back because you don't have your driver's license yet, and no, you can't drive the truck."

"All right!" he yelled, jumping up and down. "I have a pack in the truck. I put some clothes in my book pack and then I put schoolbooks on top of them so Mom would only see books. She tossed in my lunch and walked me to the bus. I snuck back and hid in the truck until Randy left. I was glad he played the stereo real loud. He didn't even hear me sneeze."

Randy went out to the truck and returned carrying Patrick's book pack and some odds and ends he found stashed in the back of the truck: Patrick's binoculars, his moccasins, the track book and bird book.

"Looks like you've been planning for a while," Randy said.

"Ever since I found out where you were going," Patrick answered.

"You little...you're just like your aunt, you know that?" Randy said in a derogatory way.

"Really?" Patrick said hopefully. Maybe that's why I liked the kid so much.

"Okay," I said, "I need to start dinner. The deer are gone for the day. The birds are probably done eating but we can try to get some to visit." Patrick and I went outside to fill up the bird feeders with wild bird seed and peanuts. He spent the evening walking between bird watching in the bedroom and watching me cook in the kitchen.

My dinner plans had changed dramatically with Patrick's arrival. I started a big pot of spaghetti sauce and left it to simmer on the stove. Sorry, Randy, I thought to myself, the kid gets precedence. I had planned on making steak but that was better cooked in the mountains, anyway, so I decided to take it with us when we went to retrieve the Jeep. I knew Patrick liked spaghetti and Randy hardly ever got spaghetti at the ranch since pasta was not considered proper ranch food.

While I cooked I listened for the sound of Rusty's car. When he finally arrived home, I met him at the front door and dragged him to the bay window.

"Look! We have horses in the corral!" He glanced through the window and then smiled at me, obviously enjoying my enthusiasm.

"He brought Shasta," Rusty said, sounding pleased.

"Yeah, and Patrick," I added.

"Patrick? Doesn't he have school?"

"Stowaways don't have to go to school," I informed him.

"Oh yeah?" he said, smiling.

"Yeah."

Patrick peeked hesitantly around the bedroom door.

"You know what I have to do if I catch kids skipping school?" Rusty asked him.

"No, sir," Patrick said.

"I have to haul them into the station and then we book them as truants and call their parents."

"Does that mean we get to go to the station again?" Patrick asked hopefully.

"You don't want to go to the station as a truant. Plus I bet we already called your parents."

I heard the sound of the back door opening then closing.

"Randy's here," I told him. "I'll have dinner on in about fifteen minutes."

I cooked the noodles, warmed up French bread in the oven and then set the table.

"You're looking a lot more settled here now," Randy observed. "Life is treating you well. It does me good to see you like this."

"Thanks, Randy."

"You never looked this content when you were with Jack."

I didn't have anything against Jack. I'd loved him deeply. But the name hit me like a slap.

"I wasn't a wife to Jack," I said simply. "I was a soldier. We just happened to be married."

"Cassidy... I'm sorry."

"It's okay. I'd just prefer to stay in the present. I like the present much better than the past."

"I can tell. I'm glad to see you so happy. Where'd you get the pictures in the living room? Those weren't here when I came for the wedding."

"They were a gift from one of my ten sixty-fives."

"Your ten sixty-fives?"

"Sorry, that's what we call the people I track down with the search and rescue team. A ten sixty-five is a missing person, although this particular ten sixty-five wasn't an official search. His parents are my neighbors. I had to go over to Santa Cruz Island to look for him. He took those pictures after I found him. He's a rather famous nature photographer and we've managed to stay friends. He's got a studio in Toronto. He even sells pictures of me in his studio."

"Pictures of you? What kind of pictures?"

"Like the ones in the living room."

"You mean I could buy pictures of you from this guy?"

"Yeah, if you really wanted to. But I don't recommend it. I hear his prices are pretty steep."

"Like, how steep?"

"He told me someone offered five hundred dollars for a set but I don't know what price he finally settled on."

"Five hundred dollars for some pictures of you?"

"I told you, he's kind of famous."

"Who is he, Mark Mireau or something?"

I smiled, then replied, "Exactly, he is Mark Mireau."

"Oh. You rescued Mark Mireau?"

"Yeah, and if you promise not to tell Jesse, Patrick has a great story to tell you involving Mark."

"I can't wait to hear this. To think, my little sister has met Mark Mireau."

Dinner conversation involved Randy trying to pry the story of Mark Mireau from Patrick who, believing he was already in enough trouble, remained silent. Not until I promised to back him up if word leaked back to his mom did he finally tell the whole story. Randy then learned of how Patrick tracked down and sent the police after Mark last Christmas when he thought the photographer was a prowler.

Randy laughed. "I can tell we're going to have our hands full with you, kid," he said. "So you got to meet Mark Mireau, too?"

"Yeah, he took my picture while I was stalking deer. He's a nice guy but he doesn't know much about stalking deer."

I caught Randy looking at the photographs in the living room with renewed interest. I took down the picture with the inscription on the back so he could read it and he studied the picture of Mark that had been taped to the back.

"He thinks a lot of you," Randy observed.

"Yeah, I expect him to come over whenever he visits his parents."

I showed Randy to the guestroom then found bedding so Patrick could sleep in the den.

"We're going to try and get an early start in the morning," I warned him.

"I hope you brought warm clothes. We will be camping out in the mountains tomorrow. It's going to get chilly."

Before we went to bed I spread a map of the area out on the dining room table. Although I bought a lot of maps of the same area I used them all. I took them on searches and left them for Rusty so he'd know my location. The maps got tattered very quickly because of the rough treatment. I traced our route for the two men so there would be no questions.

"Here's where the Jeep is now," I said, circling the end of the dead end road. "Here's where I expect we'll be able to reach with the trailer," I said, drawing an X on the road. "You can see it's quite a ways from the turnoff to the campground. I think we can pull the Jeep back to the truck the next day. If you get home from work, and we aren't back, you might drive down there and see how far we got. We can't tow the Jeep all the way out because we'll have the horse trailer to worry about first. So if you can drive the Explorer to where the trailer is we'll be in business to have the whole tow job done in two days. If you are worried about towing the Jeep through the mountains you can see if Kelly wants to help. He'd probably like to see where the Jeep was anyway."

"Cassidy," Randy said, "you're telling me you hiked out of that place? That's about thirty miles!"

"I hiked about twenty-one of it before Kelly picked me up. Now you see how I managed to drop five pounds in two days."

Chapter 10

By the time I left our bedroom the next morning Patrick was up, dressed and watching out the den window for deer.

"Let me see your pack, Pat," I said. I opened it and made sure he had what he needed for our trip into the mountains. "Those are boots you can play in aren't they?"

"Yeah, they're just my school shoes."

"But you can get them dirty, right?"

"Yeah, and I get them really dirty on the playground. Did you know that dogs visit the school when the kids are in class? Around the edges of the playground neighborhood cats visit, too, probably because there are mice in the weeds around the edges of the playground."

"You're getting more observant."

"That's because Chase told me what to watch for and I'm getting good at asking myself questions. The dogs don't chase the cats but the cats do chase the mice."

"Do your teachers ever wonder what you are doing out there looking around in the weeds?"

"Yeah, they ask me to play closer to the rest of the class. They think I'm going to ditch school or something, but I'm not."

"You're not huh? What are you doing right now?"

"Well...it's not ditching school if I have your permission, right?"

"That's between your mom and the school. Maybe if you keep up with your schoolwork while you are gone they will see you are more responsible than they think."

"Even the extra credit? What is extra credit, anyway? My teacher says I can do it because it might be more interesting to me, and I have to admit it *is* better than my normal work."

"Extra credit is work you can do to add points to your grade so you can earn a better grade than the one you were going to get. Or sometimes if you do well on an extra credit assignment you can use that grade to replace a bad grade you got."

"So I could only do the interesting stuff and still get good grades?"

"I don't think they planned on it working like that. Why, how much does she give you?"

He showed me a workbook about sea creatures. It was probably third grade level. He'd finished the book in sloppy first grade handwriting. An essay question asked: Describe a chain of life in the ocean. And Patrick had written: "The chain of life is what keeps animals alive. Big animals eat little animals. A big fish eats a little fish and a seagull eats a bigger fish. Or a bigger fish mite eat the fish. A dolphin mite eat a fish and maybe the dolphin could get cot by peepl and live in a zoo. Some times the chain of life has suprises." There was an extra piece of paper where he'd continued his thought. "I saw a big bird eat a little bird and it was sad but it is just the chain of life on the land insted of in the water. Mountain lions eat deer and that is sad too but it is the chain of life again. Im glad deer dont eat rabbits or mice. So the chain of life can start with a plant or a animal or even a big animal. Like a elefant is a big animal but if it dies birds could eat it."

The workbook had made its way into Patrick's head and become a kind of life journal. I wondered what his teacher thought of it. I looked at the early pages that she had graded. The comments started out with, "Very good!" and progressed to, "Interesting observation," to, "I can see you are quite a little scientist! Keep up the good work!"

"Wow," I told Patrick, "you ought to get an A in science. What about your real work?"

"It's boring."

I opened a book. He had to match the person with their job. Another, he had to match an animal with its home. He had to write the letter Q twenty times and he had to do addition facts. He liked the word problems: "If Taffy had four puppies and one of them was adopted by a family, how many puppies would Taffy have?" Patrick had written: "She still had four puppies but since this is a math qestion I gess she has three. My mom still has two kids even when im at school." I had to laugh.

"Pat, you're a very smart kid, but I think you can just give them the answer you think they are looking for."

"I know, my teacher said I was being a smart-aleck but I was just answering the question. She said I was either going to grow up to be a scientist or a lawyer. I don't want to be a lawyer."

"What are we talking about?" Rusty asked as he came in for breakfast.

"Here," I said, handing him the workbook. "When your day gets slow read this book. We're talking about how Patrick doesn't want to be a lawyer."

Rusty poured a cup of coffee and sat down to read. Pretty soon he was smiling. I scrambled eggs and browned sausage patties then made toast. It wasn't a ranch breakfast but it would do for the morning. I also packed the steak for the trip into the mountains. We all ate a quick breakfast and I loaded the dishwasher.

"After work tomorrow I'll drive down to the trailer and see how things are going."

"Okay, I'll do my best to have the Jeep where we can tow it back. At least you know exactly where we'll be."

"Thanks. Take care out there."

"I don't have a choice. I've got Randy along. He's worse than a bodyguard."

"You could ask Hazel to watch Patrick."

Patrick's head shot up. I laughed at him.

"No, he needs to come and do his share of the work." Patrick sighed with relief. "Besides, I don't trust her to keep track of him."

Shortly after Rusty left for work we started loading gear and then horses. Randy had brought saddles, harnesses and a tow strap, but I wasn't sure how it all fit together. I considered myself in charge of food and camping gear. I had to change the camping arrangements to include Patrick. I had to dig up an old tent that was big enough for two, increased the number of backpacker meals we brought and made an extra sandwich. I threw in fruit and a can of chips that I wouldn't ordinarily take. We loaded up the truck and got in. Patrick sat in the middle straddling the gearshift. When we reached the road Patrick asked, "Can I shift?"

"Not while we're towing horses. If you shift rough or stall the truck it could hurt the horses," Randy answered.

"Can I steer?"

"Not on these hilly roads. You'll just have to be patient. How did you stay so quiet as a stowaway?"

"I was pretending I was a stowaway, because they have to be quiet or else they walk the plank."

"Makes sense to me," I said.

I gave Randy directions to the road. When we stopped at the ranger station I hung my Adventure Pass on the mirror of the truck. Patrick was anxious to see the rangers he remembered from Christmas.

"Cassidy! Back so soon? I thought you'd have had enough of these mountains after being stuck in them for three days."

"I need to go retrieve my Jeep. If you see Kelly tell him Rusty might be heading down there tomorrow after work. Kelly will recognize the ranch truck when he gets to it."

"Hi, Mr. Paul!" Patrick said.

"Well, if it isn't the little bird stalker."

"I stalk deer too!" Patrick said.

"So I heard."

"We're headed out. We're hoping to make it all the way back in there today," I said.

"Good luck."

The turn-off wasn't easy to spot. That must have been why I tried it in the first place. We headed down the rough dirt road. I pointed the way at each turn and the road got progressively worse. It started out washboard, then got bumpy, then clearly unmaintained.

"How much worse does it get?" Randy asked.

"A lot worse. This is nothing. We've still got the trailer, right?"

"Yeah."

"When you decide the trailer can't go any further that's where we stop."

"How far in do you figure we are?" Randy asked. I got out one of my many maps. We'd gone through two intersections. Two more to go.

"Well, we're somewhere between these two intersections. We need to try to get through the next one anyway. But if we can't, we can't. I'll let you be the judge. You know how much jarring the horses will take."

"Okay." He pulled out and onto the road again. "We haven't seen a car since we got on this road."

"I know. That's one reason why it was such a long walk out."

We wound in, out, and round about seeing dry washes, deep pines, scraggly junipers, meadows and cactus. This road seemed to have a little bit of everything on it. When the road began showing signs of being washed out I knew we were close to the third intersection. Randy looked at it uncertainly, then he looked at the map again. He got out and examined the road. He chose to continue but aimed the truck directly across the ridges in the road so we wouldn't rock the horses side to side. We made it to the fourth intersection and it seemed like a good stopping place. We could park the truck and trailer off the road. We took a final look at the map. Seven or eight miles to go on horseback and it was already lunchtime.

Randy unloaded the horses and harnesses, then he packed the harnesses and saddled the horses. I packed the camping gear while Randy made sure everything was secure. I gave Patrick a hand up and we were ready to go. Shasta and Mack were good horses for a pack trip. They enjoyed a run, but they were stable and obedient when slow going was needed.

We shared stories as we rode along. If there was one thing Patrick enjoyed it was a story. When I visited the ranch it was the first thing he asked for.

"I think it's time for you to tell Randy a story," I told Patrick.

"Me? I don't have any stories."

"Sure you do. Tell him about when we went to the mall last Christmas."

"When we almost got arrested? Or in San Diego?"

"Either."

So Patrick launched into a long storytelling that almost lasted until we got to the Jeep. When his voice started getting hoarse I started telling them about the campground.

"You should see lots of deer tracks at the campground. I did when I was there the first time."

"I can't believe you got the Jeep over this road," Randy said. "It isn't even a road in spots. Why did you keep going?"

"Because I figured if I could get in then I should be able to get out. And if not very many people made it in there, maybe there would be lots of animals. As it turned out I only saw signs of deer, but it looked like they pass through there a lot."

"So why did you get stuck?"

"It's a wiring problem. Mice ate the wires but I guess there was enough of a connection left to make it in here, then all the bumping and jarring caused a short or something. It won't even start now. I checked all the obvious things. The battery seems fine, no corrosion. The wiring is a mess, though. I'll show you when we get there. I wasn't worried about getting stuck on the road. I was halfway hoping I would because I've never tried out my winch. I didn't get that kind of stuck though, the Jeep just died. It was embarrassing. I hiked for two days before Kelly found me and then I found out half the county was out looking for me."

"At least you know Rusty cares."

"Yeah, I know, and next time I better tell him where I'm going. I don't mind if he shows up and lends a hand. I just didn't like having the whole police department, half the search and rescue teams and some of the rangers out looking for me. It was embarrassing. Even Chase in San Diego knew about it. He'd have been up here too but he's a tracker and there were no tracks to follow. They could have looked for years without finding my Jeep back here. Look at the road. Do you see any tracks besides my Jeep?"

"Nope, not recently, anyway."

When we came to a deeply washed out area we let the horses find their way over it. It felt good to be riding again. It would be great to take Shasta back here on a pleasure ride. I thought about just keeping him but I worried about whether or not he'd be happy at my house after being such a big part of a bustling ranch.

Patrick rode in front of me watching the road ahead through his field glasses. Every once in a while he'd find something to watch closely and he would follow it with the binoculars. I wondered how he didn't fall off the horse as much as he twisted and turned to keep things in sight.

"What do you see that is so interesting?" I asked.

"I saw a meadowlark, and a deer but it was in the trees and it didn't want to be seen. I saw a squirrel. And I saw a big bird but I don't know what kind it was."

The land slowly slipped by beneath the horses' hooves until the road turned into the abandoned campground. We located the Jeep and unloaded all the gear. I set up camp near the Jeep while Randy looked at the engine.

"It's almost new," he exclaimed. "Why would it quit?"

"Look at the wiring."

He looked around and pulled out some wires to get a closer look, then agreed with me.

"How do you know so much about cars?"

"One summer when I broke down on the highway my dad made me learn how to replace everything that could ever need replacing on the ranch truck. He said if I'd checked the truck over before leaving then I wouldn't have gone out and I wouldn't have broken down. Then he had Old Frank and Steve teach me all about how to check fluids and change things that are easily replaced. I do a lot of my own work on the Jeep and basic maintenance on Rusty's Explorer. I'm not sure if he knows that though. He takes it in for oil changes and nothing much ever needs fixing on it but he doesn't seem to wonder why. If I ask him to leave it at home he just figures I have an extra big grocery shopping trip planned or I want to buy wood for a project. So he leaves it and I replace brake shoes or give it a tune up or check all the fluids and filters."

"He doesn't know how to do that stuff?"

"I don't know. He might but I've never asked. Besides, I enjoy doing it. Patrick, come here and help me set up camp. Kids that play hooky have to work. See this area? Clear it of all the rocks and sticks and anything sharp that you wouldn't want to sleep on."

He cleared his spot and I cleared mine, then I started setting up tents.

"Have you ever been camping?" I asked him.

"No, the ranch is too busy. But I've slept in a tent behind the ranch house once."

"Well, this is almost the same except there is no house close by."

"Where is the bathroom?"

I looked around. "See that copse of trees over there? That's the boy's bathroom. If you go over there I promise not to watch. I'll find the toilet paper in a minute. Take the end of this pole and stick it in that little pocket by the tent peg."

Step by step he helped me set up the tents.

"Now, stay within sight of camp and no climbing. Find an armload of firewood. I want to be able to see you at all times, so no wandering off."

"Cassidy, ease up already," Randy said.

"You weren't along last time we were up in these mountains. Patrick has a way of getting into trouble without breaking any rules. He's really good at it. We'll take care of the fire, if you'll take care of the horses."

Randy unsaddled the horses and tethered them to the Jeep while Patrick and I gathered firewood. We stacked it next to the fire pit then went to gather more.

"Wow, you were right, there are lots of deer that come here!" Patrick observed as he gathered wood. "Will we see some while we're here?"

"I don't know. Keep your eyes open and tell me if you see any," I answered. "Let me know if you see tracks from any other animals, too. I couldn't find any interesting tracks when I was here last time."

When the wood had been gathered I set up a fire in the pit and then cleaned the grill as well as I could. My theory on campfire grills is that the fire kills anything that might hurt you. I fried potatoes and grilled the steak that had been marinating since the previous day. We ate fruit and chips. To me it was a fancy camping meal but I knew Randy was used to Martha's cooking and so I splurged a little bit for his sake. As for Patrick, he was used to both his mom's and Martha's cooking but, if he was going to learn to be a tracker, he needed to get used to trail food. Had it been just the two of us we'd have eaten only backpacker food, jerky and trail mix all the way. We ate at the broken down picnic tables then cleaned up. I stashed all the food in the Jeep and frisked Patrick for hidden treats before we went to bed.

"No food in the tents, not even water," I explained to Patrick. "Not even a hint of food in the tents. We have never camped here before and even though we only see deer tracks we don't know what kind of animals come here. We just know they are used to coming here and having the place to themselves."

I dug my rifle out of the Jeep and put it in the tent. I handed Patrick a roll of toilet paper. "Go use the boy's room before you go to bed. You don't want to have to find it in the night."

"Aw, can't we stay up and tell campfire stories? That's what you're supposed to do on camping trips."

"You've heard them all."

"So? You never tell them the same way twice, anyway."

So we stayed up and told campfire stories and then I pressed Randy to tell me about the annual hunting trip that the ranch hands went on. He had shot a buck, just like he had every year since he was nineteen. He and Steve, the ready steady hands. Not surprisingly they were also the better shots, the more patient hunters. Zack was too jumpy and nervous while James was just one of the guys. He wasn't a particularly good shot but he was part of the group and good company.

"I don't know what we're going to do with Steve managing the ranch.

We'd look for another hand but we can't displace Old Frank, even though he doesn't do much anymore. He's more like my grandpa than my boss," Randy said. "Never had a grandpa till Old Frank came along."

"I know what you mean. He's like my grandfather, too," I admitted. "He could see trouble brewing even before I tried something. Sometimes he'd let me do it, anyway, just so I'd learn a lesson. He taught me how to think like a tracker, how to ask myself the right questions. He and Steve taught me how to ride and rope."

"What about Zack?"

"Zack taught me patience."

And what about me? Randy was probably thinking, but he wouldn't ask, so I answered it anyway.

"You taught me to listen to my trouble radar. Did you know it wasn't Dad who found you when you were homeless? It was me. We went to the same school, you know that. I was never very close to any of the other kids. Many of them didn't understand me. They could accept a tomboy, especially in the farming community, but still I never fit in. I never went to the dances. I preferred spending time outdoors instead of socializing. But as I observed the other kids, it was you I noticed. At first you were kind of a class clown but during your first year at the school you changed and I noticed the difference. Then I watched how your personality changed and how you got angry easily."

Randy was looking uncomfortable so I stopped.

"I'm sorry, Randy. I didn't know hearing it would bother you."

"I like to think the ranch is the only place I ever lived. Even if it's only been ten years of it. Go ahead, tell it."

"Are you sure?"

"Pat," Randy said, his voice filling with bitterness, "Your grandpa took me in when my parents moved away and left me behind. He made me finish school. He said if I'd finish school I could live with the ranch hands and learn to train horses. I didn't have a choice. Well, I guess I did. It was the ranch or foster homes or run away. I'd already got a taste of the running away part. It was no fun."

Not knowing the meaning of tact, Patrick asked, "How could they do that? Moms and dads can't do that! They can't just leave. Kids can't just be left."

"I guess parents can if they don't care and can get away with it," Randy said. "I'm just lucky Mr. Gordon came along. I don't know how much longer I could have lived from shoplifting food. I was stealing food and bathing in a gas station bathroom and sleeping in a shed in back of a spooky old house. The lady at the house was old and hardly ever went out so I used her shed to live in."

I continued the story from my point of view. "I saw your attitude change and I saw your clothes were getting worn. After about a month of this I followed you after school. I lost you in a store on the way and so I tracked you to the shed. When I got there you weren't back yet so I hid out and waited for you to appear. I saw you open the door and realized that you only had a small pile of clothes, a sleeping bag and some junk food. You did your schoolwork sitting on the ground. So I went to my mom and she went to my dad. My mom didn't even believe me at first, that there was a kid at school living by himself in a shed. But I convinced her it was true and then Dad asked me to show him where you lived. When I showed him the shed he looked mad, but not at you. I think he was mad at your parents and a school system that didn't step in and see a kid in trouble. He took me home and a few days later he brought you back to the ranch. I don't know what he did to get custody of you. Or if he did anything. I didn't know enough about the system back then to question what he did."

Randy filled in what had happened. "I came home from school, stopping by the Snappy Mart on the way just like I always did. I stole a can of chili and an apple and a bottle of soda. I was getting good at stashing small things in the inside pockets of a jacket. When I got home, I mean to the shed, there was a big truck and a police car sitting in front of the lady's house. I thought I was going to be arrested for shoplifting. I walked around the block and hid the things I'd stolen and then I snuck back around and watched the shed. Mr. Gordon and a bunch of people were in the lady's house. Then I worried that she had seen the stuff in the shed and gotten scared and called the police. So I thought I was going to get arrested because of that. It took me a long time to go home and face the music. I wanted to make sure the lady was okay and show her that I wasn't going to hurt anything. I never stole anything from the lady's house. I figured I owed her for letting me use her shed. When I appeared Mr. Gordon approached me. I didn't know exactly who he was but he wasn't a cop so I was relieved. Now that I know Rusty, I shoulda thought he was a detective. 'Boy?' Mr. Gordon said. 'I've got a proposition for you. You come down to the police station with me, we'll take care of a few things and you make a choice. I ain't going to force you one way or the other but you can't go on living like this.' I went with them to the police station and Mr. Gordon laid out my choices. He was very frank with me about what each decision could lead to. He told me the work on the ranch would be hard at first and it was. Lots of manual labor that I wasn't used to. I decided to give the ranch a try because I thought I could work my way into a real job. I could earn my keep and maybe I wouldn't be on the streets again when I turned eighteen. Old Frank and Steve taught me all about the horses. We found out the horses listened to me. At first I did messy stuff like cleaning stalls and feeding the horses and picking out the horses hooves when they fought Old Frank. I did a whole lot of grooming but it paid off because I got to talking to the horses and they got to know me. At first I complained to the horses about my parents and my situation. Then I complained about the ranch work on top of my schoolwork. Then I talked about…things at the ranch. And when I got settled enough to think about the horses as much as everything else I talked to them about training. When I got to thinking about training I got ideas for how the horses would respond and my ideas started panning out. When I graduated Mr. Gordon even gave me a choice of going to college, but I figured I owed him. I wasn't going to take more than I had to and I'd found my niche so I stayed on at the ranch."

"Randy, you could have gone to college. Dad wouldn't have offered if he didn't think you should go. He wanted to help you live the life you wanted to, not the life he started for you."

"I know, but I chose a ranch life. I'll make do. Maybe I'll be Old Frank for your grandkids."

"You've got to know, though, you don't owe Dad anything. He's seen his investment pay off, whether it's time or money, whatever. You've earned your way. You've paid off in a thousand different ways and he's glad to see you on your feet. You can't let Dad tie you to the ranch. What if you meet a girl and she doesn't want to live that kind of life? What would you do? By tying yourself to the ranch you are narrowing your choices for the rest of your life. If you went to college it would open up whole new worlds for you."

"I got the life I chose. Only one thing would have made it better and it isn't going to happen, so I do the best I can."

Gulp, I knew what he was referring to. He *had* met a girl and she hadn't wanted a ranch life. And that girl was me.

"It's getting late," Randy finally said.

"Patrick is in the big tent. Which tent do you want?"

"I'd just as soon sleep by myself tonight," Randy said morosely. "Come on Patrick, you've got to visit the little boy's room before you go to bed."

I put out the fire as the flashlight beam bobbed its way over to the thicket. Patrick and Randy settled in their tents and then I went and found a little girl's room.

"How come you have the rifle in the tent?" Patrick asked when I came in and settled down.

"Just in case. I've never had to use it on a camping trip. I've had a few times when I wish I'd had a rifle though, so now that I have one I keep it handy."

"When did you wish you had one along?"

"One time a dog attacked me and bit my leg. I wished I had a rifle then."

"Are there dogs up here?"

"Not that I know of. Now let's go to sleep."

"I saw dog tracks when I was looking at deer tracks."

"Those were Shadow's tracks. When I got stuck in here with the Jeep he was with me. He likes to go exploring, too. Now don't worry about dogs."

I lay awake and finally I heard Randy's even breathing in the next tent. Patrick tossed and turned beside me, unaccustomed to the hard ground. I knew he would stay in the tent. He was just frightened enough being in the big outdoors to appreciate having an adult close by. I dozed off still feeling an occasional bump as Patrick squirmed around trying to find a comfortable spot.

Finally the squirming and tossing and turning stopped but I was now getting a different feeling from the small form beside me.

"Patrick," I said sleepily, "there's nothing out here that's going to hurt you."

"What does a dog sound like when it's quiet?" he asked nervously.

"You know what dogs sound like. They don't make much noise when they're quiet unless they are walking on dry leaves or something."

The horses nickered and stomped their feet. Leaves crunched underfoot. Too many leaves. From the wrong direction.

Chapter 11

"Maybe the deer are coming through," I said, trying to ease Patrick's fear, but I knew the deer were bedded down in the woods somewhere. They wouldn't be out late at night wandering around an old campground.

The horses were edgy. They whinnied and stomped and pulled on the end of their leads, nervously trying to put distance between themselves and whatever was approaching our camp. If it were just me I'd stay in the tent. No matter what was out there, it wasn't worth a confrontation. It would just sniff around or raid the Jeep and go on its way. I wasn't alone though; it was Patrick, Randy and the horses I was worried about.

As I was deciding whether to venture outside the tent the sounds changed dramatically. The sound of crunching leaves stopped and was suddenly replaced by crunching gravel and then a soft mechanical groaning noise as something pushed down on one end of the Jeep. I heard snuffling noises and then the horses went ballistic. They reared and whinnied and then there was a crashing sound as the horses pulled the Jeep into the rocks surrounding the parking spot. I grabbed the rifle and unzipped the tent in time to see a bear following the Jeep, jerking its way across the campground like a cat toy, only this was no cat. This bear wanted dinner and it smelled food inside the Jeep.

"Randy!" I yelled, switching on the big flashlight. "We've got a bear in camp and it's scaring the horses! Patrick, stay here! Whatever you do don't go near the bear or the Jeep! Even if the Jeep looks safe don't go near it. It's what the bear wants."

Randy was out of his tent faster than I thought possible. He was unarmed but charged the bear waving his arms and yelling, "Yahhhh, yahhhh," as though he was driving a herd of horses away. The bear took one look and ran towards the Jeep, which panicked the horses even more. They took off running, the Jeep bumping along behind them. Every once in a while I heard a crash as the Jeep hit another rock or stump. As I followed the ruckus I imagined the story I was going to have to tell my insurance company. There was a loud crash and then the Jeep stood still because the horses had run on opposite sides of a tree. I cringed as I imagined the impact on their heads. I hoped they weren't injured but I couldn't see how they would come out of this unscathed.

"Let the bear have the Jeep for now. Take care of the horses!" I yelled.

As we moved toward the Jeep to unclip the horses' leads the bear moved forward, its beady eyes gleaming amber in the flashlight beam.

"I'll cover you if you want to give it a try," I said.

"That thing looks like a toy," he said, referring to my rifle. "Will it take down a bear? What are you shooting?"

"Forty-fives."

"You know how to shoot a bear with a forty-five?"

"In the dark? With only half an idea of where it is?"

"You're not helping much."

"Okay, then you cover me," I said, handing him the rifle. "Don't shoot unless you absolutely have to. I've been six feet from a charging bear and still didn't shoot. Don't panic."

I snuck around the Jeep and peered over the hood. The bear smacked the side of the Jeep with its huge paw as if to say, "My Jeep!" Then it proceeded to tear a large hole in the canvas top. I reached for a lead rope, followed it down to the bumper and shined the flashlight beam on the clip. The bear eyed me warily and faked a charge. I jumped behind the Jeep and Randy tensed. I snuck around again and unclipped the lead. The frightened horse reared, lifting me off the ground. I grabbed the rope with both hands and pulled him in, then led the horse to a distant tree. I could tell by the sound of its movements that it was Mack and he had a sore leg. I clipped the rope around the trunk of the tree and went back for Shasta. He was on the side of the Jeep closer to the bear. I followed the flashlight beam back to the Jeep and found the other lead rope. The bear threatened me, charging a little. He stopped just short, afraid to get too close to a person. I froze, then relaxed as he turned his attention back to the Jeep. Every time I approached the vehicle he charged. When I backed off he went back to his investigation. Finally I decided to ignore his threats and nervously took the time to unclip the lead rope. The bear charged to within several feet of me and I raised my hands and yelled at the bear. Randy's hands tensed and the rifle shook as the inevitable questions bounced around in his mind. How late was too late? How close should he let the bear get? Shasta bucked and snorted. The bear stopped and backed off a step. He wasn't mad enough to take a risk yet. Pesky humans. Why couldn't they let a bear eat in peace? I led Shasta away from the Jeep and the bear while Randy followed in the dark.

"Go get Patrick. He's probably scared to death," Randy told me.

I picked my way back to camp.

"Patrick?" I called as I neared the tents. "It's okay. You can come out now."

"I don't want to," came his muffled voice from underneath several layers of covers.

I unzipped the door and crawled into the tent. I found Patrick buried as much as could be beneath two down sleeping bags.

"Yahhhh," we heard in the distance. "The food's in the Jeep, you stupid bear!"

"It's okay, really. The bear is just looking for a snack. The worst that can happen is he steals all our food."

"No it's not. I'll come out when you know the horses are all right. I'm scared for the horses. Steve shot a horse because it couldn't walk. He killed it! I can't stand to see a horse get shot. If I hear a shot I'm gonna cry and if I'm gonna cry it's not going to be in front of Randy."

"I won't let him shoot either of the horses," I told Pat but the sharp crack of a shot split the air sending Patrick diving deeper under the covers.

"Pat, you don't know what that shot was. Randy was probably trying to scare the bear away. Are you sure you'll be okay here? Can I trust you to stay if I leave you? I can't be worrying about where you are. If I go help Randy I need to know you'll stay here."

"I'll stay here," he promised.

Reluctantly I left the tent and went back to help Randy.

"What was that shot?" I called as I approached.

"Warning shot," he answered.

"Patrick won't come out," I said quietly. "He's afraid you're going to shoot one of the horses."

"I might shoot me a bear, but I won't shoot a horse, least ways not till morning when I get a proper look."

We shined the flashlight up and down the horses' legs and saw that Mack had a couple of gashes from hitting his legs on tree branches. Randy wasn't sure about Shasta's knee. He'd have to check it in the morning when there was better light.

"Why don't you go get some sleep while I guard the horses? I don't think it's a good idea to walk them any farther than we have to until we know the condition of their legs," Randy said.

"There's no way I could sleep with you out here and that bear roaming around. You go sleep and I'll guard the horses."

"You expect me to leave you out here?" he asked.

"There's no use in both of us being out here," I pointed out. "I could take down that bear if I had to. I just have a slightly different version of *have to* than some people."

"Look, you and I both know I can't go home and tell your Dad I let you take first watch with a bear tearing up your Jeep. He's going to be ticked enough that the horses got hurt. I'm not going to add insult to injury, so go back to camp. At least you can talk to Patrick."

"Okay, but I'm going to be back in a few hours and I expect you to let me take over. Deal?"

"Deal."

I aimed the flashlight on the tents to point myself in the right direction and then handed the flashlight over to Randy. I felt my way towards camp and finally brushed gently up against tent fabric. I felt the tent to be sure it was the right one, then unzipped the door and crawled in.

"It's okay, Patrick. Did you hear Randy? He promised he wouldn't do anything to the horses until he could look them over in the daylight and I won't let him shoot them. I'll let them stay at my house if they need doctoring. I can fix up the barn and they will be fine at my house if they need to stay."

"Where's Randy?"

"He's guarding the horses. We didn't want to walk them through the woods in the dark. We were afraid they might hurt themselves more so he's staying with them for now. I'll take over in a little while. Let me have a sleeping bag. Are you warm enough?"

"Yeah."

"Okay, let's go to sleep. Just relax. Let the warmth relax you and try to get back to sleep."

"How are you going to know when to switch with Randy?"

"Timed sleep is another thing I learned in the military. I've got a good feel for how long two hours is. I bet the bear is long gone in two hours."

We settled down and I dozed off quickly, knowing it was going to be a very short night for me and a long watch afterwards.

After awakening I was happy to note it was still dark and Patrick was sound asleep. I pulled on my shoes and quietly slipped out of the tent. I headed in the right direction and after a short while I asked Randy to say something so I could find him.

"Over here," he said and turned on the flashlight.

I headed for the light.

"Do you think there will be any food left?" he asked.

"Well, last time a bear ate my food it only ate the things that were loose or in paper wrappers. She ate my oatmeal, hot chocolate, trail mix and beef jerky but she left the backpacker food that was in foil pouches. We'll just have to see about this guy. Go get some sleep. I haven't heard any yelling or shooting so he must be settling down some. I'll be fine."

"I don't trust you," Randy said. "If I leave you're going to try and stalk it or something. I can just see it now, you telling your dad you touched a wild bear."

"I won't stalk it. I hadn't even thought about that until you mentioned it. I prefer to keep my arms and legs. Now go get some sleep and use the big tent so Patrick won't wake up and get scared."

Randy shined the flashlight towards the camp and then started tromping off in the right direction. A few minutes later I heard cussing, then, "Cassidy? Show me where the stupid tent is again!"

I shined the light on the tent until I heard a distant, "Okay," coming back from camp.

Compared to the watches I'd kept in the military this one was actually very entertaining. At least the bear made digging and snuffling noises. I didn't hear any ripping, tearing or metal bending sounds so there was some hope for my Jeep, too. I knew the canvas top was a loss but that could easily be replaced. When the bear got tired of digging for his grub he started looking for a way out. I wished I had a movie camera as I watched, in the beam of the flashlight while the bear pushed and shoved gently against the canvas top. Each time it resisted he turned and poked at another spot as though he was wondering, "I know there was a door around here somewhere!" Seeing the bear inside my Jeep was like watching a clown car in a circus and wondering what would be popping out. I certainly never expected a whole black bear to fit inside my Jeep. When he finally found the hole he had entered through he was bent in half like a big fat, horseshoe. He pawed his way forward and gradually his back end twisted around, ripping big gashes in the back seats. When all of him was facing in the same direction he tumbled out from the hole in the canvas and waddled off into the woods. I breathed a sigh of relief and kept up my watch. Had I been able to move the horses closer to the tents I could have gone back to bed but I didn't want to walk the horses until Randy had looked them over in broad daylight.

As the night wore on and the bear stayed away I opened the door and took inventory of the contents of my Jeep. In a way I was thankful the bear had easy access to the food. Had the harnesses been in the way the bear might have tasted those first rendering them useless. I started three piles: a trash pile, an eat pile, and a keep pile. My main goal was to find enough food in the Jeep to last the next day. I was relieved to discover we still had water, however food was another matter. It took a lot of digging and sorting to find ample supplies for the next day. At least I hoped it would be enough. Three backpacker meals, powdered eggs and one bar of astronaut ice cream that had been in the floorboards for who knows how long. I'd save that treat for Patrick. He'd get a kick out of freeze dried ice cream. The trash bag was filling up fast and the pile of stuff to keep was only things that the bear hadn't been interested in or had not been in the way of more important things.

As the sun came up I looked over the horses. Mack did, indeed, have a sore leg. We'd have to take it slow walking him out. I couldn't see anything really wrong with Shasta's knee. I felt it and it didn't feel hot or swollen but I trusted Randy's opinion more than my own. I talked to the horses and petted them. When the sun was up I walked over to camp and rattled the tent.

"Randy? Wake up. It's morning. If you'll tend to the horses I'll make breakfast."

He crawled out of the tent still sleepy.

"You let me sleep the rest of the night? I was supposed to take another watch," he said.

"No you weren't. I was fine out there. It was actually kind of fun. The bear put on quite a show but he's gone now. The horses don't look as bad as we feared but I don't think Mack will be able to pull the Jeep. We'll have to walk him out. Supplies are low, but we'll get by. Rusty will meet us at the trailer."

As Randy tended to the horses I packed up the small tent. I saw him off in the distance walking Mack around watching the horse's legs while he walked. He led Mack over and tied him to a nearby tree.

"He's lame but I think if we take it easy we can get him out of here."

He left Mack with a flake of hay and went back for Shasta. I started up the little camp stove and began making powdered eggs. When they were halfway cooked I woke up Patrick.

"Hey, Pat, it's morning. The bear is gone. Breakfast is almost ready."

"The horses. Are the horses okay? Where's Randy?"

"Randy's tending to the horses. Mack's got a few cuts that will have to mend but he'll be okay. He's looking over Shasta now."

Patrick was out of bed lickety split. He looked around camp then tracked the Jeep across the campground. By the time he got there he'd have a good idea of what had happened.

"Oooh cool! Aunt Cassidy! Lookit the bear tracks! That is so cool! It looks big! I wish I wasn't so scared. I wish I saw it!"

"We barely saw it in the dark, anyway. We just saw its eyes," I called after him. I wished I could have gone with him but we needed to get going and there were eggs cooking.

"These eggs taste weird," Patrick observed.

"They're freeze dried and reconstituted. You get used to it when you've been backpacking a little."

The guys ate while I stuffed sleeping bags and packed up the big tent. I washed up the pan and packed up the stove, nesting it neatly inside the pan and strapping it all together with a little tie-down. When Randy and Patrick had eaten I washed the few dishes that were left and finished packing up camp. While I was heading to the Jeep with an armload of camping gear Randy confronted me, asking, "Cass, what did you have for breakfast?"

"We only had the eggs and three backpacker meals. That forces us to stop and cook lunch. We better get moving."

"You didn't answer my question," he pointed out.

"I'll be fine until lunch," I answered.

"So you let us eat all the eggs without getting any?"

"It's okay. I'm used to getting along on trips like this. It's only a day. When I hiked out of here alone it was two days with no food. Missing one meal is not going to hurt me."

"Damn, fool, girl. How does that make me feel? Like a heel."

"Randy, it's okay, really. Come on, we need to figure out how to get this Jeep on the road and out of here. It's going to be a slow walk. When we had two fit horses I thought we could make it out of here in good time. Now I am just hoping to get past the washed out parts of the road. What should we do if Mack can't make it? Should we split up?"

"We'll cross that bridge when we come to it," Randy answered.

As we stood there surveying the damage to the Jeep, Patrick said, "Your Jeep is never gonna be the same again."

"It's okay, Pat. What isn't fixable will become experience marks. Every Jeep needs a few experience marks to show it's had adventures."

"This one had a doozie," Pat said.

Randy harnessed up Shasta and attached the lines to a crossbeam. He attached towropes to the crossbeam and then to the back bumper of the Jeep.

"Cassidy, you steer and brake the Jeep. Keep the lines taut but don't brake so much that Shasta has to fight it. Patrick, you can ride in the Jeep or you can ride Shasta. I'm going to lead Shasta and keep an eye on Mack. If things are going easy for Shasta I might ride a little. If Mack and Shasta are both doing good maybe we can pick up the pace a little. First things first, we have to get the Jeep onto the road."

Randy guided Shasta and he gradually pulled the Jeep backwards and away from the tree. When the Jeep was well away from the tree he disconnected the towropes and reconnected them to the front bumper and we were able to move forward. He clipped Mack's lead rope to the roll bar of the Jeep and we slowly made our way through the abandoned campground and to the washed out road leading to civilization. It was mostly a long boring walk out but in a few straight stretches Randy increased the pace to a trot while keeping a careful watch on Mack. The washed out areas were very difficult and slow to cross. We untied Mack and walked him across the gap first, then eased Shasta and the Jeep over it. The wheels got hung up in the rivulets and Shasta had to use some muscle to pull the Jeep up over one set. Then it would slip down into the next. Randy urged Shasta slowly forward and the Jeep continued to lurch its way over the rough spots. Each ridge was a chore to cross over and Randy and I ended up pushing the Jeep to give it some extra leverage. We used a branch to try pushing the wheel up and over an extra high bump. When we'd crossed the washout we stopped and let Shasta rest. It was going to be a long, tiring day.

This was work for Shasta, not because of the labor involved but because he was cooped up all day. It would have been like giving me a desk job. Randy sensed this in him, too, so in the straight stretches he let Shasta trot.

Patrick was soon bored. He switched from riding in the Jeep to riding Shasta. Whenever we were stuck he'd spend time looking for birds and tracks. When he was in the Jeep he pressed me for more stories by asking questions about Rusty's family and Chase. Since Christmas Patrick had spoken to Chase more often than I had, which didn't surprise me at all. Chase had given Patrick his phone number and told him to call if he ever had questions about tracking.

"So, what did you ask Chase when you called him?" I asked.

"I talked to him for a long time. I asked him if he thought foxes would come near the house because I found red fur in the weeds. All the dogs have black or white or tan fur. None of them have fuzzy red fur. And he told me to look for other signs of foxes but I couldn't find any tracks. There was too much grass. And we got to talking about the ranch. He was glad Mom gave me more places to track and he told me things I could do around the ranch that would teach me more. Oh and he asked if any neighbors had a chow dog because a chow would have red, fuzzy fur. And he asked me a funny question. He asked if I knew how Indians track. But I don't even know how I track except I lose the trail easy and I can't do it very far. He was talking like an Indian had taught him how to track but he didn't say why. I thought it was cool and I started pretending I was an Indian tracker. That was fun. It makes me try and think how an Indian would think. Do you think Mr. Chase is crazy?"

I laughed. "No, Chase isn't crazy. He might be a little eccentric but he's not crazy, and I think he really did learn how to track from an Indian. I've seen pictures in his house and they show him with two older men: a man that looks like he could be Chase's dad or grandfather and an Indian man. It was obvious that Chase treasured those memories because those were the only pictures I saw on his walls."

From time to time I applied the brakes if the Jeep crept up on Shasta. The miles slowly inched by and I found myself thinking that next time I'd prefer to hike it again rather than sit in the Jeep and creep along at three miles an hour. We stopped for lunch and I fired up the stove again. The guys were given a choice: goulash, chicken and rice, or mac and cheese. Patrick chose mac and cheese and we were glad to let him have it. Randy and I split the goulash and hoped we wouldn't need to cook the chicken and rice. Randy refused to eat until I had dished some up for myself. I spread it around on my plate so it would look like more than it really was and then I handed the pouch over to him. Randy ate the rest of the goulash and the macaroni and cheese that Patrick had not finished. We washed up the few dishes we had used and then started on our way again, bumping and rolling over the rough road.

As the sun began to set I wondered what to do since Rusty would start worrying if we didn't appear soon. I especially didn't want him to start down this road in the Explorer.

"Ride ahead and see how far it is," Randy told me. "If it isn't far we'll keep on. If it's more than a mile we should make camp."

"We don't have enough food to make camp," I countered.

"We do if we have to," he said.

Shasta was ready to be loosed from the harness and I was weary from the confines of the Jeep so I put my heels to Shasta and let him stretch. He loped down the dirt road until I spotted the first washout. It wouldn't do to hit one of those too fast and I sure didn't want Shasta lame too.

I found another area in the road that was also washed out and it seemed to be the worse one yet. It would take a lot of patience to get over that particular washout and I feared we might be stuck for the night but I rode on anyway. Maybe, just maybe, the trailer was close.

When I finally saw the trailer I was relieved to also see the blue Explorer sitting on the road beside it. Rusty was here! Aware of the road conditions at the intersection, Shasta and I raced forward. I leapt out of the saddle and caught Rusty just as he was getting out of the SUV. I was home! As long as he was there I was home. I was even more determined to get out of these mountains tonight.

"Oh Rusty, I wish there had been time to miss you, but it's been a mess. We need your help."

Kelly got out from the passenger side of the Explorer.

"You know we'll do anything we can. What's going on?" he asked.

After enjoying my Rusty hug I set to work. I wanted to take the trailer to the washout. I knew it would make it that far.

"We need to take the trailer down the road. Will you drive it down there while I go back and tell Randy we can make it? He thinks we need to stop for the night but he doesn't know how close we are. Just stop as soon as the road looks washed out and then turn the rig around so we can load the horses easily. It's about half a mile. It's been slow going because Mack is lame and we can't leave him behind."

We talked while I turned the ranch truck around and backed it up to the trailer.

"How'd Mack get lame?"

"It's a long story," I said, trying to pull the trailer hitch over the ball.

"Cassidy, you don't have to do everything yourself. Just tell me what needs to be done."

I dropped the hitch over the ball.

"Is that how it goes? I've never hooked a trailer up before."

"Looks good to me," Kelly said.

"Will you drive the truck down to the washout?" I asked. "Just wait for us there."

"Why don't you drive down and I'll go help Randy," Rusty said.

"The washout's the worst part of it. We've already done three of them and this one is the worst. That's where we'll need the muscle. Besides, you hate riding."

"I don't!" Kelly said. "I haven't ridden a horse in years, but I'll ride down and help Randy and let you two visit."

"Are you sure?" I asked, not sure of Kelly's riding abilities.

"Heck, yeah, I used to love horseback riding."

Rusty grasped me in a hug and told Kelly, "Yeah, go on."

"Just watch for the wash out. Let Shasta pick his own way over it."

As Kelly disappeared down the road Rusty turned me around to face him and kissed me deeply. Then he held me out where he could take a good look at me.

"You run into trouble?"

"It ran into us this time. We may end up keeping the horses for a few weeks. Mack needs some quiet time to heal."

"How'd he get hurt? Is Randy okay?"

"Yeah, Randy's fine. Maybe hungry, but fine. A bear scared the horses and they took off through the woods in the middle of the night. Mack got banged up running into tree branches. The Jeep's a mess. The bear went after the food in the Jeep and the horses were tied to it."

The mental image made Rusty smile and cringe at the same time.

"Wait'l you see the washout. Then you can see what we've been dealing with and why we had to use horses."

"The road gets worse?"

I laughed. "Yeah, it gets much worse. That's what Jeeps are for. I would have gotten out, too, except for the stupid mice."

Rusty and I drove the ranch truck and the trailer down to the wash out then turned it around so it would be ready to head for home. Rusty looked at the road and shook his head.

"Cass, you took the Jeep over all that?"

"Yeah, why?"

"I'm liking the idea of that little sports car more and more."

"Not when you see the Jeep," I said hesitantly. "It wouldn't make much of a trade with the state it's in. Besides, I like it. It suits me."

When at last we saw the procession heading up the road Rusty and I left the truck and walked down to meet them. Randy took one look at the washed out road and groaned. "Cassidy," he scolded, "next time you get it into your head to go exploring stick to the pavement!"

"We'll get it over, don't worry, we've got help now. This is the last rough spot. We'll go home, get cleaned up, and have a real meal. Kelly, if the forest service ever opens up that campground I think the place should be named Starvation Valley Campground. Every time I go there I end up hungry."

"What happened this time?"

"You saw my Jeep?"

"Yeah."

"Now imagine it with a black bear inside looking for a midnight snack and two panicky horses tied to the bumper."

The washout was so extensive we had to use the ranch truck to pull the Jeep through it. The harnesses and towrope wouldn't stretch across it and we didn't want Shasta to try and pull while he was navigating the rough ground. We pulled out the cable for the winch and hooked it to the truck and worked our way over the immense segment of washed out road. Kelly was willing to handle the Jeep while Randy drove the truck but I figured it was my job.

"Do you know what to do?" he asked.

"Yeah, if you'd seen the rest of the road you wouldn't ask. Use the brake to keep the cable tight but don't drag down the truck. Steer to miss the worst parts."

I pointed the Jeep at the shallowest ruts and rode it out until finally the Jeep was on the other side and we were able to tow it home with the Explorer. Kelly insisted on being brakeman for the tow job home. I rode with Rusty in the Explorer while Patrick rode with Randy in the ranch truck. Eventually we all made it home in one piece. Of course the term *in one piece* was relative as far as the Jeep was concerned.

"Cassidy, next time you decide to take on a task that is too big for you, would you, please, say something?"

"Okay, if I come up with one I'll say something."

Rusty glared at me and said, "You shouldn't have tried to take this on by yourself."

"I didn't. Randy helped me and we did it together."

"You worked yourself to the bone just to get that Jeep out of the woods. You didn't have to do all that. If I'd known how big the job was I'd have put a stop to it."

"I don't get to decide if a job is too big for me?"

Kelly snickered quietly to himself. He knew Rusty and I would never see my adventures and risks in the same light.

"I didn't say that."

"I told you what was involved in order to get the Jeep. So a bear came along and changed our plans a bit. That's just part of what makes life interesting. I'm sorry that Mack got hurt and my Jeep was all torn up, but I'm glad I got to see the bear. If you'd have gone instead then I would have been disappointed that I missed it. This was a two man job and Randy knew the horses. I knew the area and the Jeep and what we were up against. It made better sense for me to go and for you to stay home. So don't go getting all macho on me. We did what we had to."

Rusty joined Kelly in his mirth.

"Patrick, you need a bath before dinner."

"Aw, Aunt Cassidy!"

"Do you want to take a shower instead?"

"I can't, I'm too little. I stand in the shower and the water goes all around me but hardly any of it hits me."

"What if I had a different kind of shower? Would you then? You can put the water wherever you want."

He looked at me skeptically so I showed him our shower with its two showerheads.

"See? You can spray the water wherever you need it."

I should have taken note of the mischievous glint in his eye. He showered for a long time. I figured he was enjoying the water and if he spent enough time playing he'd eventually get cleaner. I know he didn't mean to, but while he was showering he didn't know when he pointed the showerhead up the water was going up and over the shower door. Patrick never noticed he had been soaking the entire bathroom floor. He realized that he was in trouble after wading out into a bathroom sized puddle. His clothes were soaked, the towels were soaked and he was naked, so he was unable to ask for help without being totally embarrassed. He wrapped a soaking wet towel around himself, dripped down the hall, peeked around the corner and into the den.

"Aunt Cassidy? I think I made a mistake," he said timidly.

There was Patrick, wet hair plastered over his forehead, water running down his face into the sodden towel, water dripping onto the carpet. "So," I asked Rusty, "is this job too big for me?"

He looked at Patrick, dripping and shivering from head to toe.

"No, this looks about your size."
"Gee thanks, I'm glad you have so much faith in me."

Chapter 12

Goodbyes have never been easy in my family and in a way Randy was family too. All the ranch hands were. They'd played the role of big brother to me ever since I was old enough to venture outside the ranch house. Randy may have joined the family later but he still felt like a brother to me, an adopted brother who slept in a bunkhouse.

"When can we count on a visit?" he asked, knowing my mom would be asking too.

"When Mack is fit," I answered. "I'll call the vet this morning and have him come by. Patrick, when you get home don't forget to check off black bear in your animal tracks book. Now you can tell Chase you tracked a bear. Be good and catch up on your school work."

"I will. I'm going to be in big trouble when I get home." Then he smiled and flashed a look with that same glint in his eye, the one that I needed to be wary of, and said, "But it was worth it."

"Maybe you can work on some of that make up work on the way home. Randy, thanks for your help. Sorry it turned out to be more difficult than we planned."

"It's okay, it was good to see you."

"It was good to see you, too."

I waved as the truck backed out of the driveway and headed down Lost Hills Road. It looked odd to see the ranch truck driving away without the trailer. I had horses. Two horses. There was a part of me that thought I was totally nuts for keeping them while the other half was jumping with glee.

The next day found me cleaning out the barn. I had been using it as a woodworking shop to make agility equipment so I moved the woodworking tools to one side, then made the stalls on the other side useable. The weather was mild enough that the horses could stay outside but the vet had advised me to keep Mack in a smaller area so he would rest his left foreleg. He doctored the cuts and examined Shasta's knee before pronouncing him fit to ride. I felt guilty riding Shasta and leaving Mack behind. They were both working horses and Mack wanted to work too.

I called a tow truck, the driver was glad to make a run to my house for the Jeep. It was towed to a garage and work was started on the wiring. Rusty took me to town for a loner car and I found myself driving a white Ford Escort.

Every day I rode Shasta and checked Mack's cuts. The smaller cuts healed quickly and I soon decided he would heal better in the open air where he could socialize more. He watched me work in the yards and train Shadow on the agility course. He was fascinated by the deer, which didn't seem to mind the presence of horses in the corral.

In the mornings before Rusty left for work I could often catch him watching through the bay window in the bedroom as I looked after the horses. It felt comfortable taking care of them. I'd cared for horses as long as I could remember so having Shasta and Mack around felt like old times. I fell into a routine and everybody seemed happy and content and were thriving. It felt good.

When I saw the end of the horses' stay nearing I went to the feed store in town and bought grooming supplies. I had been brushing them daily but only because I'd found a brush in the trailer. I wanted them to shine when I brought them home to my father.

Driving into town had become a major event for me. If I went out I'd usually head into the hills. Trips to town were almost as infrequent as searches and it took a good reason for me to want to drive to town. Since it was already a major event I decided to do a little exploring on the way. There was a road I'd discovered a few months ago but I'd only driven a short distance down it. This time I continued driving past the burnt down house that had brought me to the road in the first place and I just kept going. One road led to another until I wasn't entirely sure where I was, but knew I wasn't lost. I knew I was between the foothills and Joshua Hills. If I headed north I would drop down into Joshua Hills. All I had to do was find a road heading north. However before I could find a road going the right direction I saw something curious that made me stop and double back. Driving past it at a normal speed I could see that the vehicle appeared to be abandoned so I did a U-turn and drove by it more slowly. It was a green Ford Tahoe. No license plates. I scanned the desert for people but saw no one.

I parked the loaner a good distance ahead of the SUV and walked back to it. If someone chased me back to my car I wanted to lead them away from the SUV. I kept the keys handy and stayed well away from the vehicle as I scanned for tracks. There had been two occupants in the vehicle when it had stopped. The tracks were old but not as old as the school shooting. I was guessing four days. The driver's tracks could have belonged to the shooter at the school but I wasn't going to bet money on it. All I could tell was they belonged to an average sized man. I'd have to see him to know if he was the man I'd seen that day at the school. The other person was male, too. Slighter build, longer feet, pronounced limp. The limp quickly caught my attention. It was not normal, but I couldn't decide what was different about it. I followed the tracks into the desert and decided I needed help. It wasn't wise to go tracking across wide open desert unarmed, particularly if I'd already shot the guy once before. He'd seen me at the school and he'd recognize me. Nope, I needed some official backup. I marked the shoulder of the road where I'd parked, just in case the SUV moved while I was gone. Then I drove home and quickly changed into my uniform. I brought my sidearm and rifle and then headed for the station. Rusty was just leaving the building when I pulled up and jumped out. He gave me a look of resignation. He didn't like that I was wearing the uniform. It usually meant Strict was calling me out on an apprehension and I was surprised he wasn't already on the phone to Strict as I crossed the parking lot. At least he was willing to hear me out first.

"You told me to come get help if a job was too big for me," I told him.

"Okay, what's too big for you?"

"We need to talk to Tom, too. He may not want to do anything but I think I need to at least follow the tracks and make sure it's nothing."

I led the way into the station right to Tom's office and knocked lightly. He answered the door, took in the uniform, and probably thought I'd been on ride alongs or out at the school with Carla again.

"What's up?"

"Green Ford Tahoe. Looks like the same one. The plates have been removed. No occupants. The tracks are about four days old but they might tell us something. I'm willing to read the tracks if you're interested in hearing what they have to say."

"No," he said flatly.

Rusty ran his fingers through his hair. He didn't like it but he knew they'd get more information out of the tracks if I read them.

"I think we ought to let her do it," Rusty said. "She'll know by the end of the trail if it's the people we're looking for. We can take the VIN number and see if it matches the plates."

Tom looked at Rusty and asked, "You're sure?"

"Have you ever seen Cassidy track?"

"No, but I've heard the stories."

"Now's your chance."

I knew Rusty wouldn't be allowed to go but I was still disappointed when Tom returned with two officers and no Rusty.

"Cassidy, this is Ben Tomlin and Raul Ramos."

I shook hands with both men. I knew Ben already. We'd met on the side of the road when my Jeep had gotten stuck in the desert. He had given me a lift into town and we'd worked together a time or two since then. Ben took in the uniform, sidearm, thought through the stories he'd heard, looked at Tom.

"Are you sure we want to do this?" Ben asked Tom.

"Michaels thinks we should."

Ben shrugged and said, "Okay, let's do it."

"Where are we going?" Tom asked, turning to me.

"Sage Brush Road."

"Got it?" Tom asked the officers.

"Where on Sage Brush? That road's twenty miles long."

"Where the green Ford Tahoe is parked. If it's gone I've got a marker on the side of the road."

"Will we recognize it?"

"No, but I will."

"Great."

When we were in Tom's unmarked car he asked me, "Does this have something to do with the shooting?"

"I don't know. There's only one way to find out and I knew I'd be in trouble if I tracked this alone, unarmed, no matter how it turned out. Actually I was hoping Rusty would just go with me to take a look. But it's your case so you get to call the shots."

"Thanks. I think," he said.

I let him head for Sage Brush Road until we got close and then I directed him in the right direction. The SUV was still there. Even before we left the car I told him, "The man that got out on the driver's side was about the right height and weight to be the shooter from the school. He doesn't walk like he's wounded but I didn't track him very far yet. I could change my mind. The other guy is shorter, lighter. The tracks are worn so they aren't going to yield a lot of information. I'll tell you what I see. Take the profiling with a grain of salt. It often turns out I'm right but I don't have any real facts to base it on."

"Then why do you do it?"

"Because I'm right more often than not. It's harder the older the tracks are. As we look at the tracks around the vehicle it's just typical getting out of the car tracks. The bigger guy steps out just like anybody would step out of an SUV, left foot first. No big hints there. The other guy, though, has a limp. See? His left foot is on the ground a shorter time than his right foot and the right foot gives an extra push with each step. Can you see that?"

"Uh, no."

"Well, see the normal looking print?"

"Yeah. I see a footprint."

"Now compare it to the other one. See the extra little bulge in the dirt? He pushes off harder with his right foot and eases over with the left foot. It's not like he's in pain. It's more like an old injury that didn't quite heal right."

"You see that, and we haven't even left the vehicle yet?"

"Yeah."

"How would it look if he were in pain?"

"Well, after four days it would look a lot the way it does now. With fresher tracks, the edges would be sharper. A new pain causes a sharp reaction and that shows up easily. That's one reason I think this is an old injury. Something this guy is used to."

"Are we through with the SUV?" Tom asked me.

"Yeah, I can't see that they got anything out of the back. There's nothing to indicate they did anything besides get out and head off into the desert."

He spoke to the officers and they went to work but I paid little attention to them. My focus was on the tracks. I followed the tracks into the desert where they faded down to nothing. Near the SUV the shoulder had been soft. A ridge of dirt and lots of brush had sheltered the tracks from the wind. Out in the desert the tracks were more exposed and eroded. It made my job tougher but in a way I liked it. I enjoyed a challenge and I enjoyed seeing tracks where the guys couldn't. After a while Tom grew skeptical.

"Cassidy, are you…"

"Yep. Look." I pointed to the ground and outlined a track. I drew a line down the outside of it pointing in the direction where it appeared to be going, then added a line slightly off from that showing the direction the track leaned. I then found a track slightly off from straight ahead and traced it for Tom.

"Okay, sorry."

The trail didn't lead us far, at first. It led perhaps half a mile and then turned in the desert and headed directly toward a plowed field. An odd thing that happens out in the high desert is that you can drive for miles and see nothing but sand and sage, Joshua trees and mesquite. Then all of a sudden there will be a bright green patch of alfalfa or carrots or onions anywhere from four to a couple hundred square acres. This field had been plowed but it wasn't green yet. A red ATV sat on the far side of the field and a lone man was arranging the pipes to irrigate the field. I still had my eye on the tracks. The soil on the edges of the field was soft. The tires of the ATV were caked with it. The ATV had obliterated many of the tracks I was following but I read aloud what I could to Tom.

"The two men came to this field for a reason. They paced back and forth here in some excitement. A group of men faced them. To me it looks like the two groups are arguing."

"What's the difference between walking or standing footprints and arguing footprints?'

"Well, think about your feet right now. They aren't still, even though we're just standing around talking. They shift around and move. You step slightly one way or the other, because standing perfectly still is uncomfortable. The more agitated people get the more active their feet become. They tend to lean forward if they are yelling. If they get very agitated they might pace back and forth or take a step towards the person they are addressing in anger. An argument looks very much like a conversation except more so. More movement, more pacing, sharper movements."

"I see."

"Talk to the worker. Ask him what happened here four days ago. See what he says. Show him McPherson's picture. See if he recognizes him."

"I don't have a picture of McPherson yet. But I'll talk to the guy."

"I'm going to figure out where the tracks went. Where did these guys go if they didn't return to the SUV and why didn't they?"

Tom went to talk to the farm worker and I followed the escalating argument. They stayed in one place for a little while, enough to leave plenty of footprints, then the group they were talking to would back off and the two men would follow them, not venturing into the field but still staying within hailing distance on the outskirts of the field. There was a small skirmish where I imagined a lot of yelling with some pushing and shoving. I didn't see evidence of a man down but the tracks dug in like a person resisting a push.

Tom called Raul over to translate the worker's Spanish for him while Ben followed me. The tracks led me around the side of the field and I discovered a road that led past the field to a house in the distance. More footprints joined the dispute. I knew those footprints. I looked at Ben's footprints. They were officers' footprints. The men hadn't returned to the SUV because they'd been hauled off for questioning. They had never been connected to the green SUV and apparently preferred it remain that way.

After much discussion Tom came my way.

"Don't tell me," I said, "the men were working in the field and two crazy gringos came up and started yelling at them. A group of the workers came over to talk to the men and an argument resulted. The men tried to go back to work but they were just heckled by the two gringos. A shoving match started and someone called the cops. Four officers showed up, sorted it out and escorted our two gringos off for questioning."

"You know Spanish?" Ben asked.

"No, I read tracks. It's all here."

"Looks like our investigation continues back at the station," Tom said.

As we walked back to the cars I felt disappointed. Although I knew we wouldn't capture a suspect in this little venture I'd been hoping for something a little more concrete. Maybe it could lead to additional information. I knew, at least in my mind, the behavior of these men fit with the profile I had built up of the shooter. There was a common thread. I knew it. This man was the same one who had frightened Mrs. T. Whether or not this person was the shooter at the school was another question. I was almost sure he was the same man, but couldn't say why I felt this way. Just because Mrs. T thought the shooter was after her didn't mean he really was.

I needed to find out more about Mrs. T. But how could I do that? I couldn't question Mrs. T without interfering in Tom's investigation. But what about going in the back door? What about Ally? Maybe Ally knew her co-workers. What common ground could I find to contact Ally? And then I remembered...

Chapter 13

I called and left a message at the school the following day, and Ally called me back that evening.

"I was wondering if you'd like to visit a deer meadow with me," I asked her.

"A deer meadow? Of course! But I can't for a while because I've got company."

"They can come, too, if they want, but it involves hiking three miles. The first part is an easy hike on a shady trail. The second part is a one-mile climb up a rough canyon."

"Will there be deer?"

"I can't guarantee it, but if we don't find any there are lots of other things to explore."

"I'll ask Mai. Hold on."

Mai? That name sounded familiar. Wasn't Mai the foreign woman who was at the restaurant with Mrs. T?

"Okay," Ally said when she got back on the phone, "I think we are on. What day?"

"You're the one with a job. You choose."

"Is Saturday okay? Will your husband be going?"

"I don't know. I wasn't planning on it. Is Peter?"

"No, I think Peter would like a break from the language barrier. I guess I better warn you ahead of time that Mai doesn't speak much English. That's why she is staying with me. She can't depend on her native language. I don't know Vietnamese or Chinese so it's English all the way at my house."

"If Peter doesn't go then Rusty probably won't either."

"Where do you want to meet?"

"If you can come to my house we can continue on from here. It's in the foothills already. Maybe Mai has never seen horses. I have two of them here right now."

"Oh, how lovely! I haven't seen horses in years. You know, I was really horse crazy as a teenager. I whined and cried for a horse for most of my teen years but my parents would never let me have one. When you were talking to the class and said you grew up on a ranch I was so jealous."

I gave her my address and directions with a warning that it would look like she was going nowhere for a while. I also told her to watch for Rusty's blue Explorer.

"I have plans for Saturday," I announced that night at dinner. "You can come along if you like or you can stay home. It's not dangerous. There's no way for me to get in trouble. I'm just going hiking with two women in the canyon but we're not going as far as the hideout. We're just going to the waterfall and the clearing where the deer graze."

Rusty gave me an inquiring look, as if I hadn't told him enough information. "There's got to be more to it than that. You're up to something."

"Okay, I'm going with Alisondra and Mai."

"Mai? Where do we know that name from?"

"I think she is the lady who was with Kima Tumibay at the Asian restaurant and she's staying with Alisondra to brush up on her English."

"And you are doing this…why?"

"Because I know there is a link between Kima Tumibay and McPherson. I was hoping that Alisondra might talk if I asked her to visit a deer meadow with me. I didn't even know Mai was staying with her, but that's an added bonus. Maybe I can learn something about what's going on with Mrs. T."

"Why would Alisondra want to visit the clearing in the canyon?"

"She went camping at Elk Meadows because her last name means *deer meadow*. She and Peter went there to see a real deer meadow. When I spoke to her class she told the kids that's why she went camping that weekend."

"I don't like it."

"You can come with us if you want to."

"No, I think that would be counterproductive."

"If I could go on a weekday I would but Alisondra is a teacher and works five days a week."

"You're not camping? It's going to be a long hike in one day."

"I know, but we can rest and recharge in the canyon."

He knew I was not going to be dissuaded and it seemed harmless. Maybe I could learn something useful and I'd get my outdoors fix at the same time. Rusty resigned himself to a Saturday by himself, and said he'd probably go to work. I felt guilty.

Friday my Jeep was returned complete with brand new wiring. After setting mousetraps all over the garage I parked the Jeep inside. It still looked awful. The front bumper was bashed in, and it had big tears in the back seat with the springs showing through. The top was ripped, the frame was slightly bent and it looked as though the roll bar was slightly bent, too. It might have been like that before or maybe the bear had bent it during his scavenging. Scratches covered the side of the Jeep where Mack had been hitched. That must have been some heavy brush he pulled it through.

Ally and Mai arrived bright and early Saturday morning. Mai was wide-eyed, unsure about doing something for the first time.

"Let me feed the horses and I'll be ready to go," I said. I had purposely held off feeding the horses so Ally could see them. I led them out to the corral where Ally squealed in delight.

"Oh! Horses! They're beautiful!"

"The gray one is mine but he lives at my parents' ranch. His name is Shasta. The bay is Mack," I told them as I carried the hay through the open corral gate. Mai shrunk back seeing the open gate and the large animals. The horses headed for the hay.

"Too bad there aren't three of them. We could take horses to the deer meadow," Ally said.

"Well, Mack is here because he hurt his leg and needs to rest it. Shasta's keeping him company. Mack shouldn't be ridden yet, anyway. As soon as Mack has recovered enough he is going back to the ranch."

"Then why are they here?"

"It's a long story. Do you want to take the Jeep or Rusty's Explorer? The Jeep is mine, but the Explorer is more comfortable."

"The Jeep is fine," Ally said.

"Are you sure, it's a little beat up."

"It's fine. What's an adventure without a beat up Jeep?"

My feelings exactly.

"Oh my," she said when she saw my Jeep. "You weren't kidding. Looks like you met up with Jack the Ripper!"

"Actually it was a bear," I said.

"Inside your Jeep?" she exclaimed.

"Yeah, it's part of the long story."

"Bear?" Mai asked, then made a growly face and held up her hands like claws.

I laughed and said, "Yes, a bear."

"I can't wait to hear this. Why do interesting things only happen to other people?"

"Getting lost in the mountains wasn't interesting enough for you?" I asked as I tossed a backpack full of lunch into the Jeep.

"Oh, that was about as much adventure as I've ever experienced, but I've never had a bear in my car or seen deer in the wild."

"Maybe we can see some deer today," I said as I started up the Jeep.

Rusty came out of the house to see us off.

"No trouble," he said. "You see trouble, I want you to run from it. Got it?"

I smiled and replied, "Got it. You know where we're going. Just to the waterfall and clearing. I'll see you tonight."

As we headed down the road Ally pressed me for the story of the horses and the bear so I told it using short, simple sentences for Mai's sake. I was glad I got to do the talking on the drive because I was hoping Ally would want to talk while we were hiking. I wasn't sure how much Mai understood but she did stop me a few times to clarify things. Maybe she found it difficult to believe and thought she hadn't understood everything correctly. She wasn't alone; I find my life hard to believe at times, too.

Creekside Campground seemed greener than usual. Mai looked around the area as though we were already lost and we'd barely gotten out of the Jeep.

"The trail hike is fairly easy. We should make good time."

Mai made sure she had a memory card and fresh batteries in her camera and then she was ready to go. I shouldered our lunch while Ally put on her daypack. We were going to have a real feast if we both brought lunch. When Mai glanced at the trail I gave a nod indicating that's where we would be heading. She took a picture of the trailhead sign, then had Ally take a picture of her standing next to it. Mai smiled broadly and held up her fingers in a peace sign. As we hiked Mai pulled ahead with swift, careful steps and I began tracking her just out of habit. I'd never tracked anyone like her before and her mannerisms deserved cataloging in my brain.

"Stop when you get to the creek," I called ahead.

Mai turned back and asked, "Creek?"

"Water," clarified Ally. "Small river?"

"Ah, water, okay," she answered.

"So," I said as Mai pulled away from us again, "you're teaching Mai English?"

"Yes, it's something I've always enjoyed doing. She's one of Kim's projects. Oh, I shouldn't say that. That's what I call it, but she really does wonders with the people she helps. I enjoy learning about different cultures and so I spend some time with Kim's 'projects' if they have trouble leaving their native language behind. It's like working with the kids, really."

"Kim?"

"Kima is her Filipino name. Sometimes she Americanizes it. To me she is Kim."

"Have you two been working together long?"

"Oh, eight years or so. She thinks helping other foreigners is the least she can do because she was given a chance to become an American."

"So she helps others emigrate to the US?"

"Not just emigrate. She interviews several people before she finds someone who will be comfortable with her rules. They have to agree to learn English and study to become citizens. When they speak enough English she helps them enroll in school, if they need more education. Many do. Occasionally she will help someone who is already educated and they just need a place to stay while they learn the language or find a job. Mai has proven to be a handful. She's a wonderful girl, really, fun and interesting. But she is going through terrible culture shock. And her nationality doesn't help at all. That's another reason Mai is staying with me. Every time Kim gets a 'client' from a controversial country this guy shows up. I think he must have fought in every conflict from World War II to present. He seems to be against everybody except Americans."

"McPherson?"

Ally laughed then said, "Is that what you heard? I guess that's what it sounds like when Kim says it. What she really said was Matt Pearson."

I stopped, dumbfounded. I'd had the wrong name all along? If I could have called Rusty I'd have been on the phone that second, but I knew I couldn't call from the bottom of this canyon. I'd tried. I'd tried from the upper canyon where we were going, too, but there was no signal. After a moment of initial shock I caught up with the conversation again.

"Did Kim really think the shooter at the school was Matt Pearson?"

"Yeah, but it could have just been a natural reaction to his threats. He threatens a lot but he's never been violent before."

"Why would he shoot up a school just because he was mad at her?"

"Well, from what I heard, if she helped one of those blankety blank commies again she wouldn't live to finish the job. He doesn't seem to understand that people are people, that the common man has little to do with their government. He doesn't seem to recognize the end of the war or its consequences. He lives in the past. Actually what he believes and what Kim is trying to do are in agreement. He says that if people are going to come to the United States they should learn the language and become citizens. But he thinks foreigners are not a positive addition to the country unless they are willing to be American one hundred percent. I'd like to ask him how far back his own family emigrated here and what would have happened if a Matt Pearson were around then, to threaten them and drive them away."

None of this information surprised me. If anything it only reinforced what I had thought before, that one of the men I had tracked from the green SUV was the same person who had frightened Kima Tumibay. So far the only surprising thing was learning that I'd had the wrong name all this time.

"You must have a lot of patience. I don't think I'd have the patience to teach someone English."

"It's just a matter of talking. You'll see at lunch. I think Mai is staying ahead of us so she won't have to talk, but you'll see. By the time we stop she will have questions. If not, I have a couple handy. I bet she has never heard of a tracker before."

"No, probably not," I said.

For the whole hike I tracked Mai. She took very short, swift steps. She wore little canvas tennis shoes but I pictured someone in little grass flip flops when I saw her tracks. Her tracks resembled her personality: quick, sharp and timid.

The day was nice for hiking. It started out a little chilly, but we warmed up as we hiked. Mai stopped at the creek, unsure and then walked back and joined us. As she led us on and the creek came into view she asked, "This creek?"

"Yes," I said, "this is a creek, a small river."

"Yes, small small river," she answered. "Fish?" she asked, making a wiggling, swimming motion with her hand.

"No, sometimes the creek runs out of water so fish can't live here."

She nodded that she understood.

"Here's where we leave the trail," I told them. "We climb this canyon for one mile. We'll stop when we get to a waterfall."

"Ooo, a waterfall?" Mai asked, making a swooshing down motion with her hand.

"Yes, a small one, creek size."

She nodded again.

I led them up the easy way. There were still a few rocks to scramble up and we'd have to climb the rocks beside the waterfall but I thought they wouldn't have any problems with it.

Mai clapped her hands with glee when she saw the waterfall. She put her hands under the falling water and exclaimed that it was cold.

"The water is from melting snow," I explained. "That's why it's so cold."

I opened the pack and dug out lunch. I knew I was dealing with city folks so I'd brought a citified lunch. As we ate Mai had some questions.

"We see deer?" she asked.

"I hope so. When we leave this place we have to be very quiet so we don't scare them."

"We see bear?"

"No, bears do live around here but we won't see one today."

"How you know this place?"

"One of my favorite camping places is further up the canyon. When my first husband died I came here a lot when I was sad. In my sorrow I explored and I found many interesting things. I love the deer meadow."

"You marry two times?"

"Mai, it's impolite to pry."

"It's okay. My first husband died in a plane crash a few years ago. I married Rusty last July."

"Cassidy, I can't believe how much you've done at such a young age. You've been a Marine and gone to police academy. You've been married twice. Now you're a tracker."

"That's not even half of it," I laughed, glad she didn't know how much I had really been through. "When we leave here we have to be quiet. No talking. Walk quietly. Pretend you are hiding from the deer. Do you want to just see them or do you want me to try to stalk them?"

"What do you mean, stalk them?" Ally asked.

"Sneak up on them. See how close I can get. It's something I've done since I was a kid."

"Can we watch them for a little bit first?"

"Of course. It helps to let the deer get used to our presence before I start anyway."

I had seen fresh deer tracks in the canyon so I was confident there would be deer in the clearing. We packed up and as I led them away from the waterfall I gave them the hush sign.

We stalked forward. I showed them how to crouch and move through the brush without startling the deer. It wasn't far. The deer would already be alert for people because they had heard us talking during lunch, but perhaps if we approached quietly they would settle down.

We came upon the clearing as quietly as could be expected for a tracker with two city slicker women. They made their share of noise, but the deer were posed nicely when at last we peered over the brush to watch the small herd. Ally and Mai looked on in astonishment. I was glad I had discovered the deer's favorite place in my canyon. If the canyon felt safe to them one or two deer could be found in the meadow most of the time. But if the deer were on the move they arrived in the late afternoon. As far as I could see a person hadn't ventured up here in months, so the five deer felt safe. The three of us sat silently observing the deer but as a wild animal they were not the most thrilling species to watch. They are attractive, will eat, glance around and walk, but they don't hold one's attention for long. That's why I always enjoy stalking them. Then it becomes a bit of a challenge and it would give the other women something to watch besides a clearing full of deer. Finally Ally gave me a "Well, are you going to try it?" look, and I passed it on to Mai. Her eyes grew large and she shook her head no. I shot her a "Why?" look. She put her hands up to her head like antlers indicating that she was worried about the buck. I gave her a dismissive shrug, like it didn't matter. Ally was game; she motioned for me to move forward. I gave both women a hush sign and picked my way into the clearing on silent feet. I felt my way forward, eyes on the deer. If I felt a stick or unsure footing I shifted my foot until it was on quiet, solid ground. When I entered the clearing I crouched low. The meadow was small, so I was already within a hundred feet of the deer. It was a stalker's meadow, too. Eyes on the deer, feet feeling my way, I slowly crossed the meadow while the deer grazed. When they raised their heads I froze. When they grazed I inched forward. I quit wondering what the women thought of this activity. Mai probably thought I was risking life and limb, and Ally was probably planning her next camping trip so she could find deer and try stalking, too.

I chose a doe and began making my way her direction. I had selected her not because she seemed calmer than the others, but because heading for her brought me within the herd. I was having fun. It had been a long time since I'd visited my canyon and it was very tempting to continue up to the hideout and just stay the night. But I couldn't do that. I had promised to be back that evening and I also had to care for the horses. Plus I didn't want to reveal my hideout to Ally, who would probably drag Peter up here if she knew it existed.

The deer's heads jolted up suddenly, which left me wondering if I had gotten careless in my distraction. Stalking took concentration and I'd let mine lapse. I could stalk deer all day but we had done what we came to the meadow to do and it was a long hike back to the Jeep, so I decided to finish the stalk more quickly and began taking slight risks. When the deer grazed I crept forward more swiftly. When I was about twenty feet from the doe and well within the herd, the deer came to attention and began shying away. I relaxed, stood, and watched quietly as the deer trotted out of the clearing. Ally and Mai also stood and we watched as the deer continued on their way.

"I've got to try that just once before I die," Ally said.

"There's easier ways than coming all the way up here. If you want to try it in the comfort of home you can come to my house after school. I have deer that come to my yard late in the afternoons. They don't always show up but they do every few days. They are probably easier to stalk than these deer. They are more used to it. I brought you up here so you could see a deer meadow. My yard isn't exactly a deer meadow."

"I wonder," she said, "how much wonderful information you have in that head of yours. You know where deer are. You can walk right into a herd. You find people lost in the woods and find your way back by different routes. You amaze me."

Everything Ally was saying had become second nature to me. If there were deer around of course I would know them, and it only makes sense to know your way in the woods. I didn't really understand why that made me stand out.

We sat in the deer meadow talking. I picked at the grasses and began weaving a mat. I found a stalk of grass that was hollow, and when we got back to the creek I demonstrated how they could drink through it. To me it was a lazy afternoon of stalking and conversation. To them it was a fascinating day of hiking and observation and learning, finding new things to try. I wish I had more time with Ally. There was so much she would enjoy learning, so much I could pass on to her that would make her time in the woods more enjoyable. Then I thought about her natural curiosity and decided she would enjoy the woods no matter how much she knew. As we walked I pointed out small things to her. I identified birds and tracks while she talked about school.

Mai slowed down and joined us on the way back. "How long I stay your house?" she asked Ally.

"Kima agreed two weeks would be enough for you to begin your English. So one more week to go."

"I miss Kima, she good person. Patient. She speak good Chinese."

"And your English is improving," Ally told her.

Mai blushed.

Ally asked her, "Try identifying things you see."

Mai pointed at the trail. "Path," she said. "Tree, grass." She looked around. That's about all there was, the trail, trees and grass. "Sky," she continued. "Why no clouds in America?"

Ally laughed then said, "There are lots of clouds in America, they just don't come to Joshua Hills very often."

"If Matt Pearson is so against Mai emigrating, why does he go after Kim?" I asked Ally quietly.

"Kim is handy and it's an ongoing thing with her. Think of Kim like a drippy faucet. The effect of a drippy faucet is minimal, but it can drive you up the wall. One person emigrating doesn't bother Pearson. But one after another has grated on him over time."

"How does he even know about Kim and what she does?"

"He was leading a demonstration and Kim thought someone needed to stand up for the other side. It was not a good time to confront Pearson. He was already agitated, had spent hours working up bad attitudes in the other demonstrators, then Kim got in his face. I guess it was not a pretty picture. It landed him in jail."

That got my attention. If Matt Pearson had a record then Kima Tumibay had a legitimate reason to be frightened of him.

"I fear for Kima," Mai said quietly.

"Why?" I asked.

"How you say… while… correct? While I stay with Ally? Is correct?"

"Yes," Ally said, "while is correct."

"While I stay with Ally, Kima say she talk Matt Pearson. I fear for her."

"Did she talk to him already? Or is this something she is going to do?" I asked. This could be important.

"I not know, but I fear. Worry? Fear?"

"It's almost the same thing," Ally told her. "Look up the difference in your phrase book."

Mai pulled a book out of her pocket and looked up the two words to get their Chinese meaning. She looked up and said, "Yes, I both. Fear and worry."

"Don't worry," Ally said, "Kima has done this many times."

"Matt, he bad person. Kima think he change, but he is angry. A very angry man. Always Kima think she can help Matt. No person can help that man. His heart is... is..." she had to open her phrase book again. Finally she found the word. "Prejudice. Kima... even in love... he hate."

When the trail neared the creek I stopped to let the women rest.

"What do you think of the mountains in America?" I asked Mai.

"Mountains are... big... and dry. Vietnam more... how you say? Tropical? Much rain. Many plants. America is wide, so wide and very dry."

"Well, don't judge the whole country by Joshua Hills. Joshua Hills is about the driest place on the continent."

"You like these dry mountains?" Mai asked me.

"I like any mountains. I have to admit, mountains with more rainfall are easier to live in. I like forest. Trees and water. I like these mountains because I know them. I work here. These mountains are almost like home to me."

"You work... here? What you do?"

"I find lost people. If someone gets lost in the mountains I help find them."

"How people get lost? Follow trail, follow canyon. How get lost?"

I laughed then said, "I wonder that myself sometimes, but some people don't have a sense of direction like you do. Some people don't remember that they stopped at the creek and followed a canyon. So I go look for them when they get lost."

"Yeah, like me," Ally muttered to herself.

"Many people get lost?"

"Yeah, many. To find them requires tracking and good timing. These mountains are very dry. Most of them are not like the canyon we visited. Most canyons have no water. I have to find the people before they run out of water. In winter it's freezing here. I must find them before they freeze. In spring it's not so bad, more water. In summer it is even drier, much hotter, very dangerous for a lost person."

"You have danger in your job?"

No, not in my job, I thought, just my life in general.

"No," I told her, "I carry water and food. It isn't dangerous for me. I try to find people before the environment kills them."

"Environ…"

"The extreme hot or cold, the lack of water…"

"I loved seeing the deer," Ally said. "I always picture deer more serene than that."

"Serene?" Mai asked.

"Peaceful," Ally said.

"Ah, peaceful, yes."

"Deer have to be alert to survive," I said. "One of the reasons they are so hard to stalk is because they are cautious."

"How did you learn how to stalk?"

"It goes along with the tracking. If I track an animal it is only natural to see how close I can get. I've stalked animals as long as I can remember. I started out easy with horses and dogs and graduated to cats and rabbits, then deer, foxes and other animals that are cautious and wary of people."

"Can I see the horses again before I go home?" Ally asked.

"Of course. If it isn't too dark, maybe you can ride Shasta."

"Oh, could I? Let's get a move on!"

I laughed. "You can always come back another day."

"I don't know how long the horses will be around."

We hiked the rest of the way out. Hiking out was easier than hiking in, because it was all slightly downhill. We still had plenty of food to snack on as we walked. We arrived at the Jeep as the sun was setting and it was dark by the time we arrived home. Rusty opened the door for us grinning broadly. As I drew near he pulled me into a hug.

"Don't tell me you were worried," I said.

"No, I was just watching the time. I wouldn't start worrying for another hour or so. I've got these things worked out."

"It's barely dark and we had six miles to hike and deer to find. We had a very successful trip, no trouble. The hiking was easy. There were deer in the clearing. You should have come along."

"I found things to do."

"You went to work. There's always things to do at the station."

I knew he went to work because he was still wearing his work clothes.

"Ally wants to see the horses one more time before she goes home. I'm going to saddle Shasta."

The horses were ready to eat when we went out there, but if I fed them they would want to eat. Horses are not speedy eaters. It could take an hour for the horses to finish their hay. I knew Ally wouldn't last long in the saddle so I let her ride before I fed the horses. I saddled and bridled Shasta and then pulled myself into the saddle to make sure he was listening to commands.

"Do you know how to ride?" I asked Ally.

"Sort of."

I showed her how to direct the horse, how to make him go and stop. I showed her the walk, trot and canter. I knew she would only walk and trot a little so I gave her a turn.

"Oh, my! He's so big!" she exclaimed.

I lowered the stirrups for her because she was much taller than me.

"Would you like some help?" I asked, and she nodded yes.

I took hold of the bridle and led Shasta around the corral. Ally grasped the horn on the saddle and rode stiffly. After one lap of the corral I instructed her, "Now, let go of the saddle and relax. Riding is a matter of balance. If trotting is bumpy push up with your legs a little, and use your knees as shock absorbers." Then I led Shasta around again increasing my pace to a jog. Shasta went from a walk to a trot and Ally bounced in the saddle. Mai laughed at her.

"You're not posting," I called up to her.

"Posting is for English," she said.

"You're right, but it's also for saving your butt. Okay, one time around all by yourself," I said, letting go of the bridle. Shasta slowed to a walk and stopped. "Kick him with your heels," I told her. "Harder, you can't hurt him. Harder." Shasta started up again. "Turn him or he'll go to the fence and stop, turn him, turn him, there you go now give him a little kick…" I coached her all the way around the corral. When she got back I said, "Okay! Mai's turn?"

Mai backed away from the corral wide eyed with fear. "Oh, no!" she exclaimed.

"Oh, come on, it's easy!" Ally said. "I'll take your picture up there."

Ally had said the key word. Mai wanted a picture of everything she did. It was worth overcoming the fear to get the picture so she approached the horse reluctantly. I turned on the barn lights and the porch light so hopefully the picture would be bright enough. I showed Mai how to mount up, then adjusted the stirrups shorter again. She went through the motions of steering and stopping the horse.

"Left, right," she said as she reined one way, then the other. "Go," kick, "stop," pull back.

"Right!" I said, "so, make him go."

She gave Shasta a kick and he walked around the corral. I walked beside the bridle but Mai was doing well on her own. She kicked him again and he trotted. She bounced at first, then posted. When she was done I unsaddled Shasta and fed both horses. Mai grinned from ear to ear.

"I rode a horse!" she said, pleased with her day.

Rusty stood behind me and wrapped his arms around my waist as I waved to the two women. Ally backed out of the driveway and headed back to town.

"You had a successful hiking trip," Rusty repeated. "Is that successful as in you saw deer or successful in that you pried some information out of Ally?"

"I didn't pry. But, yes, both."

"Are you going to tell me about it?"

"The whole trip or just the facts?"

"Both, eventually."

"Well, I need to tell you just the facts first because Tom might want to jump on some of them. First of all, when Tom checked out McPherson did he also check out the variations of the name?"

"Of course, there's more than one way to spell McPherson."

"Did you try Matt Pearson?" I asked, annunciating the t and the p.

"Matt as in Matthew?"

"Yeah."

"I don't know. Is there more?"

"Matt Pearson has a record. He was arrested in connection with a demonstration having to do with illegal immigration. Kima Tumibay was supposed to meet with him sometime between a week ago and a week from now. I don't know if she already went but if you have trouble finding Pearson she might be a lead. Mai is afraid something will happen to Kima if she sees him, so it might not be a wise thing for her to do. Kima has received threats from Pearson but apparently he has threatened before, so nobody knows how seriously to take him. I don't know how helpful that will be, but that's where things stand as far as Ally, Mai and Kim go."

"You don't know what he got arrested for?"

"No, all I know is Kima confronted him at the demonstration and 'it wasn't a pretty picture' and resulted in him going to jail. Having Mai there made it easy to bring up Kima Tumibay. Ally described Mai as 'one of Kim's projects.' Then went on to explain what it is that Kim does."

"You're right, I think we should call Tom. Did you see any deer?"

"Yeah, we did. It didn't take them long to look at a herd of deer, though, so I gave them a little stalking demonstration."

"How did the canyon look?"

"I didn't go to the hideout, but the part from the trail to the waterfall looked deserted. Nobody had been up the canyon for months. I wonder if the hideout is still livable. After we take the horses back can we go camping and see?"

"We'll see," he said smiling, but there was a concerned look behind his smile. We called Tom.

Chapter 14

Tom and I were on stakeout at the elementary school Monday afternoon. I didn't like following Kima Tumibay. Tom had assured Rusty that's all we were going to do. Our job was to follow Kima home and watch her in case she tried to see Pearson.

Pearson's house had been under surveillance and it appeared no one came or went from it. Pearson, as it turned out, had done time for assault but had gotten off easy. The green SUV belonged to someone else who had been arrested at the same protest but never served any jail time over it. Tom described the demonstration to me. Ally was right, it wasn't a pretty picture. The two men had had altercations with the police off and on, similar to the one that had occurred at the field. I was pleased to see my facts were adding up and things were falling into place. All I needed now was the man, and to see if he really was the shooter at the school.

"She's really hard to catch after school. I tried once and she just kind of vanished."

"We'll see her."

"I hate tailing Kima because she hasn't done anything wrong," I said to Tom.

"If she won't snitch she deserves it. I could demand that she fork over everything she knows. I could drag her down to the station and put her under the lamp and threaten her cat."

"She has a cat?"

"Siamese."

"She does seem like a cat person."

"Name's Marikit."

"Pretty name. How do you know all this? Did you know about Mai?"

"Some. I talked to Kima but it just made her withdraw more. Do they always line up in the same place?"

"I've only been here for dismissal once, but a kid was able to direct me to Mrs. T's line easily."

"That's a good sign."

"There are the first classes," I said, pointing.

Tom nodded as Mrs. T's class lined up. We watched as she released each child to a parent, sent several to a waiting bus, and dismissed the rest of her students one at a time to parents with more children in tow. She smiled and chatted and complimented until the last child was gone, then she turned and walked back into the school building. We waited. And waited.

"Which car is hers?" I asked.

"Black Toyota."

I looked around. "Where?"

He looked around. Cars were leaving left and right. This wasn't staff parking. These were all parents leaving with their kids. Tom gave me a disgusted look and started the car. We inched into the traffic, took a right turn onto the street in front of the school, and pulled into staff parking. We drove up and down the parking lot until Tom found the black Toyota. He parked several cars down where we wouldn't be noticed. He turned his mirror so he could observe other directions and then, with a satisfied sigh, settled in to wait again. We hadn't lost her.

Kima left the school while the traffic was still heavy. She came out from the closest wing of the building, looked both ways, and then hurried to her car. She had keys in hand, with the right key ready before stepping out from the school. Kima unlocked her car, got in and locked the doors before she put her things down. As she was leaving the staff parking lot, she waved on several small cars letting them pull ahead of her. She then sandwiched herself between a soccer mom van and an old beat up Suburban. How could she suspect that she would be followed? Or had she been driving this way ever since Pearson had threatened her?

"Do you think she knows?" I asked as we pulled out to join the traffic jam leaving the parking lot.

"I don't know how she could."

Tom had plenty of experience tailing people in traffic. By the time we exited the parking lot Kima was many cars ahead of us but Tom had noted the direction she went and passed one car after another with swift dexterity. He caught up to Kima and followed with one car between us. She headed into town, went to a big box grocery store for staples, an Asian grocery store for more specialized ingredients, and stopped at the cheapest station in town for gas. She paid with cash. Each time Kima left her car she would glance around and each time she returned to her car she had keys in hand. I thought she was being extremely cautious. I could probably take some lessons from her, too. After filling her tank she drove home. Kima lived in an apartment complex consisting of many buildings. Each building had four apartments downstairs and four upstairs. She lived upstairs. She climbed the stairs and quickly entered her unit. Tom found a parking place where he could watch her door and we settled in again.

Nothing happened that first day. Kima drove home and didn't leave her apartment. As the week passed we began wondering if she had already gone to see Pearson. The weekend neared and it was time to take the horses back to the ranch. I was hoping and fearing Pearson would get caught while I was gone.

"Four days on stakeout and not one disaster," Rusty commented. "What does Tom do that I don't?"

"We've just been sitting in a car. How can you get in trouble just sitting in a car watching a building?"

"Believe me, it can happen, especially to you."

"Well, it's not likely to if we're going to the ranch. Tom will probably get all the action while we're gone."

For the past few days I had been riding Mack in the evenings and Rusty rode Shasta just to get used to the saddle. We went up into the hills to the clearing and although we always saw evidence of deer we never actually saw any. I was beginning to think these were the rare Mojave Desert Stealth Deer. Mack seemed to be moving well and his endurance was improving. It was a mile to the clearing and he'd performed well so I declared him fit for ranch work again. Randy would take a look at Mack when we arrived and work with him too.

"Are you sure you want to take the horses back?" Rusty asked.

I sighed. No, I wasn't sure, but it seemed to be what was best.

"I like having them here. I have to admit that. But they run my life. The whole time they've been here I've been worrying about a call from Strict and what I would do if I had to be out for more than a day."

"I would have fed them."

"I know, but in the long-term they require more care than just feeding. They need grooming, exercising, socializing, and training, not to mention shots and shoes. I don't know a good farrier and I don't have the equipment to do it myself."

"We could figure it out if you really want to keep them," he said, but he only wanted me to know that he was willing to do whatever would make me happy. I didn't need the horses to keep me content. The trouble was I was feeling more and more isolated up in the hills, not because of the location, but because so much had happened to fill up my life and then it all disappeared. I missed Patrick and I would miss the horses. But they weren't a part of my life. Patrick belonged with my sister and the horses belonged at the ranch. My life, while Rusty was at work, was feeling very… small. I was never one to live a small life, but I didn't want to leave Rusty behind in my pursuit of more adventure. In some ways the horses had helped and in other ways they'd hindered.

"Thanks," I told him, "but I think the horses will be better off at the ranch."

I went outside and started bathing and preparing the horses for their trip home. As I groomed them I already found myself missing them. Once they were dry and brushed and shining again I climbed up on Shasta's bare back and lay there hugging his big, strong neck. When his mane tickled my nose I rubbed my face and realized my hand was wet with tears.

I woke up in the middle of the night still feeling sad and went to the bay window. I looked out at the horses but they were still, just sleeping. I crawled back into bed and snuggled close to Rusty. He took me in his arms. I should have known I couldn't get up without waking him.

"You can still keep them," he said softly into my hair.

I shook my head "no" because I was too choked up to talk.

"You *can* keep them. Your dad would let you."

I just burrowed deeper and he held me until I felt sleepy again.

"I love you, babe. Please don't do things that make you sad."

In the morning it was my responsibility to load the horses as Rusty didn't know how. They weren't making the job easy either. I knew they didn't want to be trapped in the trailer and I didn't blame them but it still had to be done. Rusty watched nervously while I wrestled animals ten times my size. When they were finally settled I loaded the tack and the few bales of hay that were left. Rusty would have done it for me but it felt as though it should be my job. I wanted this decision to be final in my mind and going through the motions, however difficult, helped the whole process feel more natural to me. Rusty brought out the suitcase, Shadow jumped in the back seat and we were ready to go.

The ride to the ranch was too quiet. I was so wrapped up in my sadness I couldn't think of anything to talk about. I sat there feeling more tense with each passing mile until I finally asked Rusty for some music. I tried scooting close to him but the console was in the way. When I pulled my feet up into the seat and sat curled up in a little ball, Rusty knew I was in trouble. Sadness was flooding through me but I wouldn't back down. I'd just have to get over it. Our house was going to feel empty and once again I would have way too much time on my hands. Rusty didn't have any solutions so he did something he very rarely did in front of me. He began singing, just along with the stereo, but it took me by surprise. The only other time I'd heard him sing was when he thought I was sleeping and wouldn't hear him. Listening to his voice I began feeling calmer. I couldn't bring myself to sing along, but I was able to relax and enjoyed hearing him, almost laughing when he missed the words, knowing I probably would have, too. That's how we passed the miles. And instead of sitting in a stuffy restaurant for lunch we drove through and ate hamburgers in the park, then played Frisbee with Shadow. Running after the Frisbee and chasing Shadow around did wonders to shake my mood and made the rest of the drive more bearable.

"Would you like to move closer to the ranch?" Rusty asked.

I carefully considered his words before answering. "No, I left the ranch behind for a reason. I don't want to go back to that life. I'm fine just visiting it a few times a year."

"Would you like to move back into town? If we aren't going to keep horses we don't need that big place."

"No!" I said quickly. "I love where we live. I like being able to go up into the hills from our backyard. I like the deer. I like the house. I like the space for the agility course. Shadow's doing very well running it. I've been thinking of trying him in competition."

"Oh yeah?"

"I doubt if he'd win but he could earn his certificate in obedience and agility, not that a piece of paper is important. It's just something to do."

"Is that what you need? Something to do?"

"Why is it that the things that bring us the most joy tie us down so much? I'd keep the horses but they tie me to the house. My whole life revolved around feeding the horses twice a day. In a way it was comforting taking care of them, but I guess I just value my freedom more than the comfort they brought me."

"It's not just that and you know it. Shasta's your friend and you feel like you're abandoning him. Even if it's for his own good it's still hard to do."

"It's for both of us. We just live in different worlds and he belongs in his own world, just like I belong in mine."

"Are you sure about that?"

"Rusty, this isn't a driving down the highway discussion, it's more of a hug on the brown couch conversation."

"Okay," he smiled.

He pulled off the highway, got out of the Explorer then opened the back door and climbed in the back seat. He looked at me as if to say, "Well?" and patted the seat beside him.

I laughed. "What are you doing?"

"You said this was a hug on the brown couch conversation. This is as close as we can get to our couch."

"Rusty, that's not what I meant."

"Come back here, for just a minute." I crawled through the space between the seats and he pulled me onto his lap facing him. It was snug in the back of the truck. He looked me in the eye and asked, "Are you sure about that? Because I can turn this truck around if it's the right thing to do. I don't want to take Shasta back to the ranch if it's going to tear you up."

"It is tearing me up but I'm sure anyway. We're both better off with Shasta at the ranch and me at home."

"What can I do to make this easier?"

"Stay free. I may want to get away from the ranch, go tracking. It would probably help to take the coast home and stop at the beach. You know, the usual."

"Your dad, will he have a say in this?"

"Just let him have his say and he'll be fine. Dad may rant for a little bit but if you just stand back and let him get it out of his system he'll be his old self in no time."

"And you'll just take it from him?"

"Yeah, I'll just take it from him. He's probably right."

"Right or wrong he could show you some respect."

"In his eyes I'm still a kid because I asked my daddy for help. So I get treated like a kid. I can take that. I asked for it. I goofed up. Now I have to pay the price. It won't be so bad. You'll see."

"If he…"

"Nope, you won't do a thing. I don't want there to be any rifts between you and Dad. Just let me talk to him."

He gave me a serious look, the same one that probably made criminals give up on sight. I knew that it meant he cared even if it got him into trouble.

"Just let me talk to him," I repeated.

All I got was a sigh of resignation.

Now it was his turn to be moody.

When we turned up the driveway to the ranch house we both looked at each other uncertainly. He didn't want me to face the wrath of Dad and I didn't want to have to talk about Shasta without crying. My mother's enthusiastic greeting helped a little bit. There were hugs all around, then Dad said sternly, "Randy, take the horses to the barn and check them out. I want a report after dinner."

"Yes, sir," Randy said and jumped to do Dad's bidding. Rusty tossed him the keys to the Explorer.

The rest of us filed into the house and nervously sat in the living room. I knew I was in for it when even Mom and Martha fell quiet.

I sighed, then said, "Dad, let's just get it over with, shall we?"

"Not until I hear from Randy," he answered.

"Then why don't we go down to the barn? You'll see, Mack's fine. I've been riding him and watching his movements."

He squinted at me, like I'd talked back to him or something. I just wanted to get it over with.

"Very well, we can do that."

Dad and I walked down to the barn. Randy already had Shasta in a stall and he was walking Mack around the yard in front of the barn. Dad looked at the horse, examining his movements. Randy held him still and ran his hands over the cuts and scratches. He examined Mack's legs.

"You've been riding him?" Randy asked.

"After the vet gave the okay," I answered. "I didn't have Rusty ride him so he's only born my weight but he seems fine. Try riding him."

As Randy was saddling Mack, Dad started in, "Cassidy, this whole stunt was pure foolishness. What made you get into a fix like this?"

"Mice," I answered.

"Mice? Mice caused this whole crazy mishap?"

"Yes, sir, and a few mistakes."

"Ah, and what mistakes would those be?"

"I'd like to know what I could have done differently. So I'll tell you what happened and you tell me what I should have done differently."

"Sounds fair."

I told him about going exploring and getting stuck because of the wiring on the Jeep.

"So, was there something I should have done differently?"

"You should have checked the Jeep over before you set out on a trip like that."

"And what would you have me check over before I go four-wheel driving? Nobody would think to pull the wires out and make sure they were all in casings. You can't even pull very many of the wires to where you can see them. So, what would you have me check?"

"Are you being insolent?" he asked with a Big Wayne glare that would make men's knees knock.

"I hope not, but maybe I am. I take care of my Jeep. I check the fluids and filters and brakes. I make sure all my lights and turn signals are working. I don't think you could ask a girl to do much more than that. They seemed to be working when I left the house."

Rusty was lurking out of sight. Dad was watching Randy and Mack as we talked.

"What did you do when the Jeep wouldn't start?" Dad asked.

"I checked the Jeep over and found the wires. Then I searched the Jeep for any food and water I could find and I started walking. I had half a sandwich bag of trail mix and three bottles of water to last me until I got to the highway."

"Good," he said. "I expect you made it okay?"

"Dad, it was thirty miles of mountain roads. I walked for two days and I'm guessing twenty-one miles before I got picked up by a friend who was out looking for me."

"Randy told me about the roads. He didn't tell me how far it was. What made you think to go down roads like that? It was foolishness. Washed out roads, all by yourself."

"What would you have done when you were my age? Given four-wheel drive with a lot of time and some mountains to drive around in. You might have ended up in the same place. The Jeep made it over the washouts. It would have made it out if it would have started."

"And dragging Randy into this."

"I did nothing of the sort! I made a simple request. You could have said no. You could have told me to find another way. I don't know what I would have done but you could have said no. I didn't drag Randy anywhere. Randy…"

"Would walk over hot coals for you. He would have fought the bear with his bare hands for you."

"Dad! I know that. What it all boiled down to was that we shouldn't have tied the horses to the Jeep. If we'd have tethered the horses away from the Jeep they wouldn't have panicked. The bear could have had the Jeep, and we'd have been fine. The fact is we *did* tie the horses to the Jeep so if you have a bone to pick, pick that one."

"So you know what you did wrong?"

"Yes."

"Yes, sir."

"Yes, sir."

"And what have you done to make things right?"

I could feel Rusty restraining himself from interfering.

"How right is right? I think we both learned our lesson about not tying the horses to the Jeep. I didn't put Mack through more pain by sending him on a long trailer ride home. I called a vet and doctored his cuts. I made sure he'd mended before I brought him home. He'll always have scars but no more than he might have gotten working around the ranch. He's still a good horse."

"I'm surprised you brought them back. I half expected you to keep 'em."

"I thought about it. I really did. But it wouldn't be right for them or me. They need work. I rode Shasta almost every day and I rode Mack when he was ready but it wasn't the same as being at the ranch working."

"Why wouldn't it be right for you to have them?"

"Because, they tie me down. I need to be able to come and go as I please. I liked having them but it affected everything I did."

"So you were tired of the responsibility. You can't shirk responsibilities. They have a way of sneaking up on you."

"But I'm an adult now, Dad. Part of being an adult is choosing your responsibilities. I chose to put the horses right. And I chose to hand them back over to the ranch. It's their home. They deserve better than a little corral with a small barn and an occasional trail ride."

"You think you can just hand them back, just like that. Shasta is yours."

"Are you saying you don't *want them back*? Dad, they're working horses. You know they need work. To leave them with me would be like asking you to step down from the ranch, to force you to retire. Would you like that?"

"That's fine, Randy, I'd like to hear your opinion of this after dinner," Dad said, then he turned to me. "So, you're really bringing them back to the ranch for good?"

"Yes, sir."

"So I can do anything I choose with them?"

"Why?" I asked, alarmed that he could have other plans for the two horses.

"If you turn them over to me, they are in my charge, are they not?"

"Yeah," I conceded reluctantly.

"You trust me to do good by them?"

"Yes, but…"

"No buts, either you do or you don't."

I couldn't take it any more. The possibilities were too awful. He could sell them. He could retire them. He could do anything he wanted and I didn't have a say!

"You won't sell Shasta," I told him icily. "You won't."

"I trusted you with the horses. Do you trust me?"

"No, I don't. Because to you they're an investment. They aren't your friends. I can only trust you to do what profits the ranch. I didn't call in the vet because of *your investment*. I called the vet and I doctored the horses because they're my friends."

"And now you're giving your friends away to face who knows what. If you really wanted him, you'd take him."

"You have no reason to sell these horses. They're good work horses. The only reason you'd sell Shasta would be to make me angry and I'll tell you right now, you've already done that. I couldn't be madder than I am right now. I brought Shasta back for his own good. At least I thought I did. Don't do this to him!"

He just looked at me. I'd talked back. He wasn't sure how to take that. My father knew he'd crossed a line of some kind but he was too stubborn to back down. He was sticking to his guns.

Now I really couldn't take it anymore. I stood up to him and said, "You sell Shasta, I'll buy him. And I'll take good care of him. I don't care if I'm being disrespectful or not. You *will* *not* sell my horse to anybody except me. I've never ordered you to do anything outright but I'm telling you now. You can do what you want to me but you will not sell Shasta. If you really want to sell him, call me. Rusty and I are going home now."

And I walked away. I couldn't help it. I couldn't stand it. Before I could leave, though, I had to speak with my mom. We had planned on staying a day and two nights but that was no longer possible. I'd put a rift between my dad and myself and I wasn't going to drag it out for everyone to wallow in. I was mad. I was more than mad. I was furious and I'd never been truly mad at my father before. It felt rotten.

"I'm sorry Mom. I can't stay in the same house with him. I'm too angry. I'm sure we'll both calm down but it won't be while we're together. I'll call in a few days and see how things stand."

Rusty and I left in silence. We headed for the coast and it felt like we walked every beach from Morro Bay to Santa Monica. We stopped in Santa Barbara and spent the night because I couldn't handle facing a quiet house with an empty corral. It was a challenge getting the hotel to accept Shadow. They asked for a damage deposit. I even put him through several obedience commands to show them that he was well behaved. I was so upset I couldn't concentrate on anything and didn't even track at the beach.

I seethed with anger, not just because of my father's attitude but also from the fear that he would sell Shasta just to spite me. I was very disappointed to have missed seeing Patrick and I knew when he saw the two horses again he would ask about me. It just plain hurt. When I was with Rusty it just came out as sadness. My mood rubbed off on him and although he tried his best to make things better it was no use. I would not be comforted. I was mad, sad, afraid, lonely and nothing would make it go away except to know Shasta's fate.

Chapter 15

After a couple of days had passed, when I couldn't stand it any more, I called the ranch praying I'd get a hold of Mom, or better yet, Steve. My prayer wasn't answered; it was Dad. My only hope was that he really wanted to talk to me.

"Hello?" he said absentmindedly.

After an initial reaction of shock, I calmed myself down, stilled my emotions, and steadied my voice.

"Good morning, Dad." Okay, so I didn't steady my voice.

"Cassidy? Are you okay?"

The question took me aback. "That's what I'm calling to find out."

A long pause. "You don't have anything to worry about."

"I'm sorry Dad, you'll have to be more specific than that."

"I won't sell Shasta and I won't force you to take him."

"Then I'm a lot better than I was half an hour ago but I still don't understand."

"You don't have to. Shasta's earned his place on the ranch. He won't be sold."

"Mom didn't just put you up to this?" I asked, still suspicious.

"Well, yeah, she did but I jumped the gun without thinking."

"You would have sold him just to teach me a lesson?"

"I don't know. My temper got the best of me."

"Me too. It still has the best of me, but I'm willing to calm it down."

"How do you do it?" he asked.

"Do what?"

"I almost had a full scale rebellion on my hands. Randy threatened to quit. Your mother confronted me and gave me what for. I was surprised Rusty left peacefully. Steve was fit to be tied. Zack didn't know nothin' just like always. He don't pay attention to anything but the horses. I wish you'd have stayed for Old Frank's sake. He…he really needed to see you."

Old Frank. My heart sank. I'd put my horse before my grandfather. Well, the only grandfather I knew. My parents had parents somewhere but ranch life kept my parents tied to the local area. When I needed a grandparent it had always been Old Frank who was there and now I wasn't there for him.

After a long pause I tried to mend the rift. "Dad, what was it in the whole Jeep situation that set you off? Boil it down to that and maybe we can work through it."

"You learned your lesson about not tying the horses to a vehicle?"

"Yes, sir. But I bet if you look at what you do on hunting trips you have done the same thing many times. You tie the horses to the bed of the truck when you go out in the hills. But I do know there's a difference between tying them to the side of the truck and the bumper of a Jeep. The Jeep was light and easily pulled while a truck would have to be pulled over sideways to get it to go anywhere."

"Okay, so you're thinking. That's good. What really got to me, though, was the size of the job. Even without interference from the bear you got yourself in a hell of a mess. And…and it bothers me that messes like that are some game to you. One of these days I fear you're going to lose the game. I was hoping Shasta *would* tie you down a bit. You need something to tie you down."

"That's it? You threatened to sell Shasta so I'd take him back and settle down and be a housewife?"

"Women shouldn't be traipsing off into the woods hunting for people and getting into trouble."

"Dad, you didn't raise me to be a woman. The whole time I was growing up I was a boy to you. You taught me to shoot and hunt and fix trucks and tend horses and now all of a sudden you want me to be a *housewife*? I'm not going to quit the team. It's too important. And I can't keep the horses because some of the searches take days. I need to have whole days where I don't have to worry about horses. You'd be the first to admit a person should not have a horse unless they can take proper care of them. I'm telling you now, in the long-term, I can't take proper care of them."

He paused for a long time, reflecting on my words. Guess he didn't realize what he'd done in raising me. Or maybe I had surprised him in the end by actually turning into a woman despite my upbringing. It was Rusty who had brought that about. I was still very much thinking as a boy when Rusty had met me. I still couldn't figure out what he saw in me, but gradually I was becoming more of a woman, so much so that I couldn't fool Dad anymore.

"Did I do that? If I did, then I owe you an apology. That was wrong of me."

"Maybe, but don't be sorry. I like my life. I like the way things are turning out."

"You do?"

"Yeah, Dad, I'm very happy. I'm doing something worthwhile. That's what's important to me, that I'm making a difference. You don't know what it feels like to find someone who's been missing in the mountains. They've been without food and water. Sometimes they're scared, sometimes hurt.

They are always cold and hungry. Some have thought they were going to die and I bring hope. You can't know how good that feels. I feel capable because I get along in the outdoors. I love Shasta. I'd take him if it were the only way to keep him. But I wouldn't put him before my job. So I'd appreciate it if you would take him back and keep him working like he loves to do. He likes to make a difference too. He can do that better at the ranch."

"Okay. Would you come see Old Frank?"

"There's something I need to check on first. I was helping with a case when I visited the first time. I need to see if anything happened while I was gone and if there's a way I can help now."

"What are you doing?"

"Did you hear about the school shooting down here?"

"You know I don't hear much, but it's been talked about."

"We still haven't found the guy. I've been helping the detective assigned to the case. I was at the school when it happened. I can recognize the shooter and the getaway car."

"You're after a maniac who shoots up schools?"

"Yeah."

"Good Lord, what have I done?"

"It's not like that. I won't be in on the take down. I've managed to gather some helpful information and I may end up tracking the guy. But I won't be there for the capture. That's the police department's job, not mine."

"How long will it take?"

"Either they got him while I was gone or he's still out there. If Tom found out where he's staying it's probably all over. If not, there might be nothing for me to do until they get more leads. I have to find out."

"Will you do it? For Old Frank?"

"Dad, you're talking like Old Frank isn't going to be around if I wait. It can't be that bad."

"He won't go to a home. He should, but he won't. He still makes the rounds of the horses. Won't move into the house. I offered a downstairs room in the house so he wouldn't have to climb the stairs. He said he didn't belong there, so Steve built a ramp into the bunkhouse. He wants to keep on, just like always. Only it ain't always no more."

"Okay, Dad, I'll find out."

I drove down to the station because I really wanted to see how things were going. I'd learned cops can say any number of things over the phone and they were almost unreadable in person, too, but I thought I could get a better feel for the situation if I talked to Tom in person.

First I peeked into Rusty's office. He was with someone, a young woman. Her little boy pushed a yellow sports car back and forth on the desk. I smiled. Another car gone from Rusty's stash. I wondered how many he had left in his desk drawer.

I went on to Tom's door, knocked lightly, no answer. I peeked in. Nobody home. I went to the lobby and sat, waiting. I knew it could be quite a while and there was little use waiting if Tom was out, he could be doing anything, but I waited anyway.

Rusty followed the woman out of the back offices and into the lobby. He shook hands with her and said, "Let me know if anything changes."

"I will," she said and chased down her little boy who was hurrying through the double doors.

Rusty stuffed his hands in his pockets and turned to go back to his office. He didn't notice I was there so I quietly got up and slid behind him as he returned through the fake wood, utilitarian door to the offices behind.

"Michaels, you're being followed," warned an officer walking the opposite direction down the hall. Rusty turned. He hadn't been expecting me, but he didn't seem surprised to see me. I was the only one who would follow him so closely that it would be noticeable. He grinned and playfully pulled me into his office.

"What are you doing here?"

"I'm seeing another man," I joked, then turned serious. "I need an update from Tom. If I'm not needed here I might go back to the ranch."

"Are you sure you want to do that? I can't go right now unless it's an emergency."

"I know. It's Old Frank. I need to see him. Things are okay with Dad. He's not going to sell Shasta and I found out why he threatened to. It's okay. It was just Dad being Dad. He thought I'd take Shasta back. He knew the horses would take a commitment and he thought Shasta would anchor me more, keep me out of trouble. I told him I had no intention of getting in trouble and I was not quitting the team so I couldn't keep the horses. Then he mentioned Old Frank. I should have at least talked to Old Frank before we took off, but I didn't, and he isn't doing well. I need to go see him while he can still enjoy our time together."

"Is it that bad?"

"He makes the rounds of the horses. Dad said he should be in a home. He meant a nursing home. But Old Frank won't go. They've had to make adjustments around the ranch so he can get around better."

"How important is the case to you?"

"Why?"

"Because it's gotten ugly."

"How? Is everyone okay?"

He gave me a serious look, as though he was wondering where the nearest set of cuffs were. He knew he might have a struggle on his hands with me. I thought he was probably right.

"Kima Tumibay eventually led Tom to Pearson's house. He didn't want to endanger Kima so he waited until she left, then kept an eye on the place. When she was gone he stuck around. She was in there for hours. He worried that she'd walked into something she shouldn't have. Tom thinks Kima was onto him because shortly after she left Pearson packed up and took off. Tom followed him to a house in Lake Hughes. Tom figured, if he didn't make a move he was going to lose Pearson. We went in but Pearson had the jump on us. He headed into the hills. They had whole sections of town cordoned off but it was all for nothing, except to keep people out of a potentially dangerous situation. Pearson wasn't going to use roads."

"So he's on foot, in the hills? Has anyone questioned Kima to see if she knows what Pearson's next step might be?"

"If she warned him she's not going to snitch on him."

"Where is the house?"

"You really think I'm going to tell you that? You'll be off tracking Pearson before dinner."

"No, I'd at least plan a little bit. Is he armed?"

"We have to assume he is."

"Is he alone?"

"No, there's two of them."

"And you don't want them tracked down?"

"Not by you."

"How long ago did this happen?"

"Cassidy, I'm telling you, you're not going after these guys. You're right, you need to go visit Old Frank."

"I can figure out which house it was. All it takes is some patience and a map and I can zero in on it."

He gave me a dirty look. "How?"

"Every place the police blocked off is going to have tracks from cars turning around. All I have to do is map out where the cars have turned around and it will narrow down my search to three or four houses. The houses in that area are spaced out. The roads are narrow. The shoulders are dirt. It should be no problem. It just takes time. After I narrow it down to a small area I can look for signs of life in the houses, tracks leading away. I've done this stuff before."

"And I'm asking you to stay out of it. This guy has already shot up a school and taken pot shots at three officers. I don't want him taking pot shots at you."

"He won't even know I'm there. I can radio his position in without getting near him. I can carry a tracking device and stay on his tail so you know where I am. There are ways to provide invisible backup."

"You're not going to let this drop, are you?"

"I let the guy get away. I'm going to do what I can to find him. I don't think I can bring him in but I can point the way."

"What about Old Frank?"

"Old Frank can wait a few days. Dad knows I might have things to take care of first. He asked me to find out about the case. I found out. I found out I better stay."

Rusty knew there'd be no stopping me. With a deep breath and a sigh of resignation he pulled me into his worried embrace and kissed the top of my head. "Not today. Stay with me today."

"Okay, today. I was thinking of calling Chase. I bet he'd go along if I told him what I was up to."

"If we could get Chase to do it, would you stay out of it?"

"No, I let the guy get away. I want to do what I can."

"Babe, you didn't let Pearson get away. You stopped one of them. If you hadn't been there we'd have had more loss. We'd have two guys loose. Now we just have one. You can't blame yourself."

"I can and I do, but maybe I can help correct that."

"Cassidy?" Chase asked.

"Yeah," I answered.

"Is everything okay?"

Why was it everyone automatically decided things weren't okay whenever I called?

"No, everything is not okay, actually there are lots of things not okay but I'm fine. I'm going on an apprehension tomorrow. Do you want to go?"

"You are. An apprehension. Does Rusty know?"

"Yeah, he and Tom are arranging for backup."

"And Rusty's okay with this?"

"No, of course he's not. But he knows I'm determined."

"Tell me about it."

"How much time do you have? Two guys shot up a school. One got away, one didn't. He's been linked to other disturbances. He shows signs of being a violent person. I want to stop him."

"That's not all there is to it. If it was then you'd stay out of it, at least until it came down to a tracking job."

"It has. Until I prove otherwise."

"That's still not all there is to it."

"So you don't want to go?"

"I'll be there. I just want the whole story."

"Then call Tom. And pack camping gear. We might end up on the trail a while. These guys have been on the loose for a few days."

"You think you can find them?"

"Yeah, I can find them."

"Then why call me?"

"I'll find them. I'm afraid I won't shoot them."

"Why?"

"I already had my chance to shoot them."

"And?"

"And, of the three, there's two left. And I'm calling you because I don't want a posse of noisy cops behind me. It's like scouting with a herd of buffalo. I want to track them down, get in close, then let the buffalo stampede them before they know what's happening."

"I'll call Tom."

"Good idea. And, Chase? After this is over, I'm not hanging around. There's goings on at the ranch too."

"You're just full of good news, aren't you?"

"Talk to Tom. When can we expect you?"

"Late this evening."

"We'll wait up for you."

I imagined Chase had a pack, just like mine, packed up and ready for a call at all times. He did phone Tom who then called me. Chase pulled up to the house well after dark and he was in good spirits. He was on a chase. It involved tracking. It was what he did best.

"Hey, you got a haircut!" I said when I saw him standing at the door.

"Academy finished in January. Had to get a haircut to teach tracking classes."

"Anybody with potential?"

"A few interested in learning more. One with an eye for it."

"What do you do with people like that?"

"Once they get a uniform they forget all about tracking, until they need it. A few get sent off to tracking school."

"You got the whole story from Tom?"

"Yeah, nice work."

"Yeah, right. Do you want the guestroom or the gazebo?" It would have been an odd question to ask anybody but Chase. He frequently chose to sleep outdoors. The gazebo was a nice size for hanging a hammock and Chase usually had one handy.

"The guestroom. We'll be on the trail enough afterwards."

Bright and early the next morning we met Tom in Lake Hughes. He handed me the tracking device and said, "Keep it on your person, not your pack…"

"I know. You want to know where I am, not where my pack is. Been there, done that."

"When?"

"When I searched for Kelly Green. It quit working right when I needed it most, but I get the idea."

Chase was strapping on the radio. It fit onto his belt with a microphone that clipped to his shirtfront. I was always glad when the guys took over the radio work. When I had to use the radio I felt like a little kid who would get yelled at for using someone else's gear.

"You take care of my girl out there," Rusty said.

"I will, you know that."

"Got your sidearm?"

"And rifle. I just hope I don't need it. And I'm wearing the vest."

"Don't count on it though. It's been through a lot."

"It's better than nothing."

"How about just not getting shot at?"

"It's a deal. They won't even know we're there."

"That's my girl."

I looked to Chase. "Who's tracking?"

"You are, this is your party. I'm just here for the food."

"Okay, but you might be disappointed. I just brought backpacker food."

"Rats, me too."

Tom looked to Chase and asked, "You got the plan?"

"Yep, got it."

I looked to Chase. "I don't get the plan?"

"Yep, your part of the plan is to find your man."

It was just Tom, Chase, Rusty and I at this point. They all knew the score so I didn't hesitate to give Rusty a big kiss and a warm hug then I went to work.

Getting down to the business of tracking can be a slow process. I had to find the trail leading away and in this case it meant making wider and wider circles until I was down to one trail leading off at a quick pace into the hills. When I had found my starting point I ran back and said my goodbyes to Rusty then hit the trail.

It felt odd, to be doing the tracking with Chase there. As it turned out we were both tracking because you can't stop a tracker from tracking. It comes automatically. If there are footprints they must be tracked. So I tracked them first, and Chase tracked them second. I talked as I tracked, partly because Landon and Victor expected it, and partly because it was things Chase could gather more information from.

"These are the same guys we tracked to a field. We found the getaway car, and it was parked in the desert. We followed the tracks to a field, but the men were gone. Turned out they'd gone there to badger the workers. It almost escalated into a fight, and they got hauled in for questioning. This guy we're after has trouble with foreigners. He thinks that by being a jerk he can stop people from coming here. He thinks only Americans should have rights. There's a few things that don't add up about this case. I was at the school and he comes in there shooting. I take out his buddy. I track him down, and get one shot at him before he runs out the door. Then I found out that one of the teachers thought Pearson was after her. I'm convinced that the shooter at the school and Pearson are the same guy, but it is possible that they aren't. There's one proof of it. If we track down Pearson, and he's got a fresh bullet wound to his shoulder, it's him."

"And if he doesn't?"

"Then we start from scratch. But Pearson is linked to a green SUV and so is the shooter at the school. I'm ninety-nine percent sure it's the same guy."

"What's going on at the ranch?"

"Old Frank doesn't have much time left. I should be up there now."

"He's dying?"

"Yes and no. He doesn't have a disease that is going to kill him within weeks. He is just getting old, and deteriorating very fast. Steve's built ramps to the bunkhouse to make it easier for Frank to walk. Dad won't hire a replacement for Old Frank, but he is probably thinking in those terms already."

"Old Frank taught you how to track?"

"He taught me how to think. My thinking just involved a lot of tracking when he was most influential."

"Why did you get the tracking gene and Jesse didn't?"

"Because I was supposed to be a boy. Dad never wanted kids, and if he had to have them he wanted boys, to take over the ranch. He didn't get them. I'm the closest he got to a son. Jesse and James will take over the ranch when it's time. It's the only thing Jesse knows. What I'm more concerned about in all this is Patrick."

"He's going to be fine. He isn't close to Old Frank."

"He's closer than he thinks. Oh, I know they are a world apart in age but they are very close in thought. Old Frank likes Patrick. I bet he keeps tabs on him more than Patrick knows."

"You didn't answer my question. How did you get the tracking gene and Jesse didn't?"

"Because I grew up close to the earth, and Jesse grew up close to the mall."

"Ah, that's in the genes is it?"

"Partly. I'm allergic to malls. I hate the crowds. Plus trouble knows when I'm headed to the mall. I can't go shopping without something happening."

The tracks were old, but legible. Tracking was slow going but steady. Chase didn't seem to think the pace was too slow, but there are different methods of tracking. Each tracker must use his own method and draw his own conclusions from the trail. The miles of reading, walking and talking left me wondering if I was talking Chase's ear off. Somehow I thought, though, that Chase didn't mind my conversation because he was an information gatherer. Even if it was just chit chat he was still gathering information.

"You know why Old Frank likes Patrick?" Chase asked me.

"Because he thinks. And he asks intelligent questions. And Pat doesn't think an old man's answers are dumb. He knows Old Frank is eighty-six years worth of wisdom."

"I was going to say because Patrick is like you."

I thought for a moment. "That's what I just said." I stopped reading the tracks for a moment. "We're after both men, but if it comes down to a choice we follow the heavier guy. That's Pearson."

"How do you know?"

"Attitude and previous experience. I tracked these guys a short way. I saw Pearson at the school. I saw the profile of the guy driving the SUV. He was a smaller man."

"Why is Pearson making a move now? He should be over the border and out of our reach by now," Chase pointed out. "The law doesn't take kindly to people who go on a shooting rampage through an elementary school."

"I don't think he's through with Kima Tumibay. I don't know what's going on between those two but it's not going to end peacefully."

"What makes you say that?"

"A hunch. Kima refuses to believe Pearson will never change. I can see her point. I like to give people a chance when I can, too. But I think in Pearson's case he's more likely to get worse. It's as if all her attempts to win him over to her side only deepen his grudge against foreigners."

Chase didn't answer but seemed to take note of my observations.

"You work a lot with border patrol. Are you against illegal immigrants?" I asked.

"I'm against the action. Living here illegally is a crime. I have a harder time being against the person. Can't blame a person for trying to better their life or the lives of their family. If it's so bad that living illegally is better than living in their own country, I have a hard time judging. If it's just a matter of choice. I believe people should be allowed to make a choice, but when they change countries they change commitments, too; laws, taxes, language, everything. Just like if I moved to a different country I'd take on their laws and language and taxes. And I have no problem with love of the homeland and all that. I have a love for my homeland. It happens to be in the US, but it isn't the US most people know. It's very different. I go back there occasionally, and it isn't the same but it still feels like home. People think I'm nuts to live in that mobile home out in the desert. Hell, if you saw where I came from you'd think the mobile home was luxury."

"Where *did* you come from?" I asked, since he seemed to be open enough to talk.

"Nowhere. It doesn't have a name. Right now it borders an Indian reservation. The Indians like to draw the line around the house and count it as part of the reservation but legally it's not. It's almost a hogan. No electricity, no running water, we eventually got propane out there, not while I was little though. The house had three rooms, a living room/kitchen and two bedrooms. The outhouse was dangerous. Had to watch for rattlesnakes and scorpions. But it was good tracking land. Anything that moved out there left tracks."

"Sounds like the opposite of me, except for the tracking part. And some of the conditions you grew up in I forced upon myself to learn to make do."

"You *chose* to do without?"

"Yeah, I've chosen to do without a lot of things. Food, shelter, water."

He stopped me then. "Why?"

"I told you, so I could learn to make do. I wanted to be able to live under any circumstances. It's served me well. I've had conditions get rough. I've had to live where people oughtn't have lived."

"Yeah? Where?"

"How about a cage in an illegal dog fighting ring? I was lucky I lived through that one. I'm still trying to get over my fear of dogs. I visit the K-9 unit and I borrowed Kelly Green's big Labrador retriever working on getting over my fear of dogs. I guess it's working. I'll find out next time I face a barking dog. How about a twenty mile hike down a mountain road? A hike down a road is fine if it's planned. This was not."

The tracks led us on and still the conversation flowed.

"You can't go on like this. When did that happen?"

"Last fall."

"And then you nearly got killed over Christmas. How do you get into these things? You've either got a guardian angel with nerves of steel, or you're extremely lucky."

"I prefer to think of myself as extremely unlucky, and resilient."

He burst out laughing, which was unusual for Chase. His dry sense of humor was usually controlled and kept very quiet.

"And now we're out here tracking down two guys who shot up a school. You really know how to pick your disasters, you know that?"

"So far so good."

"And you're dragging me along on this one."

"You dragged me along on the last one," I said.

"Guilty as charged. No trouble with the trail?"

"It's slow but nothing that has me stumped, why?"

"Just wondering. You seem to catch some things that I miss, and you seem to skip over other things that would intrigue me."

"I wish we had time to explore the differences. I'd like to catch up to these guys though. How many days are you prepared for?"

"Standard three days."

"Same here, although if it drags out another day I will stay on the trail. I'll be reduced to eating oatmeal, hot chocolate and trail mix though. I need to find a different kind of trail mix. I've eaten so much of it lately that I dream about it. I'm beginning to hate the stuff."

The tracks were a few days old. Wind had eroded them, kids trekking through the hills had crossed them. People out in this area walked in the hills often to visit neighbors or go for a stroll. There were plenty of tracks which meant that Pearson and his buddy had probably fit right in, just heading out into the hills. I saw several sets of horse tracks and thought about Shasta. He would like these hills. He enjoyed being ridden near my house, although it wasn't real work to him. He was happy to get out, but he was bored, too.

I was happy to be in the outdoors again. I felt at ease tracking this worn out trail that could lead me into danger, although I would know when danger was getting close. The tracks would be fresh. Right now we could walk out in the open but the end of the trail would find us using a very different tracking procedure. We would hide our tracks, stay out of sight, keep an eye on the tracks and an eye on the way before us, hiding and stealthily hiking at the same time. For now we were moving track to track.

"Did you notice the smaller guy has a limp?" I asked.

"It's hard to tell, as worn as these tracks are," he answered.

"I have to admit I didn't get that out of these tracks. I noticed it the last time I tracked these guys."

"Maybe the guy with the limp will slow them down."

"I hadn't thought of that."

Uphill and down, into gullies, around small hills, these guys just seemed to be heading out with no particular destination in mind. They had a general direction but they were taking the easy way. Whatever made for easy walking, that's what they chose. It wasn't sandy and it wasn't hard pack. The soil gave a little. After a while it became apparent the guy with the limp might indeed slow them down. They began to stop often and the smaller guy took off his pack at each stop. He sat and stretched his legs. Chase examined the scratchings on the ground at the guy's rest stops. He was trying to guess exactly what caused the guy to limp.

"From the tracking I did before I decided the limp was from an old injury. It looked like he was accustomed to walking like that."

"Still gives him fits though. That's good for us."

The land around us was mixed. The forest and desert were fighting it out. There was a lot of juniper, like around my house, but the cooler temperatures encouraged stately pines while the hot summer temperatures promoted growth like prickly pear and barrel cactus. I steered clear of the cactus. We were seeing fewer signs of other people now. The land got drier and the trees were scragglier. As the land got drier the soil became harder.

"I'm getting thankful Pearson made friends with this guy with the limp. It's the limp that shows up on this hard ground. If it weren't for him I'd be down on my hands and knees."

Morning gave way to afternoon and Chase still followed.

"Do you ever stop?" he finally asked. I was used to this question. Nearly everybody on their first search with me asked if I stop. The truth was, rarely. Usually when I am tracking time plays an important factor with the final outcome. In this situation every minute that we stopped was a minute our suspects were getting ahead of us. And tracking wasn't a strenuous activity, especially when it got slow, like this, so who needed to stop? Most people, I guess.

"Of course I stop. When I get tired."

"Or to eat lunch?"

"Actually I usually don't stop for lunch. I eat on the trail. But we can stop if you want. Sometimes Landon has to remind me to eat. When I get back I should see how he is doing. He's probably going nuts at home."

We found a spot to rest and he searched around in his pack for some lunch. I dug out a bag of the dreaded trail mix and found a piece of beef jerky. I picked the fruit out of the trail mix.

"You seem awfully calm considering what you might be walking into," Chase observed.

"No use worrying about it yet. They're still a day ahead of us. As the tracks get fresher you'll see me get more cautious, start hiding my tracks more…It's just a natural reaction, when I get careful. I go into what I call stealth mode. You've never really tracked with me, have you?"

"No, only a few blocks in Joshua Hills. It was Mickey Mouse tracking. Rusty could have done it."

"Well, I think most guys get a little freaked out when they see me change modes like that. Landon says I change when I track but I change even more when I need to be cautious. He says I morph from Cute Cassidy into Dangerous Tracker Woman. I think it's funny but he swears it is real."

"I believe him. I think switching modes is as natural as switching attitudes. Your actions show what's going on in your head. You're already hiding your tracks."

"Oh, I do that all the time. It gets worse when I'm being more cautious. Then I actually think about it."

"This is what your tracks look like when you're not thinking about it?"

"You've tracked me before. You know what it's like."

"When you disappeared and Rusty called me it was as close to panic as I've ever felt. If Rusty had found your Jeep I'd have been down here in no time. But I didn't know if I could find you even if I had a starting place. I've only met one person more untrackable than you."

"That's not saying much. It pretty much takes a tracker to think about hiding their tracks at all. I seldom run into a person who worries about the trail they leave. I can only think of two: you and Tyrone Trent, and he's probably dead. Come on, let's hit the trail. Our suspects are getting away from us."

I started thinking though, Dad wanted me to take Shasta so I'd be anchored to the house. Chase worried about me when I disappeared. Rusty worried about me constantly. Everybody seemed to be pushing me into being a housewife, but I could only stand it for so long. I remembered what had first attracted Rusty to me. It was the fact I was willing to take my challenges and deal with them. Yet now he wanted to take all those challenges away.

"Chase? Is there a happy medium?"

"Huh?"

"Sorry, guess you're not a mind reader. Is there a happy medium between being a housewife and a trouble magnet?"

"For you? Or for most people?"

"For me."

"I don't think so."

"Why?"

"Because you don't think like other people. Your thinking is part of what makes you a trouble magnet. If you could just breeze through life without seeing most of the things you do then I'd say maybe you had a chance to find a happy medium. But you can't see things the way most people do."

"I don't see how I think differently. I know I see things most people don't. I see odd behavior where other people see normal behavior. But, take this little tracking trip. How would most people handle the situation?"

"They would sit at home and watch the news and be glad it was someone else's problem."

"But it's not. It's mine."

"Only because you see things differently."

"No, that's not it. It's because I can do something about it. I can follow the tracks. I can find the guy. Most people sit at home because they couldn't do what I do."

"And the reason you can is because you see things differently."

"So it all boils down to that?"

"Pretty much."

"Why couldn't I just be a housewife or get a real job like most women?"

"Because you'd go nuts. Face it, you just aren't normal."

"But everybody wants me to be normal."

"Not everybody. I know lots of people who would be very sad to see you be normal. One of the things I worry about when you have a close call is that it will break you and you'll quit being you. Deep down Rusty worries about that too. That one of these trouble attacks will break your spirit."

I bent to see the tracks better. This hard soil was almost as bad as rock. For a while I'd been able to see the scrape of the limp from the smaller guy. Now even that wasn't showing up. I got out my pocketknife and traced the last clue I found with the point of the blade. I moved onto the spot. I thought the next one would be... nothing. I dropped down to hands and knees, my pack weighing me down. I looked at the ground sideways trying to catch any indentation at all.

"Am I missing something?" I asked skeptically.

"Want me to take a look?"

"Usually I track from footprint to footprint. If the next footprint isn't there then I take another tack but I prefer to stick to the trail."

I studied the ground from the other side. Nothing. I went back to the last track I had traced and looked down the path it was pointing to. I looked ahead, locating a patch of ground about ten feet away that appeared to be better tracking soil. I got up and walked to the spot and cast around for continuing tracks. A trail could turn any number of different directions in the space of ten feet. I returned to the original track and stood there, looking at what the men had been able to see ahead. Figuring out where they would turn, trying to determine what they would be thinking.

"Chase? What time of day do we figure the men were at this point? I don't know what time of day they took off. Do you?"

"No, but it's a good question and one easily answered."

He got on the radio as I continued to search for tracks. I headed for another likely spot to pick up the trail. I hit the jackpot on the third try. I followed the trail until I was sure it was the same men then made sure Chase was still with me.

"See if you have any cell phone reception," he said.

I got out my cell phone and flipped it open. "Yeah, I've got some."

In a minute it rang. It was Rusty.

"Hey! How are you?"

"I'm fine."

"What's up?"

"Nothing, I just wanted to hear your voice."

"You can't start worrying yet. We're still a day behind these guys. Nothing's going to happen until at least tomorrow evening."

"Babe, I can start worrying the moment I can't see you anymore. I can start worrying as soon as I know you are going."

"Well, stop it. I'm just following tracks. Nothing's going to happen while I am just following tracks."

"All kinds of things can happen when you're not looking."

"Why, what are you talking about?"

"Kima Tumibay didn't show up for work today."

"What? How can that be? Did she call in? How do you know? Did anybody check her apartment?"

"We don't know. She didn't call in. The school was irritated to have to find a sub on short notice but they weren't particularly concerned. Ally called the house and when she didn't get a hold of you there she called me at the station. Nobody's at the apartment. No Kima or Mai."

"Were there more threats? If Kima was scared either for herself or for Mai maybe she cleared out."

"We don't know. All we know is that she didn't show up for work. I thought you ought to be aware of what's going on."

"What do you want me to do?"

"You know what I want you to do, I want you home."

"Kima's actions do not affect what I'm doing out here. I still have a person to find."

He sighed. "Be careful, Cass, I don't like the way this is going. Things aren't adding up."

"Okay, the sooner I get to the end of this trail the better."

"I'm sorry, babe, I can't see it that way. If I thought Chase could fool you I'd have him lead you deep in the mountains and stay far away from all this. But I know it wouldn't work. I love you. Stay safe."

"I love you too. I'll see you soon."

Back on the trail things had gained a new intensity. I wanted to be through with this hunt. I set off down the trail as quickly as I could, but quick is a relative term when it comes to tracking.

"We should be watching for a place where they might have bed down," Chase informed me. "We've been on the trail longer than they were the first day."

"That's good news. I can use some good news."

The good news didn't last long as we tracked Pearson and company for another two miles. Pearson's buddy was having more and more trouble with his leg. We tracked them to a house in the back country.

"We better talk to the residents before we go tracking around their house," Chase said.

We went around and knocked on the front door. We heard scraping noises like chairs being moved but no one answered the door. I looked around and found a doorbell button, thinking if some one did answer the door they were going to freak out at the sight of a kid in camouflage and a sixty-year-old hippie, armed and dangerous. I rang the bell and we heard more scraping, then knock, knock, knock, pause. More scuffling, then louder bang, bang, bang pause.

Chase and I exchanged glances. This was a call for help. Chase tried the door. It was locked. We removed packs and he took his sidearm in hand. I left my pistol holstered and took my rifle. He gave the door a strong kick at dead bolt height. It took several kicks but Chase knew what he was doing. The wood finally splintered and he jerked the door open gun still in hand. I followed, rifle at the ready, like I'd practiced at academy, but never had a use for in real life. It felt weird knowing I might have to fire it at any second. We stalked our way into the living room and it appeared empty. Chase searched the living room and went on to the dining room. As he turned the corner a woman screamed through her gag. He searched the adjoining rooms before coming back to the woman.

"It's okay, we won't hurt you."

He got on the radio and called in Tom while I untied a man and woman.

"Are you okay?" I asked. "Can you describe the people who did this?"

"Who...who are you? Why are you here?" the woman asked, unconvinced we were really good guys.

"Cassidy Michaels, tracker. This is my partner, Charles Downing. We're tracking two men for the Joshua Hills Police Department."

"They were here," the man said grimly. "They tied us up, searched the house for anything useful and spent the night. They took off early yesterday morning. One of them was hurt."

"Leg? Or shoulder?" I asked quickly, cutting him off.

"The man I was thinking of had a bum leg but come to think of it the bigger guy wasn't in too good'a shape either."

"Any clue where they were going?" I asked.

"They were on the run, that's all I know," the man replied.

Chase took over. "Don't touch anything until the police get here. Do you know what they took?"

"Some. They're well armed now. They searched the kitchen. I think they were more interested in provisions than valuables."

"How much ammo did you figure they took?" I asked.

"A box for each rifle. A thirty-three and a forty-five."

"What were they armed with before they stole your rifles?"

"One of them had a forty-five. The other man didn't appear to be armed."

"Did they say where they were going?"

"Hunting. The big guy said they were going hunting."

"For what?" I asked concerned.

"A person. The big guy was after a person and the little guy objected to the violence. The big guy insisted she would show up if he called and the little guy was definitely uncomfortable with the whole situation. I think he would have ditched the big guy but he was scared of him."

"Which way did they go when they left?"

"Out the back door."

"I wonder why they didn't take a car while they were at it. It would have gotten them away easily."

"It was a game to the big guy, like an army game, only real life. It was like he made up this mission for himself and he had to carry it out."

"Well, at least he's not after me," I mused. "Chase, do we really need to wait for Tom to get here? We're still a day behind these guys and who knows what they did last night."

"Yeah, we need to wait on Tom. We need to give him a report. He'll let us know when we can leave."

"I'm going to go outside and find the tracks. I won't go far."

I was outside when Tom and two black and whites drove up. I stayed in the backyard, hoping Chase would go through proper police protocol and clear us for the trail. I couldn't fool Rusty, though; he knew where to find me. He walked up hands in pockets, worry etched in his expression.

"Get me out of here," I said.

"Okay, if you'll come home," he answered. "I'll load you up into a car and take you home now."

"That's not what I meant. I want this to be over as much as you do but it's not over. These folks were lucky. They could have been killed. They are probably alive because they are American. What if the next place Pearson breaks into is the home of a foreigner? This guy has to be stopped."

"But not by you."

"Rusty, he's still a day ahead. I need to get back on the trail."

"You'll have to talk to Tom first."

Tom outlined all the things Chase had told him. I agreed that's what had happened, just to get my marching orders. The trail was calling.

"Cassidy, do you know what you could be walking into?"

"Yeah."

"Are you sure?"

"I'm sure I've walked into worse. I'm sure it isn't going to be fun, but it has to be done."

"I can pull you off the case."

"Why, because Rusty's worried? He's worried when I go grocery shopping. If you don't think I can do the job, that's one thing. I don't think you have any reason to think that, though. I got us this far. I'd be a mile or two further if I could have kept going. I need to hit the trail before it gets too dark to track."

Now it was Tom's turn to stuff his hands in his pockets. I followed him out the door and then led him to the trail of tracks leading away from the house.

"We'll radio when we make camp," I told him. Rusty came up beside him. The house was crawling with police activity but both detectives were more concerned about keeping me off the trail. Chase joined me and I turned to go. Rusty stood there with Tom. He was miserable. When I turned back he followed. It wasn't a leisurely stroll, either; it was built up emotions driving him. He caught me up, pack and all, lifting me off the ground.

"Rusty, let me go," I said with as much patience and compassion as I could muster.

"I can't. If I let you go you won't come back."

"Yes I will. I'm just tracking. Following tracks and camping. I'll be fine."

"You always think you're going to be fine, but I've seen you not be fine. I've seen it too many times."

"I know. I know you have. Now, put me down. I can make you put me down, but I don't want to hurt you."

Chase smirked at that. I bet he was wishing he could see me try it, but I really wanted Rusty to face his emotions and let me go. He set me down then turned to Tom.

"Stop her," he demanded.

Now Tom looked miserable, too, but he didn't let Rusty scare him. He stood his ground. Rusty stalked over to Tom. "I said, stop her." I was afraid Rusty was going to hit him, but Tom stood his ground silently and miserably, standing between a man and his wife.

I didn't know if I could turn my back on him. It was one of the hardest things I've done. To just turn away, while he was hurting like that, tore at my heart. Fighting my tears as I turned to the trail, I had to stop and brush them away to see the footprints. This was going to be one fast track.

I hiked as fast as I could and still keep the tracks in view. I was verifying more than tracking. I recognized the tracks and kept them in view and hiked, cursing myself with every step until darkness fell. Then I cursed the darkness. I rolled out my sleeping bag and climbed in it without bothering to make dinner.

Chapter 16

"Cassidy, you have to eat something," Chase said, squatting next to the bag.

"I can't. I'm feeling too guilty to be hungry. I'll eat dinner in the morning."

"He's crazy about you."

"Don't start."

"You put him through hell."

"I know. I told him that when he proposed. I told him it wasn't fair to him. It wasn't fair to saddle him with a trouble magnet. But he would have been there for me married or not. He'd been with me through thick and thin when he didn't have anything to show for it but misery. If I'd have said no he'd have been miserable, but he'd have still been there. I thought, if we were married, we'd at least have happy times as well as hard times. And we have. The hard times are just catching up to him and I don't know what I can do to stop it."

"If you'd have stayed I could have finished the search with a team of officers."

"I know. And I know you would have. But this is my job to finish, at least until we locate Pearson. I don't have to finish it, but I need to help bring it about. Don't worry, I'll let the guys do their job and I won't even break a nail. My job is to track him, not cuff him."

I heard Chase call in our position, even though they were aware of our location. It was just the usual, short check-in at the end of the day.

Lying there with my emotions all tied in knots I tried to picture Rusty and what he might have been doing. It was my nightly ritual, but I couldn't come up with a picture. Usually on searches I thought he'd be getting dinner somewhere or wracking his detective brain over the computer in his office, looking for that one missing link to solve a case. That night I didn't know what he might be doing. Sitting by a radio? Maybe. I wished he'd go to work and find something to do besides imagining all the things that could happen to me. I thought I'd never get to sleep but I must have because I woke to total darkness and a skittering feeling inside my sleeping bag. I unzipped it as quick as a wink and jumped out. I opened my sleeping bag as far as it would go and shook it out, then shone a small flashlight around on the ground. I was a sight, rifle in one hand, sleeping bag in the other, waving it around. I had been sleeping in my clothes with my pistol still holstered and my rifle beside me. So getting out of bed and shaking it out wasn't exactly a simple task.

"Git! Git out of here you stupid critter!" I whispered loudly as I kicked a scorpion away from camp. It threatened me but my big foot was too much for it. I shone my flashlight around to see if any more creepy crawlies lurked nearby. I wasn't scared of them but I didn't want to be awakened by them either. I got out my tent and rolled it up until the door was on top.

"What are you doing?" Chase asked.

"I'm tired. I want to sleep without critters in my sleeping bag. So I'm getting my tent out."

"That'll learn ya."

He rolled over and went back to sleep while I crawled into my flat tent and zipped the door over myself. We were in mostly desert now. Mesquite was the tallest growth around. The forested mountains were close but the tracks led deeper into the dry hills. The morning would bring a long dry and dusty day. Come on, Cass, sleep. It's going to be a long day. But sleep wouldn't come, only that guilty feeling and a longing for home. The guilty feeling was much stronger than my desire to get Pearson. Right then I just missed Rusty. I wanted to apologize, then curl up with him on the big brown couch and just be alone together. Then the desert sounds encroached on my thoughts and brought me back to reality.

Morning came but I didn't want to stir. I didn't care about Pearson anymore but it was my job now so I forced myself up. Camp was cold, typical desert cold. People think of the desert as a hot place and it can be, but at night it doesn't retain any heat and the morning is left with a stark cold that feels like frost on the skin and seeps down in until activity thaws the frost away.

As promised, I made dinner for breakfast and had some hot chocolate, too. I didn't feel any better for having eaten. It was just routine. Follow procedure and get on the trail. Chase did the same. I packed up the stove and trash. I rolled up my tent and stuffed my sleeping bag. I shouldered my pack and paced, waiting for Chase to do the same. My rifle hung on my shoulder next to my pack like it belonged there, and sometimes I even forgot that I was carrying it. After finding the tracks I paced up and down the trail watching them, like they might change on the next pass. I'd been in a hurry the last few hours and wondered if I could have missed something. Something could have changed. But why was I thinking that? It pricked my subconscious. There was a slight difference making its way through the tracking channels of my brain. Something subtle. Chase stopped his camp duties and watched me. I took off my pack and laid my rifle on top of it. I followed the tracks a little further, then got down on my hands and knees.

"When did the smaller guy's tracks change?" I asked Chase.

"What do you mean?"

"Oh, come on, don't tell me you didn't see it yesterday. Why didn't you point it out to me?"

"What? You were tracking along so fast I was just keeping up. You sure it's the right footprints?"

"Yeah, the bigger guy is still Pearson. The people at the house would have told us if there were more than just the two men we were looking for. The man just mentioned Pearson and a guy with a bum leg. We knew that."

"Then what do you mean, the tracks changed?" He put down his half stuffed sleeping bag and walked over to me. I pointed at the tracks. Pearson was still Pearson. Same mannerisms, same size, same tread, same gait and stride. But the smaller man had changed. One foot was the same and the other was...

"Artificial," Chase observed. "He hiked all this way on a prosthetic leg?"

"Something seemed odd when he stopped to rest yesterday but he had a shoe on over the foot. Why wouldn't he have the shoe on? The limb won't take much of this desert rock and sand."

"It was bothering him yesterday. Sometimes just a slight change in angle puts the pressure on a different spot. It's not like he could go home and change shoes."

"At what point did it change? That's something that should have been obvious to me yesterday. I should have caught that but I was in a hurry. To damage a prosthesis in a situation like this seems kind of risky."

"Let's hope you never have to know what it feels like to hike for miles on a prosthetic limb. Don't knock it. You don't know how the guy feels. It's a good observation though. Good catch."

"I wonder if he has the shoe along or if it was left at the house."

"He'd be kind of dumb to leave it at the house. I'm going to pack up. I'll be ready in a few minutes."

I was thankful for the new observation since it focused my attention away from home and back on the trail again. We still tracked fast but we were both more alert to changes in the trail that might reveal the condition of our suspects.

"What was in your sleeping bag last night?"

"A scorpion."

"And you just flicked it away? I know women who wouldn't be able to sleep after being that close to a scorpion."

"It's just like a crab or a bug. I only got my tent out because we couldn't afford a delay and I wasn't sure if a scorpion sting was serious enough to affect tracking."

"It would be rather uncomfortable. You were lucky."

The smaller guy's leg was still bothering him, shoe or no shoe. I wondered why Pearson stuck with him but I was glad he did. It showed he had a little bit of heart left and it slowed them down, giving us precious time to catch up.

"Pearson isn't used to walking this far," I told Chase. "His tracks are telling on him. He's going to try something else pretty soon."

Chase began taking a closer look at Pearson's tracks.

"Tell me what made you think that."

"He's developing…I don't know how to describe it. It's not really a limp. It's more of a muscular twitch. I get it sometimes on the treadmill at the gym if I push too hard. One foot will begin acting up and it causes my foot to come down differently. I end up adjusting for it because I need to get back in rhythm. That's what I'm seeing here. The pattern changed. See here? The inside, right foot comes down just a tad too quick. It throws off the stride."

"How do you pick up these things?"

"Many years of practice and observation and cataloging of behaviors, examining my own actions, noticing patterns. It's just something I've always done. I see a track and I wonder what movement produced it. Then an image comes to mind that matches up with the action I see in the track."

"It's just something you do?"

"Yeah, you do too, I bet. I watch people everywhere, I see someone move and a track comes to mind. I see a track and an action comes to mind. Everything people do is shown through their feet."

The prosthesis was easy to follow and we walked at a steady pace. The desert sand left a good impression. We made good time.

The day heated up and with it our supply of water diminished. In a way I was glad. I didn't like the weight of carrying three days of water, but I didn't like having to worry about conserving it either.

The tracks led to another house. A pack of dogs descended on us as we approached. I found myself in a fighting stance, pistol in hand, with no memory of even grabbing it. Chase looked on, more wary of me than the dogs. They stood several paces away and barked a warning at us. I stopped to think; heads up, ears up, tails up, eyes wary. These dogs were just doing their job. They weren't attacking. I holstered my pistol and went for the beef jerky instead.

"You okay?" Chase asked.

"Yeah, just a first reaction. After I analyze their body language I can relax."

The dogs perked up right away when they saw the jerky.

There were signs of breaking and entering but no signs of people. Chase called the break-in to Tom and we kept going. We didn't want another confrontation if we could avoid it and no one was in danger. When we left the dogs tried to follow us. I didn't feel right feeding someone's pets but I had to use the jerky to get rid of the dogs. I broke the jerky into four pieces and threw them towards the house. When the dogs lunged for the food we hiked away.

"That was your lunch," Chase reminded me.

"I've got more."

"Don't tell them that."

Mid morning brought a new twist to the search. We followed Pearson's tracks. The smaller guy was left in the shade of a large juniper bush and Pearson went forward alone. His tracks changed, along with his attitude as he closed in on another house. We noticed a car in the driveway so we thought we better talk to the owners before getting shot as trespassers. We rang the doorbell and stood there in our dusty camouflage. Rifles hanging from our shoulders, pistols holstered. An older woman answered the door. Her eyes grew large in fear and she started to slam the door closed when Chase said as gently as a he could under the circumstances, "Ma'am, we aren't here to hurt you. We're with the police department. We've been tracking two men. We followed them to your property and we wanted to get your permission to follow their tracks through your land. We also wanted to make sure everybody was all right. Have you had any disturbances in the last day or two?"

In spite of the badges she looked at us suspiciously.

"Why are you tracking them? Are they dangerous?"

"Yes, Ma'am. You heard about the school shooting?"

The woman gasped. "And they came through my land?"

"One of them did. We'd like to follow the tracks to see what their intentions were in coming here."

It sounded weird hearing Chase call the woman *ma'am*. It reminded me of Patrick and Chase didn't fit the picture at all. I knew officers tried to be polite and respectful but it still felt disjointed.

We walked back to the area where Pearson had entered the woman's property. She stood out on her back porch, arms folded, lips pursed in disapproval. Pearson had walked to the house and peered in a few windows that faced the backyard. He'd stood surveying the land, which consisted of a small barn and large barbed wire paddock. He'd gone to a shed and then ducked through the barbed wire fence. Then he entered the barn. As we headed for the barn the woman ran after us. She passed us and entered the barn. She came out looking distressed then ran to the back fence and scanned the horizon. Pearson, it seemed, had stolen a horse. Chase radioed Tom.

"You go back to the smaller guy's tracks. I'll follow Pearson. They're bound to meet up soon. If we aren't back together in half an hour we'll meet back here."

"Wait, there's a couple of things I want to see."

I looked at the place where Pearson had mounted the horse. He had a hard time pulling himself up.

"He's riding bareback," I told Chase. "He's got a bridle but no saddle. See how the horse veers suddenly? A horse won't do that unless directed to. If he had a saddle he wouldn't have had trouble mounting, but it took several tries before he had enough leverage. You can also tell because both feet left the ground at the same time. There wasn't one foot left behind as he worked his foot into the stirrup."

"Why not just steal a car if he wanted transportation?"

"Because he is heading into the hills, not to the streets. He's got something in mind. He might be just putting distance in until he can quietly disappear, but right now it involves a rest from the hiking. I bet by the end of the day he'll think hiking is wonderful. Come to think of it, how often have you tracked horses?"

"Only at your parent's ranch."

"Then let me follow Pearson. I'll be able to tell how experienced he is. I'll know, by the time we meet up, how long he'll be likely to last on this horse."

"Okay."

"Let's get out of here before Tom and Rusty show up."

"Cassidy, you can't put him off like that."

"It's easier to be gone than to separate again."

"Easier on who?"

"You think he needs to see me?"

"Show him you're all right. Keep things positive. Tell him you'll be through in no time."

"Chase, they've got a horse. They can get miles ahead of us now. We need to stay on their trail."

"Give him fifteen minutes," Chase said, and then turned to find his trail.

I waited in the junipers outside the horse property. Tom and Rusty arrived first. Once the basic story had been relayed Tom sat down to get the details and Rusty walked to the back of the property, obviously wondering where I could be, reaching out with is heart.

"I want to see you, but only if we can part peacefully," I said, speaking from the bushes.

"Cassidy?"

"Will you let me go quietly?"

"Yeah."

I stepped out from the bushes and it took him a second to realize he had been looking directly at me without seeing me.

"There you are. Do I get a hug?"

I took off the pack and propped up the rifle then stepped into his arms.

"I'm sorry Rusty," I said. "I really don't want to do this to you. I really don't, but I have no choice. So don't make it harder than it already is. We're doing okay. Following the horse will be a breeze. If these guys are inexperienced on a horse we will make good time. They don't have a saddle. Trotting on a horse without a saddle is no fun. An inexperienced person going faster than a trot without a saddle is dangerous. They think they have a good deal here but they're going to wish they were walking pretty soon."

He didn't speak, just soaked up my hugs.

"Have we heard from the ranch?" I asked.

"I took Shadow to the kennel. I haven't been home since. Can I go to the ranch with you?"

"Of course. Just keep in mind I'll be spending time with Old Frank, and I'll have to talk to Dad, let him know there's no hard feelings. There aren't, are there?"

"We'll talk about it later. Just be here with me a few minutes."

"Chase will be waiting for me where the two trails meet."

"Okay."

I let him have his time and when he knew he had to let go he reluctantly released me. I shrugged into my pack, took a second to balance then shouldered my rifle.

"Every time I see you like that I relive the time you went after Kelly. It makes me feel helpless every time. The pack dwarfs you. The gun scares me, reminds me of things I don't want to think about. Seeing you move is the only thing that reassures me. Seeing you so at home even in all that gear. I don't know how you do it. Miles upon miles."

I smiled and said, "Don't get yourself worked up. I'll see you again soon."

"Can I walk with you?"

"Yeah, for a little ways."

"Can I carry your pack for you?"

"No."

"What are you watching for? You can't lose this horse."

"I'm seeing if Pearson knows how to ride. Looks like he has ridden before but this horse doesn't know him. She's giving him some trouble."

"How do you know it's a she?"

I looked at him, then pointed at the track. "See the way the hoof turns here?"

"No, yeah, I see it turns but I don't see how it's different from any other hoof print."

"It tells me this is a mare. She's older, maybe eighteen. She probably shouldn't be ridden double at all. She's light palomino. She'll be easy to spot in the woods, hard to spot in the desert."

He looked at me grinning, then said, "You're pulling my leg."

"You don't believe me? Go ask Tom. I bet he's got all the stats."

"I'll do that. You take care."

"You too."

I gave him a kiss goodbye then quickly followed the hoof prints into the desert to the place where Pearson had picked up his friend.

"Are you ready for some quick tracking?" I asked Chase. "No use spending a lot of time on horse tracks. Pearson has ridden before but the horse isn't making things easy for him. She wants to go home and he doesn't. He's got a fight on his hands."

"That reminds me, how'd it go with Rusty?"

"Better."

"That's good."

"Did your Indian tracking teacher teach you a fox trot?"

"I take it you're not asking me if I've had dancing lessons."

"It's a way of walking. And it's kind of like jogging. It's like how foxes and coyotes get around. It isn't tiring but it eats up ground. You can do it in a pack if you move smoothly."

I broke into a fox trot to show Chase the smooth, quick almost jogging motion. He followed but soon stopped.

"Cassidy, I'm twice as old as you."

"Huh!" I said. "This from the guy who landed in Mrs. Rathburn's rosebushes skateboarding down a hill and jumping over his friend just because some little kid accused him of being old."

"Who told you about that?"

"I think you can guess."

"Cody."

"Yep, leave it to Rusty's little brother. But it's okay, I heard all the stories about Rusty's family's experiences with Mrs. Rathburn's rosebushes and yours was one of the most entertaining."

"Gee thanks."

"Are you ready to give it a try? You'll find it very easy to do, just walk faster and faster until you barely have to switch modes and you'll find yourself in a fox trot. Keep it smooth so your pack doesn't bounce."

He began jogging but it tired him too quickly wearing a heavy pack.

"Okay, stop. You're jogging. Just follow for a while."

I hiked at average rate then gradually increased my pace. He had a longer stride than me so it took him longer to reach his maximum pace. Walking fast was tiring and jogging was tiring. It was that happy medium we were searching for. I broke into the trot and sped up a little, increasing Chase's pace.

"Now, just shift into second gear, don't jog, keep it smooth."

"Cassidy, this is silly."

"And useful. Once you discover it you will use it a lot."

"How did you learn it?"

"Actually, I discovered it on hunting trips, trying to keep up with a herd of deer."

"You hunt?"

"I have. Now I prefer to stalk. I hunted as a teenager for the ranch."

"You get one?"

"Yeah, I got one every year from the time I was fifteen until I left home. I already knew where I could find deer. And I could get closer to the herd than any of the ranch hands. The ranch took two deer each year. I shot one and Randy or Steve shot the other one."

"All those guys and a teenage girl gets the trophy."

"I don't think it was quite like that. More like, all those guys and they have to let the boss' daughter get one."

I stopped suddenly.

"What is it?" Chase asked.

I looked at the area. It was a mess with tracks and sign.

"Pearson might be a little sore when we catch up to him," I said.

We pieced together the puzzle. The horse had had enough. It stopped. Pearson tried to goad it on. It danced in place resisting his command. There were signs he'd given the horse a hard kick because she jumped forward dumping a rider over her rump in the suddenness. He landed hard on his backside. He was lucky he didn't have a leg when the horse backed over him grinding his prosthetic limb into the ground. He twisted away from the threatening hooves. Pearson got the horse under control and pulled around. He gave his friend a hand up again. I examined the spot where he stood and the artificial limb appeared to be bent or twisted. These guys were almost having my kind of luck.

"When do you figure this happened?" I asked.

"Mid morning today. We know the horse was stolen today after the husband fed it and went to work."

The houses in these hills were far apart on dirt roads that wound into the hills. The men were taking advantage of the lay of the land, riding from house to house. If they were noticed they could easily slip further into the hills. I worried what they would do when night came. Would they demand shelter from some unsuspecting family?

The hoof prints followed a fence line and suddenly veered off. It didn't take long to discover what had startled the horse. A playful donkey cantered up braying his heart out. He stopped at the fence and bobbed his head at us.

"Hey there little guy," I said, reaching over the fence to pet him. "Thanks for making things difficult. Keep up the good work."

"Do you always talk to animals?" Chase asked.

"Not always, only if they seem to respond to people. This little guy is a people donkey. He likes attention."

We followed the horse's frightened hoof prints away from the fence. The hoof prints bit deep into the dirt. I was surprised the men had stayed seated.

On and on we tracked. The men seemed to pause outside each house, considering the risks and what they could use, but since they had need of very little they passed these houses by. As late afternoon came upon us Chase's plan changed. He radioed to Tom our location and advised that we were closing in.

"What are you doing?" I asked.

"Calling in reinforcements. We're getting close. Two men on a horse should be visible from the air."

"No, it'll force them back to the forest. Tracking will be harder there."

"Just following the plan. The tracks are fresh. We did our job. We narrowed it down. We'll keep on following and keep the helicopter informed if we find anything."

As the tracks led on I could tell we were getting closer and there was also something in the tracks that made me cautious. I don't know how suddenly it came about but I found myself watching ahead and hiding my tracks and keeping objects between me and what lay ahead. I looked at Chase and realized he was doing the same thing. A helicopter buzzed overhead. Chase talked to the pilot via radio and waved at it when they located us. We heard the pilot pass on word to Tom that we were A-okay. Then it flew off to locate our fleeing suspects.

The clattering blades of the helicopter and the constant chatter from the radio were driving me to distraction. To me tracking had always been a quiet activity. I focused on the tracks unless something caught my attention. An hour of circling and finally we received word that there was one man on a horse headed west. One man. Which one? Chase asked for a description. Tan horse, dark mane, no saddle. And the man? Dark hair, dark shirt, jeans. That didn't help much. We'd have to track them until they split up and figure it out for ourselves.

"Pearson's on foot," I told Chase.

He agreed. It was obvious by the footprints.

"I say we follow Pearson. The helicopter can keep tabs on the horse. The cops may catch him before we get a chance to go after him. Pearson's the one we want."

Pearson headed for cover, moving faster once he was on his own. Darkness closed in, forcing us to stop. I debated whether to cook or not. The land was still very open and the glow of the fire might be seen. We didn't know how far ahead Pearson was or if he was watching his back trail. His actions seemed to indicate he knew someone might be following him. He was, at least, preparing for that event. I wanted to lay low. I didn't set up my tent. I bunched it up and set it under some cover, out of sight in case someone was paying attention. Chase noted my camp preparations.

"You're slipping," he said.

"Slipping?"

"Your caution's getting the better of you. Cook dinner. You need to eat."

"All right."

I cooked dinner but I didn't enjoy it. Chase was right, I could feel caution just under the surface of my usual tracking routine. A tenseness. A peculiar wariness. Sounds were sharp. Shadows were deep. I wasn't scared. I just wanted some warning. I'd known all along that no matter how much Rusty wanted me out of the picture when a confrontation occurred that it could happen at any moment. We only hoped we got a visual, called in the troops and let them bring Pearson in. The reality was Pearson was unpredictable, prone to violent outbursts and was just generally not a nice guy.

I caught Chase watching me.

"What?" I asked.

"You're changing. Wilson was right."

"I can't help it."

"I didn't say it was a bad thing. Better to know you're on your toes than worry about you being the kid you normally look like. Where'd you learn that?"

"I didn't. It comes with my attitude."

"Remind me not to tick you off."

"Not that kind of attitude. You don't have to worry about getting blown away if you get up in the night, either. I just feel very alert. When I feel like this differences pop out at me. Sometimes it comes on gradually. I've felt it building this afternoon. Sometimes it happens instantly. Landon will tell you it happens as soon as I really focus on a trail but what I feel tonight is more tuned to our surroundings. I don't know how to explain it."

"You spent time in Afghanistan?"

"Yeah."

"Could be post war syndrome? What did you run into over there?"

"No, it's not that. It's just part of my make up. Oh, I saw my share overseas. Never fired my rifle at a person. They kept women to more controlled areas. I remember the sounds mostly. And the car bomb. I'll never forget the car bomb. But, no, this isn't post war syndrome. I tend to think of it as trouble radar. I could be in a war zone and not have my trouble radar go off. Then again, I can be walking down the mall and have it go off instantly. I've learned to trust it. Right now it's just a vague feeling that danger is on the horizon. I can see it but it's not close enough to be a threat yet. I can feel Pearson out there somewhere. So I'm alert."

I zipped myself into my tent to avoid nighttime encounters with scorpions or snakes. Chase checked in with Tom. It was time to sleep. I went through my nightly ritual wondering where Rusty was and what he may be doing. I had hoped to be through with this search already. I was getting low on food and could stay out another day but then I'd be relying on oatmeal and water which I'd prefer to skip. Rusty, where are you? What are you doing? Feeling lonely, I finally got up again and walked away from camp. I looked around at the house lights off in the distance and then flipped open my cell phone. There was a little reception so it was worth a try. I pushed the speed dial for Rusty's cell and waited.

"Cassidy?"

"Everything's fine. I just miss you. Every night when I go to bed I try to picture what you might be up to but tonight I couldn't. So I miss you. I just wanted to hear your voice for a minute."

"How's the tracking going?"

"Easy. I thought we were closing in on him and thought we might be able to end this thing today but the helicopter is scaring Pearson. He's running for the forest again, where there's more cover. We need to close in before he gets to the thick forest. If we can catch him in the desert he'll be easy to bring in."

"How are you holding up?"

"I'm fine. I have one more day of food."

"And then you're coming home."

"No, then I keep going on little packets of oatmeal. Rusty, I *am* going to finish this. I'll be fine."

"You're going to waste away to nothing lugging that pack around, not eating."

I laughed quietly. "You're worse than my mother."

"You need someone worse than your mother to watch out for you. I admit I downplay your activities when your mom calls but you need someone watching out for you."

"Did my mom call?"

"Yeah, she was wondering when you'd be visiting. I told her you were on a search and as soon as you got back you'd call her."

"They'll know what I'm doing anyway. Dad knew I might be doing this. When mom tells him I'm on a search he'll know. He's beginning to regret helping me become a tracker. He's been worrying a lot."

"What's changed? It's not like him to worry."

"His attitude is changing about me, so he feels more protective. He worries that I take these searches too lightly, that I don't see what I'm getting into. Believe me, I see it. I know what could happen, but I can't dwell on it. All I can do is keep doing my part until it's over with and hope for the best."

"I don't want you to see the end of it. I want you to see your backup coming and stop."

"I will, if it's the right thing to do."

"Don't let yourself get caught in the middle of it. That's the worst situation you could be in."

"I know, now talk about something positive before you get all worried again."

"Like what we'll do when I finally get you back?"

"Mmm, yeah, that'll do nicely."

"I'm going to kick out Chase and send him packing for San Diego. Guess I ought to thank him for watching your back first, then I'll kick him out. Later I want a long, soapy, slippery shower. I want to feel you beneath my hands." Those magic hands. Yep, I definitely needed to end this search tomorrow. Rusty and I had one of the sexiest showers I'd ever seen. It was sexy enough to make me agree to a house that I thought was way beyond our needs. Just thinking about a shower with Rusty made me tingle all over.

"Are you saying all this in front of the guys?"

"No, I'm walking around outside. What about you? Are you having this conversation in front of Chase?"

"I don't think so, but nothing gets by Chase, you know that. I bet he knows I'm out here talking to you even though he is supposed to be sleeping."

"So are you."

"I know. It's still early but I guess if I want to wake up with the sun I better go. The sooner we hit the trail the sooner we catch up with Pearson."

"What did I tell you to do?"

"When I see backup come in, back off."

"Be careful."

"You, too."

We said goodnight and then I felt my way back to my dark tent and crawled into it. I zipped the door, settled into my sleeping bag and finally fell into a restless sleep.

A cloud hung over me in the morning. I debated whether to eat breakfast or save the food for more urgent times. Part of me was convinced the search would end that morning. The other part dreaded the confrontation. My instincts also said that Pearson was not going to be an easy catch, that he was slippery and would not give up without a fight. I ate breakfast despite feeling a lack of ambition. I knew Chase would feel better if he saw me eat something.

"You're scary," Chase said. "If Pearson saw you right now he'd turn himself in."

"You're exaggerating. Most people think I'm skipping school when they see me out in the hills."

"Not today they wouldn't. You okay?"

"Yeah, let's finish this," I said tersely while double-checking my rifle. "Let's hope Pearson overslept this morning."

Pearson hadn't overslept; in fact we came to the conclusion that he didn't stop when night fell. He slowed down considerably and did his share of stumbling and cursing while feeling his way around but he never stopped. Finally we came to a place where he'd given up and rested. The ground was almost warm. Chase and I exchanged glances, knowing we were getting close. We stopped to check our location on the map. We looked at the tracks and then looked ahead to what we might expect. There was a highway up ahead. For trackers that could mean a number of things. To the police it meant that if Pearson hadn't already crossed it, it could be a good place for an ambush. Chase put in a quick call to Tom advising him to post men on either side of the area we expected Pearson to cross.

I found myself moving in stealth mode, crouched low to be less visible. Walking silently. I looked at our back trail, almost no tracks. Chase was being careful, too.

If Pearson had crossed the highway it would be rougher tracking. It was rocky and the woods thickened. It began changing from mesquite and junipers into true forest. We had to stop Pearson at the highway. If he knew the police were on to him and got into the rocky area beyond we were set up for walking into an ambush. I didn't like it.

Hiding, tracking and hunting at the same time had my senses so keyed up I felt like I was crossing a minefield, placing my feet with care, eyes on the ground, senses aware of everything around me. Maybe that's why I saw the small movement of color ahead of us. It was just a movement but it caught my eye. I kept the area in sight as I advanced. I crouched low and followed the tracks as quickly as I dared, keeping tabs on the movement. Chase noticed the change.

"Cassidy, what is it?" he asked quietly.

"I might have a visual."

"Where?"

"Two o'clock."

He craned his neck. "I don't see it."

"I only caught a glimpse, that's why I'm trying to catch up. How far are we from the highway? Is Tom ready?"

"Tom will be as ready as he can be. We stay on the trail until we hear otherwise."

"You know what Pearson's going to do if he reaches those rocks?"

"Yeah, well, I hope not. We stay on the trail."

"Right," I said grimly. "Stick to our job. Stay on the trail."

We both crouched below mesquite level and hurried down the trail of footprints. The tracks we read showed a hasty retreat. The tracks came down hard and pushed off harder, scattering sand. Pearson knew he was being followed and wouldn't hesitate to shoot.

We were helpless to stop what happened when Pearson hit the highway. We watched as he approached the blacktop. We heard the shouts of the police, although we couldn't understand the words from this distance. Pearson fired in their direction and we heard the return shots as the police closed in. We watched as Pearson dashed across the road and dived into the cover of dense brush. Officers in body armor closed in. I headed for the altercation but Chase stopped me.

"We can get more information from here. If he climbs up into the rocks, like he should do, we can see where he goes. If he gets away we'll know where we last saw him. If we close in we lose that information and have to figure it out from the rocks themselves. Just wait."

"The officers will wipe out his trail."

"Just... wait. Give them a chance. If he gets away we'll know where to start."

It almost looked like a miniature army war game as we watched from the hill overlooking the highway. But it wasn't a game and it wasn't in miniature to the officers below. They were in the thick of it. Pearson fired towards the police. I never noticed him aiming at anyone in particular, just firing where he thought he might hit a target. When they ducked for cover he advanced up the rocks which hid him well. He would disappear from view only to appear even higher, setting off another rain of bullets on the men below. We listened to the officers over the radio barking orders back and forth.

"See the tree with the *no hunting* sign on it?" Chase said.

"Yeah."

"That's where we start once things clear out."

"You think things are going to clear out? You think we'll be on this search for another day?"

"Depends on what Pearson finds up in these hills. He'll probably make a run for it and then hole up somewhere if he finds a place to hide."

"So begin hunting at the *no hunting* sign."

"Right," Chase confirmed.

"It's okay to hunt people, just not animals?"

"Right."

"What if the people *are* animals?" I asked.

"Animals don't go shooting up schools, only people do things like that."

"And we're not going to have some angry landowner shoot at us for crossing his land carrying forty-fives?" I asked

"We'll have to see what happens to Pearson."

"If they shoot at Pearson we'll go for Plan B and pick up the pieces."

"Okay," Chase agreed.

We had to wait out the officers below before we headed down the hill. In the meantime Rusty only heard silence from our radio. When things settled down he couldn't stand it any more.

"Unit One what's your status?"

"We're fine."

"What's your twenty?"

Chase looked down the hill and located Rusty in amongst the men at the roadblock.

"Seven o'clock and up a little."

Rusty turned around and we waved our hands so he could find us on the hill. Even from this distance we could see his visible sign of relief once he realized that we were out of harm's way.

Chase and I started down the hill. Pearson was out of sight on the next hillside over but we knew where to pick up his trail. We listened as the radio chatter detailed the instructions to the officers in pursuit. When we reached the highway Rusty was waiting for us with open arms. His grin was in sharp contrast to the other officers who were not pleased with the radio description of the chase.

"Should we go?" I asked Chase.

"Give them a chance. The more they chase Pearson the easier it'll be to track him. It'll be like tracking an elephant stampede compared to what we're used to. It'll be a breeze. Maybe we can get a real lunch."

"You're kidding. You're going to go to lunch while Pearson takes off for parts unknown?" I asked in disbelief.

"You got a better idea? We have to wait and see what happens anyway. I say we restock our supplies and get some junk food," Chase suggested.

"But that'll take hours!" I complained.

"Yes, I'd like a couple of hours. How about you? Rusty, would you like a couple of hours?" Chase asked.

"I'd rather have forever but I'll settle for a couple of hours if that's my only choice," he admitted.

Rusty drove us to the nearest greasy spoon joint which seemed appropriate since I felt very greasy myself. I was very self-conscious as I sat down at the little table with a red and white checkered tablecloth and picked up a cute little menu sprinkled with graphics of Victorian china and sprigs of herbs. A woman in a faded pink uniform took our order. I ordered a bowl of fruit, a side of steamed vegetables and a slice of cheesecake. Rusty just grinned, since he had been expecting me to just order the cheesecake. Chase ordered chicken fried steak with lots of gravy and biscuits with honey. Rusty ordered the top sirloin special. He wouldn't stop grinning. The waitress looked at him strangely but he grinned anyway. I was glad he was happy to see me, but he looked a little silly.

"Rusty, we need to get back."

"Chase is right, we won't know anything for a few hours."

"A few hours can mean several miles if a man's on the run," I insisted.

"Not Pearson," Chase said. "The man's out of shape. All he's been doing is yelling at foreigners and disrupting fieldwork. He won't get far in two hours."

"We can't track as fast as he can run, and he's got a lot of incentive to keep moving."

"Eat your fruit," Chase told me. "Tomorrow it's oatmeal and we're back in survival mode."

"I'll gladly share my oatmeal to prevent you from starving to death," I said sarcastically.

I enjoyed my vegetables. Seems like backpacker food is mostly meat and filler, like rice or noodles. Occasionally there will be recognizable bits of vegetables in it but I've never been able to taste them. So I found myself craving vegetables after a few days on the trail. I shared my cheesecake. I didn't need a whole piece, just a taste to keep me from going into cheesecake withdrawal.

As we were leaving the restaurant I stuck a couple of jelly packets in my pocket, hoping they would make the oatmeal more interesting. Then we stocked up on backpacker food at a little outdoors store although I hoped we wouldn't need it.

I thought aloud, "If Pearson's out of shape and he's been on the run for three days you'd think a bunch of cops itching for a chase would be able to catch him. Maybe when we get back he'll be cuffed and on his way to the station."

"Don't count on it," Chase said. "You could give them the slip. I could, too. Pearson might be out of shape but I think he's got something in mind."

"He does," Rusty said grimly. "We picked up Woodrow Walker. He ditched Pearson, said Pearson had a mission. Walker tried to get him to quit but Pearson said there was no turning back now. Tumibay had gone too far and he was fed up with what he took to be a rebellion against him. He said Pearson was crazy. Crazy mad and unbalanced."

"He thinks Kima is just trying to spite him? A woman doesn't risk her life and put others at risk just to make a guy mad. This is something she believes in or she wouldn't do it, much less with Matt Pearson around to make things even more difficult."

"Like I said, Walker thinks Pearson has gone off the deep end. He admits Pearson was a little overzealous, even in the war. But he carried it over when he got home."

"I don't get it. He's up here running around in the mountains when all he really wants to do is kill Kima?"

"Walker said Kima will come to him. All he needs to do is call her."

"There's something going on here that we don't know about. What would make Kima show up especially if she thinks Pearson will kill her?"

"She went to see him before. Tom watched her go in, then watched her leave. I don't know what's going on between those two but it's likely to end soon."

We pulled up behind the blockade and parked. A long line of angry drivers was being waved through one at a time after thorough questioning. We walked past the blockade with curious drivers no doubt wondering what the police were doing with a couple of grungy backpackers. We stopped and spoke with Tom.

"You're still determined to see this through to the very end, aren't you?" he asked, directing the question to me.

"Yup."

"You're going to see plenty of uniforms back there. Keep your ID handy."

"Most of them know me by now."

"Yeah, they were determined to get Pearson before he gets you."

"Pearson isn't after me."

"That's because he hasn't seen you yet. They were taking bets on whether they'd have to rescue you or Tumibay."

The woods were crawling with cops. Most of them smiled and shook their heads as I passed. Chase and I climbed up to the *no hunting* sign.

"I'm glad we at least got this much of a start. Trying to figure out his path up the rocks would have been impossible."

"Last I saw he ducked behind that tree," Chase said, pointing.

We walked to the tree. Pearson's running footprints bit deep. So did the footprints of a dozen officers. I was glad I had Pearson's tread and mannerisms stuck in my head and could piece together what had happened by the tracks. He ran desperately, turned suddenly, took sloppy aim and fired. If I took the time to look more closely I bet I could have seen the tracks of the closest officers swerve to the nearest cover and the tracks of officers out of range speed up.

If two teams of police weren't able to head off Pearson on an open road what were we walking into now? Where was he going? Where would Kima be able to meet him way up here? Things were not adding up but all I could do was stay on the trail.

Rusty's grin had faded as he watched me climb up the rocks in my heavy pack, with the rifle banging against my pack each time I reached for handholds with my left hand.

Running tracks were easier to read although much of the tread marks were erased in the haste of getting away. Heels hit with force and toes pushed off leaving a peculiar humped track. Chase was right, it was like tracking an elephant stampede, unfortunately I only wanted to find one of the elephants and all of them had been stampeding. Pearson stumbled and took time while he was down to get off another shot. His kneeling stance was plain. Small plants were crushed and up rooted when he rose quickly to his feet.

"You're doing great, kid," Chase said. "I couldn't ask for a better tracking partner."

"How are we going to catch up?"

"Don't worry, he'll have to hole up soon. I'm going to spread out and see if I can get an idea of how many cops were still on his tail at this point."

"Just don't let him see us coming."

We began to see occasional houses in the trees. Was Pearson heading for a house? Did he have one in mind? We followed as Pearson ran until he couldn't run anymore. He stopped to rest for a second and take a shot down his back trail to discourage anyone still following him.

As the day wore on I began to get discouraged. We climbed up a hill and I took note that Pearson's tracks were getting weary. Upward, and still upward. This did not make sense. If he had wanted to make better time he would have stayed on the level. There were easier places to go. Why head uphill when he was already tired?

Chase rejoined me.

"How did he lose the cops? I don't get it."

"He hasn't yet."

We followed the tracks as Pearson slowed down and neared a dirt road. He walked the road until suddenly his tracks vanished. We stopped. It wasn't like he'd waved down a vehicle and carjacked it. The tracks just vanished like he'd been picked up. But who would pick up a crazy man running through the woods holding a still smoking rifle in his hands?

I turned my attention to the road. It was well traveled but I memorized the tread of the car while it was moving slowly, keeping my eyes focused to the track as it continued down the road.

"Cassidy, you can't track a car. We'll get the crew up here and they'll patrol the area."

"No! I've got it as long as we don't get more traffic up here."

"They could be thirty miles away by now."

"Get out the map. See if you can find our location. I have to keep my eye on this tread or it'll blend in with the others. Just see how long the road is and where it may lead. If the trail hits pavement then it's as far as we can go but if they are headed for one of these houses then we still have a chance."

I kept to the trail and listened while Chase checked our position on the GPS and found our position on the map. I kept walking, eyes glued to the tread. Chance jogged up.

"Cassidy, are you sure you can keep the tread?"

"Yeah, why?"

"This road is a loop. If they are headed to one of these houses we've got them."

"Keep an eye ahead. I can't look up or I'll lose the car. Watch for a green SUV or a black Toyota. A green SUV is good news. A black Toyota is bad news."

I followed the tread of the car until Chase laid a hand on my shoulder and pulled me off the road. Up ahead, parked at a two-story wood-sided house was Kima Tumibay's black Toyota. We slipped into the woods to scout out the situation.

The house was built on a manmade hill overlooking the lights of the city, so the backyard was small and then sloped away down the mountainside. The house had almost no front yard and sparse woods filled the spaces between the houses.

"You talk to Tom. I'm going to see if Pearson's really in there," I said.

"Cassidy, it's too risky. We did our job."

Chase turned down the volume on the radio and advised Tom of our position and the situation as it stood. We took off our packs and settled in for a wait, watching the house. Before the police were able to arrive a blue Honda Civic slowly drove up the road. The driver appeared to be stopping at each house to read the number. Once locating the house we were watching Mai left the vehicle and ran to the front door calling Kima's name. There was movement inside but no one answered the door.

"Someone's got to stop her!" I whispered frantically. "He'll kill Mai. He hates foreigners and she's going to throw a monkey wrench into his plans." She went around back and I stole off, staying just out of sight of the house. I crawled around the bank and when I got to a good vantage point I whispered, "Mai! Mai! Over here!" as loudly as I dared.

She walked to the edge of the yard and peered down the hill, maybe thinking I was Kima. I took a quick look at the house, saw no faces in the windows, and leapt up and pulled her over the edge. Mai panicked. She came down kicking and screaming. I put a hand over her mouth.

"Hush! Hush, it's just me! Remember? Cassidy. I'm Cassidy."

She didn't hear a word of it. She fought as we rolled down the hill and then she pushed me down the incline. Mai made a run up the hill just as the police were closing in, surrounding the house. When she saw all the guns she turned. Two officers tried the traditional knock on the door, "Open up! Police!"

They were met with a shot through the center of the door and Mai jumped. Tom used a bullhorn and called to Pearson inside. Everything was tense with silence as we waited for a reply.

"Pearson! You can make this easy on yourself or you can make it difficult! It's your choice!"

"Go to hell!" Pearson yelled from the house.

I couldn't see what was going on at the front of the house. My main goal was to keep Mai from doing anything stupid. At the moment she was standing behind the police line, shaking in her boots and obviously feeling worried about Kima. Mai wouldn't abandon the woman who had offered to help her. But she was now confronted with violence of a different kind, one she was not prepared to deal with.

"He...he no hurt her," Mai was saying. "He love her. He no hurt her."

"What's going on inside?" I asked Mai.

"Kima, she danger. She love Matt... she think he good man. He *not* good! He is very..." She reached for her dictionary but she had lost it in her hurry. "He crazy! He crazy man. Mad at all the world."

"I think he is just an extremist," I said. "He has a cause and he sticks to it. Any man who can justify shooting at kids just because of his own beliefs is dangerous. He has to be stopped."

Negotiations started at the front of the house. Tom's bullhorn bellowed out over the hillside as he tried to convince Pearson the gig was up. I moved to a better vantage point, hoping to get a glipse inside. Did they even know Kima was in there? Surely Tom had seen Kima's car and come to that conclusion. Who else was in the house? A string of foul language erupted from the front of the house as Pearson fired through the front window. Officers ducked behind cars.

Suddenly the back door was flung open and Kima ran out then stopped, startled by the crowd of policemen surrounding the house. I crept to the side of the house and watched as Pearson ran after her then jerked her back. Mai gasped and stood behind the officers, her eyes begging Pearson to let Kima go. Mai stepped forward but an officer restrained her.

"No!" she cried. "Matt Pearson you no hurt Kim. You won't! You no hurt someone you love."

Pearson's eyes narrowed, focusing all his attention to Mai. He held Kima in front of him so the officers wouldn't shoot and leveled the rifle. I realized that Mai would be lying dead in two seconds and suddenly I stopped thinking. I only knew that Mai was in trouble. I took off running as fast as my feet were able to carry me and slammed into Mai just as the bullet hit me in the back. My leap took out Mai, and an officer standing nearby, and we plunged down the incline. Unable to stop, I held onto Mai as we rolled and tumbled. I tried to shield Mai from as many of the bumps and rocks as possible until we rolled to the end of the incline and were launched into the valley below. We came to an abrupt halt and all the wind was knocked from my body as we slammed into a tree. I couldn't hold onto Mai any longer and she tumbled to the ground just past the tree, landing in a heap. I couldn't move, couldn't breathe. Mai shakily came to her feet and began crying. I would have comforted her and let her know that we were out of danger but I couldn't even suck in a breath.

"Cassidy!" I heard coming from up the hill. It was Big John Jankowski. Wow, I thought as I fought for breath, my leap had taken out Mai *and* Big John! I'd always thought it would take a Mack truck to take out Big John. "Cassidy!" he called again.

I wasn't able to do anything, much less call back to Big John. All I could do was wait it out. I knew they would find us eventually because I still had the tracking device in my pocket.

Mai was frightened and didn't know what to do. She was hurt and the valley was steep. She was shook up, with no defense, against a crazy lady and an armed man. She didn't know if she'd done something wrong. A whole slew of things can go through your mind in her situation.

"Mai, it's okay," I finally gasped, finding my voice. "It's okay. The officers will protect Kima as much as they can. They've done this before. She'll be okay."

"You crazy woman!" Mai said.

"Maybe, but I only wanted to help you. Come here. It's okay. Nobody's going to hurt you. Are you hurt? Show me where you're hurt."

She'd be covered with bruises but her forearm appeared to be the worst of her injuries. I went through the gentle feeling motions I had seen Landon perform so many times but I couldn't find anything seriously wrong. Still, after a tumble like that it needed an x-ray.

"Cassidy!" I heard again, the voice now coming closer.

"Over here!" I called back but the effort made me ache horribly when I took a deep breath to yell.

As Big John approached Mai squealed and shrank back. Big John made an imposing figure.

"It's okay," I told her. "He's here to help."

Big John hurried over. "Are you okay?" he asked, but the sound of his voice bellowed out unintentionally.

"Take care of Mai. I don't know about me yet."

When I tried to stand the world started spinning around. I stood, braced against the tree, waiting for the vertigo to pass. When I felt my head my hand came back bloody. The bulletproof vest had protected my torso from the tree but not my head. Once the spinning finally stopped I stood shakily.

"You guys got a first aid kit up there?" I asked.

"I think Victor's up there. Are you okay?"

"I think I better start climbing."

As I moved to begin the ascent Big John saw the back of my bloody head and suddenly pitched over in a dead faint. Oh great, I thought to myself, just what we need a three hundred pound cop who faints at the sight of blood. I couldn't leave Mai and she was in no shape to climb up the cliff. I crawled over to Big John and took the microphone. John's radio was dead, crushed in the fall. Shit.

"Mai, sit. We have a little wait. Sit down."

"He big, big man," she observed.

"Yes, but he has a big heart, too. He's a nice man."

"You sure?"

"Yeah. Are you okay?"

"I am worried, for Kima."

"It'll be okay. They'll send some guys down here for us as soon as things are under control up at the house."

"You are calm."

"I am? I guess I'm just used to worse things than this happening to me. There's no need to be afraid."

Big John started stirring around.

"John, next time you pass out yell 'timber' or something. Now just don't look at my head. If I were in any danger I'm sure we'd know it by now."

"Sorry," he mumbled.

"You killed your radio. We need to get word up top."

"What does 'timber' mean?" Mai asked innocently.

Gosh, how do you explain that? I wondered.

"John, send Victor down. Tell Rusty I'm fine."

I waited until John was out of earshot and then explained to Mai. "Timber is a word of warning. Like in golf they yell 'fore' before they hit the ball so people will watch for hard golf balls flying around. When someone cuts down a tree they yell 'timber' to warn people that a large heavy object is falling. Big John falling over is almost as big as a tree."

She didn't quite understand, but I guess she was used to not completely understanding everything because she didn't press for more information.

"Mai, what did you mean when you said Pearson loves Kima?"

"It's long story."

"I think we have time."

"My English no good."

"It's better than you think. I'll understand."

"Kima was young girl when the war happen. Maybe nine, ten. Pretty girl. Matt Pearson was handsome soldier. He was in Philippines on the way to fight. Kima's village was hungered...hungry? Hard times. Pearson gave Kima his food. He had a good heart as Kima said, 'in those days.' Kima loved the big, handsome soldier but she was only a child. Pearson was...I use Kima's word... 'enchanted with her.' She had big brown eyes, she has quick smile, she so skinny. After four days pass Pearson left. Kima was sad. She thought she never see Pearson again. When Kima was twelve her parents find a way to move to America. Her uncle helped her much as she helps me. When she became a woman she began looking for the soldier she never forgot and she found him. He was amazed. They had good times then. They fall in love but soon differences kept them apart. Age first, then Kima go...went to college and they were apart. Now they together but differences keep them apart. She became a citizen because she thought Matt Pearson accept her as a citizen. But it wasn't enough. It is sad."

"Why does she continue to help people like you when it keeps them apart?"

"She say, 'the people of the world are more important than one man.'"

"So she came because she loved him, because she thought the warm hearted soldier was still in there somewhere, because she trusted him."

We heard men approaching and I spotted Victor walking our way with three officers and two stretchers.

"Cassidy, what have you done to yourself this time?" he asked.

"Nothing, just give me a compress and I'll be fine."

"Not so fast. Tell me what happened first."

"We rolled down the hill. The tree stopped us."

"That's it? The tree stopped you?"

"I was lucky I was wearing my vest. It saved me twice today."

"Vest or no vest you need to be checked out."

"Just give me the ice pack and look at Mai's arm."

Victor handed me a cold compress and I held it to my head while he checked over Mai. He splinted her arm. She lay on the stretcher and allowed the men to carry her out. Victor gave me a look, aware he was going to have a struggle on his hands. I stood to follow and he noticed the blood that had run down my hair and into my shirt, and the hole where the bullet had entered my shirt and been deflected by the vest.

"Cassidy, sit down."

"I'm fine, Victor. I just want to go home. How are things going up top?"

"Tense, we need to get back."

"Then let's go."

The men lifted Mai's stretcher, revealing a second one underneath. I stared at it.

"No way," I said. "I'll help you carry it, but I'm not getting in it."

"I told you it was no use," Victor told the men.

They set Mai down, nesting the stretchers then picked up both again. I followed as they led the way around the action up top and to the ambulance parked next to the police cars. Rusty paced the area, checking the action and looking down the hill. As we came up the incline he snatched me out of the group.

"Oh, babe, you sure know how to scare a guy." His hands found the dried blood and he pulled back in shock.

"It's not as bad as it looks," I said. Seems like that was always one of the first things I said to Rusty after one of my adventures.

He turned me around, stuck his finger through the bullet hole.

"Cassidy, that could have been fatal."

"It could have been fatal to Mai, too. The tree did a job on me. Looks like I need to send Philip Cranston another thank you note."

Philip Cranston was the man who had sent me the bulletproof vest after I had tracked down his son last fall. I felt guilty every time I wore it because his son was the first missing person I'd found too late. Now it had possibly saved my life for a third time.

We found a place out of the way and sat at the base of a tree.

"I should go help Tom but it looks like he's got plenty of people over there already."

"Is Big John okay?"

"Yeah, when all the guys saw you take out Big John they all just stood there amazed. If I wasn't so busy being scared all the reactions would have been funny."

"I didn't mean to do it. I was trying to get Mai to move."

"She moved. Will she be okay?"

"Yeah, she'll be sore and bruised and she might have broken her arm but she'll be fine."

"When will you stop going into danger, babe? I thought Pearson had you that time."

"Better me than Mai. At least I had a chance."

"Pearson wasn't too pleased with your stunt. You better stay away from the house. He's angry enough to try again."

Yelling from the house was followed by Tom's voice over the bullhorn. We weren't able to understand what was being said but finally Tom resorted to tactical measures. With a large hole in the front window it was easy to launch any manner of devices into the house. The stun grenade was followed by a tirade of cursing. Rusty and I remained under the tree, staying out of trouble but also not really knowing what was happening. I didn't like what I was imagining.

"Ouch, that probably knocked out Kima," I said.

"Maybe they can deal with Pearson directly if he can't use her."

"I know, but it still bothers me. He's surrounded. Why doesn't he just give up? There's no way he can get away now."

"I think he'll give up before they shoot him because he wants his fifteen minutes of fame. He wants to be able to tell his story to the media and get more attention for his cause."

"Where's Chase?" I asked.

"Where do you think? He's in the thick of things. Although when you disappeared over that ledge he almost followed."

"Poor Chase. I think he's going to have more gray hair after this little escapade."

I was relieved to have an adventure that hadn't involved being kidnapped, beaten or shot at, well, not on purpose anyway, and I was still in one piece. This time Rusty wasn't going to have to spend days at the hospital. I was either getting luckier or I was getting better at my job. I'd be in good shape to go to the ranch when this was over.

I was relieved that Pearson gave up before they launched pepper spray into the house as that would have been harmful to Kima, lying there unconscious with no defense against it. I stayed out of sight as they led him away in cuffs. He was stuffed into a car, still yelling at the top of his lungs.

As the squad car drove away we went into the house to check on Kima. She was worried about Mai, who had been taken to the hospital for x-rays. I told her that Mai would be fine. Kima looked me over, trying to place me.

"You were at the school," she finally said. "You spoke to Ally's class."

"Yes, I've been there a few times since the shooting."

"You risked your life for Mai."

"No I didn't. I had protection."

Kent Jacobsen approached us and said, "She's humble too. Leave it to you to come out of this bruised and bloodied. Do you know how to do anything the easy way, Cassidy?"

"The easy way would have killed Mai. And it wasn't difficult at all. I just reacted on instinct."

"She's lucky you did," Kima said.

Chase and I dumped our gear on the porch.

"Chase, thanks for watching over Cassidy for me," Rusty said.

"No problemo, although I think watching over Cassidy is a team effort. When it comes right down to it there's not much a guy can do. I didn't actually do much on this search. Cassidy did all the tracking."

"You did a lot," I told him. "I needed a senior officer I could trust. I knew we could be in for some scouting so you seemed the natural choice. Thanks for coming."

"You're off to the ranch next?"

"Yeah, I need to visit Old Frank."

"What's going on?"

"Time is catching up with him. He doesn't have much left."

"Your dad is going to be looking for a new hand?"

"Not until Frank's out of the picture. Until then Dad is rather shorthanded but they'll get along for Frank's sake."

Chase looked thoughtful. I wondered if he might have connections to a person who could be a good ranch hand and help Patrick with his tracking too.

"Give your dad my number. I need to go home, visit some family of my own. Then I'll talk to your dad."

"You remember my dad?"

"Yeah, Mr. Gordon, sir. I remember."

Chase began loading his things into his Baja Bug.

"You don't have to leave tonight. You've had a long, hard day. Why don't you relax, clean up, and go out to dinner with us?"

"I've got plans to make. Wheels to set in motion. I'll be fine. Believe it or not I miss that old shack."

"Okay. Thanks, Chase."

"Next time you need a scout give me a call."

"Will do." I knew Chase had his own agenda, and it didn't always make sense to other people. We waved him off and then headed for the old brown couch.

"Rusty, how can you stand to snuggle with me after three days on the trail?"

"It might help if you take off that vest."

I smiled because he knew what was under the vest. I removed the loose blouse that covered it and then pulled the Velcro fasteners. After taking it off I examined the spot in the back where the bullet had hit. It was a glancing blow but I'd been lucky I had the vest on. Rusty had been right, without it I could have died. Underneath the vest was the lightest of tank tops which I'd worn to prevent chafing. It still rubbed a little on the shoulders but I'd gotten used to it. Setting the vest down, I climbed back onto Rusty's lap. Mmmm, that warm familiarity of Rusty's arms. I snuggled in and felt immersed in his presence. All was right with the world when we were alone on this couch. We sat together simply treasuring the time. Then the warmth from Rusty's body started making me sleepy and I found a place on his shoulder to rest my head to let the drowsiness take me. Oh to sleep like this forever. It felt so good. Not wanting to disturb me, Rusty ended up falling asleep too. Whenever I stirred his caring hands helped me find a better position. We woke to a dark house.

I reluctantly got up and headed for the shower. I left the door open and turned on the water. An open door was an open invitation. He stood there watching me, then quickly got undressed. He stood in the doorway and watched as I soaped up and got the worst of the grime off.

"Need help?"

"Yeah, I do. But first, I can't see the back of my head. I need to wash as much of the blood from my hair as possible. I don't want to invite questions when we go to the ranch and it would be better if it was less noticeable."

With tender hands he washed my hair, working the blood out.

"How did you do this?"

"I was falling down the hillside with Mai. A tree stopped me."

"You're lucky you didn't break your neck. You've got a two-inch gash back here and bruises on top of bruises."

"Then don't look, just feel," I said, standing and reaching for a bar of soap. "Just feel with those magic fingers."

Rusty always started out so gently, afraid of hurting me, not knowing how far he could go, building. As far as I was concerned my husband could touch anywhere he wanted. It all felt so good. Touches, magic touches, and after I'd rinsed off he sat on the bench and drew me close, his lips touching, fondling, his hands straying until I nearly dragged him to bed.

As we lay there exhausted and enjoying each other's company, his eyes appeared to be lighthearted, but his manner was serious.

"What is it?" I asked.

"I enjoy you so much. Feeling you be so alive. I love seeing you. Sometimes I can't believe you're still here."

"I'll always be here."

"I hope so."

"Know so. Know I'll always be here. When I'm away on searches my thoughts are wherever you are. That's why I called from camp. I couldn't find you."

"Thank you for calling."

"Thank you for being there."

"Thank you for needing me," Rusty finished softly.

Chapter 17

The road to the ranch was particularly long this time. On the way out of town we picked up Shadow from the kennel and then hit the highway, but there was a cloud hovering over us. I wished we were alone and heading for the beach or driving up to Creekside Campground to see if the hideout was still livable. It was my own camp, that I'd built when I needed a hiding place to escape from myself and to get away from life. Now I saw it as more of a crutch and something I'd used to get through a tough time. Although I no longer needed it the same way, it remained a unique place in a pleasant camping spot, with a nice creek and a canyon to explore. It stood up there in the mountains and had been calling to me softly for the last little while. I'd have welcomed some quiet time alone with Rusty there, but instead we were driving to the ranch. It's where I'd grown up and it was usually pleasant visiting the ranch for short periods of time. I loved little pieces of it for different reasons. I liked seeing my family and enjoyed the boisterous meals around the huge dining room table. I was always content riding the horses out in the hills like I did as a kid. I was amused by the old west atmosphere that my dad enjoyed, the ranch hands in their colorful western shirts, silver belt buckles, blue jeans and cowboy boots. Every once in a while I loved getting on my very own horse and taking him down to the track and running him until he tired. Shasta loved to run and I was buoyed by the powerful, free feeling as he raced around the track.

Old Frank had started working at the ranch before I was born, and he'd tried to keep up with me ever since I was allowed outside the ranch house. He had watched out for me, guided me, and taught me how to ride. He kept a careful eye on my antics and kept my trouble, or the results of it, to a minimum. He taught me how to think and in the process he taught me how to track. He knew a curious mind was a good thing and he preserved that quality in me. When I lost the trail he wouldn't say, "Too bad kid." Instead he'd say, "Have you noticed the direction those plants are bent?" or, "Why is that rock moist side up? I didn't see no rain cloud over that rock." When I was stalking and an animal ran away in fright he'd say, "Maybe your shadow fell on him," or, "Believe it or not, kid, you're big and scary to a rabbit. Maybe you need to be small and friendly." Old Frank, grumpy Old Frank, had always been full of encouragement and you couldn't beat that quality out of him. He stood up for me when I got into trouble, even to Mr. Gordon. He knew how to work my dad. Let the boss think he came up with an idea and he'd back you all the way. So when I drove the tractor into the fence he told my dad, "You said the kids needed to know the workings of the ranch. Cassidy was only learning. You can't fault a kid for learning. Now let's teach her how to mend a fence."

I was glad Steve was taking over Old Frank's ranch duties. Steve deserved the position after so many years as a horse trainer. In fact, I didn't see a whole lot of difference between their two jobs except maybe the scheduling of races. I was sure Steve would rather allocate those duties but there was no one to pass them off to. He was the one. I hoped he took to it.

The shift in positions then fell to James taking Steve's job, which was good for my sister because she was married to James. Zack and Randy were the junior trainers but Randy had a special way with horses that Zack would never have.

I came back to reality and glancing around at our surroundings realized that we were halfway to the ranch.

"Are you ready for some lunch?" Rusty asked.

"Whenever you are. I'm not hungry and I'm not going to get hungry."

"What's wrong?"

"I'm just thinking about how hard this is going to be. I wish reality didn't have to impinge on this visit."

"He's Old Frank, just treat him like Old Frank. He doesn't want to be treated like an old man. The tough old cowboy's still in there somewhere. So treat him like the tough old cowboy he wants to be. If he wants to ride, ride with him. Just do it a little slower."

"He's going to want to relive old times."

"So, you can do that. You've got old times to relive, too."

We pulled off and found a little café. I ordered light and picked at my food. Rusty was getting used to my mood being reflected in my eating habits. He knew the mood at the ranch would be warm and lively and that Martha's cooking would get the better of me so he didn't push.

Jesse and the kids were already at the ranch house when we arrived. Patrick was on the porch jumping up and down, and Wyatt was sharing his brother's enthusiasm. I didn't know my nephew Wyatt as well as Patrick. Wyatt tended to hole up indoors and color pictures while Patrick was an easy kid to get to know. Patrick ran out to the truck on silent, moccasined feet while Wyatt clumped around the porch in tiny, stiff cowboy boots. Patrick sprung into my arms with a ready hug. Gosh, how I had missed that kid. Wyatt gave us a shyer more reserved hug and Jesse doled out sisterly hugs. Mom and Martha burst out the front door.

"Cassidy, it's so good to see you," my mother said. "This time you have to stay. We're having a big get together and you have to stay for it."

"Mom, you could have warned me. I would have brought different clothes."

"It's okay, it's informal, just some friends. Frank does so much like a celebration."

"What are we celebrating?"

"I don't know, we'll make something up. Can it be Rusty's birthday?"

"Rusty's birthday isn't until November."

"Rusty, do you mind having a birthday this week?"

"Mom, your friends from town aren't going to come out for Rusty's birthday. They don't even know him."

"The girls would," Jesse muttered.

"Just say you're throwing a party for the fun of it. You're allowed to have a party for the fun of it."

Dad stepped out on the porch followed by a tense moment when everybody wondered what was going to happen. He offered a hand but I gave him a hug. He hugged me back, surprised perhaps, that I'd put our disagreement behind us. Then he shook hands with Rusty.

"Mission accomplished?" Dad asked.

"Yes, sir," I said.

"Still in one piece?"

"Yes, sir," I answered. Just barely.

"That's good."

"What do you mean, that's good? Look at the girl. She's half starved!" Martha interrupted. To Martha everybody was half starved if they hadn't been eating ranch food three meals a day.

"How long can you stay?" Mom asked.

"I don't know, Mom, it depends on a lot of things. I think Rusty's due to be back to work on Monday."

"Dinner will be ready in an hour and I expect you to eat something! Put some meat on those bones!" Martha said.

"I don't know Martha, after seeing Cassidy take down Big John Jankowski she might ought to hold off."

"Ooo," said Patrick, "Big John is huge! How'd you do that?"

"I had a little incentive. He was standing in the way of something I needed to do."

"How big is Big John?" Wyatt asked his older brother.

"He's…he's even bigger than Uncle Rusty!" Patrick said.

"Nuh uh, Aunt Cassidy couldn't do that," Wyatt countered.

"I'll tell you the story later," I offered.

After taking the suitcases up to our bedroom I walked down to the barn and checked the office. No Frank. Then I walked the grounds. No Frank. Even watching the footprints, still no Frank. I recognized Steve's even gait and size nine boot and Randy's more laid back tracks amongst the horses. Zack's nervous walk/jog was obvious. I was pleased to note that Patrick's tracks were all over the place. He'd been sneaking around the barn and tracking the dogs before wandering into the brush behind the ranch house. I saw his bright red bike propped up beside the house along with Wyatt's blue bike. His rollerblades had been placed under a chair on the big cement porch. I caught Steve walking across the yard.

"Hey Trouble!" he greeted me. "Guess you found your man?"

"Yeah, the one you're thinking of. I just haven't found the one I'm looking for now. Where's Old Frank?"

"He sleeps a lot these days. He'll be up to the house for dinner."

"So he's in the bunkhouse?"

"Yeah."

"Can you go in and make sure the coast is clear?"

"Cassidy, he'll be up for dinner."

"I know, but would you anyway?"

I followed Steve to the bunkhouse and he ducked inside, then motioned that it was okay to go in. I had spent a lot of time in the bunkhouse as a kid playing pool, poker and darts with the guys. They had rearranged it since I was in there last. Apparently the ranch hands all wanted a lower bunk so they had put all the bunks in a row on the floor. They had added a recliner, and a TV now sat on the round table where they ate snacks. The pool table filled most of the room. There was also a walker against the wall by Old Frank's bed and slippers under his bed where his boots should have been. The boots had been kicked under the bed, an obvious sign of disuse.

"Thanks Steve," I said quietly. "If you run into Rusty, can you tell him where I am?"

"Sure."

I put the balls onto the pool table and began a gentle practice round hitting in the balls that were easy pickoffs. I knew Old Frank would be uncomfortable to find me sitting there looking at him so I shot pool to make the transition easier for him. I could use the practice, anyway. He'd probably beat my socks off later. After I had hit in several balls, Randy entered the bunkhouse. Word was getting around.

"Want to play a game?" he asked.

"Shh, I don't want to wake him," I whispered.

"What, Old Frank? A freight train could go by and it wouldn't wake him. He can't hear a thing."

Another sudden reminder that I'd let time slip away. I hadn't even known that Old Frank had lost his hearing.

"Sure, I'll play you a game," I answered.

Randy racked the balls and I let him break. He got two balls in on the break, both stripes, then he sunk another stripe putting me at a distinct disadvantage. One by one the guys came in and grabbed a stick until there was no telling who was winning or losing. We were all just shooting. Old Frank woke up with only the eight ball remaining.

"Trouble! You're back! What are you doin' here? I missed you last time."

"I just came back to visit. How are you Old Frank?"

"I'm doin' good. Whose turn is it?"

"It's yours Frank," said Steve.

I handed him my stick. He sighted down the stick like a rifle. His hands were so shaky the end of the stick was bobbing around. He waited until it bobbed past the middle of the cue ball and gave a quick jerk and the cue ball sped across the table and sunk the eight ball neatly.

"Well what d' ya know, I won!"

The ranch hands all clapped him on the back. Then Old Frank hobbled over to his bed, sat down and pushed his feet into his slippers.

"If my nap timer is working right, Martha will ring the dinner bell in ten minutes. I better head for the house."

He shuffled out of the bunkhouse, stooped and worn.

"He's going to be sorry he left that," Steve said, referring to the walker.

"Should I take it to the house?" I asked.

"Nah, Old Frank left it hoping you wouldn't notice. If he needs it I'll run back for it."

"You guys spend all your time letting Old Frank pretend he's young?"

"It's just habit. It came on so gradually. It just seems the kindest way to go. We don't have the heart to stop him."

"Thanks guys, I'm going to go walk with him. I'll see you at the house, in ten minutes, right?"

"If there's one thing Frank knows, it's dinner time."

I ran and caught up with Old Frank. I watched his footprints, noting the drag marks, the short stride, the careful placing of his feet to keep his balance. His right foot hit the big porch of the ranch house just as the dinner bell rang out back. If there was one thing Old Frank knew it was dinnertime. Martha was there to open the door for him. As a kid I'd always considered Frank and Martha to be contemporaries. Now I could see that Old Frank had to be twenty years older. But Martha loved Frank nonetheless, not in a romantic way but as a part of the family. That's what the ranch was, a big family. Dad might be the boss but Old Frank was the patriarch. He had attained his place even when Big Wayne Gordon had been demanding his share of respect. Frank had quietly earned it. And when Frank was gone, it was doubtful that the mantel would fall to Dad. When it came right down to it more than likely it would be Steve, unless Dad had finally learned a lesson in all this, that you can't demand respect.

In the military the officers demanded respect. The ones that deserved it were praised behind their backs. The ones that didn't got saluted to their face, obeyed to the letter, and ridiculed behind their backs. Dad wasn't quite to that point but he'd seen over the edge when he threatened to sell Shasta. You don't sell friends. He'd learned that. I had to admit that some of the horses were considered investments and were not friends. But some of them were priceless, too.

Everyone gathered around the big ranch table. I took my place beside Rusty and noted the concern reflected in his eyes. He was wondering if everything was going okay with Old Frank. I gently squeezed his hand. Yeah, everything was fine I assured him silently.

"Candied yams! My favorite!" yelled Old Frank.

The main course that night was venison. Martha knew I couldn't get venison in Joshua Hills so she always prepared it when I visited. It wasn't a favorite of mine, but it was, at least, something different.

"Aunt Cassidy, you said you'd tell us about the search. Tell us the story! I want to hear how you took out Big John!" Patrick said.

The dinner conversation my first night at the ranch almost always involved me telling a story of my latest adventures. Patrick was notorious for asking for stories. Sometimes everybody rolled their eyes and wished they could just enjoy a regular conversation. However this time everybody knew I'd been on a serious search so they were anxious to hear the outcome too. It was hard to decide exactly where to start. I didn't want to begin with the school shooting but I had no choice. It was the reason why I'd had to finish the case, at least in my mind. So I hesitatingly began and everybody grew quiet, aware that I was treading on eggshells. A few times Rusty took over, but I finally got through the entire experience. It wasn't the most interesting story they had heard but when I finished I realized nobody had been eating and now our food was cold.

Dad's reaction was the same as it had been when I'd told him the first time. "Good Lord, what have I done?"

"It wasn't you, Dad, I'd have become a tracker no matter what."

Mom said, "Cassidy! You could have been killed!" And I quickly extolled the virtues of bulletproof vests.

Patrick said, "How'd you take down Big John?"

"I told you. I tackled Mai and he was in the way."

"But Big John is like an army tank!"

"Guess I was very determined to get Mai out of the way. I wasn't worried about Big John. He can take care of himself."

At breakfast the next morning Frank said, "Oatmeal with raspberries! My favorite!"

Nobody else got oatmeal with raspberries. Everybody else was served scrambled eggs, sausage, biscuits, country gravy and if they didn't want that there were waffles with syrup or raspberries.

"Hey Trouble, as long's you're here I got a colt for you to try out. He's a dandy! You'll love him. Faster'n the wind," Old Frank said.

Steve looked up, alarmed. I took it to mean that this horse had given him some trouble, or was only partially trained. That was okay, I'd probably ridden worse when I was a kid. I'd climb up on any horse that was old enough to be ridden and, since I was the smallest one in our family, I was the first one the colt would be able to support. I would wait anxiously for the day when a horse began its formal training. I was there when it needed gentling and when the blanket was introduced and when the saddle was introduced and often I was the first one to climb up on the back of a horse who had never felt the weight of a rider. It was like poker, though. You had to know when to hold 'em and know when to fold 'em. I'd climb up and the colt would dance around, trying to throw me off. I expected it and followed the horse's actions until it became clear I wasn't doing any good. When the ride ceased to be fun for the horse I made my escape. I was sure the horse Frank had been telling me about would be safer than that.

Steve's look wasn't lost on Rusty, but he knew to hold off judgment at the table. Rusty would take a look at this horse, but he had faith in me too. He knew I could ride a horse that scared him. He then took inventory of the rest of the table. Randy and Zack looked like this could be interesting. Dad was glad I was willing to take on a challenge. The reactions were mixed so Rusty stayed quiet.

I knew the horse had been at least partially trained when Steve wrestled him to the racetrack. Even on the lead the horse wanted to have his way. There was no way Old Frank could even lead this horse.

Frank refused to acknowledge the existence of the walker while I was around. He took a long time going anywhere but I walked patiently with him.

"Ain't he a dandy?" Frank asked.

"He's beautiful," I admitted. "He looks fast, too."

"He'd leave your horse in the dust," Old Frank said.

"I didn't choose Shasta for speed. I chose him because he was my horse. He was a tracking companion. He was freedom. I'll be the first to admit he isn't fast. But he's a fast friend and you can't ask for better."

"You're right, Trouble, you couldn't have asked for better. This horse isn't like Shasta. He was born for the track. Even if Shasta's your choice, I know you can appreciate a good run and this horse'll give it to you."

Steve held the horse for me but I took the reins.

"What's the matter, boy? You don't like me? You'll like me better in a few minutes. It's okay. Hush, shhh." I ran my hands over him gently letting him know I was friendly and continued working with him until he calmed in my presence. Rusty watched with interest. Sometimes what I did scared him but he also wanted to know what I was capable of. One of the reasons I took the time to get acquainted with the colt was to give Rusty time to see I didn't just jump on any horse. I assessed the situation first. I might ride any horse on the ranch but I'd ease his fears first. He'd see I worked with the horse, built up a little trust before I put my life in its hands. At least that was the way I was hoping he saw it.

The horse began shying away as soon as I put my foot in the stirrup. I pulled myself quickly into the saddle and found a stable seat. I had Steve lower the stirrups. They were set for racing but I wanted to make sure there was some length to grip with.

"Okay, horse, come on, show me what you can do."

I didn't need to kick him at all. He was primed. I gave him a little rein and he moved forward, danced a little. It felt light and swift. I directed the horse forward and he took off at a canter. He needed to learn some restraint so I pulled him back to a trot and then a walk. I rode him a quarter of the way around the track and then brought him back to the group.

"Okay, move out of the way. Ready?"

They moved a few feet over. Rusty moved even further since he wasn't sure what the horse would do. I sat readying myself for the leap, then gave the chestnut a sharp jab with my heels. He leapt forward and I let him go, then urged him forward. I felt his muscles tense and reach. The ranch flew by as the horse raced around the track.

"Yaaaahoo!" called out Old Frank.

I bent into the horse, more of a racing stance, the wind whipping my hair back. This horse would serve Dad well.

When I passed the group I reined in, slowing the horse and then trotting him around the track to allow him to cool off a bit. This horse wanted to run but I wanted him to be ready when I got around to the starting line. I wanted him to show Frank what he could really do.

"Got a stopwatch?" I asked as I neared the guys.

Frank always had a stopwatch. He whipped it out and readied his thumb over the button.

"Give 'em what for!" Frank enthusiastically told the horse.

I stopped at the line, paused long enough for some tension to build, talked to the horse, psyching him up. "Come on, boy, you can go faster than that! You show Old Frank what you can do!" Then, "Ready?" I called to the guys.

"Ready!" Old Frank called back.

"One, two, three…Go!" He was off the line and halfway down the stretch before I was able to catch my breath. I was ready for the burst, though, and leaned down close to the saddle, the horse's mane flowing into my face. Riding this horse was sleek as a sports car.

"Yeehaw! Go get 'em boy! Go get 'em!" Frank yelled. "I knowed you could do it! Yeehaw!"

Frank's enthusiasm was contagious. I felt the straining muscles, felt the horse reach, enjoying his run, rejoiced in Frank's delight. I asked the horse for more speed and was rewarded with a burst of energy as the horse surged forward even faster. We crossed the line and Frank was nearly jumping up and down. With any more excitement he would probably have fallen over.

"I knew he could do it! I knew it!"

Franks words faded as I let the horse take his time one more time around the track. I released the reins, sat in the saddle and rode until the horse slowed, then I pulled him to a stop and dismounted, turning the reins over to Steve again.

"Oh, Trouble! It does my heart good to see you ride like that!" Frank shouted as he clasped me in a hug. "Nobody rides like you. Aint no one can make me prouder than seeing you ride. I'd rather see you ride than see a winning horse race!"

That was a good thing, because I certainly wouldn't win a horserace. Embarrassed by the attention I let Frank go on.

"You're right, Old Frank, he's a dandy. What's his name?"

"Frank's Choice," Steve answered. "Frank's betting his last penny this horse will win."

At lunch Old Frank exclaimed, "Ham and Swiss! My favorite!"

The meals were a little different than usual. Sometimes we all ate Old Frank's favorite. Sometimes Martha didn't inflict it on all of us. We ate ham and Swiss sandwiches with potato salad and fruit. Old Frank never wondered why every meal contained something that was his favorite. After lunch Frank took his afternoon nap.

Rusty and I went for a walk to enjoy some alone time.

"Watching you ride that horse was one of the most beautiful things I've ever seen."

"You need to get out more."

"I need to watch you more. Riding that horse wasn't just a matter of getting on and telling it to go. If it was then you'd have just gotten on and told it to go. You have a way with the horses. It's always a wonder to me when you take something ten times your size and get it to do what you want."

"You could do the same thing. I could teach you if you wanted to try it."

"It wouldn't be the same. I'd rather live it through you. My heart soars when I see you fly."

"You think it doesn't work the other way around?"

He took me in his arms. "You want me to learn to ride?"

"That's not what I meant. I mean I love watching you enjoy life too. To learn to enjoy life you need to get out of your comfort zone a little."

"I'm a detective. I live outside my comfort zone."

"Now find a new zone. A fun one. I don't care if you learn to ride a racehorse. I'd just like to see you do something you actually enjoy."

"I enjoy you."

Old Frank appeared at the ranch house door a minute before Martha rang the bell. He had used his walker but left it on the porch when he saw me inside.

On the table Martha had served roast beef, potatoes and gravy, carrots, tossed salad and soup but Old Frank said, "Liver and onions! My favorite!"

"Aunt Cassidy, can we go stalking? You said you knew where the deer go. We did stalking at your house. Can we go to the deer clearing? Please?"

"Did you talk to your mom and dad before asking?"

He looked guilty. "I was hoping you would do that."

I looked to Jesse and James. "Well?"

"It's up to you. It's your time here," Jesse answered.

Old Frank would be taking a nap all afternoon the next day. "Tomorrow after school, if Uncle Rusty can come, too," I told him.

"Yay! Do I hafta go to school?"

"Of course you do!" I said quickly. "School is important."

"Aw shucks. How can a kid think about school when he's thinking about *after* school?"

"I'm sure you'll manage," I said. "Kids have thought about after school for centuries and I bet it didn't hurt them at all to apply themselves to their work and wait a little while."

After dinner Old Frank sat back and started reminiscing.

"I remember you two girls when you were just little tykes. Jesse was always so prim and proper and Cassidy was always the go-getter. I always had to sort out which one I was dealing with. Did I have to be careful she didn't chip her fingernail polish or did I have to be careful she didn't kill herself and set the house on fire? I don't know which one was worse. A chipped nail could be a catastrophe. At least Cassidy's catastrophes took some thinking and planning. I could see the wheels turning and that got me to thinking. A few things I never did figure out, like how did she get on top of the barn roof when she was eight years old? I sure knew how she got down! She jumped! But how'd she get up there?"

"I'll show you, but Patrick and Wyatt can't watch," I promised.

"Aw, Aunt Cassidy, that's no fair," Patrick said.

"Every kid has to make up his own trouble," I told him.

Chapter 18

When Jesse took the kids home I walked with Old Frank to the rear of the barn. There was a washroom and an office at the back of the barn that used both water and electricity, so a panel of meters ran up the back wall outside the washroom. Electrical lines ran from the meters into the ground and a line ran to the roof and then out to a telephone pole behind the property. The men looked at the arrangement wondering what the meters could possibly have to do with kids being on the barn roof. I took a quick look and scrambled up the meters. I was on the roof in ten seconds.

"Well, I'll be hornswoggled," Old Frank said in amazement.

"Steve, you might think about covering these up somehow. Patrick is bound to figure it out," I suggested.

Steve nodded in agreement. Now that Patrick knew there was a way, he'd find it, no problem.

Rusty beamed up at me from the ground below. He always found my antics as a kid humorous.

I walked to the corner of the barn and jumped off, landing on bent knees.

"It makes my bones ache just watching you do that," Old Frank said. "How did you win that bet with Randy, when you was sixteen?"

"Which bet? We were always making bets."

"You bet him he couldn't track you across the ranch. It was when he first came here."

"Oh, that was easy. I just didn't touch the ground," I told him matter of factly. "But at that time I could have done it walking on the ground too."

"That's impossible. How could you cross the whole ranch without touching the ground."

I sighed. It was going to get dark soon.

"Okay, one more quick demonstration and then we need to head for the house." I climbed back up onto the barn roof, walked to the front of the barn and lowered myself onto a stall wall. I walked the fence that formed the outdoor section of the stall. "The tractor was parked here," I pointed out. "I lowered myself onto the wheel of the tractor and followed the contours of the machine to the other wheel. Then I had to touch the ground but there was a patch of grass."

I climbed up onto the pasture fence and followed it around the front of the property. It wasn't difficult. It was a four by four beam. In just a few minutes I was at the front of the property by Jesse's house. I followed the fence to the middle pasture and back up to the front of the house and jumped down. "No tracks, no tracking."

"An' how did you get back to the ranch when your mom took you for x-rays and you didn't want to have to wear a cast on your leg?" Old Frank asked.

"I walked."

"With a broken leg?"

"It wasn't too broken. I had a barrel racing competition the next day. I was afraid they wouldn't let me sign up if I was wearing a cast and it would just get in the way," I explained.

"So you walked from town. How come we couldn't find you?" Steve questioned.

"Because I didn't want to be found. If you found me Mom would just take me back to the doctor."

"We didn't find her 'til the competition," Steve explained. "By the time it was over she was ready to come home. Laid her up for six weeks but she got third place in the competition."

"Saaay, how'd you get Shasta to the competition without us seeing you?"

"Very quietly. Basically I stole him. I snuck in at night, saddled him up and took him away. I rode him to the competition. That's why we only came in third. Shasta was really tired."

Rusty leaned against a fence post. "Do you folks ever run out of stories to tell? Seems like every time I come up here there's at least one new story."

Old Frank said, "They're only new to you. It was nothing new to us. In fact, it didn't worry Betty none that Cassidy up and vanished in town. She just called us and sent us out looking for her. We spent about an hour driving the roads between the doctor's office and home and gave up, figuring she'd come home when she was ready."

"You left her out there with a broken leg?" Rusty asked in disbelief.

Old Frank said, "If Cassidy don't want to be found ain't no way to find her. If she ever disappears on you ain't no use looking unless she wants to be found."

"How'd you break your leg?" Rusty asked.

"We're not sure," I answered.

"How can you not know how you broke your leg?"

"Well, it was a two disaster day. I got in a fight at school. Barton Fartston was picking on Colin Oliver and I told him off. They were going to stuff him in a locker and I got in Barton's face."

"I remember that," Randy admitted. "You were spooky mad."

"The bell rang and everybody ran off to class except Barton and his goons, Colin and I. Colin tried to leave and Barton stopped him. They stuffed both of us into lockers and left. So it could have happened in the struggle. After school I was punching bag mad but we didn't have a punching bag so I took off on a dirt bike out into the hills. I was going too fast, taking risks I shouldn't have and wrapped the bike around a tree a couple of miles from home. We'll never know if I broke it in the crash or if Barton's goons did it trying to stuff me into the locker. Anyway, I walked home and told Dad about the bike. First he grounded me and gave me extra chores. Then he scolded me about the fight at school, said now they couldn't do a thing to Barton because we had no way to prove he hurt me in any way. Then I got sent off to the doctor for x-rays. It was a long two days."

"Did it occur to you that one high school girl could not hold off a bully and his gang?" Rusty asked.

"Ooh, Rusty, you're treading dangerous ground!" Randy warned.

"It didn't matter," I answered Rusty. "I thought I could do anything I put my mind to. It didn't matter to me if I came out ahead as long as somebody stood up for the underdog."

"I see that in you a lot," Rusty observed. "It's what made you shield Mai from that bullet."

"Holy smokes, I'm late for an appointment," said Old Frank.

"Hop in the truck, I'll give you a lift," said Steve.

"What could you possibly have to do at this time of the day?" I asked him.

"It's important. If'n I don't get there soon I'll miss my chance."

Steve grinned. "Dominoes game with Patrick. If Old Frank isn't there by seven-thirty Jesse says it's too late to start a new game."

"It's good for him. Keeps his mind going. That kid's got a head on his shoulders," Old Frank said. "He keeps score an' everything."

Eighty years difference in the two and they still had respect for one another. It was an unusual thing to see these days.

The next day Old Frank was late getting out of bed. I wandered around the barn area and watched the horses in the pastures before walking out to see if they would approach me. These were different horses than the ones I grew up with. They didn't know me. As a kid I'd have horses following me, nuzzling my shoulder for attention. Why the change? I decided it was me. I'd become distant, distant from my family, from my surroundings, from everything except Rusty. At least I hoped I wasn't becoming distant to Rusty.

I tried walking up to a horse but I had to make friends first because she didn't trust me. I held out my hand and approached slowly. Running my hand down her blaze, I felt a pang of sorrow for losing all the familiarity of my childhood. I was a stranger here. Heading back to the barn again I noticed

Steve and Rusty leaning against the fence watching me. I walked over.

"Why so melancholy?" Rusty asked.

"The horses don't know me anymore."

"You can't expect them to," Rusty said. "Shasta and Mack know you."

"And Satan. He still charges the door when I enter the barn."

"It's not because he knows you. It's because he's ornery," Steve said. "Nobody can do a thing with that horse."

"Why do you keep him?"

"He's a good looking horse. He's a picture perfect quarter horse. He's kind of a mascot. Sometimes we put him in the pasture up by the road and people stop and take pictures of him. Then soon as a kid climbs the fence it's back to the barn with him."

Old Frank finally stepped out of the bunkhouse holding onto the doorway for balance.

"You up for a ride?" he asked me.

"Where to?" I asked.

"To find some tracks," he answered.

I thought for a minute. How far was it to the best tracking grounds? There was a place a little over a mile away. At least it had plenty of tracks when I was a teenager.

"Sure," I decided.

"Do you want to go?" Steve asked Rusty.

"Me?" Rusty asked, not thrilled with the prospect.

"If you don't go I'll send Randy," Steve said as he motioned towards the barn. Rusty followed, knowing there might be a reason he should go.

When I got to the barn Steve was giving Rusty instructions.

"Put the stirrup down where he can reach it, way down. When he tries to mount be ready to give him a boost. Then, after he's up on the horse, raise the stirrup to just above where his foot reaches. Cassidy could help him up but I don't think she could support him if he needs more than just a boost."

By the time Old Frank caught up to us, all the instructions had been given, and I busied myself while Steve went through all the machinations involved with getting Old Frank in the saddle. I noticed Old Frank was riding Chet, probably because Chet was the shortest workhorse on the ranch. Being short, he was easier to mount. I handed Rusty Shasta's reins and I took Mack.

Once in the saddle, Old Frank was a cowboy again. He moved with the horse and Chet obeyed him implicitly. It didn't take long for us to get to the wood I had in mind and we walked the horses around until a trail caught my eye.

"What is it, kid?"

I dismounted and knelt by the tracks.

"Dogs, I think, based on the various sizes of the tracks."

"How many of them?"

"Three, one big furry dog, one more along the lines of a German Shepherd and a smaller one."

"Tony Macaluso's dogs. I bet he doesn't know they're loose again. How old are the tracks?"

"Not a day, but the weather's been mild. They could have come through here last night."

"Can you see the toe nails?"

"Yeah, it's very clear that it's dogs."

"I was hoping for wild animals," Old Frank said.

"We can keep looking. I'm sure there's other tracks out here somewhere." I strolled around looking for more, watching for game trails, burrows, anything that signified animal life. Rusty dismounted, too.

I knew there had to be other animals in this wood because the dogs were canvassing the area thoroughly. We saw so many dog tracks that it became a mystery of what they were looking for. I found a rabbit's tracks. The dogs had chased it away into a burrow. We saw a few gophers, the bane of the horse ranch. Gophers were common and their burrows were a danger to the horses in the pastures. We fought them relentlessly.

Suddenly a commotion of barking and snarling startled me. I instinctively drew near to Mack and sought out Rusty who suddenly was in cop mode with a take-charge look about him. A dark brown blur rushed past the horses followed closely by the same three dogs I'd just described to Old Frank. Mack was startled at the sudden appearance of the fight and knocked me into Chet. The two horses jockeyed for position crushing me in between.

"Ha! Ha! See, Trouble? You were right! A Shepherd, a Malamute and a Springer Spaniel. Cain't fool you, no sir!"

"Frank! Move! Make Chet move! I'm stuck!" I called over the ruckus.

He didn't hear a word I said.

"Rusty! Grab Mack's reins! I can't breathe!"

Finally Rusty was able to snag Mack's bridle and pull him away from Chet. I painfully worked my way clear of the two horses and stood, hands on knees gasping for breath.

"Cassidy! Are you okay?" Rusty exclaimed.

"Yeah, just give me a second."

"There's your wild animal," Rusty said to Old Frank. "What was it?"

"It's a marmot," I told him. "But I bet we can't even see the tracks. The dogs were hot on his trail."

I climbed up onto Mack so if he was startled again I could control him. We followed the dog's tracks and found them lunging at a burrow in the ground. They weren't going to catch a marmot today. That critter was long gone, deep in the ground or out his back door.

We wandered around the hundred-year-old oaks and discovered deer tracks pointing toward the clearing. I found myself hoping there would be deer there for Patrick after school.

"I guess there just aren't as many animals out here as there used to be," Old Frank observed. "Them dogs don't help none either. He usually keeps 'em on his property but they're hard to keep at home with no fences. I remember when you used to come out here and spend most of the day just wandering and tracking, poking your nose into dens and game trails. I often wished I could take off like that. Now, it seems, I can. I just don't got the get up and go to do it."

"You can do it, Old Frank, you just have to take your time and be careful."

"Kid, I cain't even get back up on the horse once I get off. If I got down from here I'd have to walk back and I cain't walk neither. I just have to stick closer to home now. Sometimes Steve drops me off in town and I sit outside the barbershop and play checkers or dominoes with Hector an' Bert. That's the extent of my travels anymore. I can't even say I need a haircut when I go there. I got more hair growing out my ears than they trim off my head. I always admired the way you took off after life and you never let tough times get you down. You're always right back at it. If I ever had kids, don't *think* I did but you never know. If I ever had kids I would want them to live like you, out there in it, not cooped up on a horse ranch. It's such a small world, this ranch. At least I got to travel to the racetracks. When I was at the tracks I saw the sights. When I saw the sights I got more than I was lookin' for a time or two. Thought I was really livin'. But you, you got a way with life. Adventure, happiness, sadness, love, it takes a little of all that to make a good life. You done good, Trouble, and I'm happy for you. You done real good."

"Thanks Old Frank," I said with a lump in my throat. I got the feeling the whole purpose of coming out here was so he could talk to me in private, let his opinion of me come across as clear as he could make it.

"An', Rusty, if there was ever a man I'd entrust our Trouble to, it's you. I was sixty-two when Cassidy was born. I barely kept up with her for eighteen years. It takes a quick man with a lot of guts to keep her in line, but I know you're the best man for the job. I never seen her happier, so you must be doing something right."

"You done good, too, Frank," Rusty told him.

"Training horses was only a part time job. Once the young ones came along they worked me into a full time job. Think I shoulda gotten time and a half for Cassidy. Double on holidays. Holidays jus' gave Cassidy more idle time to plot. I cain't remember a holiday we didn't have some excitement round the ranch. It's been a mite quiet lately, though Patrick is starting to get the best of me. He's a quick one, he is. Why is it only one kid is a handful?"

"Because parents couldn't handle more than one. I think I gave you more gray hair than my parents because you were my go between."

"No you didn't, Trouble, all my hairs was gray by the time you were born. Maybe you made 'em fall out but you didn't turn 'em gray. You showed me how I shoulda turned 'em gray. I shoulda gone out looking for ways to turn 'em gray. Hell, gray hair ain't the end of the world. Some day, though, you run outa options. I'm glad you're lookin' over all the options while you're young. Don't ever stop." He looked thoughtful for a moment and then added, "But don't let 'em kill you either."

We went back to tracking and continued finding dog and deer tracks. We backtracked the dogs and the marmot looking for a decent marmot track, but the dogs had been very thorough in wiping out the marmot's paw prints. Finally Old Frank needed to get back to take a nap before the "big shindig." He rode with grace and style but as soon as he moved to dismount all the aches and stiff joints got the better of him. Rusty caught him as he struggled with the saddle and stirrups.

I doubt if Patrick's feet hit the ground when the bus pulled up to the bus stop on the highway. He was home and onto his bright red bike before Jesse could even say hello. From up in my old bedroom I heard Dad bellow from his office, "Young man, there will be no running in this house."

"Yes, Grandpa," he replied respectfully, a little too respectfully as far I was concerned. Let the kid be excited, I thought. Rusty and I appeared at the top of the stairs.

"Are you ready?" Patrick asked.

"Yup, ready."

"Did you wear your moccasins?"

"I even wore them to school and the kids thought they were funny looking 'til I told them I made 'em myself. They all think I'm weird so who cares what they think of my shoes."

"I saw some deer tracks in the hills today so hopefully there will be deer at the clearing. Remember, these deer are going to be even harder to stalk than the deer at our house. They scare easier because they aren't used to people."

"I gotta go get my horse," he said and headed for the door.

"Your horse?" I asked.

"Yeah, well, only temporary. He's mine and Wyatt's but Wyatt doesn't care to ride yet, so I call him mine. Dad keeps him in the far pasture and makes me catch him before I ride him to keep my throwing arm in shape. He isn't hard to catch. He wants to go too. I talked to him this morning and told him we were goin' on a ride, so he's expecting me. I'll meet you at the barn."

It amused me the way Patrick thought he could talk to animals. I never saw anything to doubt his ability, but I didn't talk to animals believing they could understand my words. When I was halfway through saddling the horses Patrick walked up leading a diminutive pinto horse. It wasn't quite a pony. It had a sturdy toughness to it coupled with a gentle look. I suspected the horse had been chosen specifically with the boys in mind, an older horse that some other ranch kid had outgrown so it was used to children and familiar with their quick movements. He seemed like a good horse for Patrick and Wyatt.

"What's his name?" I asked Patrick.

"Snoopy, because he has markings like Snoopy."

He did, sort of, and would probably stand out like a beacon to the deer, but we always stopped on the outskirts of the clearing, anyway. Patrick knew exactly where to find all Snoopy's tack and, with some help lifting, he had his little horse saddled in minutes. He stood on a stool to get the right angle to pull the girth tight enough then had me check it just in case.

Rusty looked at Chet appearing as though he'd have preferred to stay on his own two feet.

"You can stay here if you want to," I told him.

"No, I'll go. I want to watch. I just had my share of riding already."

"I know you did, but Old Frank and I were glad to have you along."

"Come on guys!" said Patrick impatiently. We did need to get a move on so we could find the deer and stalk them. Then we had to get home in time for my mom's party. Getting back in time wasn't much of a problem, since we couldn't stalk deer in the dark.

We loped our horses out the back of the ranch and pointed them towards the clearing. Patrick rode like he was born in the saddle even though his legs barely straddled the horse. Snoopy couldn't have felt a kick even if Patrick's legs had been long enough to bend in that direction. I watched the horses for signs of strain. They were used to being ridden frequently, but only for short jobs around the ranch. Repeated long rides were not part of their usual routine. Snoopy looked like he could go all day, determinedly plugging along. He looked like he was part mountain goat.

Only two lazy mule deer were dozing in the clearing. We stopped on the edge of the clearing and left the horses in the shelter of trees. Rusty found a comfortable vantage point as Patrick and I headed for the does. Patrick followed his usual ritual of showing himself to the deer and then knelt down and began silently talking to them. I still wasn't sure how that worked but it made Patrick feel better and it was harmless so I left him alone to make his introductions. In a moment he was finished and gave me an "are we ready?" look. I started walking toward the deer, eyes on the does, alert for signs of fear. They ignored us at first but as we drew closer they began getting edgy. We stopped and froze in place. Patrick seemed to have a good understanding of how the deer were feeling. He froze at the appropriate times. He tended to take more chances than I would, but risks stalking deer were not a danger, simply a disappointment and a learning experience. I certainly had taken my share of disappointing risks as a kid. I was convinced the only reason Patrick really needed me along was because he was only six. He could use some fine-tuning but that would only come with practice. He was certainly exploring the confines of the ranch and had been seen investigating all kinds of animals in the brush. As I walked around the ranch I'd find his bicycle in odd places behind the ranch house, and eventually I would find blue jeans and cowboy boots poking out of the undergrowth or hear little, stealthy footsteps in the leaves.

After signaling Patrick to head for the closer doe I let him copy my movements for a while, but eventually felt he was ready to decide how to continue on his own. Inch by inch he grew closer to the doe, freezing when it moved, moving forward while it was distracted or grazing. A few times he startled the doe but he would immediately stop and freeze in place, sometimes for unbearingly long durations. He had the patience of a much older kid, but he seemed to live closer to the deer's timetable than that of any person. It seemed as though he was a part of their world so their rules applied, just like they would if he was visiting a friend. If Pat had been spending the night at his best friend, Ricky's, house where bedtime was at eight p.m., Patrick followed the same rules. If Ricky wasn't allowed to play outside the yard, then Patrick wouldn't either. He was used to these different rules and it seemed to apply to the deer as well. So if the deer said, no leaf crunching or impatient hurrying then he agreed to not crunch leaves and to slow down. The deer was over a hundred feet away when it ran away. Three blurs on the hunt ran after the deer and then veered in our direction barking. Rusty leapt to his feet and I made a dash for Patrick, my heart in my throat, not because the dogs were dangerous but because I was scared to death of them! These were not the ferocious police dogs I was used to. Still, from my perspective, they were feral dogs. I snatched Patrick off the ground and then stood my ground. My instincts said to run but I knew that was just fear talking. To run would invite a chase. I held Patrick close, glad he was only six. I raised my free arm and, assuming a threatening posture, stepped towards the dog yelling, "Yaaah! Get out of here dogs! Yaaaah, go home!"

Rusty was advancing, sidearm drawn but it wasn't necessary. The dogs were on the run again.

"I'm going to talk to Tony Macaluso. This is dangerous. That's twice today we've caught his dogs up to no good. He's got to know the repercussions of his actions."

"Those dumb dogs!" said Patrick. "We were doing good, an' they ruined it."

"It's common when stalking to have disappointing things come up: a car going by on the road, a predator, your own silly mistake. That's why stalking takes patience. You were doing a great job. All you need is practice and to get practice you need permission to come out here on your own. To do that you just need to be older. That's what's really going to take patience, waiting for your age to catch up with your capabilities."

"I hope Tony Mac catches his dogs before they catch that doe," Patrick said. "She's hurt and I don't know if she could run faster than a dog."

"What do you mean she's hurt?"

"Look at her tracks. One hoof is different from the other three tracks. I think she hurt her leg."

I looked at the doe's tracks. Sure enough, there was an odd or missing track in her trail.

"That's a very good observation," I told Patrick. "I'm proud of you for spotting that. You didn't see it as she ran away from the dogs?"

"No, I saw it in the tracks as I was stalking her. I forgot to look when she ran away. I was just scared for her."

We took our time on the way back to the ranch. I was watching Snoopy. Yup, I decided, he was a mix all right, welsh pony, mountain goat and pinto horse. Patrick seemed to love the little horse and talked to him as he rode along. When we stopped at the barn Pat already knew the rules. He removed the saddle and blanket. The saddle nearly knocked him over when he dragged it down and he fought it all the way to the tack room with firm determination. Rusty watched Pat thinking I'd probably done the same thing when I was six. Pat returned with a brush and groomed his horse as far as he could reach, then got out a stool and finished the job. Patrick gave Snoopy a chance to take a drink of water, then took him back to his pasture. Rusty helped me with Chet and Shasta. It felt good doing simple, quiet things together, tasks that were familiar to me. It eased away the fear of the dogs. We put the horses in their stalls then went back to the ranch house to change our clothes.

"I'm really proud of you," he told me once we were finally alone. "You faced those dogs without any signs of your old fear."

"That doesn't mean I wasn't scared of them," I pointed out.

"Bravery doesn't mean you don't have fears. Bravery is facing things despite your fears. You've confronted a lot of things you've been afraid of.

And you've faced things I wished you were more afraid of."

"Speaking of facing things, half the town's people will be here in about an hour. We need to get ready."

I hadn't brought any dressy clothes but decided to wear my newest jeans with my most flattering knit top. Hmm, it was a little low cut but I'd only bought it because I thought Rusty would appreciate it. However, now I was wondering if it was suitable for my mother's party. Oh well, I thought, I could always change if necessary. After curling my hair I applied a thick coating of mascara then finished my make-up. I was beginning to look like a normal woman these days. I wasn't sure if I was pleased with my assessment since I never wanted to be normal.

Chapter 19

Half the town was not an exaggeration. When I saw the crowd downstairs I thought, if that's half the town then it's grown a lot! Old Frank caught me coming down the stairs and I was dragged helplessly to the couch in the living room.

"This is Cassidy, Mr. Gordon's older girl," he said, introducing me to two elderly men. They were both seated on a couch so cushy they'd never be able to stand without asking for help. They tried standing to meet me but couldn't lever themselves up enough to stand. "Cassidy, this Hector and Bert, my two closest friends outside the ranch."

I sat on the coffee table so they wouldn't feel obligated to stand.

"It's good to meet you," I said sincerely.

"Cain't be," Bert said.

"Can too," argued Old Frank.

"This kid is not a Marine," Bert said.

"Cassidy, tell them you were in the Marines."

"Yes, I was a Marine for four years but I've been out for a few years."

"Did you really track down a man who'd been missing for a week?"

"Yes, that's my job. Most of the people I look for haven't been missing that long, though."

"Who was the last person you tracked?"

"He was a man wanted for opening gunfire inside an elementary school. I invited a tracker from San Diego to help me and we tracked for two days before we found him in a house. The police closed in and made the arrest."

"Amazing, I'd never think, by looking at you that you'd be capable of the things Frank has told us."

"I never claimed to be capable. I do what I can and when things go awry I deal with it. I guess it works because I'm still here. Frank might tell some doosies but I've never known him to lie."

A shadow fell across the coffee table.

"Well, well, if it isn't the tough little tracker, returned from the wilds. Looks like you've developed a *different* wild side."

His voice was an octave lower than I remembered it, but I looked up into the face of Barton Fartson, I mean Farthington. I quickly stood to prevent him from looking directly down my top but it didn't help much because he still towered over me. He was still big but he'd stretched out and filled in some, and still had that cunning look to him.

"Barton, I'd tell you to pick on someone your own size, but from what I've heard, Cassidy could best you now," Bert said.

"Bert, I think you're exaggerating," I said. "If I remember right, I graduated from high school several years ago. So I thought maybe Barton and I would have both grown up a little. It's good to see you again, Barton. How have you been?"

"Fine," he said suspiciously.

"Oh, come on, you don't think I'd carry a grudge this long, do you? I only carried a grudge against you during the school year. And it only acted up when you were being a bully. School's been out for a long time now. I think the grudge is gone."

"So, what are you doing these days?" he asked.

"Still tracking. I find lost people for the Joshua Hills search and rescue team…"

"And violent criminals, too!" added Hector.

"Only rarely do I track criminals. My husband kind of has a thing against violent criminals. They tend to do bad things like shoot at me and kidnap me so he discourages me from having anything to do with them."

"It don't always work, though," Old Frank said.

"Mind if I introduce you around?" Barton asked. "There are a few people from school you haven't seen for a while."

"I'm not sure that's a good idea, unless you don't mind my husband tagging along."

"Why? What's he going to do? He's not the jealous type is he? Those jerks are a pain in the ass. I thought you'd be smarter than to marry a man like that."

"He's not the jealous type, or I wouldn't be able to do my job."

I found Rusty and we exchanged introductions. "Rusty this is a friend from school, Barton Farthington. Barton, this is my husband, Rusty Michaels."

Barton took one look at Rusty and turned white, not because he was scared of Rusty, but something else was going on inside his head.

"You better march him upstairs, lock the door and tell Jesse not to say a word."

"Barton, are you okay?" I asked.

"Barton, the guy who stuffed you into your locker?" Rusty asked.

"Yeah, but I'm sure he wouldn't do it again."

"Cassidy, I'm not kidding," Barton insisted. "Misty Montague is here. And recently divorced for the third time."

"I can't just walk out on Mom's party. She waited until we came just so we could be part of it."

However, a part of me really did want to run Rusty upstairs and lock the door. Misty Montague. Of all the people I didn't want to see it was her. She even scared Barton. I wondered if Barton was scared of her because he was one of her victims.

"Misty Montague?" Rusty said.

"Remember when I was being stalked by Tyrone Trent?" I asked.

"How could I forget?" Rusty answered. "I thought he'd killed you."

"Misty doesn't actually kill people, but she makes Trent look like an amateur and you are the perfect bait. Unfortunately she isn't violent or clinically insane or anything, so we can't lock her up. She's just incredibly good at what she does."

"Which is?" Rusty asked, trying to get to the point.

"She likes to steal husbands. In high school it was boyfriends. Now it's husbands. She collects them, lures them away until she gets tired of them, then divorces them and takes half of everything."

Rusty looked skeptical.

"And you're worried about this Misty Montague stealing me away?" Rusty said laughing.

"Ask my sister," I said.

"Okay, let's ask Jesse."

I steered Rusty through the crowd carefully avoiding the lilting laugh of Misty Montague.

"Jesse, Barton told Rusty about Misty Montague, but he thinks we're exaggerating. Tell him all about her."

Jesse's mouth fell open in surprise. "Mom invited *her*? How could she do that? Mom knows the history. Is she here?"

"Yeah."

"You better march Rusty right up those stairs and lock the door. I'm going to talk to Mom."

Rusty was really amused now. I think his curiosity was working overtime. What kind of a woman could this be, who thought she could just run off with another woman's husband? That was part of the allure. Local guys knew she was deep trouble but they still wondered what it was about the temptress that attracted her victims. One by one they found out and she had married and divorced three of them since high school. In high school it had only taken months, not years to lure her prey away and then break up with the guys. Misty adapted and had to develop some patience in the adult world but it probably had paid off monetarily.

Barton reappeared with Jason Kilby. Seems like he was bent on letting all the guys in town know I was back, if only temporarily.

"Cassidy, you remember Jason."

"Of course." Jason had been Joe Average in school. He was nice, had a car, made decent grades, ended up with a lousy job but smiled his way through it all.

"How's life been treating you?" I asked.

"Oh, about average," he said, "can't complain. How about you?"

I looked to Rusty. "Anything but average," I said to Jason. "This is my husband, Rusty."

One by one Barton made the rounds, except for Misty Montague.

Music began on the big porch and people wandered out there to dance. There were tables of hors d'oeuvres and little desserts, glasses of wine inside and coolers of beer outside on the porch. Martha had her daughters come to the ranch to help with the serving. Some of the guests were wearing suits while others wore jeans. Old Frank had dressed for his shindig in his usual pressed jeans, bright western shirt and bolo tie. His boots had been shined and his hair carefully combed. Misty Montague, I noted had worn an evening gown that sparkled from the plunging neckline to the floor. It clung to every curve of her body and had a thigh high slit up the skirt. She was busy working the crowd. She laughed at rotten jokes and laid a hand on the shoulder of the man she was standing next to. I knew that part of her pathetic hobby of collecting husbands was psychological. She made women feel inferior and most men don't like women who feel inferior. They like women who project an air of confidence. So I stood taller and carefully avoided getting anywhere near Misty Montague. I caught Rusty glancing at Misty from a distance. He could figure out who she was without any introductions. I came up beside him.

"She's the shallowest person I've never met," he said.

"She'll be interested in anything you say to her. She's like a social chameleon. She's been a cowgirl, a cheerleader, and an avid collector of antiques. She even learned to play golf and make wine. By the time she gets to be Old Frank's age she'll know how to do just about anything."

Old Frank was having a great time. He was swapping tall tales with the local police chief. Later I found him on the porch with a group of young ranch hands. Most of them wore jeans and t-shirts, but not our hands. He laughed and traded training tips. He sure got around, if slowly. I also saw him talking to Patrick who was feeling a little left out of the adult festivities.

"Patrick," I said, "go get your rope and show the folks what you can do with it."

"They don't care about ropin'," he said, discouraged.

"You'll be surprised. I bet only a couple of people here can even turn a rope and none of them have tried the things you can do."

"Really?"

"Yeah, really. I bet your dad can't even turn a rope like you can. Give it a try and you'll see what happens."

He rode his bike down to the barn and got out a lasso. He went to the coatroom and retrieved his black cowboy hat. What a ham. He even had to dress the part. He found a clear spot on the big front porch and started turning the rope. I gave him time to get a consistent pattern going and then found Rusty.

"Go look on the front porch," I told him.

Then to my sister I said, "Hey Jess, you've got to see what your son can do. Come here," I said, dragging her off to the front porch, too. We found Rusty there grinning at his little nephew. He had seen Patrick do this before but I didn't think Jesse had, which became obvious as we watched him.

"How did he learn that?" she asked me.

"James made him practice roping and he got bored," I told her simply.

"And you know this because…"

"When he spent the night at my house I talked to him and realized he knows a lot of things that will surprise you."

"But he's jumping in and out of the loop. Do you know how much practice that takes?"

"He said James has him practice roping a little bit every day."

"Well, yeah, but not this! We only wanted him to be able to catch Snoopy!"

"He doesn't need a lasso to catch Snoopy. That horse adores him because Pat spends time with him. You know how attached horses can get. Oh, but don't call what he's doing a rope trick. He gets very offended if you call it a trick."

"I'm going to find James," she said and rushed off. I grinned to myself, glad that Patrick finally had a chance to show his parents a thing or two of his hidden talents. Pretty soon I saw Jesse lead James over to the side of the porch and they stood watching as Patrick kept the rope going, leaping and turning, twirling the rope over his head, then down by his side. I could think of a few moves that professional trick ropers were able to do that he hadn't thought of yet but he was amazing all who stood on the porch, including the band members, who all stopped playing to watch Patrick's performance. The guitarist started playing a country western riff to match the mood and Patrick began timing his rhythm to the chords of the guitar. When he got tired and needed to stop for a drink of water the crowd broke out in applause. Patrick looked embarrassed. He slipped into the house on his way to the kitchen and Jesse took off after her boy. I followed to make sure she gave him the credit he deserved.

"Patrick! That was fantastic! How did you learn to do all that?" Jesse beamed.

"Dad made me practice, so I practiced," he said matter of factly.

"It's not exactly what I had in mind," James said from across the room. "It takes real talent to do that. I just wanted you to be capable of lassoing your horse. Long as you can lasso Snoopy then you'll get along fine."

"Dad, Snoopy don't need lassoing. He follows me without a rope. I only use the rope because I'm supposed to. And even if he did need lassoing I could do that the first week you had me work the rope. I got bored practicing so I made up other things I could do with the rope. Don't know why everybody is so surprised. Hey! Aunt Cassidy!"

"Yeah, Pat?" I said.

"I learned something new since I got my bike. I can lasso fence posts while I'm riding my bike. I thought that would come in handy when I have to rope one horse when I'm riding another."

"Good thinking," I told him. "It's easier to lasso something from a horse. A good roping horse knows what to do. Bicycles aren't very smart. What do you do when you hit the end of the rope?"

"Well, the first time I got yanked off my bike. Now I let go and ride back for the rope."

The night was a success as far as I was concerned. Old Frank got to see half the town turn out and made the rounds of all his friends. Patrick had finally shown his parents he knew a thing or two. Mom happily played hostess while Dad made his connections.

Everyone was slow getting up the next day, except Martha, Zack and Randy. Zack and Randy were up early for the morning chores and Martha was in charge of breakfast. We had one more day at the ranch before we needed to head back home and it was a quiet day. I played Chicken Foot with Old Frank, placing his dominoes where they belonged when his shaky hands couldn't get them in place without ruining the whole line of dominoes on the table. Then we played penny poker. He let me use quarters now that I was old enough to decide for myself how much I was willing to risk. Rusty threw his pocket change into the game too. It was really useless. Nobody wanted to win all that change. In the end Patrick watched the game with interest. We counted up all our winnings and proclaimed Old Frank the winner.

"Wow! You won three dollars and seventeen cents!" Patrick said.

"Yup, I tell you what kid. If you can add up everybody's winnings, we'll give them all to you. Cassidy ended up with two dollars and forty cents and Rusty ended up with two dollars and ninety-five cents. If you can tell me the grand total you win it all."

Pat ran off quickly.

"No fair using your grandpa's calculator. Use your brain!" Old Frank called after him.

"Aw, shucks, can I use paper?"

"Course you can use paper, gives your brain somewhere to wrastle with it."

Patrick found a piece of paper and a pen and then wrote down the numbers. He calculated furiously, double checked, and handed the paper over to Old Frank who checked the math.

"By golly, I do believe we have a new winner!" Old Frank proclaimed. "Boy, you are eight dollars and fifty-two cents richer!"

"Oh boy!" Patrick said, jumping up and down. Everyone pushed their piles of change across the table and watched as Patrick tried to stuff it all into his pockets. Half an hour later Jesse wandered into the room.

"Why is Patrick three pounds heavier this morning?" she asked.

"Because he is the grand prize winner!" declared Old Frank.

"How much did he take from you?" Jesse asked.

"It weren't so much a taking as a getting rid of," Old Frank told her.

"And how much did you get rid of?"

"Eight dollars in change."

"Well, that's a good chunk to go into his savings," she said.

"Wait, just a minute, a kid wins a measly eight bucks and you make him put it in savings? He cain't buy nothing with it anyway."

"He's the one putting it in savings. He's got his eye on what he calls 'Army field glasses.' I call them camouflaged binoculars. He thinks he can sneak up on birds easier if his binoculars don't stand out. I say he stands out enough all by himself and his binoculars are not going to make one whit of difference."

"Jesse, one quick trip into town and I'd buy him the field glasses."

"Don'choo dare!" Old Frank exclaimed. "The kid wants to save his money for field glasses, you let him! It shows real character for a six-year-old to save up that much. If'n you want to help him, give him a job to do to earn money, but don't jus' go handing it to him."

"What did he have to do to get your winnings?" Jesse asked.

"He correctly added them all up and it weren't easy math for a first grader. It weren't an even eight dollars." He handed the paper to Jesse and she did the math, too.

"How does he know to carry over from one column to the next?" she asked.

"You'll have to ask him that. We didn't tell him how to do the math. We just told him if he gave us the right number he could have the winnings," I told her.

She wandered into the kitchen and I heard her say, "Mom, look what

Patrick did..."

I smiled to myself glad to have one more piece of evidence in Patrick's favor and I was also glad to see Old Frank was definitely on Pat's side.

I had mixed feelings when Sunday arrived and it was time to go home. I unenthusiastically packed the suitcases and helped load the Explorer. I was anxious to get back home where Rusty and I could do as we pleased. But at the same time the ranch had been peaceful and I treasured my time with Old Frank. I didn't know how many more visits I'd have with him. Then I reminded myself that after I left he'd probably need to sleep for a few days to recuperate. He'd feel more comfortable using his walker again and could slow down again. He probably needed that.

Shadow was reluctant to go home as well. When he was at the ranch he became a ranch dog. He was able to play with the other dogs and had free run of the property. He played with the boys and followed Steve around. At home it was boring for him so I was determined, after loading up the Explorer, that we would get more involved in polishing his agility skills. That would help both of us because our house was going to feel way too quiet again.

We took the scenic route home. Rusty had pretty much decided that I needed some tracking breaks to get my mind off the ranch, so on the way home we always headed for the coast. As we walked the beaches I couldn't help but read the footprints in the sand and it gently eased me back into my own world again. How did Rusty know to do these little things for me? How did he know I needed the time, the distraction, whatever it was? I knew he liked the beach, too, but there was more to his stopping than just a need to stretch his legs. He watched me as I tracked and he could tell when my mind was finally at ease and it was time for the next leg of the drive.

The house was dark when we got home, as it always was when we took our time on the scenic route. Rusty went in first and turned on enough lights to make the place seem cheery. He dragged me over to the old brown couch and we sat for a long time, like we always did, with me sitting on his lap, my arms around his neck. He probably felt the silence even more than I did. Rusty would have packed up Patrick and Wyatt and brought them home with us if he could but he knew it wasn't a solution.

Over the next few weeks, Shadow and I applied ourselves to the agility course. He flew over the obstacles except for a few glitches that we had to work on. I knew if he balked at them at home he'd be even more likely to balk at the competition. So we worked on the dog walk. Shadow didn't like looking down and seeing the ground so far away so I lowered the beam. He still didn't like the height of it, but he obeyed me better with the beam closer to the ground. There was a pet competition in town, Bark in the Park, and I quickly signed us up just to see how we would finish. It wasn't a stiff, formal, official kennel club competition. But it was official enough to issue the certificates that the American Kennel Club offered. Once we made it up the ranks locally maybe we'd try a larger venue. For now the annual city pet festival would have to do. It would acclimate Shadow to working in a crowd and it would force me to work amongst dogs of every shape and size.

I was leading Shadow over the lowered dog walk and wondering if he'd even try the seesaw when the phone rang in the house. After placing Shadow in a heel I ran for the house with my dog on my tail. I got to the phone just as it stopped ringing. I checked caller ID and it was the ranch. I sat down, wondering what to do. I should call back but I wasn't ready for the news I had been fearing most. I decided there was no point in putting off the inevitable so I called the number with a sinking feeling in the pit of my stomach.

"Hello?" It was my dad. That was bad. If it had been an invitation or a chat, Mom would be the one to call.

"Hi, Dad, you called?"

"I did," he said wearily as I sat down. "I called to tell you Old Frank's gone. He fell last night in the bunkhouse and Steve called an ambulance. Turned out Frank had a stroke. He died last night. We were there. He didn't know it, but we were there. Came as close to dying with his boots on as he could. He didn't want a service. Said he didn't want folks to think of him like that. There'll be a burial next Saturday if you want to come."

With my heart aching for Old Frank all I could say was, "Thanks, Dad, I'll try."

"I wanted to thank you for coming back and seeing him. It meant a lot to him to have you there. When you left he kept saying, 'It's too durn quiet around here without that young un'.'"

"I know how he felt. I felt the same way when I got home."

When I'd hung up the emotional pull from the hideout was calling like crazy but I couldn't run. I couldn't leave Rusty behind like this. Besides, he wouldn't let me stay up there by myself in my present state. So I threw myself on the bed and cried until I couldn't cry any more and then I slept. I woke up when I heard Rusty arrive home and I flew into his arms.

"Whoa, babe, let me put my stuff down," he said, but I couldn't let go. All I could do was hurt. He set his things down on the entryway floor and wrapped his arms around me and, when I didn't respond, he carried me to the big, brown couch. I cried until I thought it was impossible to cry anymore but then I cried some more.

"How long have you known?" he asked softly.

"All… afternoon," I sobbed.

"You could have called."

"No… I couldn't."

"Thank you… thank you for not running. You don't know how much it means to me for you to choose to stay and not run. I'd rather be here with you than traipsing off after you wondering what's wrong." He talked quietly, hugging me close. "I know it's sad. I know it hurts. It'll get better, you'll see."

So ended an era in time that only a few people really noticed, in the large scheme of things. The ranch would never be the same. Now the ranch would truly be too quiet.

Chapter 20

On the day of the competition I told Rusty, "Now remember, this is just for practice. We can't think about actually winning one of these events until we see what the competition is like. I think he will make it through the course, but we are not going to have anywhere near a top time."

"Okay."

"Part of the learning process is running the course with a hundred people yelling in the background and other activities going on. Just like we train the horses to stay calm around other people, animals and cars, Shadow has to learn the same thing, to perform under unusual conditions. So we're not out to win. We're still training."

"Hon, I'm just here to watch. As long as you're happy with the results I'll be happy too."

"Okay. I just didn't want you to set your sights too high."

"I'm not setting anything. Just do your best and I'll celebrate with you afterwards."

"You even want to 'celebrate' an agility competition?" I asked.

Rusty's way of celebrating usually involved sex. He said he loved to feel me alive beneath him. So we often celebrated after a bout of trouble when I could actually show him that I was still very much alive. We celebrated birthdays and anniversaries. We 'celebrated' many things, but celebrating a favorable outcome for an agility competition would be a first.

"Number eight? Calling contestant number eight to the starting line," we heard over the loud speaker.

"That's us," I said as I stood on tip toes to give Rusty a kiss before we left. "Okay, boy," I told Shadow. "You just ignore the people, dogs and cars. Watch me. Heel. Good boy, heel."

Shadow trotted by my side as I found the starting line. I didn't know why I was feeling nervous and hoped it didn't rub off on Shadow. He knew how to complete all the obstacles in the course, but there were still a few that he didn't like. I'd watched the other dogs run the course and a few of them flew through it rejoicing with each accomplishment. Those dogs were overjoyed to be working and thrived in competition. Shadow wasn't quite that enthusiastic, and he wasn't used to working with a lot of distractions, so I really only had hopes of making it all the way through the course. Even that would be a victory for us. In the world of agility only the top few had any real hopes of winning. The rest of us were just trying to get better at it and have fun with our dogs.

I had walked the course to familiarize myself with the order of the obstacles but this was my first time at an agility competition, too. So far one dog had balked at an obstacle and ran off the field. I'd heard that wasn't unusual. So if we could just get through all the obstacles and finish I'd be happy. When I walked the course I was pleased with the arrangement. This was a family friendly event, Bark in the Park, and so the obstacles were arranged in order to make the dog and handler ease into the competition. They could have placed something challenging as the first obstacle but they chose to ramp up to the more difficult ones. I thought we could do this.

I unclipped the leash and stuffed it in my pocket. The timer began after we crossed the starting line but that didn't concern me. I jogged to the first obstacle and Shadow breezed over the hurdle and then over the paneled hurdle after it. He loved to jump. After the hurdles we had to turn and Shadow started toward the next obstacle in his sight.

"Ak! No! Shadow, heel!" I called to correct his route. Many of the other handlers used a clicker to communicate with their dog but I had never learned how to train a dog to respond to the clicker so it was just Shadow and myself out there on the course. He veered in my direction disappointed that he wasn't able to try the tunnel. He liked the tunnel, too, but one of the challenges in an agility match was to get the dog to obey the handler and not just do whatever they wanted. The obstacles were numbered. Each one had a cone beside it with a number taped onto it, but of course Shadow couldn't read the numbers. He had to rely on me.

"Heel Shadow! Now up! Up you go!" He walked up a short ramp. "Now stop! Stop. Stay." An official came over to the platform and pet Shadow, scratched him behind the ears and ran a hand over his back. Another area of obedience was having a well socialized dog that was friendly with other people. When the man stepped back I continued. "Okay, down, heel, good boy." The officials had really taken beginners into consideration when arranging the obstacles. Shadow had to climb a ramp to reach the pause table which was directly followed by a slightly more challenging ramp, the A-frame. Shadow was getting distracted by the crowd and looked like he was feeling uncertain so I tried rushing him through the A-frame. He went over it with barely a pause but was still watching the people outside the course. "Shadow, heel!" I called as I made the turn towards the tunnel Shadow had always loved. At home I had to keep him from doing it twice. After passing through he gave the tunnel a glance and I knew he wanted to go back and do it again. "Shadow, heel! Here's another one! Heel!" He looked at the collapsed tunnel and dashed through, then leapt through the tire jump. I wished he hadn't done that, but it was the next numbered obstacle, so it didn't harm his score. He was supposed to check with me before proceeding. "Shadow, wait," I commanded. The next obstacle took some coaxing from me. "Heel." We came to the weave poles slowly. The enthusiastic dogs nearly ran through it but it had to be taken with caution. If the dog even missed one turn, points would be taken off. The obstacle consisted of poles placed in a line and the dog had to weave in and out of the poles until reaching the end. Shadow could do it, but he didn't like the focus it required to complete it. He would begin weaving and then wanted to do something more interesting like tunnels or jumps. "Shadow heel." The crowd watched as I worked with my dog. The spectators were a mixed bunch but most of them had seen an agility match before. They waited to see what the dog would do. Anticipation mounted as they sensed this was an awkward obstacle for us. Would Shadow complete it? Or would he screw up? We had already lost the match time wise. The fastest dogs completed the whole course in a minute or less. The dogs who lived for agility only needed to know the next command and took the whole course at a run. We could almost do that at home, but not in a park full of people. "Shadow, heel, now weave, weave. Come on, boy, weave, one, weave, two, good boy." He was slow. He didn't like it. He was distracted. He almost stopped. "Ah ah! Keep going, weave, weave, there you go! Good boy! Now heel!" I jogged over to the dog walk. This was another obstacle that Shadow had never liked. It was high off the ground and he didn't like being able to see down. "Up, go up!" I commanded. He started ascending the narrow ramp. "Good boy! Up!" I wanted to tell him to heel but he associated heeling with being on the ground so I just continued on quickly so he wouldn't have as much time to think about heights. "Come, Shadow, come, good boy, almost through, okay down! Shadow down!" Only two more obstacles left but the next one was the hardest. It wasn't as high but this structure moved underfoot. "Shadow heel, now up, good boy!" He reached the pivot point and stopped. "Easy, come on, you can do it." He stepped forward, felt the teeter totter move and almost jumped off. "Ahah! No. Stay." I moved to the end of the board and commanded, "Come! Shadow, come!" He ran down the board as though he was afraid it was going to bite him. "Okay one more jump! Jump, Shadow!" He cleared the broad jump and the run was over. I heaved a sigh of relief. "Good boy! Good Shadow! Now sit." He sat and I clipped the leash back on. Whew! We had made it!

Rusty clasped me in a hug.
"I was holding my breath for the whole run," he admitted.
"You can breathe again."

"Did you win?"

"No… and yes. We didn't win the competition but we completed our goal. Maybe next time we'll do better."

An Australian shepherd won the match, but Sparky lived and breathed agility. His eagerness to run the course was evident from the moment his owner walked him to the starting line. He was a spring waiting to be sprung. And when his owner spoke the first command he practically read his handler's mind as they ran the whole course at a sprint. He was a winner through and through. Several of the dogs were like Sparky and there was stiff competition amongst the top dogs.

"Do the bigger dogs scare you?" Rusty asked.

"No! Wow, I hadn't even thought about it. Even that Rottweiler doesn't seem to frighten me. Guess I'm in obedience mode."

Dogs in every size competed. The smallest was a Pomeranian. There were shepherds and hounds, lap dogs and working dogs. The variety of dogs was astounding. The largest was a Rottweiler bigger than me. Then there was a lighter but taller Great Dane. It was encouraging to see so many people who valued a well trained pet.

We achieved three goals that day. I overcame my fear of dogs. Shadow's speed had been nowhere close to a winning time but he received two certificates, one in obedience and the other in agility. While part of me thinks it's silly to strive for a piece of paper confirming what I already know my dog can do, part of me looks at the piece of paper and says, "We did it! We made it through, so we can make it through again. And again." That's what life is all about. Making it through no matter what comes at us. Sometimes we laugh through it. Sometimes we cry. But no matter what we must come through, dust off our boots, and look for more adventures.

www.ingramcontent.com/pod-product-compliance
Lightning Source LLC
Chambersburg PA
CBHW050424260626
47156CB00003B/1140